T0274424

CALL
FORTH
A
FOX

CALL FORTH A FOX

MARKELLE GRABO

PAGE STREET YA

FOR ANTON, WHO ENCOURAGES
ME TO EXPAND MY WORLD.

AND FOR ANYONE WHO THOUGHT
IT WAS UNFAIR THAT ROSE RED
MARRIED THE PRINCE'S BROTHER.

CHAPTER 1

The first snowfall arrives while I'm sprinkling ashes across the cottage doorstep.

I set down my bucket and breathe deeply, my chest filling with brisk air and the promise of winter. Flurries settle on the ground as I lean against the doorframe. They don't melt—a good sign. Though snowfall won't make foraging easier, the western wood is most beautiful when covered in white. An undeniable smile pulls at my lips, and my feet itch inside my boots, begging me to abandon my bucket and stride toward the trees.

Doing so would be risky; I'm supposed to complete my morning chores before going to the wood. It's part of a deal my sister and I made after Ma left. In return, Eirwyn won't pester me if I stay out until sunset. Inviting as the snow might be, sprinkling ashes is the last of my tasks. Better to wait a little longer now than tempt Eirwyn to renegotiate later.

I bend over the bucket and dip my pale hand into the soft, cool ash, withdrawing a handful and scattering more layers over the doorstep. These ashes will keep us from slipping as the world turns to ice, and whatever's leftover in spring will enrich our garden.

Well, that's how we would normally use the leftover ashes. But come spring we're leaving the village, so there won't be a garden. No one will be around to scatter the ashes, to see anything grow. Not that much has grown in the four years since Pa died.

"Almost finished, Ro?" Eirwyn calls from inside the cottage.

"Yes, be right in," I answer. I've scattered plenty of ashes; I should return the bucket to its spot beneath the coat rack and leave to forage in the western wood. Instead, my eyes are drawn to the soil plots beside our cottage.

Before she left, Ma told us not to waste time clearing weeds or dead plants from the garden. She advised we let nature reclaim the land because we don't need it anymore.

Well, maybe she doesn't. But I do.

Three purposeful strides bring me to the garden. With my ash-dusted fingers, I pull up the shriveled leaves before they're covered with snow. Pa kept our garden thriving for years. He worked the soil until the day he couldn't stand. Sure, since he passed the harvest has been hardly enough to feed our family, but that doesn't mean I'm ready to abandon his life's work. Not yet. Not while there's still a chance we could stay. If Ma were to change her mind—

"Ro, what's taking so long?"

Startled by my sister's voice, I turn away from the garden, and in my haste to reach the door before Eirwyn comes out looking for me, I knock over the bucket. Ashes spill onto the doorstep. I groan, shoulders slumping. I can't let my sister see this. She already thinks I'm sloppy with my chores.

"Just a minute!" I call, hoping she's patient enough to stay inside.

I kneel and shovel as much ash as I can back into the bucket. It's a good thing we're not using ashes to make soap anymore. Before she left, Ma sold bars to compensate for our poor harvests, along with floral arrangements made from the rose trees that haven't wilted like our garden. Neither brought in a great deal of coin, which is why Ma's gone across the river to Poppy, the prosperous town she believes is the answer to all our misfortune.

My aunt runs a tavern in Poppy and owns the rooms above, so Ma's staying in one for the winter while she secures a trade. She'll return to collect Eirwyn and me once winter's breath turns warm and the river thaws to slush. She's been gone for three weeks now and missing her is a strange thing. I want her home with us, of course, but her return also means our departure from the village, and I'm nowhere close to ready for that.

When I've cleaned up as much as I can, I draw in the layers of ash left behind with my finger: a cottage with a garden and two rose trees intertwined, a line of forest beyond. Home. But only for winter.

A familiar pair of sock feet enter my line of vision, just beyond the doorstep. "Ro, what are you doing?" asks Eirwyn.

Startled, I wipe away the drawing and stand to meet my

sister. "Nothing," I answer, smacking the lingering soot from my hands.

Her gaze narrows like she knows I'm lying, but she doesn't say so. "Well, come in then. You should eat before you go to the wood."

I follow her inside and set the ash bucket beneath the coat rack. Eirwyn returns to the kitchen to continue preparing plates of bread and hard cheese at the free-standing counter. Nearly eighteen, she's the eldest sister by two years. She's tall and slender, like the stem of a rose, whereas I'm more like the bloom—short and a bit thicker around the middle, with strength earned from years of navigating the western wood.

All the cupboards behind my sister are open, as she often forgets to close them. The sight makes my fingers twitch, but I hold back a complaint. We've been bickering more than usual, and I don't want to add to that if I can help it.

"Water should be hot enough for tea," Eirwyn says with forced brightness, tucking a loose strand of wheat-blonde hair behind her ear.

I resist the urge to roll my eyes. My sister is in good spirits more often than not, but she's been especially cheery since Ma left. All part of her misguided attempt to make the most of our last winter here, and to keep me from shouting about all the reasons we should stay—reasons she and Ma have heard dozens of times yet refuse to understand. Yesterday Eirwyn praised my foraging finds, even though they were meager, and she didn't frown at the dirt on my collar. But extra cheer won't be enough to distract me from what's coming.

I cross to the stone fireplace in the sitting room to remove the iron kettle from its hook. Beneath my feet there's a crack in one of the floorboards where I once dropped it, having forgotten to cover my hand with a thick cloth before grasping the handle.

The scalding heat against my palm was brief but severe. Pa heard me cry out and brought a damp cloth to press against the blooming red welt, but when I apologized for ruining the floorboard, he only shook his head. Pa said he was glad for the crack because it would serve as a reminder for me to never forget the cloth again. He was right, as I haven't forgotten since.

I kneel and press my fingertips to the wood fracture, feeling its rough edges against my skin as a sad smile curves my lips. Pa never made me feel foolish over being wrong about something. He joined a lesson to every mistake, and the memories of his teachings are tied to this cottage, to our garden, to the western wood. I hate to think about what will happen to those memories in Poppy. Without tangible reminders to keep them alive, what might I lose?

Gloomy and in desperate need of that cup of tea, I cover my hand with the worn cloth and remove the kettle. I pour the steaming liquid into two clay cups, each holding a tiny pile of dried rosehips and mint leaves foraged by my hand. Eirwyn joins me then, a platter of food in the crook of each arm.

Plates balanced on our laps, we sit on the cushioned wooden bench facing the fire, gazes trained on the flickering flames as we eat. The bread is a little stale and the cheese a little too hard, but I don't mind much because at least I'm eating something filling. There was a time before Ma left when we couldn't afford bread or cheese, and we lived on the remnants of our poor harvest and the mushrooms, nuts, and berries I foraged in the western wood. But when Ma wrote to alert Aunt Meara of her plan to move us to Poppy, the woman sent back an envelope full of coin along with a note that read, "You should have done this years ago."

Aunt Meara's certainly not wealthy, but between running her tavern and renting out rooms, I know she lives comfortably. She's sent us coin each year since Pa passed, but not so much as when she learned Ma would finally be heeding her advice to leave the village and join her across the river. Ma didn't seem bothered by this, too overjoyed knowing the coin would help Eirwyn and me survive the winter. All my sister could do was list the things we could finally buy again: bread, cheese, fish, spools of thread for mending.

I'm grateful, too, but I also can't deny the resentment behind that gratefulness, knowing my aunt could have helped us more these last years if she'd wanted to. Maybe if she had, we wouldn't be leaving.

"I think I'll walk to Maple Square once the snowfall stops." Eirwyn pauses to finish chewing a mouthful of bread. "Stock up before winter sets in and there's less to choose from. How do you feel about smoked fish? Shea says her catch is larger than usual this week, which means she might sell at a discount."

"Hmm," I say, slurping my tea.

"You can come along if you'd like," she offers. "Help with the shopping, say hello to people other than me for a change."

Bristling at the suggestion, I shake my head with perhaps more force than necessary. "We have a deal," I mutter into my cup.

"I know, but you don't need to forage every day."

That hardly matters. Can't she sense my disinterest?

I set down my tea. "I don't want to go."

I feed her the words slowly and deliberately to ensure her understanding. As silence stretches between us, I wonder if I've gone too far. Whereas Eirwyn has been especially cheery in Ma's absence, I've no doubt been especially sour. I can see it's weighing on her.

I do believe Eirwyn deserves my sourness some of the time. She continues to side with Ma about the move, after all, which I consider a grave betrayal of our sisterhood. But lately, even on the rare occasions when I want to be the good younger sister, I can't seem to make myself do it. It's as if the moment Ma left, a great, angry beast came to inhabit me. Short of Ma changing her mind about leaving, I don't see what will make the beast go away.

Finally, Eirwyn clears her throat.

"All right," she says softly as if I'm a babe in need of coddling. "Careful in the wood today. The snow makes it easy to lose one's way."

I'm tempted to say I've never gotten lost in the wood a day in my life. But I refrain, because beneath my frustration is affection for my sister, who rarely insists I do anything I don't want to do. Much unlike Ma.

I nudge Eirwyn with my shoulder. "Tea's good."

I do the foraging, but my sister's in charge of blending. She always manages the right balance of rosehips to mint so the taste is never too tart, sweet, or spicy, but the perfect mix of all three.

Eirwyn smiles. "Thank you, but I'm afraid that's the last of our blend. Should I get something while I'm out? Just enough to last until you forage more ingredients?"

I bite my lip, thinking of something Ma said before she left. About spending our coin wisely, about not being frivolous.

But she also said to enjoy our remaining time here, so I ask the question anyway: "Do we have enough for ginger spice?"

"Let me worry about that," Eirwyn says, grabbing a book from the end table.

Like all her books, this one's been read at least a dozen times. The brown leather binding is worn and cracked, and some of the pages have folded corners, marking her favorite passages.

I flop back against the cushions. "Bet Poppy has lots of new books for you to read."

"Mmm," she agrees, flipping a page.

I breathe heavily through my nose, feeling prickly. Whenever I make snide comments to Ma about Poppy, like how ridiculous its name sounds on my tongue, I'm rewarded with a stern lecture. Eirwyn is harder to prod. She can be unaffected and silent in response to my remarks, which is worse in a way I can't explain.

I'm determined to get a reaction from her this time, so I say, "Bet you're excited about the soap."

That seems to do it, because Eirwyn lowers the book to her lap. "What?"

I shrug, picking at the crust of my bread. "You'll have more time to read since you won't need to make soap anymore. Who needs homemade soap in a thriving town like Poppy? Ma will start buying it for sure."

Likely soap that's overly scented with herbs and flower

petals, and I'll choke every time I scrub my hands.

Eirwyn sighs, a warning that I've descended too far into dramatics. "Moving to Poppy won't mean we can suddenly buy everything we need instead of making it ourselves. We're moving because we're poor, not because we're tired of making soap."

Crust crumbles between my fingers. "You sound like Ma, saying 'we' as if this move has anything to do with me."

Eirwyn's book shuts with a thump. "Do you enjoy weeks of little more than mushroom and acorn stew? Adding extra fabric to your clothes year after year instead of stitching anything new?"

I lower my gaze, finding I can't lie to her this time. "No."

"Then this move has as much to do with you as it has to do with Ma and me."

I cross my arms against my chest, wounded but unwilling to give up so soon. "You know Pa wouldn't want us to go. He loved the village and the western wood. He'd want us to stay here and keep trying."

She sets her book aside and rises from the bench, another forced smile stretching her pale pink lips. "Snow's not falling too hard. I think I'll go to the square now."

"Eirwyn."

"Don't worry, I won't forget your tea."

"Eirwyn," I repeat.

"I'll be back before dark," she says, fastening her golden brown wool cloak. "Mind the fire before you leave."

She's out the door before I can say her name a third time.

I lean forward, elbows on my knees, the fire hazy through my half-lidded eyes. Shame warms my face for invoking Pa when I know it does awful things to my sister. But how else can I get through to her, make her understand that leaving Sugar Maple Village, the only home we've ever known, is a mistake?

Doors to bedrooms stand on either side of the fireplace. The door on the right, which leads to Ma's bedroom, has remained mostly closed since she left, as there's no use in heating an empty room. Now I envision Ma inside as if she never left for Poppy. Imagine her opening the door, but slowly, because she hates the scraping sound of the rusty hinges. See her fussing with the ties of her apron, pale cheeks ruddy with frustration because it always takes her three tries to get it right. Picture her stepping into the sitting room and announcing that she's finally persuaded Aunt Meara to help us more, and so our family will spend the rest of our lives in this cottage, this village.

I've daydreamed such a scene quite often over the last three weeks, adding more details to prolong it. Sometimes I nearly convince myself that my imaginings are real. But each time I run out of details, all the breath rushes out of me, and I'm forced to confront the truth that the scene will never take place. Because Ma did leave. When she comes back, it won't be to announce we're staying.

I turn to the window, toward a forest slowly being covered in white. A tugging sensation has started below my chest, a pull I can't ignore. I take up the iron poker and stab it into the fire, moving the half-charred logs around until the flames begin to dwindle. I grab my foraging satchel and throw on my own dark brown cloak.

Stepping outside, I'm finally able to breathe once the door closes.

The snowfall is gentle as I plunge into the forest. Flakes are sticking, and a light layer of white already blankets the ground. I keep my gaze on my boots as they make thin tracks in the snow, and then birdsong draws my eyes upward.

High above, the tops of winter-bare and evergreen trees stretch toward the bright gray sky. A striking red cardinal perches on one of the branches. Ma's favorite bird. I look back down at my feet. She's not here to admire it, so why should I?

The windless air makes the cold less daunting, and the more I walk, the warmer I get. I remove my hood to free my dark auburn hair and roll up my sleeves. I breathe deeply, slowly, collecting each breath like a treasure. The cottage holds a hint of smoke all through winter, but the forest never smells fresher than when it snows.

Because the snowfall is light, I make quick work of uncovering the red oak acorns and black walnuts scattered around the trees. The squirrels always get to them first, but I find enough to make the venture worthwhile. With Eirwyn in mind, I visit the wild rose bushes for more rosehips, then collect the last of the season's mint. Not much remains, so I pick up a few fallen pine branches too. The needles are no mint replacement, but they'll help make a decent tea.

I forage for mushrooms last. Their delicate caps and stems mean it's unwise to keep them at the bottom of my satchel. Though I've gathered most of the season's harvest, I manage to find the last of the fall oyster mushrooms, their white caps nearly blending in with the snow.

Once my fingers are sufficiently dirt-stained and I'm satisfied with the weight of my satchel, I pause to rest atop a tree stump, half my height, where I found my last mushroom. I sit cross-legged and lift my face to the sky so the snowflakes bathe my cheeks, flushed from the hours of foraging.

It's rare to find a stump so well cut in the forest. Trees here are cut down only if they've rotted or been irreparably damaged by a storm. Villagers say that when Sugar Maple Village was first founded, and most of the trees were cleared to make way for cottages, all the faeries who inhabited the region gathered west, in the forest left untouched.

They say this because every time a healthy tree is cut down in the western wood, strange occurrences are rumored to befall the woodcutter responsible. Missing coin, missing tools, missing food, even missing children. So tree cutting in the western wood is widely regarded as an invitation for faeries to wreak havoc on one's life and home. That's why all of Sugar Maple's wood comes from the eastern forest.

Yet I've spent more days foraging in my wood than any other living villager and never once come across a faerie. I'm old enough to know losing one's coin is often touted as an excuse for overspending. But if the legend protects the trees, I'm happy to play along.

Pa did more than play along. He watched for faeries in the wood. He blamed them for strange noises or things moved out of place. *When a glove goes missing, blame the faeries*, he'd say. *When food spoils too early, blame the faeries.*

He'd give them credit for good things too. A rose that blooms even after you've forgotten to give it water? Must be the work of faeries. Eirwyn's eyes sparkled every time he told one of his stories, but for me, his tales never held any weight. Perhaps there are faeries in this wood. It's terribly difficult to prove that something you've never seen doesn't exist. But more likely the tales are entertaining fodder for children, a warning for them to behave.

Pa was never discouraged by my indifference. He'd remind me often of the ways I could seek out faeries of the western wood: rituals with bowls of water, gifts of honey and cake, and meeting times among the trees. Simple steps, but ones I've never been tempted to take.

I drop my hand to my side and trace patterns against the rough bark of the tree stump with dirt-soiled fingers. The snow-fall has ended, and a breeze has picked up in its place. Clouds of flurries skim across the ground, tumbling like dancers. My eyes follow each graceful lift and swirl.

I don't yearn for faeries, because I know that nothing could be lovelier or more invigorating than this wood. Nothing.

A burst of new color and the snap of a twig pulls my gaze to the right, where a slender red fox stands frozen.

CHAPTER 2

I hold back a gasp as the fox lifts one black paw—perhaps meaning to step forward but still considering the act—while the other three paws remain buried in the snow.

Her coppery orange coat is gleaming, her tail bushy and brown. Her ears stand straight up and her whiskers twitch ever so slightly. Yellow eyes squint at me, a gaze that is both a question and a challenge.

I don't speak or move. I breathe thin and quiet as the fox slowly lowers her paw to the snow, cocks her head to the side. The fox watches me watching her. She doesn't come closer, but she doesn't retreat either.

I can count on one hand the times I've seen foxes in the wood. They move quickly and stealthily, and whenever I do spot one, it's usually a tail disappearing into a bush or the tips of ears behind a rock. I get to see the whole of this fox, and she doesn't disappoint. She is striking, particularly against the white backdrop of snow.

The fox takes a tentative step forward, and I hold my breath and body completely still. She takes another step, lifts her muzzle, and sniffs the air. Another, and her head turns side to side, as if checking for lurking predators. Then she's padding toward me, and her nimble paws kick up tufts of snow.

She pauses a tail's length away from my tree stump, looking up at me with that same questioning, challenging gaze. And the hint of a smile.

Warmth rushes to my cheeks. It's a foolish thought to have. Foxes can't smile, can they?

And yet, it sounds strangely right. My fingers twitch, and I yearn to reach out and stroke the fox's gleaming mane, brush the tips of her soft ears. Anticipation stirs in my gut. I don't dare move.

A distant bird call sounds somewhere among the trees, and the fox swings her head to the left. Her ears stand straighter. I follow her line of sight and squint but see nothing, not even the source of the call. She swings her head back to me and pushes her forepaws toward the tree stump, bringing her body lower to the ground. She bows her head.

Then she turns and darts into the trees.

"Wait," I call.

But the red fox doesn't wait.

I sit in stunned silence. What a strange encounter. And the sun, so low in the sky already, orange-yellow hues dappling the white ground. My time with the fox felt like minutes, but could an hour have passed? Or two?

And before she ran, she bowed. A red fox bowed to me as if I were royalty.

I uncross my legs and dangle them over the tree stump. I knock my heels against the bark, creating a soft rhythm not so unlike the beating of my heart. I draw a shuddering breath.

The red fox made me forget, for a little while, about overly scented soap and Eirwyn's weathered books. About Ma's absence and the last first snowfall I will ever see in the western wood.

And now she's gone.

"Was that a fox I saw?" a familiar voice calls.

I turn to see my neighbor, Deidra, approaching with her patch-quilt foraging satchel slung over her shoulder. I clear my throat, unable or perhaps unwilling to speak of the fox aloud, and ask instead, "Isn't Shea selling fish in the square?"

Deidra nods, removing her hood to reveal tight black braids draped over her shoulders, the ends decorated with the tiny shells her wife finds on fishing expeditions.

"Then who's watching Orla?"

"Shea took her along if you can believe it."

I lift my eyebrows. Shea is mostly pleasant, except when it comes to her work. One time when I was six, I tried to hang around her during selling hours, eager to escape the dullness of Ma's vegetable cart. I made two dead fish kiss each other in front of customers and nearly lost my hearing when Shea caught on. I can't imagine her selling fish with a baby on her hip.

"I all but spit out my tea when she suggested it," Deidra says, echoing my thoughts. "But she feels poorly about being away so much."

Shea's trade used to be hunting and trapping, but a few years back she switched to fishing because she heard it would provide a steadier income. She was right, but now instead of daily trips into the forest, she takes days-long trips upriver for the best catch, meaning she's often separated from her wife and daughter.

"Well," I say, shifting on my tree stump so there's room for Deidra to join me, "I hope the villagers don't give her too much trouble."

"I imagine if they do, Shea will know how to handle them even with Orla in her arms." Deidra holds up her satchel. "Gather a good haul?"

I pat my bag. "Should please Eirwyn."

"Likely the last good day we'll have until spring," she says, sitting beside me on the tree stump. She's much taller than I am, so her boots brush the snow.

This close, I can smell the rosemary oil she uses in her hair. The comforting aroma chases away some of the unease that's been clinging to me since my argument with Eirwyn. I'm tempted to rest my head against Deidra's shoulder, as I so often did in the weeks following Pa's death. We'd be foraging together and suddenly the loss of him would overwhelm me. I'd freeze up and close my eyes, unable to take another step in the forest he loved so much. Deidra would guide me to a log or a boulder, and she would stroke my hair and sing nonsense songs about the trees until I felt safe enough to open my eyes.

But as comforted as I am by Deidra's presence, I find I'm still feeling too prickly to revert to childlike ways.

"I like winter foraging," I say. "The challenge of it, you know?"

"I don't," Deidra laughs. "But you've always had a bit of a hunter in you."

Ma thought so too. She even took me to the eastern forest to hunt when I was eight. The first rabbit I caught in a snare had a wounded leg, so of course I bandaged it and set it free. Ma ruffled my hair and told me to stick to foraging with Pa.

Eirwyn took to hunting much easier and became quite skilled with a bow. Nowadays, it's hard to catch anything in the eastern forest when there's so much competition from other villagers, and Ma won't let her hunt in the western wood because of the faeries. Not that Ma's blessing would make a difference. My sister hasn't so much as touched her bow since Pa passed.

I watch Deidra rub her deep brown hands against the chill. Curiously, I'm not cold at all. "I see quite a bit of Eirwyn," she says, "but you haven't come by since your mother left. I was beginning to fear you'd taken ill."

"You could've looked for me if you wanted," I tell her, lifting my chin in a gesture toward the trees. "I'm always here."

"Yes, well, you ever think about venturing a different way?"

I roll my eyes. "You sound like my sister."

She bumps her shoulder against mine. "Your sister wants what's best for you and so do I. You know, there are young people your age here in Sugar Maple."

"So?"

"So," she says, drawing out the word, "perhaps you should invite one over for tea. Or take one of them foraging."

I frown at my palms, which are beginning to sweat. I wipe them on my cloak.

Deidra releases a heavy breath. "You need friends, Ro. Eirwyn can't be your only one."

"You're my friend. Shea is, too." I swallow against an ache

in my throat. "And what's the point of making more now that we're leaving?"

She hesitates a moment before answering. "Could give you practice for when you meet people in Poppy."

"I don't want to meet people," I say. "People ask too many questions."

"Like what?"

Childhood memories drape over my shoulders like shadows. Blushes, downcast eyes, sweaty palms. My ears are teased with the echo of whispers that follow whenever I venture to Maple Square. I scratch the tree bark with my fingernails, adding more grime to hands already soiled from digging in the dirt.

"You know," I murmur, "like if you have your eye on some-one, and if that someone is a boy or a girl."

Because according to the villagers of Sugar Maple, it must be one or the other.

Deidra offers me a soft smile. "There will always be those who refuse to understand you, Ro, but there are plenty of peo-ple who will. You need only to find them like Shea and I have."

I don't want to roll my eyes at her again, so I resist the urge by inspecting my fingernails, dirtied with bark shavings. I'll gladly take my forest hideaway over an exhausting search for acceptance, thank you very much.

"And whatever questions you face," continues Deidra, "you're the one who decides whether to answer or not. That's a bit of power, I think."

I want to believe she's right. I do. But I can't ignore the stab of frustration in my chest. Deidra's situation is different. She's dealt with her own share of poor looks and harsh judgments, but she's never been a question for our village to puzzle out. Deidra and Shea have been together since they were young. They have a child. Their family is the picture of stability.

Meanwhile, I remain the confused girl who can't make up her mind.

Deidra asks, "Have you tried talking to Eirwyn about this?"

I shake my head.

"I think she'd want you to confide in her so she can offer counsel. It's what sisters are for, after all."

I shrug. Maybe there's some truth in that, but I don't want my sister's counsel. Not when she has little use for mine regarding the move to Poppy. Besides, though Eirwyn loves the whole of me, her desire for a dashing prince, and only that, has never wavered. How could she possibly understand?

We sit in silence for a while longer until Deidra yawns loudly, her shoulder jostling mine again as she stretches her arms to the sky. "Well, time to head back. Shea and Orla will be home soon."

I'm fighting my own yawn, but I'm not ready to leave the wood yet. "I'm going to stay a bit longer."

"All right, but leave before it grows too dark." She slides off the tree stump and adjusts her satchel. "There are creatures larger than foxes in this wood."

"I will," I say, eyes drawn back to the trees by her words, hungry for another glimpse of a coppery orange coat.

"And visit more," she adds over her shoulder. "I know Shea misses you too."

I nod, but I'm not sure I will. Seems smarter to distance myself from Deidra and Shea now, so when spring comes and I must leave them, the leaving won't be so difficult.

Once Deidra's long out of sight, I hop off my tree stump to study the line of fox tracks leading deeper into the wood. My neighbor might've scared her away, but the fox could be waiting for me somewhere among these trees. Perhaps she wants me to follow her tracks, find her like she found me.

I'm tempted to do just that, yet night draws near. While Ma encourages independence in her daughters, her one rule is to never be alone in the forest when it's dark, and it's a rule Eirwyn's enforced since she left. Besides, my sister's likely returned from Maple Square by now. She'll be waiting for me, on the bench reading or hopelessly attempting to rebuild the fire. My sister can no more successfully kindle a flame than I can prepare a decent meal.

I find the will to turn away from the tracks before the temptation to follow seizes me completely, but I drag my feet toward the cottage, thoughts of the fox wrapping around me like rose vines. My boots clomp through the snow and I imagine them as nimble fox feet prowling past the trees. I shift my head right and left, wrinkling my nose as if scenting the air for signs of prey. I imagine the glowing moon illuminating my coppery coat, turning its fire into faerie light.

If only I were a fox. No one would take me to Poppy, then.

I lift my eyes to the dark opening ahead, the one that leads to the clearing before the cottage. I squint, and through the dimness, I can make out the square windows glowing faintly. Either Eirwyn figured out the fire, or she's lit every lamp we own.

Icy unease pricks my skin. Now that I'm closer, I'm not sure I'm ready to go home, ready to face Eirwyn so soon after our quarrel. I still feel awful for invoking Pa's name the way I did. I linger in the developing night, breathing in the cold until it nips at my chest. All around me, snow glistens like the stars slowly appearing overhead. Shadowy trees bend and creak in the wind. A few stray leaves—left over from fall—flutter quietly to the forest floor.

Then, a streak of copper leaps across my path, mere inches from the tips of my boots.

I jump back, but I can't find my footing. I fall to the ground, and the sudden drop is so jarring that I wince. I press a cold palm to my forehead, blinking away the haze in my eyes in time to see the red fox bounding in the direction of the cottage, paws kicking up snow like a small windstorm.

An ache spreads down my neck as I rise to my feet, and my backside is covered with snow, but neither matters with the fox running ahead. I'm about to chase after her when I hear a deep huff.

I breathe in sharply through my nose. Slowly, I turn.

A bear, its massive form crowding the forest, lumbers toward me.

Muscles ripple beneath dark brown fur. Ears stand straight up. Each puff of breath is a steamy cloud beneath the moonlight.

I try to swallow my rising terror but it's so thick in my throat that I choke. I cover my mouth, fingers trembling. My chest plummets to my gut, over and over.

A bear in the wood. A creature much larger than a fox. Fur bristling. Eyes gleaming. Mouth hungry. Cold fear drenches me, seeps past layers of clothes to soak my skin.

My teeth chatter. I know I should do something, but I can't

remember what. Ma's voice is insistent in my ears, but I can't comprehend the words. I'm caught. Gasping. Trembling. Prey.

The bear huffs again. I can't breathe.

Then something inside me snaps, and Ma's lesson slams into me like a gale of frozen wind. I don't wait. I lift my arms, wave them slowly. "Hey! I'm backing away, I'm backing away."

I step backward as he trudges forward. Enormous paws make deep grooves in the snow. I veer to the left, straying from his path. Dread grips my gut like bear claws. The itch to flee has never been stronger, but I keep my pace. Never try to outrun a bear.

I bump into something solid. Only a tree, but a yelp escapes my lips before I can stop it. The bear groans low.

I shudder against the bark. "I'm backing away," I repeat. "Please, I'm backing away."

Moving around the tree, I lose sight of the bear for a few precious moments. But my knees weaken in relief as soon as I regain my view. Despite my yelp, the bear isn't following me. Ma's lesson worked.

I wait until I can no longer hear the bear's heavy tread, then collapse against a tree, my forehead pressed hard against the bark. I release a rush of breath, lips pulling upward in a cautious smile. No longer caught. No longer prey. No need to tremble.

But a sharp wail pierces the night. *The fox.*

I imagine the scene clearly: Teeth clamping. A coppery coat drenched in red. A broken body in the snow. A triumphant roar.

A swell of rage much stronger than my fear burns its way down my throat.

I dash after the lumbering bear, my satchel thumping

against my side. My clothes are damp with snow and sweat. When I reach the edge of the forest, my breaths have turned hoarse and painful.

The bear has the fox cornered, pressed up against a thick oak tree. My ears ring, the sound overcoming all whispers of Ma's lesson. I must save her. I must stop him.

With fumbling hands, I remove my boot. I blink hard, find my aim, and hurl my boot at the bear. It spirals chaotically until it hits the top of his back. He grunts and turns his head.

"Hey!" I scream, clenching my fists. "Hey!"

It's not enough. The bear's head swings back toward the fox. The cornered animal wails again—sharp, insistent, and loud.

I yank off my other boot and throw. "Leave her alone! Get away from her!"

The second boot hits the bear's side. This time the beast turns fully in my direction. Gleaming eyes latch onto me. He huffs, lifts one large paw, takes one step forward. His ears flatten against his head.

It seems I've become the fox.

The bear charges. I spin on my heels and sprint toward the cottage. A mere hundred feet away, but I fear I won't make it. My chest is tight; I can't get enough air. I can't move fast enough. My sock feet slip and slide. Above the ringing in my ears is the sound of the bear's heavy tread. At such a speed, not even a fox body could save me now.

With a grunt, the bear's head rams into my back and I'm thrown forward. My body smacks against the ground and my face meets the snow. Crystals of ice sting my cheeks. Unlike the fox, my resulting wail is low and quiet.

A fleeting hope flares in my chest at the thought of the fox leaping onto the bear's back, nipping at his ear to save her new ally. But of course, foxes don't think like foolish girls. Foxes don't provoke a bear; they run from one. I hope the red fox is running now.

A massive paw batters my side. The assault turns my scream into a whimper. I bring my knees to my chest and cover my head with my arms. I wait for another swipe; I know it will come.

Until it doesn't.

Instead, the bear emits a low groan, and my eyes flutter open. There's an arrow embedded in the beast's right shoulder. He stumbles. I uncoil and drag myself across the snow. He drops to the ground like an overturned boulder, huffing and making clicking sounds with his tongue.

In the open doorway of the cottage stands Eirwyn, bow in hand. Her slender frame is illuminated by the light from within.

"Ro," she calls, starting forward.

I stagger to my feet and run to my sister. We collide and Eirwyn's bow smacks my back, but I barely register the discomfort. I bury my face in my sister's neck, smell her rose perfume. Eirwyn grips me tight and murmurs calming words into my ear, stroking my snow-drenched hair.

"I'm sorry," I tell her. "I didn't mean to be out so late. I'm so sorry."

"You're all right," Eirwyn says, breathless and trembling. "I'm here."

Thank goodness for that. After years of neglect, she took up her bow to save me. I'm relieved she never threw it away.

"Did you kill it?" I ask. "Is it dead?"

"I don't know, I—"

I feel Eirwyn's body stiffen, then she shrugs herself out of my embrace. Her eyes are wide, her lips parted. She stares past me as if I'm no longer here.

I tug on her sleeve. "Eirwyn, what is it?"

"Ro," she breathes.

She lifts an arm and points. My eyes follow.

Lying in the snow is a boy. A boy where there should be a bear. A bleeding, naked boy.

He groans, and he sounds like a bear. But he isn't one. He's not massive and he doesn't have fur or sharp claws. He's pale with messy brown hair and long limbs. He's human.

But he's lying in the snow where a bear was, with the arrow Eirwyn shot protruding from his shoulder.

Numbed by the sight, I reach for my sister's hand, grip her fingers as if touch will rouse me from this strange, terrible dream.

The not-a-bear boy lifts his head. "Help," he moans. "Please."

Eirwyn drops her bow. "What have I done?"

CHAPTER 3

"**Q**uick, help me bring him inside," Eirwyn says, rushing forward. When I make no move to follow, she adds, "Come, Ro, he's bleeding."

"Because you shot him." I'm breathing heavy and fast, still not quite certain what I'm seeing. "Because he's a bear."

A bear that's not a bear. A boy that should *be* a bear but isn't. I rub my eyes. I blink three times. The scene remains the same. I need to steady my thoughts, need to understand. But how?

Eirwyn kneels before the boy and touches a tentative hand to his bare back. "He's not a bear anymore. Help me."

"No." I begin to back away, clutching my throbbing side. "He tried to kill me. He almost ate the fox."

"What fox?" Eirwyn shakes her head. "Never mind, it doesn't matter."

"It does matter," I insist, shuffling in the snow because I can't seem to pick up my feet. "That boy, or bear, or whatever he is—he's dangerous. We can't help him."

Anger sparks across her features. "We can't let him freeze and bleed in the snow. He's a person. He asked for our help."

I bring my fingers to my temple. She's not making any sense.

"I won't be responsible for a boy's death," she snaps. "Help me, Ro. Please."

I groan, the sound not so unlike a bear, and stomp over to my sister. I cross my arms against my chest, pouting like a child, but I think I have the right to, all things considered. "What do you want me to do?"

"You take his uninjured arm. I'll take the right."

Together we lift him from the ground. The bear-boy stirs but doesn't speak. Pressed against his naked side, I use my free hand to shield my eyes.

"Ro," says Eirwyn.

"I've never seen a naked boy, and I don't want to see one now." I keep my eyes shielded. "Lead the way."

"Fine," she mutters.

He's as heavy as a bear, so it takes us a while to drag him to the cottage. The boy appears to be unconscious, as he doesn't speak again nor offer to hold any of his own weight. I yearn to drop him in the snow, but Eirwyn's determined breaths keep me from leaving him to the night.

My sock feet are numb with cold, but sweat breaks across my forehead and pools under my arms. A sharp pain pulses behind my eyes, and my side continues to throb where the bear-boy struck me. Thankfully his claws ripped my cloak and not my skin.

"Almost there," Eirwyn says.

With my eyes still shielded by my free hand, I can do nothing but believe her.

Inside the cottage, we carefully maneuver past the dining table, then lower the boy onto the cushioned bench before the fireplace. I step away while Eirwyn fusses over something.

"You can look now," she says.

Cautiously, I lower my hand from my eyes. A blanket covers the bear-boy's legs and waist.

I bite back a grin. "Thank you."

Eirwyn nods. "Fetch Ma's whiskey and the garden shears."

What follows is a process I fiercely wish I didn't have to see.

Cutting the arrow. Pulling it free—so much blood. Drenching the wound in whiskey. Sewing it shut with a needle and thread—how does he not wake in agony? And finally, the bandages.

"Where did you learn all this?" I ask Eirwyn, my throat thick.

My sister pulls the blanket up to the boy's neck. "From books, mostly."

"Books taught you how to remove an arrow from a bear-boy's shoulder and stitch his wound?"

Eirwyn's brows lift. "Bear-boy?"

"What else do I call him?"

"I suppose we can ask him when he wakes."

I wrinkle my nose. I'm not sure I want him to wake.

My sister wipes her hands on the last, mostly clean cloth. "We should change. We look awful."

She's right. Her white linen shirt is smudged with blood.

My clothes aren't faring too well either, ripped and drenched in melted snow and sweat. But leaving to change means leaving him alone. I voice the concern to Eirwyn, all while peering warily at the bear-boy.

Her lips twitch in amusement. "Do you think he'll turn into a bear while we're dressing?"

"He *was* a bear," I say through clenched teeth. I wish she'd take this seriously. I wish she'd stop treating this like an ordinary night. "Whatever strangeness holds him could start up again at any moment."

"If it does, I'll grab my bow." She squeezes my shoulder and disappears into our shared bedroom.

I linger in the sitting room, watching the rise and fall of the boy's chest. He stirs and I jump back toward the fireplace, but thankfully my cloak doesn't catch because the fire is nothing but embers. I draw a steadying breath. Despite the creaking floorboards, the boy's eyes remain closed.

Eirwyn seems to have already forgotten what this creature did to me, how he hurt me. But I haven't, and I won't. The bear's huff echoes in my ears. He charges toward me every time I close my eyes. My hands continue to tremble. I hate being alone with him, but I also don't want him left completely alone. It's a maddening contradiction.

When my sister returns, she brushes past me to kneel beside the bench, fixing her eyes on the bear-boy's calm, sleeping face. She wears a pale blue skirt and a matching linen shirt, and I recognize the outfit as one of her favorites, as if she's trying to impress the creature that attacked her younger sister. Gooseflesh pricks my arms. What's gotten into her?

At her prodding, I leave to change, but keep the door to the bedroom cracked open. I set my satchel on the dresser. No doubt the mushrooms are battered beyond usefulness, but that's a concern for tomorrow. I strip off my dirty clothes, tossing them in a corner to also deal with later, then inspect the damage done by the bear. Thankfully, my thick cloak kept his claws from breaking skin, but my side is red and tender where he struck me. Bruises are sure to form by morning.

Heartsick and bone-weary, I pull out a worn pair of leggings and a long-sleeved shirt that belonged to Pa. It has a few stains and holes and stray threads. Ma's offered to mend it many times, but that would make the garment more mine than his, and I don't want that.

I count silently while I dress, and when I reach twenty, I peer out into the sitting room to check on Eirwyn, but nothing's amiss. The bear-boy remains asleep. Once I've finished, I take a moment before the mirror that hangs above the dresser. My dark auburn hair is in tangles, my cheeks red. My eyes are cold and empty. I can't remember looking so grieved, not for years, not since Pa passed.

Before tonight, I never had reason to fear the western wood. The forest was as much my home as the cottage, perhaps even more so. The betrayal tastes bitter on my tongue, like tea that's steeped too long.

"He's waking up," Eirwyn calls.

My body tenses. I consider pulling back the covers and crawling into bed. But I'm a girl of fifteen, not a child. I can't abandon my sister.

I slip past my bedroom door without making it creak, but

even my smallest sounds draw the eyes of my sister and the boy. He's propped himself up on the bench, though he's still reclined. The blanket has slipped from where Eirwyn tucked it around his chin, gathering just above his waist.

"Roisin," he says, the moment our gazes lock.

Panic seizes me, implores me to run from him as I ran from the bear. "How—how do you know my name?"

He gives no answer, only watches me with something like wonder in his eyes. I can't think of a single reason why he'd look at me like that, the girl he tried to kill.

Eirwyn swats away the question. "He must have heard me say it."

"No." His voice is deep—much too deep for a gangly boy. "I knew it before."

"Before what?" Eirwyn asks, looking at him strangely.

He shakes his head, eyes squinting to slits. "I . . . do not know."

Who is this boy? This boy who knows my name, who had claws instead of fingers a mere hour ago. His stilted speech more than hints that he's not from Sugar Maple Village, or from any village like it. Even with the blanket covering his legs and waist, much of his skin is exposed, pale and smooth, bearing no scars or marks to show he's lived any sort of life. Lingering by the fireplace mantel, I exchange a wary glance with my sister.

"What's your name?" Eirwyn asks.

His eyes take in the room as if he's searching for the answer, as if something in our cottage will tell him what he seeks.

"Brend," he says finally.

"Brend," repeats my sister. "All right, what about your family name?"

"Family name." He says the words slowly, not quite a question but not an answer either.

"You know, a name your relatives share, which marks you as family," Eirwyn explains, amusement bleeding through her tone.

His thick eyebrows draw together. "I do not remember any family name."

"Perhaps you're an orphan," I murmur.

"Ro, that is quite unkind to say," Eirwyn scolds.

I'm tempted to challenge the reprimand, as I don't think it's so unkind to suggest the boy who was once a bear might be an orphan, but my sister moves on before I can form the words.

"I'm Eirwyn Birch," she says, adjusting her braid so it drapes over one shoulder rather than down her back. She must've re-braided her hair after she changed, because this one is too neat to be the same one she had earlier. "Roisin is my younger sister, but she goes by Ro."

"No one calls me Roisin," I add.

Which makes the fact of him knowing my full name all the stranger.

Brend has no comment for that, though. He moves his right arm, wincing. "How did I get here? My arm . . ."

"You don't remember anything that's happened tonight?" asks my sister.

Before he can answer, I blurt, "You were a bear and you nearly killed me."

"Ro!" gasps Eirwyn.

"What?" I jerk my chin toward Brend. "He needs to know what he did."

He can't hide from it. My sister might let him, but I won't.

He seems to look past us, out the window into the night. "So, it was not a dream. The fox. Snow and trees. Claws . . ." he trails off, shuddering. "I was a bear?"

"It seems that way," says my sister.

"How?" Brend asks. "How is this possible?"

Eirwyn shakes her head. Her voice is subdued when she says, "We don't know."

He looks at me. "I am sorry. For whatever I did, I am sorry."

I turn away from his heady gaze, rubbing my arms against the chill. The burning oil lamps provide ample light but not much warmth, so I kneel to rouse the fireplace embers into flames. As I add kindling and strike a match, I feel Brend's eyes on the back of my neck. Like the sun bearing down on me while I slice delicate mushrooms from tree bark in the summertime. A searing, inescapable heat.

Sounds of Eirwyn cleaning up fill the cottage—the toss of bloody cloths into the wastebasket, Ma's whiskey returned to the top cabinet in the kitchen. Once the flames are steady, I place the kettle, half filled with leftover water from this afternoon, on the hook over the fire and wait for the water to heat, for my own body to warm. My clean clothes are dirtied by ash dust, reminding me of the bucket I dropped this morning—a time that already seems so long ago.

Brend remains quiet, assumedly from shock. I'm grateful to lose the sound of his strange, deep voice, if only for a little while. Sometime later, I brush the ash dust from my leggings and help Eirwyn prepare the tea. I breathe deep as I lift a cup to my lips. Ginger spice.

To think that while Eirwyn purchased tea, I locked eyes with a red fox, a fox that led me to a bear-boy named Brend. Where is the fox now? If Brend wasn't here, taking up space on the bench and fascinating my sister, I would search for her, make sure she's all right.

When I return to the sitting room, the boy who was once a bear holds the broken pieces of the arrow in his hands. His fingers graze the sharp tip of the bloody arrowhead, his eyes closed. When he opens them, they appear wet. But it could just be the glare of an oil lamp.

"I'm sorry I shot you." Eirwyn holds a steaming cup out for Brend. "You were threatening my sister, and I didn't know you were also a boy."

I gape at Eirwyn, my ears growing hot. "Threatening? Are you sure that's the right word for it?"

She gives me a measured look and shakes her head, wordlessly telling me to be silent in the way elder sisters do. I scowl at her, then at him.

"I understand," says Brend, in that same, unnervingly deep voice. He sets the arrow pieces aside and takes the offered cup. For a moment I don't see hands holding the clay, but claws. I blink, and the vision leaves me.

"Can you remember anything other than your name?" Eirwyn asks. "How old you are? If you have a family?"

I tap my foot against the floorboards, wishing she would get on with telling him to leave. Why so many questions? What does it matter how old he is, or what family he hails from? He's a bear, not a guest.

"Sixteen winters, I think," he answers. "I cannot remember any family."

Sixteen *winters*? Doesn't he mark time according to years? Well, if it wasn't already clear before, this confirms he's not from anywhere near here.

"You have no idea how you became a bear?" continues Eirwyn.

He shakes his head.

"Maybe the faeries cursed you," I say, leaning against the mantel of the fireplace. A healthy distance from the bench. From him. "If that's the case, you should leave. They probably cursed you for a reason, and by sheltering you we might be angering them."

Eirwyn sighs. "You hardly believe in faeries, Ro."

"Before tonight, I didn't believe in bear-boys either."

"That's enough," she says under her breath.

I lift my shoulders in a shrug. I can no more say that faeries are responsible for Brend's predicament than I can say they don't exist. All I know is what happened: A bear attacked me, then turned into a boy. Eirwyn stitched up his wound, and now he should be on his way.

"Roisin is right." I bristle at his use of my full name. "I know nothing of faeries or curses, but I do know that I have caused you enough trouble. I should go." He struggles to a seated position, wincing again.

Eirwyn gently pushes him back down. "You can't leave in the middle of the night. You're hurt. Where would you go?"

"That's for him to figure out," I say.

Eirwyn glares at me. "Ro, follow me to the kitchen for a moment, will you?"

"Fine."

I avoid looking at Brend as I follow my sister. Though the kitchen isn't separated from the sitting room by a door, Eirwyn leads me far enough that our low murmurs won't easily reach our visitor.

"What he did as a bear no longer matters," Eirwyn says, righting a jar of herbs that must have toppled over amid the melee of the night. "He's a boy now—a boy our own age who's alone and confused and hurt. He needs us."

"What if he becomes a bear again?" I ask, pushing stray crumbs—remnants of our midday meal—into a tiny pile on the countertop.

"He might," she admits, biting her lip. "But we can't send him away. Not while he's wounded."

"Ma wouldn't approve." I hope that by bringing up our sensible mother, my sister will also return to sensibleness.

Instead, she says, "Ma's not here."

The reminder doesn't bring me any sort of satisfaction. I'd rather endure a hundred of Ma's lectures than spend another moment listening to Brend's heavy breathing. I'm not given a chance to say any of this because Eirwyn's already heading back to the sitting room, back to him. I brush the stray crumbs into the wastebasket and follow her.

He looks up as we return. He was studying the arrow pieces again, and now his eyes have a haunted look about them. I have the sudden urge to chuck the pieces into the fire.

"It's decided," Eirwyn says. "You're staying. At least until your wound is healed."

What did she just say? "I didn't agree to—"

"Excuse my sister," she interrupts. "She's a little shaken, but she understands."

I press my lips together, fuming. I certainly do not understand. It's as if my sister hasn't heard a word from me. Or simply doesn't care. I fear it's the latter.

"Are you sure?" Brend asks, handing his empty teacup to Eirwyn. "Roisin?"

Is he trying to taunt me? "I said don't call me that."

"Right, I apologize." His eyes meet mine. "But are you sure you want me to stay?"

I rein in the urge to scoff, but only because Eirwyn is watching and listening, and will punish me with more than a glare if she senses another hint of dissent. Of course I don't want Brend to stay. Of course I'd rather Eirwyn chase him from the cottage with a broom and tend to my bruises. But Eirwyn is the elder sister, the one Ma left in charge. Much as I'd like to be rid of him, the decision isn't mine.

I close my eyes and take a deep breath, holding it until my chest is near bursting. Breathing out, I say my next words in a rush, "If you become a bear again, I'll shoot you myself, and I won't be aiming for your shoulder."

Before my sister can scold me, I withdraw to the bedroom. I leave the door open so warmth from the fire can trickle in, but once I crawl into bed, I pull the covers over my head to hide from the lamplight and murmured conversation between Eirwyn and Brend. I hug my knees to my chest like I did during the bear attack. Alone in the dark, tears I've held since I fell onto the snow slip freely down my cheeks.

Drifting off, I think again of the red fox—her coppery coat, her peculiar smile, her paws sliding forward into a bow. I wish the fox was sleeping in the sitting room, instead of the boy who was once a bear, and who could very well become a bear again in the night.

CHAPTER 4

Eirwyn is not in her bed.

As I open my gritty eyes to the morning light, my sister's absence is the first thing I discern. Someone who doesn't know Eirwyn might suggest she rose early. But her bed is made, and Eirwyn never makes her bed. I'm the one who makes it for her every morning.

Which can only mean my sister did not sleep in her bed last night.

Chest thumping, I sit up too quickly and groan at the ache in my side, a reminder of what happened last night. I wait for the pain to pass, then search beneath my pillow until I grasp the small knife I've kept there since Ma left. I unsheathe the blade from its leather and grip the handle tightly, abandoning my bed and tiptoeing to the cracked-open door. Slowly, I pull the knob until I can slip through without bumping the wood.

The sitting room is quiet, lit by the gray winter light streaming through the windows. The fire holds dwindling embers and the lamps no longer burn.

The bear-boy—*Brend*—still sleeps on the cushioned bench, bare chest rising and falling with his even breaths. His right hand clutches both arrow pieces, stained with his blood. What sort of boy sleeps with a weapon between his fingers? Surely not a safe one.

Meanwhile, Eirwyn is curled up on the floor before the fireplace without even a blanket, arms wrapped around herself and chin tucked to her chest. Her hair's come loose from its braid. Soot clings to her clothes. Scowling, I sheathe my knife and tuck it in the waistband of my leggings.

I lay a blanket over my sister, rebuild the fire, then tread lightly to Ma's bedroom. The space is crisp with cold from keeping the door closed, and I rub my arms as I hurry to the set of drawers beside her bed. I rummage through the one with Pa's clothes until I find something suitable. The shirt and trousers will hang on the boy, but at least he'll be properly dressed.

As I pull the clothing from the drawer, I can't help but recall the way Brend said my name last night. *Roisin.* Assuredly, as if he already knew me. As if our first introduction wasn't in the wood. As if his first *hello* wasn't a terrifying huff followed by the strike of his enormous paw.

I place a flat palm against my tender side, an injury Eirwyn didn't think to ask about last night, too busy tending to Brend. I lift the hem of my shirt and the sight of the ugly purple bruise brings a feeling of sick fullness to my chest. That bear could have killed me. I came close to leaving Ma and Eirwyn like Pa left us. I've ached with hunger. I've wondered what we would do when the food stores ran out. But until last night, I've never thought I could die at fifteen. The sudden shift in perspective is a sobering weight upon my shoulders, like a satchel filled to the brim with walnuts and acorns.

There's a soft knock at Ma's door. I look up to see Brend in the entryway, a blanket wrapped around his thin waist. He cradles his injured arm to his chest.

I drop my shirt. "What are you doing?"

Brend's eyes widen. He takes a step backward. "I—I did not mean to startle you."

Outraged and, all right, a little embarrassed, I hurl a wad of clothing at him. Despite his injured shoulder, he deftly catches the pile. I bite the inside of my cheek.

"Don't follow me," I order, brushing past him.

In the sitting room, I check the kettle and find it filled with water, meaning sometime before she fell asleep, Eirwyn must have made a trip to the well. Oh, the irony! I practically live in the forest, and yet it's *Eirwyn* who ignores Ma's rule about going out after dark. At least the most dangerous creature in the wood slept in our cottage last night. Eirwyn might have been safer outside, away from the bear-boy who sleeps with the arrow that wounded him.

I place the kettle over the fire then return to the kitchen to grab the last remaining apple, maybe a day too soft, from the basket on the counter. Slicing off pieces with my knife, I witness a fully clothed, possibly ganglier Brend emerge from Ma's bedroom and proceed to do exactly what I said he shouldn't.

I'm finished slicing when he reaches me, but I don't look up. Instead, I arrange the apple pieces into the shape of a flower on the counter. One piece doesn't quite fit in the design, so I plop it into my mouth and chew slowly. Too soft, like I thought, but still tart and sweet. I try and fail to ignore the bear-boy's heavy breathing.

"Roisin—*Ro*," Brend corrects quickly.

I scowl. It can't possibly be so hard for him to use the name I prefer. Sourness thickening on my tongue, I start chewing with my mouth open, hoping I'm off-putting enough to drive him away.

"I know you do not want me here," he says.

I keep chewing.

"You do not trust me."

I wipe juice from my chin.

"Well, I cannot say that I trust myself either."

I close my mouth. Swallow.

"I know three things. One is my name."

I lift my gaze to meet his. I didn't notice last night, but Brend's eyes are a rich, dark amber. A bear's eyes. I shudder.

If Brend notices, he doesn't let on. "The second is that I owe you and your sister a debt, one that I mean to repay."

I blink at him, surprised but thoroughly unconvinced. I can't imagine what he could do to repay us. His stilted speech could mean he's highborn, yes, but what good is a highborn boy cursed by magic, without his memories? If he does have treasures to offer, he's likely forgotten where he hid them.

"And the third," he says. His eyes flit to one side briefly.

"Yes?" I ask, suddenly impatient.

"Your sister is waking."

I pour every ounce of my irritation into my resulting glare. "That's the third thing?"

"What?" Brend's eyebrows pull together. "No, of course not. But she is waking up."

"How could you possibly—"

"Ro? Brend?"

I swallow and it feels like I still have an apple piece stuck in my throat. Lying on the floor, Eirwyn is hidden from view by the free-standing counter, yet Brend knew she was waking without so much as turning. How? Is it because he's half-bear? Or is the explanation stranger?

"Coming," I answer. I look at Brend. "The third thing?"

His face, a moment ago messy and full, is now completely blank. He's so still and silent that I question if he's even breathing.

"Oh, what, have you forgotten?" I ask.

The fire hisses. More smoke than usual stings my nose.

"Ro, there's something wrong," Eirwyn calls.

"You should attend to that," says Brend quietly.

Then he walks away.

After my morning chores, I bring my cloak and the sewing kit to the dining table behind the wooden bench, where Brend sits quietly while Eirwyn changes his bandages. Though I try to keep my eyes on the needle while I mend the tears in the wool, Eirwyn's cheery voice draws my gaze.

"No sign of infection. In fact, you seem to be healing rather quickly."

"Which means you won't have to stay much longer," I mutter, earning an eyebrow raise from my sister and a pained look from the bear-boy.

I ignore both, continuing, "You know, Pa used to say a curse is a sickness, one you can catch if you get too close. So we shouldn't house—"

"Stop peddling Pa's beliefs as if you've ever believed them yourself," Eirwyn snaps. "Goodness, Ro, how can you want to chase away someone who needs our help?"

Her words are needle pricks to my chest. What he needs? What about what I need?

I drop my half-mended cloak onto the table. "That beast," I say, pointing a finger at Brend, "came close to killing me last night, and now you want to help him? What's wrong with you?"

A look of hurt crosses Eirwyn's features before it's quickly replaced with one I've seen on Ma's face many times: a look that says I don't understand anything and never will.

Brend clears his throat. "Roisin, please do not be angry with—"

"Don't call me that," I say. "And don't talk to me like you know me."

Brend grips the arrow pieces so hard they break apart in his hands. Stunned, I rise from the table, the backs of my knees knocking against the chair. If he sets those hands on me, those hands that were claws . . .

"Let's all settle down," murmurs Eirwyn, "before someone gets hurt."

But I was already hurt. Last night. She didn't care. Still doesn't.

Seething, I snatch my half-mended cloak from the table and yank open the front door, slamming it behind me and muffling Eirwyn's call of protest. I stomp to the tree line in sock feet and find the boots I threw at the bear lying in the snow. I brush them clean, then pull them onto my feet. They are stiff with cold, but walking will loosen them.

I venture into the forest. The needle pricks in my chest soften with a few deep breaths of winter air, but shivers quickly overtake me. The temperature plummeted overnight and now it's even too cold for snowfall. My eyes are too dry and my nose stings. The ground is hard and a little slippery. My steps are slow and careful.

Yet though the air is frigid, my mind begins to calm, draped in the clear winter quiet. I didn't bring my satchel, so I forgo foraging in favor of loops around the trees searching for animal tracks, specifically the set that will lead me to the red fox. I walk for more than an hour, seeking her curious smile, but the sets of tracks I find belong to rabbits or deer. Even the line near the tree stump has vanished.

I don't want to leave the wood, and yet the air is no warmer than it was when I began and my bruised side is beginning to throb. Since there's little to do in the forest when it's bitterly cold and one is alone, I reluctantly head home.

I used to spend winter days in the western wood with Pa. On afternoons when Ma and Eirwyn weren't selling goods in

Maple Square, my sister would follow along as well. We'd catch snowflakes on our tongues, make shapes in the snow, and build tall castles that would freeze to ice overnight and glitter beneath the next day's sun.

Until the winter Pa passed away.

A fever stole many lives that winter, including his. During the first few months without him, Eirwyn kept to her bed, surrounded by her books even while she slept. She has only one shelf full, as they are hard to come by in the village, but she must have read each book at least three times during her grief—stories about romance and daring rescues and enchanted kingdoms. Stories very unlike her own life.

Every so often a book or two would slip off her bed in the middle of the night and jar me from sleep. Once an apple core got lost under a pile and tiny flies invaded our room for over a week. Whenever Eirwyn cried, I couldn't comfort her because the books were always in the way.

Because it was easier than mourning, I complained and complained. About the noise and the smells, and the barriers between my sister and me that never existed before. To each grievance, Ma said, "Hush. Your sister will heal in her own time, as we all will."

And Eirwyn did heal, eventually and rather suddenly. One spring day, she returned all the books to the tiny shelf below the bedroom window. The following afternoon, when she returned from using the outhouse, she didn't hurry to her bed. When she cried, she didn't stiffen as I stroked her hair.

Eirwyn healed, yes, but not quite enough, for she's never wanted to spend another winter day in the forest—not even when I've asked her, not even when I've begged her.

This will be the fourth winter I spend alone in the wood.

I'm at the edge of the forest now. Squinting, I can make out the blurry shapes of Brend and Eirwyn through the cottage window, still on the bench where I left them. A dark feeling spreads through my limbs, threatening to turn loose fingers back into clenched fists. I know our village is small, but there must be other boys for my sister. Boys who don't turn into beasts.

"Is that where you live?" a voice asks from behind.

I whip around to face a girl my own age dressed in a striking blue cloak. Tight raven curls frame her face, and her brown cheeks are freckle-dusted and flushed from the cold. Slender like Eirwyn but short like me, she leans against a tree, one booted foot crossed over the other.

She might be the loveliest girl I've ever seen.

"Are you . . . following me?" I ask.

Her eyes are warm honey. They widen at my accusation. "What? Of course not."

"Then what are you doing here?"

I didn't mean for the question to sound so aggressive, but now the sharp tone of my voice hangs in the air between us. I want to explain that it's rare for me to come across anyone other than Deidra in the western wood. Most villagers won't risk an encounter with faeries. Unlike the rude question, the apology sticks in my throat.

The raven-haired girl frowns as if the answer is obvious. "I'm hunting."

I cross my arms. Her answer is clearly a lie, which makes me feel better about my rudeness. "Hunting? Where's your bow, your knife?"

She lifts her eyebrows. "I didn't say I was hunting animals."

My hand strays to my bruised side. I consider taking a step backward.

The girl laughs—a bright, rich sound—and pulls a weathered pouch from the pocket of her cloak. "I'm sorry, I didn't mean to alarm you. Hunting is my more exciting term for foraging. I hear there are good mushrooms in this wood."

I decide to keep my feet where they are. For now. "Many varieties too. But the ones for cooking are scarce now that it's so cold. You should have fine luck with the medicinal types, though."

She smiles. "Sounds like you have experience."

I shrug. "I've been foraging here for years."

"Have any other tips?"

"I don't know. Not really."

I bite my lip, immediately wishing I could recant the dismissive response. Not counting Brend, it's been a while since I met someone new. I'm out of practice, not that I was any good at meeting people in the first place.

But she doesn't seem to take offense. Her nose twitches. I have the oddest desire for it to happen again. "You don't remember me."

I blink. "Should I?"

"I suppose it's been a while," she says, making circles in the snow with her boot. "Years, even. I'd come by your mother's cart in Maple Square, and you'd be there sometimes. Until you weren't."

Now it makes sense why I don't remember her. I've worked hard to forget all the dreadful times I was forced to help Ma in Maple Square, and she gave up bringing me after Pa died. My palms begin to sweat, and I curse myself for forgetting my gloves.

"Oh, well," I say, wiping my hands down the front of my half-mended cloak. "I favor the forest over the square."

"That's fair," she says. Then adds, rather proudly, "I happen to favor trees to people myself."

The answer endears her to me in a way not even her loveliness could before. Deidra also values the wood but sees it as a means to nourish her family, not her spirit. Might this girl see the trees the way I do, the way Pa did?

The girl cocks her head to the side. "Your name is Roisin, right?"

I nod. "But I prefer Ro."

"Ah, well, I'm Colette," she says, holding out a gloved hand. "I don't prefer Lette."

I cover an unexpected grin with my fingertips. "All right, Colette, no shortened names for you."

I take her hand, warm from the glove, as she laughs again. Heat blossoms in my cheeks. Is she laughing because she finds me amusing, or odd? I can't tell. I don't know how much it matters.

"So, this is where you've been hiding all these years," Colette says, gesturing to the trees. "Well, it's much lovelier than the eastern forest. My cottage lies at the edge of that wood, so it's where I normally forage."

"Woodcutters and hunters," I mutter.

"Hmm?"

I feel my blush deepen. "They prefer the eastern forest."

"Oh, yes, you're absolutely right." She nods vigorously, curls dancing like tree leaves caught by a breeze. "The woodcutters are especially loud. It's much quieter here. But don't you worry about faeries?"

It takes me longer to form a response than it would have yesterday. If last night hadn't happened, I'd scoff at the very suggestion that faeries might keep me from the wood. Now, knowing a cursed bear-boy rests in my cottage, the answer isn't quite so simple.

"The western wood is as much my home as that cottage over there," I say. Perhaps not a direct answer, but it's the truth I can manage.

"The faeries must be used to you by now," Colette proposes, tapping a finger to her chin. "They might even like you."

"I doubt that," I murmur, again thinking of Brend. If I had the favor of faeries, they wouldn't have sent a bear after me.

Silence befalls us both. Colette still wears half a smile, but I can't meet her eyes. I stuff my hands into my pockets. They no longer sweat, but now they're cold almost to the point of numbness. Colette shifts her weight, gloved hands squeezing her empty foraging pouch.

I can't think of anything else to say, other than an uninteresting comment about the weather, which is more likely to put her to sleep than continue the conversation. I want to hold her attention, but I'm hardly what one would call a captivating presence. I can tell you where to dig for the best acorns or how to build a fire without causing too much smoke or how to irritate your elder sister until she won't speak to you. I doubt any of that would interest Colette, except for maybe the acorn bit if she intends to forage for something other than mushrooms.

Yet the thought of even sharing such knowledge is frightening; in the company of Colette, I feel more like a child than a girl of fifteen.

After an uncomfortably long stretch of silence, her honey eyes flit upward to meet the bright winter sky. "Well, I suppose I shouldn't lose any more daylight."

I swallow. I know this is my final chance, but I can't manage more than, "Good luck."

Her smile falters. She dips her head, then starts away.

I feel a tugging in my gut, not so unlike the sensation I get when I've been away from the forest too long. Colette's curls lift as she walks, her boots treading upon the snow with a lightness I could never achieve.

I recall Deidra's suggestion to invite someone to forage with me. Suddenly and inexplicably, I want nothing more than to ask Colette. The desire reveals itself too late, for before I can begin to utter the words, the girl has already vanished from sight, swallowed by the trees.

CHAPTER 5

Though I make a point of stomping my snow-covered boots over the frayed doormat, neither Eirwyn nor Brend react to my entrance, too immersed in their conversation.

Unlike Colette and me, they seem to have plenty to say to keep each other's interest, and their relaxed bodies are turned toward one another like they're old friends.

"I'm back," I announce to get them to stop looking at each other.

Their heads turn. Eirwyn's cheeks are pink. Brend shifts so there's more distance between him and my sister. I clench my fists.

Appraising me, Eirwyn says, "You look cold. Sit and wrap a blanket around your shoulders. I'll add more wood to the fire."

"No need," I say. "I'll take care of it."

Truth be told, with the tugging in my gut and the warmth in my cheeks and the nails digging into my palms, I hardly notice a chill. I add logs to the fire before Eirwyn can protest, then retreat to the bedroom.

I pull off my boots and damp socks and toss them in the corner with last night's clothes. Then I lay on my bed, staring at the ceiling. Most of the wooden planks above me are dark with age, but a few bright spots remind me of the times we've had to replace rotten or damaged boards. Pa used to handle such repairs, but Ma took his place even before he died, when a horde of mice made a home in the attic at the start of the same winter he fell ill with fever.

I remember Ma climbing up the slender, unsteady ladder leading to the attic, a broom in one hand and a lantern in the other. She brushed out every nest she could reach through the attic hole, and dozens of mice fell like a rainstorm, plopping onto the wood. Eirwyn and I shrieked and laughed as we chased the mice out the front door. A few broke from the pack and darted into the bedroom where Pa rested. Later he swore he woke to a mouse sitting directly on his chest, but when I ran in to chase them out, I found him sleeping and two mice running across the floor. Even when struck with fever, he couldn't resist telling a story.

When the mice were gone and the cottage grew quiet, Ma carried fresh wooden boards up the ladder and repaired the holes in the roof without once consulting Pa. She was brave and smart and strong that day and has been every day since.

I blink away the memory, catching a glimpse of Colette's smiling face in my mind's eye. I should have been brave today.

I should have asked Colette to go foraging, or at least found a way to stop her from leaving. The feverish heat of regret flushes my neck.

"I need to go out for a while," Eirwyn says from the doorway, already dressed in her cloak and boots. "Shea was supposed to stop by this evening, but I think it's best if I visit her and Deidra myself."

"Why?"

"Well," she says, "I'm not sure how to explain our current guest without making them fret."

"Oh." I nod, considering. If Ma wouldn't like Brend staying here, I doubt Shea and Deidra would either. I could run to their door and tell them everything to be rid of the bear-boy, but then I'd have to suffer Eirwyn's bitter disappointment all winter, and that sounds too exhausting right now. "I suppose that makes sense."

"Do you mind watching over him while I'm gone?"

I frown. "You mean I can't come along?"

"I'd rather you didn't," she says softly. She clears her throat and glances briefly over her shoulder.

My chest lifts. The reason she wants me to stay must be Brend, whom she's clearly fond of but maybe doesn't trust. At least not enough to leave him alone in our cottage.

But enough to leave him alone with me.

I swallow my disappointment. "How long will you be gone?"

"An hour or two at the most." Eirwyn offers me a fleeting smile. "He's truly quite polite as a boy. You should talk to him."

I scoff. "No, thank you. Watching is enough for me."

"All right, have it your way. I'll give Deidra and Shea your love."

"And give Orla a kiss for me."

"Of course."

I close my eyes, imagining my sister taking the short path to Deidra and Shea's cottage, then Deidra beckoning Eirwyn inside and asking about me. She will be disappointed that I'm not with my sister, but at least I have a suitable excuse this time . . . not that she will ever hear it, since I've decided—at least for the moment—to be the compliant younger sister and play along with Eirwyn's foolishness. Hopefully Brend leaves before anyone suspects we have a visitor. Rumors spread quickly in the village, and the last thing we need is curious folk knocking on our door to ask questions.

I'm debating a nap when the floorboards in the sitting room creak, announcing Brend's movements. Soon there's a soft rap against my open door. Well, that didn't take long, did it?

"Yes?" I ask.

"Are you hungry?"

I open my eyes. "Why?"

"Because I am," says Brend, fiddling with a splinter poking out of the door frame.

"Eirwyn said to watch you, not feed you," I mutter, laying back.

"She believes I need watching?"

"Don't you?" I say to the ceiling. "You were a bear yesterday."

Brend doesn't respond right away, but the scuffle of shifting feet and the sound of wood creaking pulls my attention. He leans against my bedroom wall, arms loose at his sides but his expression stern. He huffs a loud breath, the act so bear-like that it makes me startle. "So you keep reminding me."

"I'm not going to stop either."

"Fine," he says. "I am going to the kitchen. Hopefully I recall how to prepare a meal, or, at the very least, how to avoid setting fire to your cottage."

I clench my jaw as he exits the room, fighting the temptation to shout a retort because doing so would only draw him back. I try to conjure an image of Colette. Her curls, her freckle-dusted cheeks. Instead, all I see when I close my eyes are the ashy remains of the cottage after Brend burns it down, and Eirwyn shaking her head.

Groaning, I rise and head to the kitchen.

To my surprise, Brend stands before the free-standing counter, already dicing potatoes. He must have gone through the pantry, where we keep the week's food stores to avoid multiple trips to the cellar. He's using his uninjured left hand and seems quite confident. He hasn't sliced off a finger either. Not that I'm impressed.

"Too concerned or too hungry?" he asks, keeping his eyes on the knife.

"Both," I answer. "What are you making?"

"I have no idea. I grabbed the first edible item I could find."

"Edible item," I mutter, shaking my head.

He sets down the knife. "What?"

I hoist myself onto the counter beside the potatoes that haven't been chopped. "You say strange things," I tell him, picking one up.

I frown at the potato, which hasn't been thoroughly cleaned. Specks of dirt cling to its rough skin. I start flicking them off one by one.

"I apologize."

I glance sideways at him. "That isn't what you should apologize for."

"I am truly sorry for last night," he says softly.

"All right," I say past the ache in my throat.

"I am."

I blink to clear the moisture from my eyes. "What should we make?"

Brend frowns at the potatoes. "I was hoping you had a thought or two."

I shrug. "Eirwyn's the cook, not me. But we could boil them with other vegetables and add some seasoning?"

"Do you have any meat?"

I stiffen. I breathe. He's *not* a bear, he's *not* a bear. The refrain doesn't help, and my bruised side begins to throb.

"I think Eirwyn bought fish yesterday," I say, in a shaky voice I don't much like. "It's in the cellar, but I wouldn't know how to prepare it. We'd have to wait for her to come home."

"Vegetables are fine, then."

I slide off the counter as Brend resumes chopping. In the cool darkness of the pantry, I press my forehead against the wall free of shelves, inhaling wood and garden earth. My pulse is quick, and there's pressure behind my eyes. I breathe in and out, in and out.

I tell myself I'm all right, even if I don't quite believe it.

I grab carrots from one shelf and an onion from another. I'm pleased to find the oyster mushrooms I foraged yesterday, a bit smushed but otherwise still intact. Eirwyn must have gone through my satchel. I add the least damaged mushroom to my haul and bring everything to the counter. I rub the vegetables—including the remaining potatoes—with a damp cloth to remove any lingering dirt. I leave Brend to continue chopping so I can make a trip to the well to fill a pot for boiling.

Outside, the shadows of early evening are still and quiet, but the cold is harsh enough to steal my breath. I pull up the hood of my cloak and head left toward the well, which stands a short distance from the side of the cottage without a garden.

I remember the day the well was dug. I was young, maybe five, and our parents decided they'd had enough of walking deeper into the village to gather water. When I saw the hole, my first thought was to jump in, to see what the world was like below the ground. Eirwyn must've sensed my wild curiosity because she pulled me back, distracting me with chases along the tree line until Ma and Pa finished laying the bricks.

I lower the bucket, the rope so cold and frayed that it scratches my bare palms. I think of what it would've been like to jump into the well, to not have Eirwyn there pulling me back. I can't decide if the feeling that floods my body is one of thrill or fright. Perhaps a bit of both.

The bucket is halfway up when I turn my head and spot a ribbon of copper standing before the line of trees leading to the western wood. Even from far away, I know it's the red fox. My red fox.

The rope slips from my hands. I take a step forward, holding my breath and willing the fox to remain where she is. She doesn't appear to move, but she's so far away that I wouldn't be able to tell if she took just one step.

The sound of the rope moving fast against the rung draws

my focus back to the well, and I manage to grab the rope before the bucket hits the water. I gather a steadying breath, cursing my thoughtlessness as heat graces the tips of my ears. I'm glad Brend is tucked away inside, and not here to witness my foolishness. I pull the bucket the rest of the way up, pour the water into the pot, and set the pot onto the frozen ground.

I turn back to the tree line, but the fox is gone.

A sudden heaviness descends upon my shoulders, making them sag. My feet itch to carry me into the wood, and any other time I would let them. But Brend is in my cottage, a cursed boy with no guardian, and I told my sister I would watch him.

My eyes rest on the last spot I saw the fox. "I hope you learn to trust me again," I whisper to the trees. "I won't let him harm you."

I lift the pot, water sloshing over the rim and turning my hands to ice. My teeth chatter as I take measured steps back to the cottage. Before I open the door, I look back to the trees one last time, but the fox hasn't returned. Very little wind stirs the forest tonight, and my promise must not have carried far enough to reach her.

Inside, I secure the heavy pot over the fire as my brief encounter with the fox melts from me like snow on hot skin. In my absence Brend has moved on to the carrots. I use the iron poker to move the logs and lower the height of the flames, then step away only to catch his left hand trembling as he slices.

"Let me take over," I offer.

"Bears are not accustomed to chopping vegetables," he says, stepping back.

I can see that he's tried to make a joke, but I can't bring myself to laugh. Neither can he. The knife handle is warm in my hand. "Watch the fire. If the flames get too high, use the poker to spread out the wood."

Brend's eyebrows lift, and he presses a palm to his chest in mock disbelief. "You trust me with the fire?"

This time he manages to make me grin, much to my displeasure. I face the vegetables so I can hide it from him. "Don't let me down."

"I will not," he says quietly, in a tone that's all too serious.

My knife stalls against the carrot. My grin falters.

He has no right—no right to be chivalrous or make promises. Not when he doesn't know who he is. Not when he can't control *what* he is.

I will myself to continue chopping, pretending I haven't heard him. Hopefully he believes me.

Later, at the dining table, we drink hot tea and eat overcooked vegetables seasoned with dried herbs I foraged during summertime. Though mushy, the food is warm in my mouth and chases some of the lingering cold from my skin. I keep my eyes on my plate as I eat, but I can feel Brend watching me.

"Eirwyn tells me you like to forage," he says after a prolonged silence, and the deep thrum of his voice startles me into dropping my spoon. "Is that what you were doing when you found me?"

"You found *me*, remember?" I scoff. "No, I guess you don't. How convenient for you."

"There is no need to be cruel," says Brend.

He might be right, but I won't admit it.

"I was on my way home," I tell him, trying to keep my voice even. "A red fox darted across my path, and the bear was—*you* were chasing her."

"Go on," Brend invites.

Irritation prickles my skin. "Why? You know how it ends."

He sets down his spoon. "Contrary to what you believe, being unable to remember what happened is not . . . convenient for me. I know almost nothing of my life. I would like to at least know this."

I lift my gaze from my plate, trying to imagine myself with an empty mind. A Ro who doesn't know she loves the forest, who doesn't remember Ma and Eirwyn, or the years she had with Pa. The thought of such a life stabs my heart.

"You came toward me, so I did what my mother taught me to do. I waved my arms and told you I was backing away."

"Did I listen?"

"You did."

He rests his chin on his hands. "What happened next?" Brend reminds me of Eirwyn when she was younger, always eager for another of Pa's stories. His eyes hold the same gleam.

I'm not like Pa. I don't relish telling tales, especially those of my own experience. But I understand why Brend wants to hear this one, so I'll oblige him. "You left me, then I heard the fox wail. I didn't want you to kill her, so I caught up with you both. I threw my boot at you, but—"

"You threw your boot at a bear?" I can see he's fighting a smile.

"Yes," I hiss. "Don't interrupt."

His lips twitch. It's not nearly as pleasing as the twitch of Colette's nose. "I apologize. Please continue."

"Like I said, I threw my boot at you, but you wouldn't leave the fox alone. So I threw my other boot at you, and that's when—" I stop, barely able to swallow the rising pain in my throat.

"That's when . . . ?"

I let my gaze fall to my plate. I can't look at him as I say the rest. "That's when you turned and charged me."

Silence fills the room. Then: "Did I hurt you?"

I nod. Tears fill my eyes, threatening to drip onto mushy vegetables. My body shudders, and I must hug myself to still the quakes. I hate that I'm reacting like this. I hate that I can hear the bear's huff in my ears again, so terribly loud. That I can smell his wet fur and feel his hot breath.

"When I saw your bruise this morning, I knew—" Brend breaks off, cursing. He remembers how to do that, at least. "I hoped I was mistaken."

I don't know what to say. I have no words to ease his pain. I have none to ease my own.

"I am so sorry, Roisin. No wonder you hate me."

I shake my head. It's worse than that. Hate is easy. Hate is uncomplicated. What's clinging to me like soot is *fear*. I fear him, and that frustrates me as much as it grieves me. I thought I only had the villagers to worry about. Their questions and their judgments. Now I've been menaced by a creature of the wood—my western wood. The place I run to when I want to feel safe, when I want to hide.

The chair creaks as Brend shifts his weight. His spoon scrapes against his plate.

"These vegetables . . . are very good," he says.

I nearly laugh. I'm startled by the urge, by a reaction to him I can't explain. A tear slides down my nose. "Liar."

Brend manages a chuckle and I pick up my spoon, scooping up a few vegetables before bringing it to my lips. My body hums with the strangeness of the evening. I'm dining with a boy who was a bear yesterday, sharing a meal with someone other than Ma or Eirwyn. Living at the edge of the village has made seclusion quite simple for me, but in a single day, I've met a cursed boy and another girl who loves the trees.

"Who was the girl you were with?"

I almost choke on my food. It's as if he can read my very thoughts. I swallow and dab my lips with a cloth. "You saw me?"

He nods. "Who was she?"

I scoop up another chunk of potato but don't take a bite. "A girl from the village."

"Something about seeing her with you . . . made me feel odd," he says.

"Don't tell me she's a bear too."

Brend frowns at his near-empty plate. He does a lot of that—frowning. I suppose he has plenty of reasons to, what with his curse and his empty mind and his vegetable dinner.

I let the chunk of potato slide off my spoon and drop back onto my plate. I glance at my full cup of tea, bereft of steam and likely cold by now. I was hungry earlier, but now each bite of food is like a stone settling into my gut. Each sip of tea tastes like muddy water.

Maybe Brend asked about Colette out of mere, innocent curiosity. Or maybe he's like the villagers who pester me when

I look at any boy or girl for too long. Either way, it's time to change the subject.

"I noticed you were cutting with your left hand." I set aside my spoon, too full of other things to eat. "Is that because your right arm is wounded, or are you left-handed?"

"I have no idea," he admits. "But the act felt natural."

I lean over my plate. "You seem awfully calm for a boy with no memories."

Brend's left hand starts trembling again. His spoon clangs against his plate. He drops it and covers his left hand with his right one.

"Perhaps I do not need them." His tone has sharpened. "I do not want to remember hurting you, and if I have more memories like that, maybe it is better to lose them forever."

"I don't think so," I say, thinking of Pa, of my burn and the kettle. "If you don't remember what you did wrong, who's to say you won't do it again?"

"I will not make—" he breaks off, looking down at his hands. His right one is trembling too.

"Are you all right?" I ask.

He clasps his hands, but the trembling increases, snaking up both arms until his shoulders are shaking. "I do not know, I—"

His jaw goes rigid. His right eye twitches and beads of sweat appear on his forehead. I lean back in my chair.

"Brend," I say, and I recognize the fear at the edge of my voice.

"*Roisin.*" My name begins as a breath and ends as a painful groan.

I stand. The legs of my chair scrape against the wood floor. "Brend?"

"Something . . . is happening."

A visible shudder runs the length of his body. He groans again, and this time it doesn't sound quite boy-like.

Realization steals the breath from my throat. Something *is* happening, and I can't let it happen here. My eyes dart to the door and back to Brend. "You need to go."

Tears well in his eyes, but I can't pity him. Not when he's like this. Not when he's *changing*.

I rush to help him out of his chair. He's halfway up when his body spasms violently and he falls against the table. Dishes clang and slide. A cup overturns, spilling tea onto the floor.

I jump back, hugging my arms to my chest. What happens if I can't get him outside? What happens if he becomes a bear beside my dining table? Black spots dance across my vision. I don't think I'm breathing enough.

Another beast-like groan rouses me from my panic. I pull Brend to his feet and drag him toward the door. He stumbles and cries out, but I don't stop moving, can't stop moving. My arms burn beneath his weight. Thankfully the distance we must cover is short. I fling open the door and shove him out onto the snow. He staggers a few feet then falls to his knees. His back arches in another spasm.

I brace myself with one hand against the door frame and cover my eyes with the other. Whatever wicked magic reigns over this boy, I don't want to see it.

He groans again, whimpers my name. I imagine the spasms, each one more violent than the next. I squeeze my eyes shut as tightly as I can. I wait in anguish.

Then, a familiar huff prompts me to look.

A bear stands on four massive paws next to a pile of rags. The sight of Pa's clothing, torn to bits, strikes my chest. I tear my gaze away from the pile to lock eyes with the bear. Does he recognize me? Does he know his name? The bear huffs again, and my foolish thoughts disappear. I grip the door, prepared to slam it shut and build a barricade of furniture if I must, if he charges.

"Did you know it was coming?" I shout at him, my voice strained beneath the evening chill.

The bear doesn't answer. His amber eyes glow beneath the dusk like embers. I try to see past the bear, to see Brend. The boy who apologized. The boy who ate mushy vegetables and called them good. I can't.

"Don't come back," I tell him.

Then I close the door and wait at the window until his large form ambles into the night.

CHAPTER 6

I'm adding logs to the fire when my sister returns.

She steps inside and kicks the snow off her boots before removing her cloak. I know I should speak first, tell her about Brend, but I'd rather pretend he was never here. I'd rather pretend this is a normal night and that the one before never happened.

"Sorry I'm so late, Deidra made—Ro, what happened to the chair?"

I dig my nails into the log I still hold, muttering a curse. Can't very well pretend nothing happened in the face of over-turned furniture. I can clear away dishes and mop up spilled tea, but it seems I can't remember to right a chair.

Eirwyn's eyes rove over the empty bench and the dining table, then finally return to the chair. The one Brend claimed before he started changing.

"Ro," she says.

I drop the firewood back onto the pile. "It all happened very fast."

Her bottom lip quivers. Her cheeks, moments ago red from the cold, are drained of color.

"We were eating dinner," I say, "and I noticed the trembling earlier, but I didn't know what it meant, and by the time I figured it out I was too late, and—"

"Where is he?" she asks. "Where did he go?"

"I got him outside before he changed. I didn't see where he went."

Eirwyn nods slowly. She tugs on her left ear, which means she's trying not to cry. She tugged on her ear a lot after Pa died—so much so that for weeks her earlobe was perpetually red. Problem is, the trick only works for her about half the time.

"Are you okay?" she asks, her voice breaking.

"I'm all right," I tell her. "I didn't get hurt this time."

I don't mean for my words to bite, truly. But they do. Eirwyn's fingers go still against her earlobe. She averts her eyes.

"Ro, I know I've been acting . . . but he was hurt and—" She shakes her head. "That's no excuse. I left him alone with you knowing full well what he could become." She offers me her hand. "I'm sorry."

I almost smile; this is the apology I've been waiting for since Eirwyn first welcomed Brend into our cottage. But I hold back the urge, not wanting to ruin the fragile moment between us. I rush to my sister, ignoring the offered hand and pulling her into a tight embrace.

"I'm sorry too," I say. "I know—I know you cared for him."

"Cared for him?" Eirwyn pulls back. "I wanted to help him."

I don't believe her, but I try not to show it. "I'm sure he's grateful."

Eirwyn nods again, then turns to the window as if she's already searching for him. Frustration heats my ears, spreading down my neck. I nearly demand that she keep looking at me, at my bruised side and haunted eyes. But demands won't make her see me, won't make her stop wanting him.

"His curse is unfortunate," I say. "But there's nothing we can do."

"He might come back."

"I don't think he will." I bite my lip. Do I dare say it? I feel I must. "I don't think he should."

Eirwyn's expression is built from stone. "That's not for you to decide."

She withdraws to the bedroom without saying goodnight. The following morning, when I step outside to begin a day of foraging, I find a pile of Pa's clothes neatly folded beside the doorstep. On top of the pile lies a note held in place by a rock.

A note that reads: *Come in.*

A full week passes without sight of Brend, as a bear or as a boy. Eirwyn watches out the window while she does her morning chores, but the pile of clothes remains undisturbed.

I'm not oblivious to the faraway look in my sister's eyes. Even when she's speaking it's as if she's also dreaming. Likely dreaming of Brend, imagining his return as if he's an adventuring prince from one of her stories, and she's a waiting princess. I'd like to tell her that if Brend is anything, he's certainly not a prince. But with her so often tugging on her left earlobe, I know the remark would hurt her too much.

I try to distract her with complaints about our upcoming move, but I'm met with silence. No list of reasons why I'm wrong. No insistence that Ma knows what's best for us. It's as if she's no longer interested in changing my mind about Poppy.

Otherwise, our routines proceed rather normally. We keep the cottage tidy, play table games, mend our clothes, and decorate for Yule with evergreen branches. I ask Eirwyn how to prepare a fish, and we spend a quiet day cooking together. Eirwyn makes trips deeper into the village to see friends and replenish what supplies we have the coin for; I forage in the wood on clear days, alert for signs of the red fox I saved.

The logical voice inside my head insists there's nothing special about her, but another voice—a voice that sounds curiously like Pa's—believes there must be a reason we crossed paths when I'm so close to leaving the western wood behind. There must be a reason she bowed to me like royalty, a reason she strayed near my cottage so I could save her. I keep a watchful eye for Brend as well, a hand splayed over my fading bruise.

Yet it's not Brend or the red fox I find in the western wood on a clear, bright morning.

It's Colette.

The village girl kneels in the snow, carefully picking penny bun mushrooms from the base of a pine tree. The fungi have miraculously survived the early days of winter, and if my satchel wasn't already full, I'd be envious of her find. Dressed in her blue wool cloak, her hood is pulled back to reveal her obsidian curls, shining beneath the dappled sunlight streaming through the trees. The loveliness of the scene catches my breath.

"I know you're there," she says in a singsong voice that makes me blush.

"Hello," I reply, unsure of what else to say. I don't need to explain my presence in the wood, do I? Would that be the polite thing? "That's—that's a great find."

Mushrooms can be hardy when they want to be, but I've never found penny bun mushrooms after the first snowfall. In fact, they usually disappear from the wood before the end of autumn. I know what Pa would say about this: he'd credit faeries for the find. Despite last week's events, I'm still not inclined to credit the creatures of the wood myself. There must be something special about this pine tree. That's all.

Colette rises from the snow to face me. "There's still a few left if you'd like." She gestures to where two mushrooms have yet to be picked.

"Oh, I couldn't," I tell her, though it'd be a lie to say I'm not tempted. The mushrooms are in perfect condition, the bulbous stems a healthy white and the caps like a crusty brown roll straight from the oven. "They're yours. Besides," I say, lifting my satchel. "I've got a good enough haul."

But Colette shakes her head. "I insist. As you said the other day, this wood is your home. You've a right to these as much as I."

I'm not so certain of that. When Deidra and I forage together, we share what we find, but I'd never expect her to offer something that she's found on her own. She has a family to provide for, same as me, as I'm sure Colette does too. But when I make no move to approach the log, Colette bends to pick them for me. I've once again forgotten my gloves, and I can't help wishing she would've done the same as our hands brush. I carefully set the mushrooms in my satchel atop my other foraging finds, hoping they will remain undisturbed until I get the chance to show them to Eirwyn.

"There," says Colette, smiling. "Consider it payment for foraging in your wood."

I blink at her, skin prickling with discomfort beneath my cloak. "I don't own the wood."

When I called this place my home, I only meant to share how much the trees mean to me. I hope she doesn't believe I'd chase her out as if she can't belong here either.

"No," she agrees, "I suppose that honor belongs to the faeries."

Her honey eyes sparkle with amusement, but I can't play her game. No one owns the wood, not even faeries. I grip the strap of my satchel, bare fingers flushing red.

Colette's smile softens but doesn't disappear. "Sit with me, Ro?"

I nod and follow her to a fallen log, too surprised she wants to continue spending time with me to think of an excuse. We sit with our satchels between us. Hers is colorful and beaded. My brown burlap is drab in comparison. "I like your satchel."

"Thank you." Colette brushes her hand over the bag. "That old pouch you saw the other day was a temporary fix while my mother mended a tear in this one. Quilting is one of her trades."

"She's very skilled." If I had the coin, I would express interest in purchasing one for myself.

"She tried to teach me. I didn't take to it," admits Colette. "Too much stillness in quilting. Foraging is movement."

Her words are so similar to my own thoughts that they chase away any lingering discomfort. "Constant seeking."

"Right, you understand," she says, nodding. "My mother doesn't, but she's always supported me. She just doesn't like that I've started foraging here."

"Because of faeries," I assume.

Colette sighs. "Because of faeries."

I chew at my lip, remembering Brend. The wild spasms that overtook him. The wet gleam in his amber eyes. There's magic in him. There's no denying that.

"Do you believe in them?" I ask Colette.

In answer, she points to the pine, where a large owl perches upon one of the thicker, outstretched branches. I sit up straighter, startled that I didn't notice the creature until now. I'm usually aware of the western wood's fauna. "That's a great horned owl," she says.

I nod, recognizing the brown, ear-like tufts and piercing yellow eyes. "I've only seen them in drawings." I swallow past a thickness in my throat. "Because they're nocturnal."

"And yet," says Colette, her voice almost a whisper, "one watches us beneath a full sun."

Succumbing to the owl's intimidating stare, I drop my gaze to my boots. Is Colette implying that faeries have something to do with the creature's unnatural presence? The thought prompts an unnerving flutter in my gut.

"My mother told me a story once," says Colette, "about a woodcutter who ventured into the western wood."

I glance at her sidelong. "Woodcutters know to avoid the western wood."

"Yes, but this one was desperate," explains Colette. "A storm had damaged his roof, you see, and the season for cutting in the eastern forest was over. So he took his son with him to the western wood, where they found a scrawny tree offering just enough wood to repair the damage. The woodcutter didn't think it would be missed."

I scoff. "The woodcutter sounds like a fool."

"Hush," says Colette, but with amusement. "Reserve your comments until the end."

I roll my eyes. Colette doesn't know me well enough yet to understand that patience is not one of my virtues. But it's hard to refuse a request from someone so lovely.

"The day after he repaired the damage, the woodcutter noticed an owl perched upon his roof." Colette gestures to the horned owl in the pine, who doesn't seem to have moved since she began her tale. "Sightings continued in the days that followed, and always at daylight. Just like our friend here."

"Maybe the owl was ill," I offer. "Or injured."

Colette nods. "That's what the woodcutter thought, too, until the night he woke to smoke filling his cottage. He and his son panicked, believing a spark had been tossed from the fireplace. Yet nothing inside was burning, so they opened the front door to a line of fire surrounding the cottage, moving in steadily like a closing snare."

I gape at her, enraptured. "What happened? Were they killed?"

"No, with help from neighbors, they managed to quell the flames before everything burned. But they suffered injuries.

Burns that left terrible scars. The woodcutter had to abandon his trade as a result. They never saw the owl again after that."

I frown at the bird in the pine. "So you're saying the owl sought revenge for the downed tree?"

"An owl," says Colette, "or a faerie in disguise."

I turn to her. Her slender eyebrows are raised, as if daring me to challenge her.

For all his tales, Pa never spoke of faeries' appearances, likely because he couldn't know them himself. There's truly no way for Colette to know, either, unless the owl speaks the truth to us.

But I think of Brend in our cottage. His flawless skin. His formal speech. His hands fingering the arrow pieces. His words: *Sixteen winters, I believe.* Sixteen winters. Not years. As if he marks time according to a different structure, a different name.

Names.

I do not remember a family name.

Perhaps because he's never had one. Perhaps because faeries do not have family names.

Yet if Brend's a faerie—and that's a rather large if—why did he look and act so much like a boy while staying in our cottage? And what of his transformation into a bear? What would cause a faerie to lose his memories? To lose control of himself?

"You tell a good story," I say as a distraction from my thoughts. Brends's gone, and I can't follow these questions further just now, not when I'm beside a lovely girl while an owl that should be sleeping watches us with a heady gaze. "My sister would be impressed."

Colette's nose twitches, the answer to a desire I've held for days. "Are you?"

"Am I what?"

She leans over her satchel, close enough that my eyes can't help but fall to her lips, full and slightly chapped from the cold, as she says, "Impressed?"

The word is both a caress and a spark, equal parts soothing and stirring. I think of leaning in myself. I think of shoving our satchels onto the snow and closing every bit of distance between us. But a creaking branch pulls my attention before I gather the courage. I turn as the great horned owl spreads his wings and takes flight, disappearing over the trees.

When I return to Colette, her posture has straightened, her satchel slung over her shoulder. "I should get home," she says apologetically. "My mother will worry."

"All right," I say, disappointed but understanding. "Thank you for the mushrooms . . . and the story." I draw a breath of strength. "I was impressed, you know."

"I know," she says, rising from the log. "I hope to see you again soon, Ro."

CHAPTER 7

I return home to a cottage filled with mouthwatering, savory scents, and a pot of stew cooking slowly over the embers of the fire. Eirwyn is on the bench reading a book, but she shuts it when I join her and hold out the two perfect penny bun mushrooms from Colette.

"Ro, those are beautiful," says my sister. "I'll add them to the stew."

She takes the offered mushrooms and brings them to the kitchen for chopping while I put away the rest of my haul. When I emerge from the pantry with an empty satchel, Eirwyn is carrying the mushroom pieces to the fire. I sit on the bench, knees pulled to my chest, as she adds them to the stew. My stomach rumbles, though the meal won't be ready for hours.

I'm considering a return to the pantry for a handful of nuts to keep me sated when Eirwyn steps away from the fire. "It's been a month, you know." She brushes her hands down her apron. "Since Ma left."

I'm ashamed to admit I didn't know. I've been so keen on tracking the days without Brend that I've left thoughts of Ma to the wayside. With no one to carry news over the icy river, I don't know how she's faring in Poppy, if she's found a trade that'll give us enough coin to make our fresh start, or if she's getting along with Aunt Meara. The distance hits me in a way it hasn't before. Winter has barely begun. We have so much longer to go without her.

My sudden melancholy must be obvious, because Eirwyn offers me a sympathetic smile and says, "Come to Maple Square with me."

Frowning, I pull a pine needle from my sweater and flick it at the fire. "No, thank you."

"I've been careful with Aunt Meara's coin, but I want to use some to sew a dress for Ma, one she can wear in Poppy over the summer. I need your help choosing the fabric."

"I don't know, I—"

Eirwyn throws her head back. "Come on, Ro. It's been ages since you came to the square with me. Aren't you tired of spending so much time in the cottage?"

I sit up straighter, preparing my argument, but Eirwyn speaks first. "And don't mention your time in the forest because it's nearly the same. You don't interact with anyone, and you do the same thing over and over."

I almost mention Colette but refrain at the last moment.

I'd feel guilty boasting about her when Eirwyn is clearly still missing Brend. I'll wait until that faraway look in my sister's eyes disappears.

"Time for a change in routine," Eirwyn says. "I think we're both due for one."

I want to disagree, yet I can't deny a certain restlessness that's overtaken me since my time with Colette. The thought of spending the afternoon waiting for stew is just as unappealing as interacting with villagers in Maple Square, but at least there I'll be moving. Seeking.

"All right," I tell my sister. "Just this once."

The shop is as colorful as I remember. Rolls of fabric line the walls and clothing samples hang above them. A leather-bound book rests on a nearby pedestal, filled with patterns for patrons to study for their projects, but we've been sewing for so long that we rarely consult those instructions.

"What do you think of this?" I ask, pointing to a roll of brown fabric patterned with stitches of green ivy.

Eirwyn makes a face. "I don't know. I don't think of Ma when I look at it."

I shrug, but she's probably right. Ma likes bright colors and bold patterns. She's uninterested in blending into the background of things.

My sister sighs. "I haven't liked a single piece of fabric I've seen so far."

I lock arms with her. "Come, let's check over here."

I lead her to the front of the store, closer to the exit. In truth, I'm hoping she finds something quickly so we can leave. Coming to Maple Square hasn't cured my restlessness. If anything, it's made it worse. While Eirwyn compares samples, I study the passing villagers through the window, though there aren't many due to the snow. The quiet is a relief, but I still find myself rubbing my arms more often than not. Being in Maple Square, inside or outside a shop, always gives me a cagey feeling. My eyes can't help but dart to the door each time the welcome bell chimes. Voices, both familiar and strange, make me step closer to Eirwyn. My head constantly itches as if an insect is crawling across my scalp.

Before Pa fell ill, the agreement was that I help Ma sell our vegetables once a week with Eirwyn assisting otherwise, leaving me and Pa to spend most days together in the wood. We'd climb trees, study birds, and forage, and we'd return well after dark to find Ma worrying and Eirwyn with her nose in a book. My sister enjoyed the forest then, too, but usually preferred a day in Maple Square whenever I announced we'd be digging up mushrooms.

But when Pa's fever began, Ma started sending me to the square with Eirwyn every day so she could stay home with him. Pa opposed the change, insisting he could look after himself, but Ma couldn't be swayed. She believed it'd be good for all of us, especially me. Supposedly, I was too isolated in keeping to the wood, and I needed to see more people.

Trouble is, I don't like being around other people, and I didn't try to like it then either. Despite Ma's encouragement,

I'd hide behind Eirwyn whenever a customer approached the cart. If anyone spoke to me, my responses were quiet and muddled, and I'd agonize over them as I lay in bed at night.

Any time spent in Maple Square left me with ill feelings, especially once villagers started asking me personal questions. *Why is your cloak always dirty? What makes you so quiet? Do you fancy Lucy Mackenzie's boy, or is it the older sister who draws your eye? Come now, we're merely curious. We won't mind the answer.*

One day, I protested going so vehemently that Ma relented and let me look after Pa instead so she could accompany Eirwyn. That meant a lot of time stuck inside the cottage, but I didn't mind, because I was with Pa, someone who made me feel safe, who never asked me questions I didn't want to answer.

"Ro? Are you listening?"

"What?" I ask, but I don't turn away from the window.

"Which do you like best?" asks my sister.

It's at that very moment I spot Colette across the way, inspecting a cart of firewood. I recognize her instantly by her striking blue cloak.

I glance at the fabric samples in Eirwyn's hands, point to the left one, then dash past her and out of the shop. I've already forgotten what the samples looked like as I hurry to the firewood cart. Eirwyn calls for me, but I don't call back.

Colette's face is mere inches from a log when I reach her. "Looking for termites?" I ask.

She straightens. "Well, one can never be too careful."

"Seems I found you again," I say, grinning so wide my cheeks hurt.

Her lips break into a smile. "Seems you did." Colette wipes her hands down the front of her cloak, leaving behind a light smear of dirt. She doesn't seem bothered by the mess, which I appreciate. "Twice in one day. I'm flattered."

"Are you alone?" I ask.

She cocks her head. "Not presently."

"No, I mean, are you here with anyone? Your mother?"

"Interested in meeting my family, are you?" she teases.

My neck flushes with heat. "Can't you give me a simple answer?"

She shrugs. "You don't ask simple questions."

Our gazes meet, and Colette's warm irises glow like honey beneath the sun. Oddly, every bit of my frustration slips away. "What would be a simpler question?" I ask, my voice much breathier than I intend.

Colette leans forward, so close that I smell the fresh mint on her breath and the rosemary oil in her hair. "Hmm, how about: Why does your sister look so flustered?"

I squint at her, thoroughly confused. Then I hear, "Ro, why did you rush out like that?"

Oh, right. I ran away from Eirwyn without telling her why.

"Sorry," I say, reluctantly drawing back from Colette and turning to meet my sister.

"You should be," says Eirwyn. "I feared you were experiencing some sort of panic, like when you were younger."

I cringe. Her words make me sound fragile and strange. I hope Colette immediately discards them from her mind. I offer my sister what I hope is my most apologetic smile. "I should have said something. Forgive me."

"All right, but you better not regret the fabric you chose," she warns, then turns away from me, her expression brightening. "Colette, how's your mother?"

Colette dips her head. "Quite well, thank you."

I blink. "You know each other?"

My sister rolls her eyes. "She used to come by Ma's cart, don't you remember?"

No, but of course *she* does. I give her my blankest stare. Eirwyn sighs.

"It was some time ago," Colette says. "I'm glad we've been reacquainted."

"Ah, well," says my sister, "Ro tends to keep to herself."

"I'd like to change that," says Colette, and my stomach flips.

"Then you should come for dinner tonight," says my sister, never one to let an opportunity slip away. "How do you feel about stew?"

Colette puts a finger to her lips in contemplation. "I suppose I feel very good about stew."

A flurry of snowflakes swirls in my chest, and I bite the inside of my cheek to keep from smiling so wide I look frightening. This is progressing so much better with Eirwyn's help. I promise myself I'll thank my sister later.

"Perfect," Eirwyn says. "Do you need directions to our cottage?"

"I don't, actually." Colette glances my way with a conspiratorial smile, and I'm taken back to our first meeting in the wood. Her warm hand in mine. The sound of her laugh.

Eirwyn's brow rises considerably. "Hmm, all right then. See you soon." She takes my arm and steers me away from the firewood cart.

"Come at sundown," I call over my shoulder.

Our eyes lock once more as she nods, and the burn of her gaze melts all the snowflakes inside me. I'm tempted to linger in Maple Square rather than run away. Endure the stares and the whispers if it means I can be near her.

"Don't trip over your feet staring," teases my sister. "I'm terribly cold and in need of a warm fire."

The cottage is always clean, but tonight I want it to be spotless.

Eirwyn busies herself with finishing the stew while I tackle everything else. I sweep the floors, wipe the counter, fluff the bench cushions. I sprinkle ashes across the doorstep and gather logs from the covered woodpile beside the cottage. Refill the oil in the lamps. Clear away the cobwebs in the pantry. Make two trips to the well.

I put on three different outfits before settling on a burgundy wool dress, the only one I have that doesn't show its years' worth of alterations. I braid my hair like Eirwyn does, wipe my face clean of dirt, and pinch my cheeks until they're red, like I've seen Ma do.

I ask Eirwyn when dinner will be ready four separate times. I set the table. Eye the pile of clothing outside the door and consider removing it. Eye my sister, wondering how much it would anger her. I decide against it—too risky.

Everything tonight must be perfect.

I practice sitting because my sister says I'm awful at it,

tending to look ready to bolt rather than relaxed and comfortable. First, I try both legs side by side, hands in my lap. Then the left leg over the right. Then the right leg over the left. Then both legs tucked beneath me. When nothing satisfies, I try standing, but that feels strange too. I can't decide what works best.

I run a finger along the fireplace mantel—dusty, so I grab a cloth. I dust the mantel, then notice dust on the windowsills I can't ignore.

I check my braids in the mirror, lick my palm, and smooth it over the top of my head to taper the loose strands. Pinch my cheeks one more time.

I do all of this and by the time I'm done, sundown still hasn't arrived.

I bounce on my toes in front of the window. Watching the sun must be the most boring thing I've ever done. I'll do it anyway, for her.

"Ro," Eirwyn calls from the fireplace, where she's bent over stirring the stew, "why don't you start on Ma's dress? That should keep you occupied."

I press my face to the glass. "I don't like the fabric you chose."

I hear her scoff. "The fabric I chose? You chose that fabric!"

My breath turns the window foggy. I wipe it with my fist. "Couldn't you tell I was in a hurry? That I was distracted?"

"Honestly," she says, "I didn't know what to think. I certainly wasn't expecting you to chase after a village girl."

I turn away from the window. "Why not?"

Eirwyn sets aside the stirring spoon and rises. "Well, you rarely show interest in anyone, you are so content with your trees and wild animals."

"And you, and Ma," I add.

"Yes, yes, I know." She wipes her hands on her apron. "But you don't have to seek us out; we're always here. It's different with friends and . . . with those who are more than friends."

Heat blooms in my cheeks. Have I been so transparent? "Eirwyn, I—"

Eirwyn holds up her hands. "I'm not going to push you, Ro. All I'm saying is Colette is a nice girl from a good home."

"She is nice," I say, perhaps more wistfully than I intended.

I turn back to the window. The sun is finally setting, hues of orange and blue slowly mingling. Shadows cling to the trees, and the snow-covered ground appears to glow.

A rustling sound starts beyond the door.

She's here. I bite back my smile and smooth the folds of my dress. Before she has the chance to knock, I turn the knob and pull with vigor. But it's not Colette standing on the doorstep.

It's Brend. No longer a bear and halfway dressed in Pa's clothes.

A disappointed sigh whistles past my lips. I didn't try to fight it, really, and I don't think I could have if I'd wanted to. He's here, though I told him not to come back. She isn't here, though I told her to come at sundown. So much for a perfect night.

Brend's hair is ragged, his hands and feet dirty. He reeks of smells I would rather not identify. But his eyes are bright, and as he slips into the sleeves of Pa's shirt, I see that no trace remains of the arrow wound, not even a faint scab or scar. How he managed to heal so quickly, I've no idea. Perhaps fast healing is part of his curse.

"I found the note," is all he says before Eirwyn rushes to the door.

"You're back," says my sister, not even attempting to rein in her delight.

Eirwyn throws her arms around him but jumps back just as quickly. Brend's lips part in silent surprise as she clears her throat and tucks loose strands of hair behind her ears. I make a gagging sound and am rewarded with two sets of glaring eyes.

"I'm sorry," Eirwyn tells Brend, pink creeping into her cheeks. "I'm happy to see you."

"I am as well," Brend says. "And relieved."

"Of course, you must be. Come in, come in."

Brend follows Eirwyn to the bench, while I linger by the door. I check the window for signs of Colette but spot none. My shoulders sag, my posture turning terrible.

"You've been gone for over a week," I hear Eirwyn say. "What have you been doing?"

"Searching, I think," says Brend.

"Searching for what?"

"I . . . I do not remember. Something important."

I release a heavy breath. Looks like nothing's changed. Still no memories. Still turning up where he's not wanted. "That sounds very intriguing, but we're expecting company." I tear myself from the window. "It might be best for you to go."

"Ro, don't be ridiculous," says Eirwyn, a hint of humor in her tone as if I've made a moderately funny joke. "Brend will stay with us. I'm sure Colette won't mind."

"Colette?" Brend lifts his head. "Who is Colette?"

My sister grins. "Oh, a girl Ro—"

"Eirwyn," I snap. The bear-boy is the last person I want to know my business.

My sister doesn't seem to agree, throwing up her hands and remarking, "What's the harm in him knowing?"

"I am intruding." Brend's eyes widen in alarm. "I did not know. I saw the clothes on the doorstep and I——"

Eirwyn places a hand on his arm. "It's all right. There's plenty of stew for one more guest."

I groan and retreat to the window. My eyes search the clearing and the first line of trees. Maybe Colette decided to fit in another hour of foraging before dinner. Maybe she found another cluster of penny bun mushrooms she couldn't pass up.

But there's still no sign of her. It's past sundown now, and she hasn't come.

Eirwyn brings a cloth and a basin of water to Ma's room so Brend can clean up. She hums while she stirs the stew, no longer needing to tug on her left ear. She informs me that dinner's ready, but I don't answer. My eyes ache from staring out the window for so long. I can't see anything in the night, but I keep looking anyway. Keep looking and waiting. Why hasn't she come? I consider other possible excuses—strict mother, getting lost, succumbing to nerves, falling ill—but none of them make me feel any better.

All that work. All that dusting and sitting and dressing, and the one to witness the result of my efforts is a dirty, cursed boy.

Maybe I should blame Colette for her absence, but I *want* to condemn him. I want to take this white-hot ire in my chest, shape it with my hands, and hurl it at him. For being there when I opened the door. For coming back after I ordered him not to.

Why couldn't he stay away? Why couldn't she have been the one on my doorstep?

I catch Eirwyn's reflection in the window. She puts an arm around my shoulders and draws me close, strokes my hair.

I blink, hard. "It's only stew."

"It's more than that," she says.

She's right, of course. I thought I'd found someone I could take foraging, someone who loves the forest like I do, someone who'd accept the answers about myself I'm willing to give. But sundown has come and gone, and that someone has turned out to be no different than everyone else. As much as I want him to, Brend can't harbor all the blame for this horrid night.

I turn into Eirwyn's embrace. My sister's arms are warm and strong around me. I tell myself this is all I need.

A door creaks as Brend steps out of Ma's bedroom. His hair is wet and tousled, his cheeks red. When he meets my gaze, his eyes aren't quite as bright.

His lips part as if to speak. I shake my head against Eirwyn's shoulder and close my eyes.

CHAPTER 8

Knees pulled to my chest, I sit before the fireplace, watching the flames bend and flicker. Behind me at the dining table, Eirwyn and Brend trade murmurs and scrape up spoonfuls of stew. The savory smells make my gut clench with hunger, but I don't move to join them. I can't decide what would be worse— to taste the penny bun mushrooms on my tongue or be unable to discern their flavor among the acorns and onions.

No one asks me to help clean up. Eirwyn refills the washbasin while Brend carries dishes to the counter. He drops a plate, and the resounding clang rattles my ears. I shut my eyes and try to imagine Colette in my kitchen instead of him. I can't.

Perhaps there's a reason seclusion is so easy for me. Perhaps I'm meant for it.

Once the cottage is tidy, Eirwyn bids Brend goodnight and strokes my hair once more before she goes to bed. Brend doesn't sit on the bench with me, but I sense him lingering nearby, hear his heavy breathing. Sometime later, he clears his throat as if to remind me of his presence.

"Well, you'll be wanting your bed," I mutter.

"I am all right with waiting," he says.

I bite down on my bottom lip until it stings. I can't take any more of his pleasantries. "I told you not to come back."

He shifts his weight so the floor creaks but doesn't answer.

"You were a bear, standing outside the cottage next to a pile of my father's clothes, and I looked at you and said, 'Don't come back.'"

"I heard you."

"Then why didn't you listen?"

"I do not kn—"

"Don't say that." I rise to face him, anger crackling in my chest. "That answer doesn't work for me."

"All right," he says, holding up his hands. "I came back because of you. I believe you can help me. Help me stop this . . . changing."

I nearly laugh; the idea is so absurd. "Why would you think that?"

"I knew your name before we met. There must be a reason."

"Like what?" I challenge.

"Tell me why else I would know your name," he says.

"I don't know, all right?" I grab the ends of my braids and pull until the stinging in my scalp becomes too painful to withstand. "I don't know."

None of it makes sense. Not his transformations, not my name on his lips. Pa would've invited the chance to deal with the unknowable, the impossible. Not me. All I want is the comfort of my western wood, and perhaps a raven-haired girl at my side. I can't even change Ma's mind about moving away. I'm not meant to handle magic.

But one side of Brend's mouth lifts into a smirk. "That answer does not work for me."

I press my tongue against my cheek, annoyed I've been caught. "Fair enough."

"I know you do not want me in your life." He steps toward me, his amber gaze bright again, imploring. "Nor do you want me in your sister's life. So, I will make you a promise. Help me, and once I am free, I will disappear from your lives for good."

The idea is tempting, I'll admit. Not so tempting that I can ignore the questions that bloom from his declaration. "What if it isn't a curse? What if you've always been half-bear?"

"I cannot accept that," he answers simply. "At least not until I have exhausted all other possibilities."

I look toward the window, toward the blackness of the night. The angry, resentful part of me asserts that Brend charged his way into my life. That I owe him nothing and shouldn't hesitate to reject him. To send him on his way while my sister sleeps and return to sulking over Colette.

But the truth is . . . I invited him.

To save a red fox, I challenged a bear, a boy with a curse. I chose to interfere. Though I can't explain why Brend knew my name, perhaps if I want him out of my life and away from Eirwyn, I must now do my part.

More than that, if I were cursed like Brend, if I couldn't remember the trees and the family I love, I'd want someone to help me. I'd want someone to help me remember. Since Brend has no one else, and I certainly won't risk Eirwyn's safety, that someone will have to be me.

But how do I help him? Brend's . . . affliction isn't natural. Though I've heard trauma to the head can steal a person's memories, I've never heard of such trauma turning someone into a bear. The only explanation for that seems to be a curse. A faerie curse.

Thanks to Pa, I know how to meet faeries. Using this knowledge might reveal me to be nothing but a fool, yet right now, it's all I have.

"All right, I'll help you," I tell him. "Wait here."

Meeting the faeries means leaving the cottage, means stepping out into the snow and traveling through the winter wood. Since Brend's no longer dressed in bear fur, I must find something to protect him from the cold. In Ma's room, I open the wardrobe and push past dresses and skirts. One gives me pause: a worn dress of mismatched fabrics, of conflicting patterns and colors. The first dress Eirwyn and I sewed for Ma. Eirwyn was nine, me two years younger. We collected scraps of cloth for months. We sewed in secret at night while our parents slept.

Clumsy hands. Bleeding fingers. Bright eyes. When one sister's eyes fluttered shut, the other took up the needle.

When the dress was complete, we expected a warm smile and a good-natured laugh. Maybe Ma would wear the dress once to be nice. After all, we knew what it looked like.

We certainly didn't expect that Ma would wear the dress for

every Yule, every birthday, every celebration. Of course, she did. She wore a dress with patches of dots and stripes and flowers, a dress with patches from old dishcloths and wool socks. She still wears the garment often, though she decided against bringing it to Poppy because she assumed the chaotic patterns would frighten Aunt Meara—and they would.

Ma wears the dress because she never does anything halfway. She sticks to each decision she makes despite any fear or uncertainty that may come along. Sometimes I find this sort of attitude frustrating, like when her decisions affect me and I'd rather they not. Mostly I admire her commitment, her resolve.

I press the patchwork dress to my nose, breathing in faint traces of pine wood and rose perfume. I will be like Ma. I will help Brend. I know little of curses, true, but I'll do for him what I can, and I'll do it wholeheartedly. Once he's gone, Eirwyn and I can return to our disagreements and forced smiles, to weathered books and forages in the wood. To an ordinary final winter in our cottage.

Resolute, I rifle through a few more garments until I find what I need, then return to the sitting room with Pa's gray wool coat.

"What is this for?" Brend asks, slipping his arms through the sleeves. Like all of Pa's clothes, the coat is too large for him but should keep him warm.

"Have you never worn a coat, or have you simply forgotten why you should?"

Brend gives me an exasperated look. "You know what I mean."

I refuse to fight my grin of satisfaction. Just because I've pledged to help him doesn't mean I must be entirely kind. "My father told me how to meet faeries. The quickest way involves leaving the cottage."

"Why faeries?"

"They might have answers."

I add a few more logs to the fire so it doesn't die out while we're gone. I don't want Eirwyn waking to a cold cottage, wondering what's become of us. At the door, I stuff my feet into boots and pull on my cloak. I light two lanterns and hand one to Brend.

My eyes rest on the doorknob, scuffed from years of calloused hands turning and tugging, coming and going. I'm not supposed to go to the wood at night. Ma always speaks of dangers that come with the dark, dangers I now know to be real. But with a bear-boy beside me, I've already put myself at risk. It's not too late to change my mind, but I don't want to. Helping Brend is the only way to be rid of him.

I grasp the knob, ignoring the echoes of Ma's warning. "Ready?"

He nods.

Outside, a frosty wind bathes our faces, and snow crunches beneath our feet. I lead Brend into the trees, both lanterns providing ample light to travel by. Winter has driven away insects, so the only sounds of night are the rustling leaves and the occasional hoot of an owl, which reminds me so much of Colette that when Brend begins speaking, I'm unexpectedly grateful for the distraction.

"From the way Eirwyn talks, everyone in your village believes in faeries," he says. "What took you so long?"

"Pa's stories were always stories to me." I duck beneath a low-hanging branch. "I never tied them to truths."

"Yet you still remember them."

I think of the crack in the floorboard, and the shirt I refuse to mend. "Forgetting his stories would mean losing parts of him."

I pause then, an ache for Pa building in my chest. He should be the one leading me through the night, bringing me to meet the faeries. Instead, I'm guiding a strange boy who wears Pa's old coat.

"I am glad you did not forget," says Brend, his shoulder brushing mine.

The contact is so fleeting I might've imagined it, but comforting in a way I would rather not face in the dark. I force my boots forward, and we walk the rest of the way in silence.

Our lanterns have burned through half their oil when I finally stop in the center of three trees arranged in a triangle. I hold my lantern out toward each one—an oak, an ash, and a hawthorn—confirming I've found the right place. I nod to myself, satisfied.

Missing nothing, Brend asks, "Why here?"

"Pa brought me here once," I explain. "He said a good place to meet a faerie is at the center of these three trees, late at night or early in the morning."

While some memories of Pa are dimmer than they once were, this one remains exceptionally clear. He was in the late stage of his fever on the morning he roused me from bed well before dawn, pressing a finger to his lips so I wouldn't wake Eirwyn. I was half-asleep as I dressed, pulling on mismatched socks and missing a button on my cloak. I stumbled after him, following deep into the western wood until he halted in the middle of three trees.

I remember his hand pressed against the oak, remember him asking aloud to speak with a faerie. When he received no answer, I suppressed my fifth yawn and asked why he brought me to the wood so early.

"I've told you many stories, Ro," Pa said, palm tapping the tree as if to rouse a faerie from slumber. "But there are some tales only the faeries of this wood can tell, and I need you to hear them."

I never did hear them, though, because even after hours of pleading, no faeries answered Pa's summons. Frustrated and delirious, he finally gave up, and I led him home beneath the beaming afternoon sun. We found Ma and Eirwyn seated at the dining table, Ma with a stern look and Eirwyn with tears in her eyes. Ma shouted for a while, then placed her hand against Pa's sweaty forehead and sent him to bed.

I was startled by her reaction. Pa hadn't left a note, but that wasn't unusual. Ma and Eirwyn should have assumed where we were. Fearing I'd be scolded, too, I apologized for following Pa to the western wood when it was still dark, but Ma simply shook her head and gave me the fiercest hug she ever had.

Pa passed a week later.

Despite the strangeness of that day, I've never given much thought to what Pa wanted me to hear from the faeries. He was simply ill, confused. Trying like he always did to bring his stories to life. Now, as I instruct Brend to do as my father once did, I can't help but wonder what I would've learned if Pa's summoning had worked, and why he wanted me to know the stories so badly.

Brend steps up to the oak and places a flat palm against its bark. Closing his eyes, he says, "I wish to speak with a faerie."

We wait. I cup a hand around my mouth, releasing puffs of hot breath to keep my fingers warm, once again having forgotten my gloves. The lantern light illuminates Brend's features, showing stubble across his sharp chin that I'm just noticing.

Studying the rest of his body, I debate who Brend was before he was a bear. Slender and tall like Eirwyn, he doesn't have a woodcutter's thick arms or a gardener's rough hands. He knows how to chop vegetables, so maybe he was a cook. His lack of scars and calluses could also mean he's a wealthy merchant's son or an inexperienced traveler who wandered into the wrong forest and angered a faerie or two.

I consider what's to be gleaned from my own appearance: stains on my cloak and dirt under my fingernails; dark auburn hair that's a mess of tangles if not in braids; eyes on my boots if I'm not surrounded by trees. I'm certainly not like any girl who belongs in a town like Poppy, and I seem to have more in common with a fox than a wealthy merchant. No wonder Colette changed her mind about coming to dinner.

"Nothing is happening." Brend's voice chases away my dark thoughts as he removes his hand from the bark.

"I don't know what I expected," I say. "It didn't work for Pa either."

"What about you?"

I blink at him. "Me?"

He inclines his head toward the tree. "Did you ever try?"

"No. He didn't ask me to."

"Maybe you should now. What if the faeries are ignoring me because I am cursed?" My hesitancy must show because he adds, "This was your idea. At least see it all the way through."

"All right," I huff, joining Brend by the oak, "if it'll make you stop pestering me." I press my palm against the tree, its roughness tickling my skin, and close my eyes. "I wish to speak with a faerie."

We wait again. I don't trust that the summoning will work. How could it when it didn't work for Pa, the one who genuinely believed in faeries? My doubt grows heavier as my palm grows colder against the bark.

But a voice, deep and gravelly as if woken from a thousand years of slumber, speaks in the night, "I did not expect to meet you so soon."

When I open my eyes, I'm no longer in the western wood. Or at least not the western wood as I know it.

This wood is sharper and brighter. The black sky remains, but the trees and leaves are hemmed in a sliver's width of glowing blue light. A light that makes my eyes dance, unsure of where to land. A light that makes my skin itch with the yearning to move. To run. To dance. To lose myself completely.

Standing in the center of three trees is something that resembles a man but is clearly not human.

I hold up my lantern to better see the figure in front of me. Snow-capped branches wrap and twist around his body, and his skin is rough and gray-brown like oak tree bark. His ears are slightly pointed, his eyes a piercing shade of green, vivid even amidst the blue-tinged shadows and yellow lantern light.

I sway from a spell of dizziness. I'm looking at a faerie,

hearing him speak. He's real. Pa was right. Despite Brend's curse, I couldn't truly believe it.

Now I've no choice.

"This is," the faerie continues, "quite unprecedented."

The air is thick with the scent of roses, almost cloying in its strength. "Where—where am I?" I ask, trying not to breathe through my nose.

His bark-rough lips creak into a smile. "The western wood."

But the wild roses in the western wood don't carry so strong of a scent, and I've certainly never seen this strange blue light, nor felt its pull. "What happened to it?"

"Nothing happened to the wood." He pauses, smile deepening. "Something happened to you."

"I don't understand." I close my eyes, but the dizziness remains. The scent of roses remains. The strangeness and allure remain. It takes so much strength to keep myself still.

"You brought yourself beyond the veil."

The veil. Pa's answer every time I asked why I couldn't see faeries. A layer of magic that separates the ordinary world from their enchanted dwellings, keeps them out of sight unless they want to be seen. I thought he was making up excuses, but he knew. How did he know?

I look up at the stars to find that they, too, are edged in radiant sapphire. My breath escapes me in wonder, puffs of steam that sparkle. Nothing in this wood remains untouched by the blue glow.

"How did you know to do it?" the faerie asks, regaining my attention. "Why did you do it?"

It's then that I realize Brend isn't with me.

"The boy," I say, panic sharpening my tone, "where is he?"

"He stands beside you, on the other side of the veil." The faerie's green eyes drink me in like water to roots. "Again, I ask you, why did you cross it?"

I swallow thickly. "I didn't mean to. I only want to ask about the boy. I think he's cursed."

"Ah, well." The faerie shifts and his branches groan. "He is indeed cursed, but I am not meant to interfere in that. Neither are you, for that matter."

I grit my teeth. "Then why speak to me at all?"

"Curiosity," he says. "As I said, I was not—"

"Expecting me," I finish, irritation expanding in my chest, tempting me to shout. "I heard you the first time. I'm here anyway." I put my hands on my hips, the anger like a weight, keeping me from floating away. "So, what can you tell me?"

The faerie's eyebrows lift, two dark shards of wood. "My, my, you are striking. No wonder they sought you out despite the rules."

I breathe heavily through my nose. I've lost nearly all my patience. "Who?"

"The bear. And the fox."

"What does the fox have to—"

As if summoned by our words, a woman strides into the blue-tinged clearing. "What is the meaning of this?" she asks, her voice low as she addresses the oak faerie.

Copper fur covers her body. Soft ears peek out from dark curls and a fox tail wraps around her middle. Her eyes are a muted shade of yellow. Based on her build, she must be somewhere around Shea and Deidra's age, older than me but younger than

Ma. She is beautiful and strange, animal and woman. Faerie.

And unmistakably familiar.

"Tamsin," says the oak faerie, green eyes widening. "I understand what this must look like—"

"You are offering counsel," says the woman, Tamsin. "To help *him*."

"I have done nothing of the sort," says the oak faerie, a hand to his chest. "She summoned me, yet I have told her nothing."

"That's not true," I say. "You confirmed that Brend is cursed. But is he also a faerie? Like you? Like her?" I point at the fox woman. The woman who might be my fox. The one I met in the wood, the one I've been searching for.

"He is no faerie, foolish girl," says Tamsin, and the disparagement in her voice wounds me. I never expected that the fox who bowed to me would speak to me like this. "Now, leave us."

I stumble as my vision darkens and a sharp pain slices my forehead. I bend over, placing my hands on my knees to steel myself against another bout of dizziness. I suck in deep breaths, drinking so much frigid air my chest burns.

When I'm feeling well enough to gingerly lift my head, the oak faerie and Tamsin are gone. Brend stands before me instead, fear in his eyes and confusion turning down the corners of his mouth.

I take in my surroundings. The trees are draped in ordinary shadows. Every trace of the blue-edged light is gone. Did I cross back to the ordinary world by accident, or was it Tamsin who pushed me out? Either way, I doubt I'd find success in summoning her or the oak faerie again.

"Where did you go?" asks Brend.

I shake my head but instantly regret it. Pressing fingertips to my forehead to fight the ache, I answer, "A place I didn't believe existed."

A place Pa was right to believe in. I thought he was a fool. I groaned whenever he pointed to a ring of mushrooms or a uniquely well-trodden path. Giggled at his stories.

But everything he said is true. Now I'm in the midst of my own peculiar story. A story he will never hear.

Guilt unfurls its wings in my gut, flies up my throat, and bursts from my mouth as a sob. My body is overtaken by shudders. I hear Brend take a step forward, can feel the nearness of him, can almost sense his hand hovering over my back. But he never touches me.

Eventually, I lead him back to the cottage. I know I ought to, but I don't share my conversation with the faeries, what I saw. I add wood to the fire and leave Brend to sleep in my sitting room another night.

CHAPTER 9

I wake with bleary eyes. My skin feels tight, like dry soil in need of water. I can't remember at what hour I finally fell asleep, except that I saw a faint gray light outside my window. I was kept awake by tumbling thoughts of faeries, the veil, and Pa.

Now, harsh strokes of sunlight paint my sheets, and slipping further beneath my blankets won't keep out the light. I rub a hand against each of my cheeks, working the rigid muscles of my jaw.

Faeries are real. I spoke with two, creatures of oak wood and fox fur. I crossed beyond the veil and saw a land edged in blue light.

No escaping the truth of Pa's stories now, not after all I've seen.

Clanging sounds in the kitchen incite me from bed. I stumble from my room to find Eirwyn at the counter slicing a loaf of bread and Brend at the dining table with a steaming cup.

Eirwyn greets me with an apologetic smile. "Sorry about the noise. Tea?"

I nod and take a seat across from Brend. The arrangement is eerily reminiscent of the dinner we shared. My eyes draw to his hands, but they remain still against his teacup. No trembling. No changing. I release a steadying breath.

"Are you well?" Brend asks.

I yawn into my palm. I can't meet his eyes. Not after last night.

Eirwyn places a cup before me. "You slept in your dress?"

I look down. Sure enough, the burgundy dress I chose for Colette is rumpled from sleep. Now the dress will be remembered as the one I wore to meet faeries for the first time. I'm not sure I'll ever wear it again.

I watch tendrils of steam rise from my tea. "Has he told you yet?"

"Told me what?"

"I thought it best to wait for you," Brend murmurs.

"What are you two talking about?" Eirwyn asks.

I look up at my sister. "You should sit."

Her eyebrows draw together. "But I was—"

"Please."

Eirwyn holds up her hands in surrender. "All right. Now I'm worried."

I wait for her to join us at the table, then begin. "Last night, Brend and I went to the wood to summon faeries."

Eirwyn's eyes noticeably widen. "Ro, why would you—"

"Let her explain," interrupts Brend, surprising us both.

"Fine," says my sister, crossing her arms.

I recount the rest of the night's events, though I don't include the deal Brend and I made—that in exchange for my help breaking the curse, he's promised to leave for good. An ill feeling churns in my stomach for keeping such a secret from my sister, but it doesn't change my mind. Brend is a danger to our lives, both as a bear and as a boy. I don't need Eirwyn arguing against the decision I've made.

"Pa was right, then," my sister says, her voice solemn. "He was telling the truth all those years."

And I didn't believe him. Those unsaid words hang between us. I can't meet her eyes now, either. "He was."

Brend, who remained quiet while I told my story, asks, "What now? Neither faerie seems to have been very forthcoming."

"The oak faerie mentioned the fox—Tamsin—before she interrupted us. She must be tied to your curse." I set aside my cup of tea. "I'm going to find her."

"What if she ignores your summons?" Brend asks.

"I'm not going to summon her." I can't trust myself beyond the veil—those odd, alluring feelings, the dizziness. I need to confront her where I'm most comfortable, and that's the western wood of this plane. "I'm going to track her."

She's a faerie, but she's also a fox. If she's returned to an animal form since last night, I can find her. Eirwyn doesn't seem convinced, but I won't waver. Tamsin is involved, and I'm determined to find out how.

I also hope that our next meeting will prove last night was

a fluke. That she called me a foolish girl because she was upset, not because it's what she truly thinks of me. I've held closely our first encounter in the clearing since it happened. It would ruin me to know that moment, and those feelings, were one-sided.

I finish my tea and eat a slice of bread, then dress in leggings and a hooded, long-sleeved tunic, adding a leather vest to help cut the wind. The vest was Pa's. It fits surprisingly well when I pull the laces tight enough. I haven't worn it in a while, too afraid to ruin the garment like I do with most of my clothes. But I want him with me today as I search for the fox. I remember to pull on my gloves but leave my cloak hanging on the rack; I'll move more freely in the wood without it.

Brend meets me at the door. "Let me come with you. This is my curse."

"A curse I promised to help you break," I remind him. "Besides, you nearly ate the fox last time."

He grimaces. "Do not make fun."

"I'm not. I'll find her. Trust me."

"I do," he murmurs.

He draws closer and his fingertips brush my elbow, gentle and warm. I breathe sharply without meaning to, taking a step back. "You should help Eirwyn with the morning chores."

Brend's hand hangs in the air for a moment. "I did not mean to—"

"It's all right," I tell him, even though it's not. Nothing about him is all right.

I turn toward the door and grab the knob.

"Good luck," he says.

"Thank you," I answer, before escaping into the cold.

I don't immediately go to the wood. Instead, I follow the snow-covered path to Deidra and Shea's cottage and knock quietly in case Orla is sleeping. I breathe warmth into my palms while I wait, bouncing on my toes to fight the chill.

The door creaks open, revealing Shea. Her dark blonde hair is a tangled knot atop her head, and the skin beneath her eyes is puffy. The threadbare wool tunic over her trousers is decorated with an array of stains, which upon further inspection I suspect might be from spilled tea, stewed carrots, and fish guts.

"What?" she greets, in a scratchy voice I used to cover my ears against as a child.

"I assume this is a poor time?" I ask, peering over her shoulder to survey the sitting room. I don't see Deidra or the baby, which means they must be in the bedroom.

"Oh, not at all." Her fingers scratch at her messy mop of hair. "Simply witnessing Deidra outshine me as a mother. Come in."

"Actually, I was wondering if you would come outside."

Shea is suddenly narrow-eyed. "Why?"

"I need your help," I tell her. "I'm tracking a red fox."

"I fish." She tugs at her collar. "It's why I smell so delightful all the time. Haven't tracked forest animals in ages."

"You're still the best tracker I know," I insist. "I really need to find this fox."

"Why?" she asks again.

"I can't tell you."

She rolls her eyes. "Right. Well, I'm sure your reasons are sound, but I promised your mother I'd keep you out of trouble if I could."

I frown. "How do you know finding the fox will put me in trouble?"

"Why else keep secrets?"

"Shea, please," I say, trying not to whine but coming dangerously close. "This is important."

Somewhere in the cottage, Orla screeches like an owl. Shea winces, signaling with a hand to her ear that this isn't the first time today her baby's made a fuss. I bite my lip to keep from smiling. No one screams at Shea the way Orla does—they wouldn't dare. But the baby is too young to have those sorts of fears, and I'm glad for it.

I hear Deidra begin a lovely tune to calm Orla down, but the song prompts another scream. And another.

Shea winces again, then twirls a stray tendril of hair around her fingertip. "All right, fine, but I'm not agreeing to this for your benefit. My ears happen to require the rest."

This time I fail to fight my grin. "Right, of course."

"Promise you'll explain yourself once we've found the fox?"

"Deal," I say.

The second bargain made in less than a day, and I've no idea how I'll keep it.

Shea withdraws inside to grab her coat, leaving me to dwell on the unsoundness of my own plan. Though I've promised to explain myself, I can't let anyone else get wrapped up in Brend's curse. Eirwyn and I invited Brend into our lives—me by challenging him, Eirwyn by wounding him. But Shea didn't ask to be put in danger, and neither did her family. I need her help to find the fox, but that's where her involvement will end. Brend is mine and Eirwyn's burden, and no one else's.

I consider telling Shea about my meeting with the faeries without mentioning Brend. Unlike her wife, who studies faerie lore and even collects crystals of varying properties, Shea doesn't believe in faeries. But she's always said she would change her mind if someone she trusted claimed to have witnessed their magic. Maybe I can say faeries told me to seek a fox for an undivulged reason.

Yet if we find Tamsin and it's possible for her to shed her fox form on this side of the veil, Shea will be involved anyway. My boots squeak against the snow as I turn away from the cottage. Maybe this was a poor idea. I shouldn't have come for help. I'm no tracker, but it might be safer for everyone if I find the fox on my own.

Before I can commit to retreating, though, Shea appears with a bag thrown over her shoulder.

"What's in there?" I ask.

"Trapping supplies. I doubt your fox wants to be caught."

My mouth is suddenly dry. I hadn't thought of that. If Tamsin resists us, trapping her might be the only way for me to garner information about Brend's curse. But I don't want any harm to come to the fox no matter how fierce my desire for answers. I risked my own life to save her from Brend, after all.

Peering at the bag, I ask, "Are they fatal? Your supplies?"

"Not unless you want them to be," Shea says, but doesn't elaborate.

We pass my cottage on the way to the wood. Discreetly, I glance at the window to make sure Eirwyn is all right. To make sure Brend hasn't become a bear since I left.

I can see the back of Eirwyn's head from where she sits on the bench before the fire. Brend is out of sight, perhaps making himself useful by cleaning up the kitchen. A relieved breath loosens the tightness in my chest.

"Eirwyn know we're doing this?" Shea asks.

My glance must not have been as discreet as I intended. "What did you tell Deidra?"

"Not much," she admits, setting a quicker pace. "Said I'd explain later."

I rush my stride to keep up with her. "That's not part of the deal we made."

"You should be honest with those you love." Shea's shoulders lift as she sucks in a deep breath. "Especially if a child is involved."

"Do you like it? Having Orla?"

I haven't decided if I ever want children of my own. Ma says I have plenty of time yet to make up my mind.

Shea keeps her eyes toward the trees as she says, "Orla's the most precious part of my life."

I sense there's more to it than that. "But?"

"Every time I'm away on a fishing trip, I can't stop thinking of her. When I'm home, all I think of is how I should be fishing—providing more for her and for Deidra."

"You provide so much already," I say. "Ma says it all the time—you put her to shame."

"But is it enough?" Shea shakes her head. "Village life is hard, Ro. You should be grateful to your mother for what she's doing for you and Eirwyn. It's a risk to leave, surely, but a good one."

Bitterness blossoms on my tongue. Why must I have this conversation over and over? Shea, Deidra, Eirwyn, Ma—they tell me the same thing with different words. Be grateful. Be supportive. This change will be good.

Two people in my life refrain from telling me what to do and how to feel. One is half-bear. The other is a mystery.

I catch myself before my mind wanders further into dangerous territory, into thoughts of Colette and why she didn't come to dinner. I can't dwell on last night's disappointment; I'm tracking a fox.

We enter the forest, and Shea asks me to bring her to the spot where I first saw the creature. In winter, so much of the wood is indistinguishable, but only to the unfocused eye. I pick up the little details: a long scratch in the bark of an ash tree; an evergreen with needles on one side; a frozen stream I drink from in the summer. I use these details to bring us to the clearing, to the tree stump I sat upon that fateful day.

I perch on that same stump while Shea inspects the area. She picks up twigs and touches her fingertips to fallen leaves. She bends low to survey the snow, searching for tracks and other disturbances in the smooth layer of white. She curls her fingers behind her ear, listening to the wind and the birds.

Then, she kneels beside a boulder. "Here."

I slide off the stump and go to her. There's a dip in the snow next to the rock, exposing a few of the leaves and branches beneath. The impression is fox sized.

"A fox lay," says Shea. "Your fox might've spent time here. Recently, as there was snowfall yesterday."

Shea explains that because the prints lead in a straight line, it means the fox was trotting when she left. Apparently, when foxes trot, the rear paws land where the front paws stepped.

I point ahead to where the line of prints stretches into the trees. "That's the direction she left the day I saw her."

Shea grins, showing slightly crooked teeth. "Been a while since I've pursued something instead of waiting for it to bite."

We follow the tracks, and Shea's careful not to miss any change in their direction. The trail takes us through clusters of bare trees and around snow-covered boulders. At another frozen stream, the paw prints end, but before I can be discouraged, Shea notices that they pick up on the other side.

A few times Shea pauses to listen to the forest, chin raised and eyes alert. She inspects some prints closely, dark blonde eyebrows pulled together in concentration. Her hand hovers over the snow, and one slender finger outlines the paw print's shape. She doesn't explain her actions to me, and I don't mind. This isn't a lesson.

The fox path stretches further than I anticipated, twisting and turning seemingly at random. Shea says a fox will expand its territory during winter to compensate for less abundant prey, but I can't help but wonder if Tamsin is toying with us. If she knows I'm after her.

Finally, Shea finds a second fox lay, this one with a tuft of copper fur and what she calls "a strong fox scent." We're close. I tug on the cords of my vest. Anticipation is a rock in my gut.

It starts to snow.

Thick flakes of white shower the forest like rain, only this rain sticks. I pull up the hood of my tunic to keep my hair dry, but snow clings to my leggings until they're drenched, the dampness leaking down into my boots.

"Eyes on the ground," Shea says. "Don't lose the tracks."

She takes my hand, and we walk side by side, the fox path between us. We pick up our boots slowly and place them carefully so as not to disturb the prints. When I look up to give my neck a break, the snowfall has grown heavier. I can barely see in front of me, and the bright swirling white is harsh against my eyes. My face is warm from the lengthy pursuit, and snowflakes melt against my skin and slip down my cheeks like tears.

The line of paw prints curves, heading deeper into the trees with no sign of ending. If the snowfall keeps on like this, we could easily get lost. We need to move quicker. We need to find her before it's too late.

"Ro, we should turn—"

"We can't lose the tracks," I protest.

Shea squeezes my hand. "Snow's falling too hard."

I look longingly ahead, my gaze following the tracks as they're steadily overtaken by snow. Soon they'll disappear completely, forcing us to wander with no path.

Yet turning back now will mean failure. Failing Brend. Failing myself. I shudder. Not from the cold, but from the thought of Brend remaining as he is, unpredictable and animal. Growing closer to Eirwyn. Growing closer to me.

I shake my head, a few snow-drenched strands of hair whipping across my face. "We have to keep going."

Shea halts, tugging on my hand until I'm forced to stop as well. "We'll try again another day. The tracks are already fading."

Panic crackles like a flame in my chest. If I can't fight this snow, how will I fight a curse?

"You can go back," I decide, fixing my determined eyes on the trees ahead. "I'm following these tracks until I find her."

Shea groans. "Enough of this, Ro. It's just a fox."

I squeeze my eyes shut. I remember her curious smile, her bow. No. She's more than that.

"Careful walking back," I say.

Then I take off running.

I slog through the accumulating snowfall, boots kicking up torrents of white that are carried off by the wind. I ignore Shea's pleading calls, and soon they are lost to the gales slamming against my ears. Even the trees creak and moan, struggling to maintain their hold in the forest.

I can't see the fox tracks anywhere. The snow has erased every trace. I move by instinct, predicting where the trail leads based on the tracks I've already followed.

Finally, I squint, and in the distance, through the snowfall, I spot a flash of color. Coppery orange beneath an evergreen. The sight stalls my breath.

I've found her.

I press onward, though the snow makes my pace frustratingly slow. The ground before me is white and endless and the red fox seems unreachable. Fear of losing her clutches my throat. But I don't stop. I trudge forward, boot after boot, the creature's name like a wish on my tongue.

As I get closer, I know I'm right. That *is* my red fox beneath the tree, snow dappling her coppery coat. The needled branches are missing from the front of the trunk, giving the fox enough room to take shelter from the storm.

I crouch before her, shifting until I, too, am sheltered by the evergreen. The fox backs against the tree, fur bristling. Her yellow eyes are wide and panicked. Her tail slaps against the snow until it's covered in white.

"Woah, easy now," I say gently. "I won't harm you."

The fox doesn't look so sure of that. She presses tighter against the tree, eyes darting as if judging her chances of getting past me. Unlike the bare front, the evergreen branches aren't missing on the sides of the trunk. They are sharp and thick and impenetrable for a fox, leaving no pathways for escape. I block the way out.

A strong gust of wind blows back my hood, exposing my dark auburn hair to the cold. I leave my hood down, worried that any sudden movement will further frighten the fox.

"Tamsin? Is that you?"

The fox dips her head, nose to the snow. Her eyes become slits. She growls low.

Unsettled, I shift to gain a bit of distance. Faerie or not, right now this fox is still a wild animal, like Brend when he's a bear. I can't forget that. I must be careful.

I try another way. "Remember that day in the wood? When you bowed to me? You did that for a reason. You must have."

The fox doesn't lift her head, but her fur settles, and she no longer growls.

"Were you trying to reach me? To see if . . ." I break off, frustrated. I don't know the right questions to ask, the right words to say that might convince her to trust me. "If you can understand me at all, show me. If you know me at all, show me."

The fox finally lifts her head. Full yellow eyes bore into mine, holding me captive. Making me incapable of thought. Incapable of movement.

But I still have my voice, and I use it again, this time with intensity: "*Please, show me.*"

Then the trembling begins.

Trembling that turns to shuddering, and shuddering to bones snapping, muscles stretching. Body contorting. My shock keeps me still, keeps my eyes open even though I'm desperate not to witness the agonizing change.

The red fox yelps. The red fox whimpers. The red fox is becoming something *not fox*.

The red fox is becoming a girl.

A girl I know, with brown skin and tight curls.

CHAPTER 10

"Colette," I breathe, when the transformation's ended.

"Ro," says Colette in a rough voice.

Our lips fall silent then, unable to progress past the utterance of names. Breaths labored and mouths agape, we hold each other's gazes. Colette's eyes are still the muted yellow of a fox, and the look is so eerie it makes me shudder.

No other traces of the animal remain. Colette's cheeks show freckles rather than whiskers, and her damp curls hang heavily to skim bare shoulders.

Bare shoulders. Bare body, trembling and slick with sweat. My eyes trail downward, taking in curves I only imagined her having until this moment. Looking at her now, I can almost forget she was a fox. Can almost forget the sickening cracks of her animal bones as they changed to fit a girl's frame; the sight of her body convulsing against the evergreen.

Because right now every inch of Colette is a girl, from her wet curls to her smooth stomach to her bare knees pressed into the snow. A warm ache starts low in my belly, urging me to draw closer.

She jerks forward, and my body reacts first, hand jutting out to pin her shoulder against the tree trunk. Her skin is hot beneath my gloved hand. I pull back when her yellow eyes widen in fear.

"I'm sorry, I didn't want you to run. I—" Suddenly Colette's nakedness is too much. Shame burns my throat for looking at her, for touching her so aggressively. I shut my eyes. "Do you have any—would you like my shirt?"

She doesn't answer. I cover my closed eyes with my hand then carefully peer between my fingers, intending to look at her face.

But Colette is gone.

I blink, shake my head, but the gestures don't bring her back. My sight hasn't failed me. Somehow Colette got away.

No. I'd have heard her move, would have *felt* Colette crawl past me. Many things are possible—bear-boys and fox-girls and bark-skinned faeries. But she couldn't have escaped without me noticing. Not so quickly.

I shift backward, little by little, until I'm out from beneath the tree and able to stand without hitting branches. I suck in a startled breath.

The evergreen is edged in blue light.

I've crossed beyond the veil. Again.

"You should not be here," says a voice.

I turn. Standing in the small clearing of the wood is a faerie. She has bark-skin legs, but she's covered in evergreen needles from the waist up. Her eyes are easy to miss because they are the same shade of green. She has no hair, but the needles point upward at the top of her head, like a piece of wood that hasn't been cut clean. The curves of her body and her voice are the discernible cues she might be female.

I pull up my hood. Even in the faerie realm, the snowfall remains heavy. "Why not?"

The faerie takes a step backward, shedding evergreen needles that color the snow. "The rules. No one may interfere."

The oak faerie also mentioned rules and interference. Do all the faeries of the western wood know about the curses? Did they play a part in creating them? Brend and Colette must be worth a lot to garner such attention.

I hold up my hands. "Please, don't go. I'm sorry. I don't know the rules."

"You are not meant to know anything, not until the end."

"The end of what?" I ask, desperate to know more. I'm not sure how much longer I have here, if I'll be pushed out like the last time. "The curses?"

"If I told you—" But the evergreen faerie abandons whatever she was about to say, shaking her head and shedding more needles. "Stay away from the girl. He is watching. He will not like this."

The faerie turns and runs, leaving a trail of green in her wake. I could follow the path, but that would mean abandoning Colette. I'm not so desperate for answers that I'd leave a cursed girl trembling against the trunk of a tree.

But how do I get back to her?

"Foolish girl," says a familiar voice.

I whip around to face Tamsin. The fox faerie watches me disapprovingly, furred arms crossed over her chest. I'm grateful to know she's not my fox. But could she still be tied to the curse? Tamsin's a fox faerie, and Colette can become a fox.

"Are you the reason my friend is cursed?" I ask.

Tamsin scowls. "I am not here to answer your questions. I am here to make sure you leave."

"Fine." I don't have time for her anyway. Colette is waiting for me. I glance toward the evergreen. "How do I cross back?"

"Last time, I pushed you." The fox faerie lifts her chin. "But you do not require my help. You can send yourself back the same way you came."

She makes it sound so easy, but she's forgetting one thing. "I didn't mean to come here."

"Think, girl." Tamsin taps her temple with one black claw. "What happened moments before your first crossing?"

I swallow, remembering last night. My hand against cold bark. "I summoned a faerie."

"And what did you do before this crossing?"

Snapping bones. Yellow eyes. "I asked Colette to show herself to me."

"What do those instances have in common?"

I bite my lower lip, searching my memories, looking for similarities. This line of questioning reminds me of Ma's teachings when I was younger, the lessons I could rarely sit still for but Eirwyn devoured. "I . . . asked for something."

The faerie shakes her head. "You commanded."

I bristle at the word. *Commanded* makes me sound like a cruel authority. Like the villagers who insist I pick one kind of person to love. Like Aunt Meara in her letters to Ma, telling her it's time to leave the cottage behind.

"I didn't mean to command anyone," I tell her. "I only want to help."

Tamsin sighs heavily. "I am not here to be your conscience. You asked how to return to your world, and I gave you the answer. Command yourself back across the veil."

"Um, all right." I clear my throat, still vexed by her word choice but, more than that, motivated to return to Colette. "I command myself back across the veil."

If I sense the weakness of my tone, Tamsin surely does too. But I can't summon the passion I used with Colette, now that I know there was more than a plea behind my words.

The fox faerie closes her eyes, seething. "I do not possess the patience for this." Her clawed hand juts out, and though it doesn't make contact, I feel a force against my chest. I stumble backward, blinking through the discomfort.

When my vision clears, Tamsin and the blue light are gone, and the world is bright-white again, though the heavy snowfall has finally ceased. I kneel, and I'm relieved to find Colette still beneath the evergreen. Sometime while I was away, her honey-brown irises replaced the eerie fox-yellow. She rocks back and forth against the tree trunk with her knees pulled to her chest.

"Where—where did you go?" she asks, her teeth chattering.

I shake my head. I can't explain the veil now. "Never mind that. We need to get you clothed before you turn to ice. Do you have—"

"I have a stash of clothes behind a boulder."

"How far?"

"Not far. A few trees away from this one, to my right."

I nod. "Wait here."

I stand and brush snow off my knees. My limbs are stiff, but I force myself to move quickly, concern for Colette driving me past three evergreens before I spot the boulder, partially obscured by a barren birch tree. I limp toward the rock and find a lump of clothes mostly covered by snow.

I shake them out as best I can: leggings, linen shirt, cloak, gloves, boots. I bring them back to Colette, then wait beside the evergreen as she dresses, though my cheeks burn as I recall the sight of her smooth brown skin.

"I'm finished," she says quietly.

I hesitate, holding a hand against my aching chest. Two curses now instead of one. More faeries opposing my involvement, and a mysterious *he* watching me defy the rules. Is this what I deserve for not believing in faeries all those years, for resisting Pa's stories?

"Ro? I'm finished."

I push Pa from my mind. The vulnerability bleeding through Colette's voice brings me back beneath the evergreen, keeps me from running away out of fear. I sit, mouth dry and throat tight. I don't have a plan. I don't know how to break these curses. But I can offer Colette support, let her know she's not alone.

"How are you feeling?" I ask. Then, remembering what Tamsin said about commanding her, add, "I'm sorry about what I did before. I didn't mean to—"

"It's okay," Colette says in a rush. "I didn't want to run from you. I was only scared, and I was . . . still coming back to myself. I'm all right now."

I'm confused for a moment, until I remember what happened after she changed, when she jerked forward and I pushed her back against the tree so she wouldn't leave. "Oh, right. Yes, I'm sorry for that too." I bite my lip. "But I was referring to what happened before." I twist my hands in my lap, suddenly nervous. What if she decides I'm awful? Could I blame her?

But I must be honest. I owe her that. "I think you changed into a girl because of me. Because of something in my voice."

Colette studies me with a peculiar expression. "Ro, I'm not sure how your voice could do something like that," she says, "but if it did bring me back, I'm grateful."

My tense shoulders ease. I remain unsettled by what I've done, but at least Colette doesn't despise me for it. "All right. That's good to hear."

"You know," she says, drawing up the hood of her cloak, "I remember you from that day in the wood. I remember bowing to you. I can't explain why I did, only that when I'm—when I'm a fox, I get these urges. To go somewhere or do something. If I fight them, I feel . . . wrong."

The admission is unnerving. I try not to show how much I'm affected by it. "Do you know how—"

"No." Colette's lashes press tightly against her cheeks. "I don't know why I'm like this, if it was something I did. The first change happened the night I turned sixteen. That was almost two weeks ago."

"And you can't control it?"

She shakes her head.

Just like Brend. But Colette has her memories. She knows who she is. What makes her different? Perhaps even more important: what makes them the same? Why were they both cursed to take the forms of animals?

"Colette." Her name sounds strange on my lips, as if I'm tempted to call her something else. "I think you might be cursed."

Her gaze is hard, wary. "What do you mean *cursed*?"

"There's another who's like you, who becomes an animal against his will, and we—"

"Who?"

I look down at the snow, reluctant to utter Brend's name. Hesitant to remind Colette of the night she nearly died, because I don't want to give her the waking nightmare I still face—the claws, the hot breath, the low groan. But we can't shy away from such things if we mean to understand what's happening.

"Colette, what else do you remember about being a fox?"

"A bear. I remember a bear. And you—you—" I hear her sharp intake of breath. "You saved me," she finishes, drawing closer. "You saved me from that bear."

We watch each other, bodies still save for our breathing. A shiver runs across my skin, hot and feverish, not at all to do with the winter air. The distance between us is short; I could easily close it. Even if Colette wants that now, will she still after I confess the rest of the story? Because I can't hide this truth from her either. Not if I want her to trust me.

"The bear is cursed like you," I tell her. "He's a boy our age, his name is Brend, and he's staying in my cottage."

Colette draws back, booted feet scuffing snow. "He tried to kill me."

I hold out my hands, the same gesture I made when she was a fox. "I know, I know. He hurt me, too, and I didn't want him anywhere near me at first. But he needs my help. He doesn't remember who he is, or why he was cursed."

She blinks, long and slow. "Maybe he's lying."

I don't have any proof that he's not, except the feeling in my gut. "I don't think so."

Rather than argue the matter further, she grows quiet. I watch her fingers trace the cracks in her leather boots, fingers that can become claws.

Fox. Girl. Fox. Like Brend and the bear, Colette and the fox are vastly different yet also inseparable, even when one tries to hide the other. "Colette, does the name Tamsin mean anything to you?"

The fox faerie wouldn't say whether she cursed Colette, but there must be a connection there.

Colette's brow furrows. "No, should it?"

"Maybe, I—"

"Ro?"

The familiar voice wrenches me from my attempted explanation. *Shea.* She's finally caught up with me. I curse softly. Colette's eyes narrow in a silent question.

"My neighbor," I whisper. "She was helping me track you, but we were separated during the storm. She's going to have questions. I don't know what to say, how to explain—"

"Let me." Colette leans forward. "I've been working on excuses to use on my mother since this all started happening."

I frown, unconvinced. "You don't know Shea. She's sharp."

Colette grins, granting me a brief glimpse of the girl I invited to dinner. "I'm sharper."

She crawls past me to leave the safety of the evergreen, and I scramble after her.

Colette tells Shea she was foraging when the snow started. She tried to find her way out of the wood, but the severity of the storm forced her to take shelter beneath an evergreen, where I found her soon after. I hold my breath throughout her telling of the story, waiting for Shea to mention the fox, how I left her behind when she wanted to turn back.

But she doesn't say anything. Perhaps because she doesn't want to yell at me in front of Colette, whose mother, it turns out, is a dear friend. Shea and Colette's mother often sell their goods in Maple Square together, and Deidra commissions a new quilted satchel each time hers becomes too worn to use.

The reason for Shea's silence could also be the snow, which starts up again almost as soon as Colette and I come out from beneath the evergreen, and quickly becomes as thick and torrential as the earlier storm. With me as our guide this time, we abandon the clearing and begin our trek home through the snow-drenched forest, though our journey is anything but neat. I turn at the wrong markers as snowflakes sting my eyes. Colette trips over her boots, as if unused to human legs. Shea shouts against the wind. But we keep moving, and soon the last few lines of trees are visible up ahead.

We reach the clearing and are greeted by a clear sky and a thin layer of snow on the ground. The scene is quiet, cold, and undisturbed.

Behind us, the snowstorm still rages within the trees.

"Strange," Shea mutters.

Colette and I are both quiet. I'm not sure what she's thinking, but I suspect faeries are to blame. The faerie responsible—Tamsin, the oak faerie, the evergreen faerie, or a faerie I've yet to meet—matters little. It's a clear threat, one meant to deter me from my promise to Brend, a promise that now extends to Colette. But no amount of poor weather will stop me from trying to free them both.

An entire wood of faeries might, though.

Shea decides we could all use a cup of tea, so she leads us to her cottage. Deidra greets us warmly, Orla swaddled in her arms. We shrug out of our outerwear, leaving it to dry by the fire; Deidra hands the baby to Shea and sets to work brewing tea. Orla coos and giggles, tugging on strands of Shea's wet hair, showing not a trace of her earlier tantrum.

Side by side on the cushioned bench, Colette and I share stiff smiles. I want to continue our conversation about the curses, but I can't while Shea remains in the sitting room, while Deidra prepares tea in the kitchen.

We wouldn't fare any better in my cottage, with Eirwyn asking questions and Brend hovering like he does. The wood seems like the only place for us to be alone, and yet we were chased out by the storm. How will we possibly come to understand these curses if we can't speak of them?

As if reading my frustrated thoughts, Orla starts fussing,

and Shea takes her to the bedroom for her nap. Deidra hands us each a cup of tea, then withdraws to join her wife and the baby. I breathe a heavy sigh of relief. Alone. Finally.

"I'm sorry too," says Colette.

I squint at her, wondering if I've missed something. "What for?"

"Last night. I wanted to come to dinner, but I was a—" She pauses, checking over her shoulder, likely to make sure Shea and Deidra are still in their bedroom. Her voice is softer when she says, "I was a fox for most of the evening."

"Oh," I say, fighting a guilty smile. I shouldn't be giddy over Colette's predicament, but knowing she failed to come for dinner not because she changed her mind about me, but because of her curse, alleviates some of the gloom I've carried. "I understand."

Colette smiles, but it's tight and doesn't quite reach her eyes.

"Are you all right?" I ask.

"No shaking." Colette holds up her hands. "That's a good sign."

Her tone is light, but her expression has darkened. I can't imagine what she must be feeling, knowing that at any moment she could transform against her will.

"How often does it happen?" I ask.

She shrugs. "Sometimes every few days, sometimes twice in one day. If there's a pattern, I haven't figured it out yet."

"You're very brave," I blurt, but immediately feel foolish. I sound like an awestruck little girl.

Colette's eyebrows quirk upward, but she doesn't laugh. "Why do you say that?"

I look down at my lap. I normally keep my impressions to

myself, but something about Colette makes me want to share. "If I kept changing into a fox, I'd never leave my cottage. I'd be too afraid."

Colette sighs. "I leave my cottage *because* I'm afraid. Afraid of my mother seeing me change, afraid of the villagers finding out and calling me wicked. If I were truly brave, I wouldn't run." She rests her hand on my knee, her touch solid and warm. "You stood up to a bear. You're the brave one."

I don't know if I'm truly brave, but from Colette's lips, the word sounds right. I lift my head to find her gazing at me, eyes so warm and deep and un-foxlike that I can't help but get caught up in them.

I lean in first, but she meets me just as quickly. Our lips brush, then linger. Colette's hand slides from my knee up my thigh, the pressure of her fingers light and achingly slow. I draw a startled breath, because the loveliest girl I've ever seen is kissing me, and all my imaginings hardly compare to the thrill of her touch.

I kiss her harder, cupping a hand behind her neck to bring her closer, and pinpricks of heat blossom across my skin. My fingers find the hem of her shirt, slip beneath to skim her soft waist. Colette shudders, her fingers curling against my thigh as she sighs against my mouth.

I've yearned for her since the day we met. Since the moment she spoke of her love for the trees, a love we have in common.

Too soon, she breaks the kiss, touching her forehead to mine. Our quick breaths mingle in the small space between us. "Roisin," she says.

Oddly, I don't mind that she uses my full name. I do mind

that we've stopped kissing. "Is something wrong?" I've never kissed anyone before. Maybe I'm lousy at it.

"I'm not very brave." Colette's voice catches on the words. "I need to know, before this goes any further, that you won't tell him about me."

"Who? Brend?" I can't think of any other *he* she'd reference. "Why not?"

"He's dangerous. He's already come close to killing me once."

I pull back. The reminder of what Brend is, of what he's done and what he's capable of, suppresses my desire for more kissing. I want to say he'd never harm Colette as a boy, but one shared dinner and a walk in the dark doesn't mean I truly know him.

So, I do as she asks. "I promise, Colette, I won't tell him."

"Thank you. I'm sorry for—" she hesitates, biting her lip against a smile. "For ending our kiss so quickly. I had to be sure."

I nod, swallowing a sour taste in my mouth. I'll have to keep Colette's identity from my sister as well. I can't risk her telling Brend, knowing how much she wants to help him. Add that to my deal with Brend, and that's two secrets I'm keeping from my sister.

Two secrets. Two curses.

I pick up my vest from the floor. "I need to go."

"Oh," says Colette. "What about—I mean, what do we do now? About my . . . curse?"

"We can meet tomorrow, in the wood," I say, as I finish tying the laces. "Figure out our next step."

Right now, I have no idea what that next step will be, but hopefully I will by the time we meet again.

Her eyes brighten at the suggestion. "Tomorrow, then."

"Tell Shea and Deidra I had to leave." I force a wobbly smile to my lips. "Be careful walking home."

I go to the door, and a sudden pounding in my ears nearly overwhelms Colette's goodbye. I barely manage to mutter my farewell before stepping outside, and guilt chases me down the path to my cottage, insistent and loud.

So much for being brave.

CHAPTER 11

After the warmth of Deidra and Shea's fire, the cold air is biting. I rub the sleeves of my tunic and look to the trees, but no storm rages now. The forest and clearing are equally still. Not even a slight winter wind stirs the damp ends of my hair.

I wonder what would happen if I dared venture into the wood. Would the snowfall start up again, or would the faeries ignore me because Colette is beyond their reach? I'm not keen to find out. I seek my warm bed and a dry set of clothes. For the first time in my life, I'm glad to be out of the western wood. If Ma were here, she'd be equal parts shocked and delighted by my sudden preference for the refuge of the cottage.

When I step through the front door, the pounding in my ears is met with silence. No Eirwyn in the kitchen, no Brend at the dining table. I check my bedroom, then Ma's, then the pantry. All empty.

I clutch at the collar of my vest, fighting to keep my breaths even. I didn't expect to return to an empty cottage, but that doesn't mean Eirwyn and Brend are in any danger. There are no signs of a struggle: no overturned chairs, no dishes on the floor, nothing out of place. I check the rack by the door and let loose a relieved sigh when I discover Eirwyn's cloak and Brend's coat are missing, meaning that when Brend left the cottage with my sister, he left as a boy.

But where did they go? Certainly not to Deidra and Shea's, but I can't think of any other place Eirwyn would take our cursed houseguest. To Maple Square for more supplies? She must know that would be irresponsible. Then again, most of Eirwyn's choices when it comes to Brend have been less than sensible.

I go to the window, eyes focused on the first line of trees. Maybe they noticed the peculiar snowstorm. Concerned, they might've ventured into the wood to search for me. The idea is hard to believe due to Eirwyn's staunch avoidance of the western wood for the last four years, but not impossible to consider when coupled with threats from faeries and curses.

If they did go out searching for me, maybe they'll find their way back now that the storm has cleared. Yet the sun is already beginning to set, and each minute that passes without sight of them adds to the foul taste in my mouth.

My worried breaths fog the window, turning the white world outside to gray. My sister can't be in the wood at night, not with a boy who could change into a bear at any moment.

I rub the glass with my palm to clear the fog, wondering if I should go after them, but then a familiar figure breaks past the line of trees. Eirwyn. Alone.

I throw open the door and run toward her. We meet halfway between the cottage and the forest, hands reaching, then clasping tightly. Eirwyn's breathing heavily and her braid is half undone. Her face glistens with sweat.

"It's Brend," she says, drawing a gulp of air. "He changed while we were looking for you. He couldn't stop it."

"You got away safely," I say, squeezing her hands. "That's all that matters."

"No, you don't understand." She shakes her head as more strands come loose, reminding me of the evergreen faerie shedding needles. "The fox. He chased after it. I tried to follow but lost their trail. They were moving so fast."

I pull my hands from hers. That can't be right. Colette is on her way home. She's supposed to be a girl. She's supposed to be safe.

Guilt bears down on me like another snowstorm. Why did I leave her alone? Why did I let shame over secrets chase me away?

"Ro," Eirwyn says, the urgency in her voice snapping me out of my thoughts, "what do we do?"

I can't let Brend catch her. "Can you take me to where you lost the trail?"

Eirwyn looks to the trees. "I think so."

Colette called me brave. I want her to be right.

I take my sister's hand. "Let's go."

Eirwyn doesn't lead like a girl who's afraid of the forest.

My sister pulls me through close-knit clumps of trees without a trace of uncertainty in her steps. Tall and slender in her brown cloak, she reminds me of a maple whose roots have come loose from the dirt after a lifetime of stillness, not wasting any time because the spell granting her freedom could end at any moment.

All the memories of our shared days beneath the trees come rushing back, stirring a hunger that's slept deep within me. I've missed running through the wood with her. I've missed having her by my side in my favorite place. I wish we were sharing this moment under different circumstances, but I'm still grateful for it.

The evening sun casts an orange glow over the wood. Night is a while off yet, so we should have enough time to find Brend and Colette before darkness settles over the trees. Evergreens heavy with snow brush our shoulders with cold caresses as we pass. Bushes shake, and I don't know whether to blame animals or faeries. *He is watching*, the evergreen faerie said. Whoever he is, is he watching now?

We come across a pile of Brend's clothes, and Eirwyn scoops them up before I can tell her to let them be. Then, as the first shadows begin to fall over the western wood, my sister shows me where she lost the trail. Both sets of prints, bear and fox, end abruptly between two barren birch trees. I suspect faeries are behind this, as the snow beyond the tracks is neat, far too neat for someone to have smoothed the layer of white with their hands or boots. Thankfully, the attempt to cover the trail was only a partial success, as I notice a line of fallen branches leading deeper into the trees, suggesting a big animal may have crashed through.

Hand in hand, my sister and I follow the branches. Though our pace is swift, each time I blink I see us arriving too late, see Colette's broken body lying in the snow. Not as a fox, but as a girl with blood drenching her curls. Nausea grips my throat.

"Don't worry." Eirwyn must notice the pallor of my skin even amidst evening light. "We'll find them."

I nod, but the gesture is out of fierce hope rather than belief. I almost don't say it, but the words slip out: "Thank you for coming to the wood to find me. I know it must have been hard for you." As if in answer, a tremor runs through Eirwyn's hand. I strengthen my grip. "Pa would be proud."

Her lips are tight. "Let's focus on finding Brend, all right?"

A sharp wail rises through the trees. *Colette.* I drop Eirwyn's hand and break into a sprint, not even following the branches, just the direction of the fox's cry. I know my sister's close behind by the sound of her breathing and the crunch of her boots, but I don't slow.

I surge past one last group of trees, needles catching in the wool of my tunic, and into a new clearing. The space is scarcely big enough to hold a girl my size, let alone the thrashing bear I nearly collide with. Something's caught between his teeth. The wild thrashing shows little more than a blur of copper, but I'm almost certain it's the fox's tail he clutches.

I can't tell if the fox is alive, or if the thrashing has proved fatal, but I pound the bear's side with my fists. I scream for him to drop her. He swings his head toward me as if intending to clamp his jaws around me too. I pound harder. I kick at his legs. I shout.

The bear groans and finally drops Colette. He opens his jaws wide and roars, hot breath and spittle blasting my face. I stumble backward, whacking my head against a tree. I slump to the ground, dizzy. Eirwyn shouts my name, but the dark spots dancing across my vision keep me from finding her.

I do see the fox sprint away, and I'm granted a sweet moment of relief. At least Colette is safe. At least I was brave.

The bear curves his body until he faces me, heavy paws beating the snow. My heart crashes against my chest. Just like last time. Only now, Eirwyn doesn't have her bow.

The bear huffs. Defeat weighs heavy on my shoulders. What about the curses? Who will break them if I can't?

I close my eyes, waiting for the bear's first strike.

Two flashes of memory come to me, unbidden. First, Tamsin beside the evergreen. Her disapproving gaze. What she told me: *You commanded.*

But that's not the word Pa used. I know this because of the second memory. Walking with him in the western wood on a clear winter day, our boots kicking up snow. The feel of his garden-soiled hand in mine, the sound of his fingers scratching his thick brown beard. *Learn to use your voice here, Ro. Sing to the birds. Call to the trees. When you're older, you'll be amazed by what your words achieve.*

I reach for a tree branch and use it to pull me to my feet.

I didn't believe Pa then, but I believe him now. Because with words, I summoned a faerie. I brought Colette back to herself. Now I will survive the bear by seeking the boy within.

The call builds in my throat.

"Brend," I say, "can you hear me?"

The bear thrashes his head. I want to run, find my sister. But this won't work if I give in to weakness. I won't succeed with fear.

"Brend, listen to me."

The bear opens his jaws. Sharp teeth. Dark mouth. Low groan.

"Brend," I repeat. "Come back."

I hold myself completely still, look directly into his amber eyes.

The bear lowers his head.

I stretch out a quivering hand. I cup the side of his face, burying my fingers in his coarse fur. I feel his hot breath on my arm. "You don't want to hurt me. I know because you told me. So come back. Please."

I hold my stance, hold it even against the cracking of bones and the stretching of muscles. Against the huffs that slowly turn to heavy sighs, as the bristled fur disappears and is replaced with stubble-rough, chilled skin.

When it's over, my palm finds Brend's cheek. The edge of my thumb feels the parting of his dry lips, but he doesn't speak.

I drop my hand and step away. My eyes are wet. I rub them fiercely.

"You were warned."

I whip around. The evergreen faerie stands before me, green

eyes narrowed to slits. Behind her, night bathes the western wood, and the leaves are edged in sapphire.

The veil. I've crossed it for the second time today.

"What's happening?" I wipe my eyes again. "How do I keep doing this? Why?"

"You should have stayed away from them. It could have been over." The faerie dips her head. "If you had only let him finish."

"Finish?" My nose twitches at the strong scent of roses. "Finish what?"

But I needn't wait for the evergreen faerie's response, because the answer slams into me like an icy gust of wind. Brend had Colette in his jaws. He would have killed her if I hadn't stopped him. Brend would have killed her, and that's what the evergreen faerie wanted.

"No, he can't—she's just a girl, she's . . ." I swallow against the threat of sickness. My tongue is heavy. "Why—why would you want that?"

"What *he* wants. The answer to a long-held question. This is what he seeks, and he should not be defied."

"Who is he?" A flare of anger quashes my revulsion. I'm tired of her riddles. "I deserve to know that much."

"You deserve nothing," the faerie spits, and a spray of needles shoots from her evergreen mouth to strike me, embedding themselves in my cheeks as I shout for her to stop.

Frantically I pull out the needles and toss them onto the snow, droplets of blood falling with them. I bend over, shielding my wounded face with my arms and closing my eyes, but a second assault doesn't come. I lift my head.

The evergreen faerie is gone, and with her the sapphire light.

"Ro," calls my sister.

Eirwyn rushes forward, pulling her scarf from her neck and using it to wipe the blood from my cheeks. Brend lingers behind her, dressed in Pa's coat, the only garment other than his boots that survived the change.

We trudge silently through downy snow. Eirwyn holds tight to Brend's hand as if she fears letting go will return him to his beastly form. Brend leans against my sister as if she's the only one keeping him up.

I wish I could take Pa's hand, wish I could lean against him and let him hold me up. I hear him so clearly now, telling me to use my voice. To never forget again. I utter silent promises, promises that would've drawn laughter from my lips when I was a child. But the child didn't know. She didn't know the truths Pa held, didn't know that one day she would have to face those truths without him. I hug myself, cheeks stinging where the evergreen needles struck me.

In the cottage, silence continues to hold us captive. Eirwyn and I guide Brend to the bench before the fire. I put the kettle on for tea. My sister brings out extra blankets from Ma's bedroom. She drapes two over Brend's trembling shoulders before handing another to me. The last she keeps for herself.

Later, I sit with my sister at the dining table as Brend warms himself before the flames. Over a cup of ginger spice tea, I tell Eirwyn about the evergreen faerie's warning to stay away from Brend and the mysterious *he*. But I say nothing of her disappointment in me for preventing the fox's death. I fear what it might mean. I don't think I'm ready to know.

Eirwyn is undeterred by my story. "He needs our help more than we thought."

But can we help him? Can we stand against faeries who watch, who warn, who sting?

"What you did to bring Brend back," says my sister, "do you think it's permanent?"

I touch my fingertips to the dried blood on my cheek. I wish I could answer yes. I wish I could comfort her with my assurance. But tonight, Colette was a fox again, not long after I called forth a girl beneath the evergreen, so I doubt I hold enough power to forever keep Brend as he is simply because I will it. I don't think that's a power I'd be comfortable possessing, in any case.

But yesterday I didn't believe I had any power at all. So who's to say for certain?

"I don't think so," is what I tell my sister. It's all I can offer her.

Her cup scrapes wood as she sets it down. Then she asks, in a voice so small she may be unaware she's speaking aloud, "Why you?"

"I don't know." My vision blurs, a haze of flames. "I don't know."

Whatever this magic is that I wield, it's growing, and it seems to have been triggered by the curses. But I've no idea why.

Eirwyn's hand grips my shoulder. "Whatever this is, we'll figure it out. Together."

I set down my cup to embrace my sister, Eirwyn's smooth cheek pressing against my wounded one. I breathe in the rose oil scent of my sister's hair, allowing myself a moment of relief from the doubts and questions that plague me.

Eirwyn withdraws to bed soon after, so I bring Brend a plate of food. Hard cheese and bread hardly make a fitting meal after the day we've endured, but he takes the dish without complaint. For a boy who was a ravenous bear mere hours ago, he chews slowly and quietly. We sit watching the fire crackle and spark.

"Thank you," he says when he's finished, "for bringing me back."

I shrug, his gratitude making me uncomfortably warm. "Thanks for listening."

He takes my hand. I let him hold it for three counts before I pull away. I don't know why I wasn't faster. He doesn't try again.

"Ro." It's the first time he's used my name without being prompted, and it sounds different on his tongue. Almost reverent. "I know how to break my curse."

Colette's name tempts my lips. "How?"

"After you brought me back, a memory came to me. A memory from before."

Fear spreads across my skin, a sickening chill. I'm not ready to know, but my mouth forms the words: "Tell me."

"I knew the oak faerie before I was cursed. He told me to catch the fox."

I swallow past the sting in my throat. I can guess what he's about to say, but I'll ask the question anyway, in the hopes that I'm wrong. "Why?"

"So I can kill her," he says. "To break my curse, I must kill the fox."

CHAPTER 12

My sleep is haunted.

Haunted by the bear's roar, his thrashing head. Haunted by the red fox's wail, her bloody tail. The evergreen faerie spitting needles. Tamsin calling me a foolish girl. Brend's confession before the fire, his words lingering as I rise much later than usual and dress quietly so as not to wake my sister.

He told me to catch the fox.

I stand before my dresser, watching myself in the mirror as I braid my hair. Shadows beneath my eyes. Lips a hard line. Jaw clenched.

So I can kill her.

My fingers falter, so I start over, sucking in a haggard breath.

To break my curse, I must kill the fox.

I leave my braid half finished and grip the edge of the dresser, nails biting into the wood. Colette was right. She was right to make me promise, to make me keep secrets. Brend was hunting Colette as a bear, but now he wants to hunt her as a boy, too. His two selves have aligned. If he finds out Colette is the red fox . . .

My fingernails grate audibly against the wood. No. I won't let it happen. Whatever game the faeries are playing, I won't let them win. I'll break both curses without anyone dying. Somehow, I will.

I hear Eirwyn stir behind me. "Let me help."

My sister's voice is groggy and her eyes bleary, but her nimble fingers make quick work of my hair. She lays a braid over each of my shoulders. "There."

I want to thank her, but the words stick in my throat.

"Are you going after the red fox again?"

"No, I'm going to see Colette," I say, the answer both a truth and a lie.

My skin itches with the thought of venturing into the village, but I must make sure Colette's all right after last night's encounter with Brend.

"Ah, well, be sure to tell her she can apologize with sweets." Eirwyn squeezes my shoulders. "For you, of course."

"Apologize? What for?" My heart pounds so fast I feel ill. Does Eirwyn somehow know about Colette? Is she blaming her for what happened last night with Brend?

"For not coming to dinner. What else?"

My sister turns away and slips back beneath her blankets. Once my heart settles, I follow her and sit at the edge of her bed.

I watch her eyes flutter closed.

"Eirwyn?"

"Hmm?"

"Brend wants to kill her."

Eirwyn opens her eyes.

"The red fox, I mean," I add quickly.

"Why?" she asks.

"He says it will break his curse."

"Do you believe him?"

"No." Another lie.

Eirwyn throws back her covers and scoots over. She pats the empty spot next to her. I slide into bed beside my sister. Eirwyn hugs me tight, enveloping me in sleepy warmth. I try to match her even breathing, but my heart's beating fast again.

"You care about this fox."

A breath hitches in my throat. If only she knew.

But for once, I'm thoughtful with my words. "The red fox isn't Tamsin. I know that now." I don't explain how, and thankfully Eirwyn doesn't push me. "But she's still involved somehow. Maybe even cursed herself. If she is, would you be all right with Brend killing her?"

Eirwyn sighs deeply. "No, I wouldn't be."

Unexpected hope surges within me. Does she mean it? If I tell her about Colette now, will she understand why Brend can't know? Will my sister help me keep her safe?

"But if it is the only way, we might not be able to stop him," she adds, and dismay rattles my chest.

I can't tell her about Colette. Not when there's still a chance she might take Brend's side.

"Go see Colette," Eirwyn says, waiting for a yawn to pass before continuing. "When you get back, we'll go to the wood together to search for the red fox."

I sit up in bed. "Brend can't come with us."

"No," Eirwyn agrees through another yawn. "He'll stay behind."

I grab fistfuls of her blankets. "What if he changes?"

"Then we'll have a mess to clean up."

"Eirwyn, that's not—" But I break off as movement from the window catches my eye. "Oh, no."

It's Shea, walking purposefully down the path toward our cottage. Her tangled blonde hair is covered by a woolen cap, and she wears her ice fishing gear. A full pack is slung over her shoulder, and her rod is strapped to her back.

"Why would she be checking in now?" Eirwyn asks. "I stopped by the other day."

"This might be my fault." I bite the inside of my cheek. I probably should have tied up that loose end, but it's not my fault Brend and Colette took me on a chase through the trees before I could. "Yesterday I sort of left her cottage without saying goodbye. I can't face her, Eirwyn. She'll ask about the fox."

"All right," sighs Eirwyn, throwing back her blankets. "I'll take care of it. You get Brend into the pantry and stay there until I come for you."

I give her arm a quick squeeze before hurrying to the sitting room. Brend's still sleeping, brown hair disheveled and mouth open as he snores. I shake him awake and he sits up in a daze, unfocused eyes surveying the room.

"Follow me," I say. "Now."

We're cloaked in darkness as I close the pantry door. I lean against a shelf of cranberry preserves and drink in the scent of root vegetables. Brend's eyes glow faintly, reflective like an animal's. All I can think about is last night, seeing Colette's tail in his jaws, hearing him say he must kill the fox. My throat is thick. I clear it as softly as I can.

"Ro, why are we hiding?"

"Why are you calling me Ro?"

A pause. Then: "That is your name, is it not?"

"Hush."

I hear the knock, then the creak of the front door opening. Eirwyn and Shea exchange polite greetings. Eirwyn invites her in for tea and comments on Shea's state of dress. Shea explains she's leaving for an ice fishing trip. She asks about me. Eirwyn says I set off early this morning to forage.

Their voices are clearer now. Likely they're in the kitchen.

"Isn't that Ro's satchel hanging there?" Shea asks.

I curse my neighbor for being so observant. It's no wonder Ma chose her to look out for us. Sweat pricks my palms.

"Oh, yes, but that one has a hole in it that I mean to repair today. Ro took a different bag."

"Ah," Shea says, the sound of a heavy thud nearly obscuring her response. She must've dropped her bag onto the floor. "Let her know I won't be able to track her fox until I get back from my trip."

I don't hear a response from Eirwyn.

"She tell you much about that?" asks Shea.

I hear the clink of cups and spoons as my sister prepares the tea. "Not much, no. But you know Ro and her animals.

Remember when she used to bring us baby birds?"

I grin at my sister's adept use of deflection. I wish I were so talented in conversation. The villagers of Sugar Maple might've stopped asking ignorant questions if I'd known how to avoid them.

"Rabbits too," Shea muses, then clears her throat as if to catch herself before following Eirwyn's tangent. Curse Shea and her sharp mind. "Ro also left a village girl in my cottage yesterday. Nanette O'Connell's daughter. Know much about that?"

The shelf I'm leaning against creaks. I hold my breath, but there's no comment from Shea.

"I'm afraid I don't," Eirwyn says, a slight, unmistakable edge to her voice.

Shea tells the story of finding Colette in the wood during the snowstorm, then adds, "I understand Ro's not one for company, but she seemed to like this girl. Even saw them, uh, kiss before she bolted."

I hear Brend draw an audible breath. My eyes flick upward to meet his reflective gaze. I didn't want either of them to find out this way, from Shea's lips rather than my own. Of all the new experiences from the past few days, kissing Colette is one I certainly don't regret. Yet this feels like the exposure of another secret, one I didn't mean to keep. I press myself tighter against the shelf, rattling a few jars.

"Got something hiding in your pantry?" asks Shea.

"Likely squirrels keeping out of the cold," Eirwyn says.

"I can take care of those when I get back."

"Thank you."

Brend's glowing eyes hold mine, and as much as I want to, I

can't look away. Shea and Eirwyn continue speaking, but I hear little of their conversation. There's a whirring in my ears, and my neck is flushed with heat.

Sometime later, a chair scrapes against the floor, startling me out of my trance. Eirwyn thanks Shea for stopping by. Their voices grow muffled as they presumably head toward the door.

But Shea's final words are clear: "Remind Ro to be vigilant in the wood. Deidra found signs of a bear the other day. I've set traps, just in case."

Suddenly Brend is at my side, sweaty hand gripping my wrist. I hold myself still beside him, our shoulders brushing. We already have the faeries to contend with. Now there are traps to avoid as well. If Brend becomes a bear and gets away from us again . . .

The front door rasps open then closes. My sister's quick footsteps beat across the floorboards. Brend releases my wrist and steps away, but the ghost of a feeling remains where his fingers rested.

Eirwyn opens the door. I squint against the sudden light, heart thumping because I know she'll ask about Colette, about why I didn't share what happened yesterday.

But she says, "Wait for Shea to gain some distance, then you can go."

"Go where?" asks Brend.

"Ro is taking care of an errand." I notice the emphasis she places on the word *errand*, a subtle hint that the Colette discussion will happen at some point, but not now, in front of Brend. "Come, it's nearly midday. You can help me with her chores."

Brend frowns but says, "All right."

I leave the pantry before the other secrets I'm holding escape past my lips, but Brend follows me to the coat rack by the door.

"You didn't tell us about Colette," he says.

I roll my eyes. "I was a little preoccupied with you turning into a bear again."

"Do not use me as an excuse."

I tug on my boots. "I'm not." I feel his gaze as I button my cloak. "Why do you care who I spend time with, anyway? Once I break your curse, you're leaving."

I wince at the bite of my words, and the hurt I see in his eyes tempts me to apologize. But doing so would ignore the truth in what I've said. Our deal stands. I want that to remain clear.

He says, "Good luck with your errand."

He waits a moment as if giving me room to answer, to make amends.

I dip my head and turn to the door.

I'm not familiar with the parts of Sugar Maple Village that lie beyond the square, but I remember Colette mentioning that her cottage lies at the edge of the eastern forest. I take the long way to avoid a trek through Maple Square, passing a string of cottages before crossing through a potato field currently barren and covered with snow, though a few dead remnants of the last harvest remain.

I reach what I presume to be Colette's door when the sun is at its highest. I knock softly, then chastise myself for knocking *too* softly. I'm about to knock again when the door creaks open, revealing a short, round woman with a rosy flush to her pale cheeks and wrinkles at the corners of her hazel eyes. Her hair is long over her shoulders, chestnut-brown tinged with streaks of gray.

The woman smiles warmly. "Why if it isn't Roisin Birch. I see so much of your father in you, especially that auburn hair."

I blink at her, startled by the greeting. I'm certain I've never met this woman in my life. "I'm looking for Colette?"

"Ah, yes, she mentioned the two of you were acquainted," the woman says. "I'm her mother, Nanette. Come in."

She ushers me inside the cottage. The sitting room is well-lit and warm from the roaring fire. Patterned quilts, expertly stitched, drape the sparse furniture. Nanette leads me past the dining room where a table is set for the midday meal.

"We're about to sit down," she says. "Colette is resting, but she'll be out soon. Would you care to join us, Roisin?"

"It's Ro," I correct quickly. "And sure, thank you."

Truthfully, the last thing I want is to share a meal with a stranger, but I didn't know how to tell her no without sounding rude. Now suitable excuses run through my mind, but it's too late to say them.

"*Ro*, that's right. Your father always called you that, didn't he?"

"He did," I say, again startled by Nanette's familiarity with my family.

From the dining room we pass through a door to enter the kitchen. The space holds a second, smaller fireplace. A delicious, hearty smell wafts from the cooking pot over the flames.

"Who built your home?" I ask, marveling at the size and wondering what the bedrooms must look like.

Nanette chuckles. "My husband was a woodworker. The first year we were married, he used his entire stock to build us this. Never mind we nearly starved that winter since we barely had an income. But he wanted a grand life for us, as grand as you could get in the village."

Was. Did Colette also lose a father? Shame burns my cheeks for not knowing. We might've shared a kiss and a secret, but we haven't shared much else of ourselves.

Nanette picks up a ladle from the counter and moves to the fire. She stirs the contents of the pot while I linger beside the round kitchen table.

Normally I'd be all right waiting in silence, but today my curiosity prompts me to speak. "How well did you know him? My father, I mean?"

Nanette continues stirring as she says, "He helped me out a great deal after I lost Liam."

"Liam was your husband?"

She nods. "Passed while I was with child. Then Callum—my boy, he was born still. Maybe because of my grief, I don't know." She releases the ladle, but the soup's current carries on, spinning the spoon lazily around the pot. "Every week your father hand delivered vegetables to my front door. He wouldn't accept payment for them until after Colette started walking and I'd found a trade."

"I—I had no idea."

"He wasn't one to boast, your father."

It's not what I meant. The story about the vegetables is one I've never heard, but not so surprising. Pa was a kind man. "I mean I didn't know . . . about your son. I'm so sorry."

To lose a husband is heart-shattering; I know that much from witnessing Ma's grief. But to lose a child you never got to know? I can't imagine the pain of that. I don't know Nanette well enough to offer an embrace, so I pull out a chair and sit because I feel I must do something.

Nanette turns away from the pot and affords me a weak smile. "Thank you, Ro."

I draw a finger down a crack in the table. "So, Colette is . . . "

"Adopted as my own, yes," she confirms. "She came to me when I needed her most, and she's been my light for sixteen years."

I murmur a curse I hope Nanette doesn't hear. Colette is adopted. Another thing I didn't know about her. And she's like Orla, a child with a mother who doesn't resemble her in appearance. I know the fact has troubled Deidra at times, especially when their differences are rudely pointed out by villagers. I hate to imagine Colette and her mother facing similar strife, especially after all Nanette's been through, and knowing Colette's kindness. But maybe that's part of why Colette prefers trees to people.

Nanette moves to the counter and begins slicing a loaf of bread. The air grows heavy with the sound of the knife against the cutting board and the aroma of simmering soup. I look over my shoulder, hoping the scents and sounds of cooking will draw Colette to the kitchen, but the doorway remains empty. I'm tempted to ask the way to her room, but I don't want to make it seem like I'm trying to escape after Nanette's confession about the losses she's suffered. I also don't want to accidentally reveal why I'm so worried about Colette. Nanette said she was resting and didn't sound concerned, so that must mean she's all right.

Curiosity over the adoption pricks at me like stray pine needles caught in my sweater, but I don't want to pry for more information. Nanette and I are little more than strangers, after all, and I know how irritated Shea gets when villagers ask too many questions about Orla.

Though in Shea's case, the questions have more to do with her and Deidra's capabilities as parents. The village is mostly accepting of their marriage, but some people have the frankly insulting habit of wondering aloud whether a child should be raised without a father. Perhaps Nanette has faced similar judgments as a single parent.

I lean back in my chair, frowning at the idea that having one mother or two mothers is somehow less than. It's true that Pa left behind holes for Ma to fill when he died. He left a garden to be tended and rotted boards in the roof to be replaced, a daughter who expected adventures in the western wood and another who wanted nothing more to do with the trees. But with patience and practice, Ma found a way to manage, to fill those holes. We all did.

Nanette turns away from her loaf of bread. "Ro, why don't you call on Colette for the midday meal? Her door is the first one off the sitting room."

"All right," I say, nearly knocking over my chair in my haste.

My breaths sharpen as I hurry through the dining area and sitting room to reach Colette's closed door. I'm not sure why I'm so nervous; I know she's alive, and not wounded badly enough to alert her mother. Then again, a lot happened yesterday. The red fox reveal. The kiss. The attack in the wood. I feel as though Colette and I have traveled miles together despite being so newly acquainted.

I hesitate after knocking, listening for some sign that she's awake. I hear nothing. With one palm flat against my chest to contain my heartbeat, I gently open the door. Colette sleeps on her side, facing me, both hands pressed beneath her cheek. A wrap covers her curls. Her leaf-patterned quilt has been kicked to the end of her bed, and her nightdress is bunched up high on her thighs, revealing the curves of her legs.

And the blood that spatters the sheets.

CHAPTER 13

I quickly shut the door behind me, fearful that Nanette will come upon us and see the blood. Colette's eyes blink open. She follows my gaze to the mess, then reaches for the blankets.

Softly, so my voice won't reach the kitchen, I say, "Wait, don't cover that up."

She sits up, wincing. "The wound must have opened in the night."

"The one he gave you?"

She nods, hand sliding up her leg to rest at her hip. I notice the bandage, dark with blood, through the thin fabric of her nightdress.

"I made it halfway home before I changed back. Thankfully I had some clothing stashed nearby." The dullness of her tone tugs at my heart. "Limped the rest of the way, though, bleeding."

I press back against the door. "Colette, I'm sorry." She must be exhausted, having endured the aftermath of Brend's attack on her own.

"Where is he now? Is he still a bear?"

"No," I tell her. "I—I think I brought him back. The same way I helped you change yesterday."

Her eyes flash, and for a moment I see only fox. "He's still staying with you, then? Even after last night?"

"I told you he needs my help." I wish she would see that. I wish she would understand that, while I didn't ask for any of this, I can't give it up now. "He can't control the change, and he's probably following the same urges that you are."

"We're nothing alike," Colette insists, her voice trembling, and I realize my mistake too late. "He's trying to kill me." She scoffs. "I suppose I should thank you for stopping that a second time."

My eyes burn. I've made a mess of this already. "Don't thank me."

She buries her face in her hands and draws a ragged breath. I press even harder against the door. Last night, bringing Brend home felt like mercy. Now, standing in front of Colette, I feel complicit in his actions. I chose to help the boy who hurt her, rather than make sure she was all right. Maybe I'm as bad as Eirwyn, bringing Brend tea that first night rather than tending to my bruises. Brend didn't ask to be cursed, but neither did Colette ask to be attacked. Like I didn't ask to be attacked.

The heavy ache of guilt spreads throughout my limbs, making me suddenly weary. "I should have been with you. I should have walked you home."

Colette lifts her head. Her eyes are red-rimmed but dry. "Can I go back to resting, now?"

I clench my fists so hard my nails dig into my palms, the resulting pain not so unlike the sting of evergreen needles. I wanted to share what I've learned about the curses, but the trust between us is undoubtedly crumbling, and divulging the evergreen faerie's words and Brend's recovered memory might demolish it. I'd rather accept the weight of yet another secret than risk losing the girl who calls me brave.

So instead I say, "Your mother sent me to fetch you for the midday meal. I'll tell her you're sleeping."

Colette sighs. "No. She'll ask questions."

"Maybe you should tell—"

"She can't know anything about this," says Colette, with a severe shake of her head.

I don't agree, but it's not my choice. "All right, would you like help—"

"I can dress myself, thank you."

Too startled to fight further, I leave without another word. I follow savory scents back to the dining area, where steaming bowls of soup and a basket of bread await me. I sit on the side of the table with two places instead of one. I don't want to sit next to Colette now, but I want to meet her eyes from across the table even less. I hope Nanette claims the lone spot on the other side.

Thankfully, she does. Silently we sip tea and wait for Colette. When she finally joins us, she's wearing dark leggings and a long tunic to hide her bandages, and her curls are tied back. Her movements are slow and stiff, but she doesn't wince as she bends to kiss her mother's cheek in greeting. Nanette brushes back a curl of Colette's hair that's come loose from her bun and gives her ear an affectionate tug. Witnessing the tender moment makes me miss Ma so much that I have to look away.

Nanette invites us to begin the meal. The warmth of the soup is soothing as I sip my first spoonful. It's earthy and nutty with just the right amount of spice. It tastes like the western wood. "Delicious," I say.

Nanette blushes. "Thank you, Ro. Winter's hard for all of us. I try to do the best I can."

"Soup's great, Mama," Colette says, slurping her second spoonful. "As always, you turn my meager offerings into splendor."

Her voice is light and doesn't tremble. I marvel at how quickly she's managed to compose herself after our fraught conversation. She did mention she's been practicing for Nanette, but I didn't expect her to be this good.

"Oh, hush," Nanette says, blushing harder. "She's never this polite, Ro. Don't let her fool you."

Colette beams at her mother before returning to her soup. I force a laugh and reach for a slice of bread, then dip it in my soup and take a bite, relishing in the warm meal despite the tension in the air.

Nanette scoops soup onto her slice. "How are you feeling, Colette?" Glancing at me, she adds, "She was foraging in the western wood yesterday when she took quite a fall. Came home with a limp, and this is the first time she's been out of bed all day."

"I can tell her myself, Mama," Colette says. "I'm perfectly well. Simply needed time to rest and recover from my embarrassment."

My most recent bite of bread turns sour on my tongue. If I hadn't seen the blood on her sheets, I might be convinced by

Colette's performance. She hides the truth from her mother well, but I wonder if that's the right course. I'm keeping secrets from Eirwyn, but that's because of Brend. Nanette doesn't have a bear-boy competing for her attention. She could be supporting Colette through this ordeal. I don't understand why Colette doesn't trust her.

Nanette frowns. "Perhaps you should stay out of the western wood for a while. You do fine for the two of us with what you find in the eastern forest."

"But you promised," says Colette, "and you've seen my haul lately. The western wood is much better suited to foraging."

"I know, but you don't want to tempt fate."

"Fate?" I ask, drawn back into the conversation.

"She means the faeries," Colette mutters into her soup.

"I know the stories." Nanette waves her spoon, causing drips to fall onto the table. "Being a frequent visitor to the western wood will bring you nothing but trouble."

Colette jerks her head toward me. "Ro's a frequent visitor."

Nanette smiles. "Ah, but Ro was marked by the faeries long ago, weren't you, dear?"

My next bite of bread is hard to swallow. "What?"

"It's why they tolerate you in their wood," explains Nanette. "Your father was kind to them, leaving offerings and the like, and that secured your place."

I drop my spoon into my bowl, and a splash of soup jumps over the rim, staining the tablecloth. "He did what?"

"You didn't know?" Her eyebrows scrunch together. "How odd."

My hands begin to tremble. I bury them in my lap. Marked

by the faeries. Is this why I can cross beyond the veil? Change animals into mortals? Did a faerie give me these gifts without my knowing?

I think of all the time I've spent in the western wood, the faeries might've been watching me. Altering me. An ill feeling churns the meal in my gut. I thought the forest was safe. A place I could hide from villagers who've never liked who I am. All the while, I was in a different kind of danger. Is there no sanctuary for me here, then?

"Let's talk about something else," Colette suggests.

"What's wrong with what we're talking about now?" Nanette tears her slice of bread in two. "Ro is a fortunate girl. Faeries can be wicked, but to be in their favor is a blessing."

I think of Brend, of his claws and his curse. Of the oak faerie's devouring grin and the evergreen faerie's needles and yesterday's snowstorm. Having the attention of faeries doesn't seem like much of a blessing to me.

Colette asks Nanette about her current quilting project, which consumes her mother's attention for the remainder of the meal. I abandon my bread but manage a few more spoonfuls of soup so I don't offend my hosts. Afterward, Nanette suggests that we continue our visit in the sitting room, but Colette declares exhaustion and retreats to her bed. As heartsick as I am over our quarrel, I'm equal parts relieved, because I have questions for Nanette, questions that can't wait. I offer to help clean up, and Nanette cheerfully accepts.

Carrying the empty bowls, I ask, "Did you and my father talk often about faeries?"

"Oh, yes, every chance we could," she says, leading me

to the kitchen. "You know, most villagers say they believe in faeries, but few can attest to having seen them, or being on the receiving end of their favors, like me and your father."

I set the bowls on the counter harder than I intend, causing a loud clang. "What favor have you received from faeries?"

She grins. "Why, she's resting in her room as we speak."

My hands drop to my sides. Had I still been holding the dishes they'd have crashed to the floor.

"I told you my Callum was born still shortly after I lost my husband. Well, the faeries knew my grief, and they gave me Colette."

I lower my voice in case Colette can hear from her bedroom. "How—how do you know this?"

"Well, she was left on my doorstep, for one." Nanette's voice remains cheery and loud as if her story isn't a secret. Perhaps it's not. "No one in the village claimed her as their own. A few suggested an unfortunate mother left her as she was passing through, but that doesn't explain the gifts that followed. Floral crowns. Sprigs of herbs. Even pouches of coin. Your father wasn't the only one who helped me in those early years."

I follow her back to the dining table. "Does Colette know?"

She nods. "I keep no secrets from my daughter. She knows about the rituals I've performed too."

"Rituals?"

"To make sure she's not a faerie herself." She collects the cloth napkins like flowers. "I couldn't keep her if she was. Wouldn't be fair to keep her from her true home."

I'm startled by the admission. Ma wouldn't give me or

Eirwyn up for anything or anyone. She'd fight faeries bare-handed before she'd relinquish her daughters. No wonder Colette doesn't want to tell her mother about her curse. If she does, might Nanette take it as a sign that her daughter belongs with the faeries instead of her?

Picking up the spoons, I ask, "So if Colette's not a faerie, why did the faeries give her to you?"

A bundle of napkins in her arms, Nanette shrugs. "I assume they found her orphaned somewhere, scooped her up, and brought her to Sugar Maple Village." She passes me on her way to the kitchen. "I try not to question a gift too much. It's not polite. Once my rituals confirmed she wasn't a faerie, I stopped wondering."

If this were a month ago, her story would make me desperate to excuse myself from the silly lady who believes in faerie rituals. I'd be fighting an embarrassed grin. Not now. Now I listen without squirming. I even want more.

In the kitchen, I set the spoons next to the bowls. "These rituals . . . could I see them?"

"Why, of course," says Nanette, dropping her napkin bundle on the counter and reaching up to a cupboard with a brass knob in the shape of a leaf.

From the cupboard, she produces a thick stack of birch bark, which she brings to the round kitchen table. Some of the strips—mostly the ones near the bottom—are weathered with age. The sheet of bark on the top is covered in a fancy ink scrawl that reads: *Leaving Gifts for Faeries.*

"During the summer months when my quilts aren't as popular, I often sell these to curious villagers or those who are having trouble with faeries." Her smile stretches wider. "You know, your father was one of my best customers. I gave him many rituals over the years in exchange for his kindness."

My hands hover over the stack of bark, imagining Pa in my place, one of his garden-soiled fingertips tracing the swirls of ink. Did one of these rituals teach him to commune with faeries in the center of three trees?

"Look through them," Nanette encourages, briefly squeezing my shoulder. "Take one or two if the desire strikes. Call it a thank you for helping me clean up."

I nod, fingers already rifling through the stack, eyes skimming each title and the instructions below. Rituals for keeping faeries out of your home, for inviting faeries into your home, for making amends if you've angered a faerie, for borrowing a faerie's magic.

One finally makes me pause: a ritual for seeing past glamour, something faeries use to hide themselves, or their magic, from humans. I draw my finger down the list of supplies: a bowl of water, a crystal, and a drop of the suspected faerie's blood. Simple steps to reveal a faerie-made disguise.

Could this be one of the rituals Nanette used on her daughter to determine she was human? What would happen if I tried it on myself? Nanette says I've been marked by faeries. This ritual might reveal if she's right. Resolute, I slip the birch bark into my pocket.

I help Nanette with the rest of the cleanup and bid her goodbye, but I pause before the front door, wondering if I should check on Colette again, try to reclaim the trust I've lost. Sudden nerves fill me—more than the ones I'd felt at the midday meal.

Maybe I've done and said enough for today. Colette needs time to recover; I can visit again tomorrow.

To complete the glamour ritual, I need a gem for clarity, so I stop by Deidra's on the way home, grateful that Shea is fishing on a frozen lake somewhere.

Deidra opens the door with Orla on her hip. "Ro," she says, smiling. "I expected Eirwyn might come by, but you're a lovely surprise."

I shrug. "I need your help with something."

Her eyes narrow, but her smile remains. "All right, come inside."

Because I don't intend to stay long, I don't accept the offered chair that Deidra pulls out from the dining table. Rather, I get right to the point. "I need a gem for clarity."

Deidra switches Orla to her other hip, bouncing her playfully in the process and causing the baby to giggle. "Might I ask what for?"

Thankfully, I took time to make up an excuse on the way over. "I'd like to hold onto it for a while. I'm hoping it helps me sort through my feelings about Poppy."

My neighbor nods approvingly. "That's quite mature of you, Ro. I know you've struggled with your mother's decision."

"Yes, well," I say, looking at my boots. "I don't feel like struggling anymore."

Oddly enough, those words are true. Consumed by curses and

faeries, I've no time to fret over the upcoming move. I hardly have time to miss my own mother. How naive I was to think that leaving the village behind would be the hardest challenge I'd ever have to face.

"Wait here," says Deidra. "We'll be just a minute."

She carries Orla into the bedroom, returning moments later. A clear-white cluster of thin crystals rests in her outstretched palm.

"It's called apophyllite," she explains. "Should help you work things out."

"Thank you." I pocket the crystal with the birchbark ritual. "I should be going now."

I turn, then feel Deidra's hand on my shoulder. "Ro, wait. I just want to say that I think your father would be proud of you."

I whip around, the burn of anger in my throat. "No, he wouldn't."

Before Pa passed, the vegetable garden beside our cottage flourished. Ripe tomatoes, onions, carrots, all kinds of squash. Pa grew them, Ma sold them. Villagers loved them. Pa liked to say our garden thrived because of faeries. He claimed they came while we slept to sprinkle magic over the soil, touch their fingers to sprouts, and sing to vegetables to keep them happy.

Before the fever consumed him, Pa told me to always mind the garden. Those were his last words to me. He made me promise.

But I haven't been able to do what he asked, because the garden lost its magic after Pa died, and we haven't been able to bring it back. This past harvest, we didn't grow enough for the three of us to last the winter, which is why we're relying on the coin from Aunt Meara. It's why we're moving to Poppy.

If I'd just been able to keep my promise, we could have stayed.

"This is the last thing Pa would've wanted," I tell Deidra. "No matter how I end up feeling about the move, that will never change."

I leave before Deidra's expression of shock can become one of pity or disappointment. I can't bear either right now. I take the path to my cottage, the apophyllite heavy in my pocket, and I fight the prickly threat of tears. I've failed Pa. I've failed Colette. I'm no garden-tender, no curse-breaker. I'm just an unfortunate girl marked by faeries.

I intend to escape to my room early to perform the ritual, but Eirwyn insists we all have tea after dinner. As I sit with my steaming cup, I try not to let impatience dictate my movements, afraid that the rustle of birchbark in my pocket will draw my sister's attention, that the sound of a gem knocking against the chair will alert Brend. But neither asks if I might've brought something home with me.

Wood creaks as a strong gale batters the walls of the cottage. A storm approaches, and tonight isn't the night for venturing into the western wood. I want to imagine Colette sharing the evening with her mother, safe and warm with no hint of trembling. But when I blink, I see a red fox caught in the wind, hail pelting her copper coat.

I'm here with Brend, prepared to call him back if he

trembles. Who's protecting Colette? Another pang of guilt tightens my throat. I pick up and set down my cup three times before I manage a sip.

Forcing a yawn, I say, "I'm exhausted. You wouldn't mind doing your reading out here, would you, Eirwyn?"

My sister nods, sipping. "Of course. Did you have a nice visit today?"

I'm staring at my cup, but I'd bet a day's worth of foraging that Brend's watching me. I don't want to lie, so I grasp for the only truth I can manage. "Colette's mother is a kind woman."

"She is," agrees Eirwyn.

I consider asking my sister if she knew about Pa's friend-ship with Nanette O'Connell. If she knew about the vegetable deliveries and their shared love of faerie lore. But providing any details of my visit seems dangerous, too close to the truth—that tonight I plan to perform a faerie ritual in secret, because I have a power my sister doesn't seem to share.

Eirwyn stirs more honey into her tea. "Did Colette say she'd come for dinner again?"

I turn my cup in circles, the clay warming my fingertips. "I don't know. Maybe."

My sister points at me with her spoon. "If she hasn't been kind to you—"

"She's been kind," I insist. "It's me who's the trouble."

And a certain bear-boy.

"Ro," says Brend.

I look at him. "What?"

He shakes his head and returns to his tea.

"What?" I ask again, but he's ignoring me now. I wish I

could ignore him, too, but his heavy breathing never allows for it.

"There will be others, is all I'm saying." Eirwyn takes a sip. "I happen to like Colette, but I don't want you settling for anyone."

I cover my burning cheeks with my hands. "Eirwyn, enough."

Brend remains noticeably silent, but I know something waits behind his lips. An accusation. An argument. An insistence of some kind. Brend doesn't know Colette's the fox, but he might have other reasons not to care for her.

Once Eirwyn's on the bench with a book, eyes already drooping, I carry a bowl of water into the bedroom that I've said I'll use for washing up. With the door closed, I sit on the floor beside my bed, a blanket and Nanette's ritual in my lap. I draw the bowl of water closer. My hands shake, and a bit of water sloshes over the rim, darkening the wooden floorboards. I draw a deep, even breath. Release.

With a clean sewing needle, I prick my finger. A bead of blood gathers on the surface of my skin. I hold my finger over the bowl until the tiny drop falls. The spot of red, at first in stark contrast with the clear water, billows until it dissipates completely.

Next, I pick up the apophyllite and press my bloody finger to the gem. Red slowly seeps out, staining the white. Finally, I lean over the water so my face is reflected.

"Show me what is hidden," I say in a clear voice that surprises me.

The effect of my request is instant. My reflection blurs and reshapes itself, and I drop the gem cluster so that a hollow thud sounds as it hits the floorboard.

Because in the water, I find pointed ears.

Piercing green eyes.

A latticework of vines on my skin.

Red roses in my hair.

I haven't only been marked by faeries. According to this ritual, I am one.

CHAPTER 14

Pa often told stories about changelings.

His favorite tale was about a skilled healer who had a baby boy only to have that baby taken in the night, a faerie child left in his place. The healer knew the babe wasn't her own because it wailed and screeched, whereas her baby always slept peacefully.

One day, she took the faerie child to the western wood and laid him down on a bed of leaves. The healer begged the faeries to return her true son but received no response. She stood there all night while the babe wailed, and when morning came, the faerie child was dead from the cold.

Delirious, the healer wandered the village crying for the baby she allowed to perish. For the child that was stolen from her. Villagers reasoned that the healer's baby must have been taken because the faeries wanted a healer of their own, believing the boy would grow to be as skilled as his mother.

Pa meant for the story to be ominous. Ma never took it that way, insisting that Eirwyn and I be glad our parents didn't have any enviable talents, so the faeries were never tempted to snatch us when we were babes. I found the dark joke amusing, but Eirwyn frowned in disappointment, making me wonder if my sister wished she'd been stolen.

Staring into the bowl of water, I wonder if that is what I am. A changeling. Somewhere beyond the veil, the true Ro—the Roisin my parents were meant to have—may live among blue light. Might that be why Pa took me to the center of three trees? Perhaps he wanted me to know the truth before he died.

My finger still bleeds, and I press it to my mouth, tasting blood on my tongue. I should grab a cloth, but I can't move.

Vines on my skin. Roses in my hair . . . .

The scent of roses—that makes sense now, why I got a whiff of them whenever I crossed beyond the veil. Because I'm dressed in roses, halfway made of them it seems. Like the oak faerie and the evergreen faerie, I'm part of the flora.

I feel so full I could burst. Burst into what? I'm not sure. Tears? A scream? Both responses are equally likely.

"I heard a noise."

I startle, lifting my head to see Brend in the doorway. The sight takes me back to when he first stood in my doorway like this, when I was bruised and fearful. Now the bruises are healed and fear of him has been replaced by fear of myself. Why? Because I'm a faerie. A faerie with the power to summon and transform. To influence others according to my will. How could I not fear that? Given the chance, Brend will fear me too. They all will.

"How long have you been standing there?" I dare to ask.

Brend doesn't speak, merely glances at the bowl of water, but that's answer enough.

I bolt to my feet, striding past him to the sitting room. Eirwyn sleeps on the cushioned bench, an open book spread across her chest, lifting and falling with each breath. I don't wake her. I don't even consider it. I pull on my boots and carry myself out into the snow. I fight the wind as I close the door. I haven't brought my cloak or a lantern, but that was deliberate. I want to be consumed by darkness, by cold.

I take slow steps to the tree line, the crunching ground beneath my boots nearly inaudible due to the howling gales. I stare into blackness, waiting to feel the familiar pull that will draw me in, carry me through the forest. Maybe that pull has always been my faerie blood, called to by the western wood. Perhaps my love of the trees was never something I could control, but predestined. It's not a comforting thought.

A warm weight settles upon my shoulders, the scent of pine and smoke enveloping me. My cloak. Someone's brought it to me. Someone with heavy breathing to rival the wind. He moves to stand beside me, his pale skin glowing beneath the moon.

"Brend," I say, leaning close so he can hear me, "what you saw back there—"

"I saw you," he says, his lips tight, "nothing more."

And he's here. He hasn't cursed my name or cast judgment. My throat aches as if I've howled like the frosty gales. I didn't know how much I needed acceptance until he offered it to me.

"What will you tell Eirwyn?" he asks.

"Nothing. Not yet." This revelation has already reshaped my memories of our childhood. I'm not ready for it to affect my sister's memories too.

Please don't tell her, I don't add, because I'm ashamed to need his help. He's supposed to need mine. He's the one who's cursed.

But he says, "I understand. You can trust me, Ro."

I nod, even though I don't. Not enough to tell him everything. Not enough to speak Colette's name.

There's a break in the wind, and Brend must see it as an opportunity. "I trust you," he says, his voice quieter now but weighty. "To me, it does not matter what you are because I am certain of who you are." He draws a breath, and the intention I sense behind it prompts me to watch the trees rather than him. "You are all that I am certain of."

I used to be certain. I used to be certain of the western wood, of my life and how it fit in the spaces between the trees. I used to be certain that leaving the village for Poppy would be the greatest mistake my family could ever make.

But the trees are no longer trees; they're faeries. And leaving the village seems so much smaller than dealing with curses and claws, and my own nature that I'm just now discovering. There are so many mistakes I could make between now and spring, mistakes that could easily amount to more than a journey across the river to a town I've never seen.

I'm not certain of anything.

I won't tell Brend that, not when he's counting on me. Not when he's *certain* of me.

Instead, I linger by his side in the cold, attentive to the sounds of faeries: Branches moaning as if the wind disturbs their slumber. The high-pitched chirp of a sparrow that should have migrated south for winter. I shiver. I never noticed the oddities before. Now they compete for my attention.

I lean my head against Brend's shoulder. Not the first person I'd seek comfort from if I had a choice, but no longer the last either. He drapes an arm around me and brings me closer. I can't say what'll happen next, only that neither of us can endure it alone.

"Thank you for the cloak."

No, I'm not certain. But I'm warmer than before.

"You are welcome."

The winter storm arrives in earnest overnight, forcing us to remain inside the cottage the following day. I move through my morning chores only half aware of my actions, mind preoccupied by roses and vines and changeling stories. Though I never lock eyes with him, I sense Brend following my movements, perhaps noting how I'm handling things. Not well, admittedly.

I startle at the quietest sounds. Crackling flames. Boiling water. Gusts of wind against the windowpanes. I drop things—buttons and sewing needles and matches—prompting me to the floor for embarrassingly lengthy searches. I catch myself scowling at things I normally take comfort in: my foraging satchel hanging from the coat rack, the cracked floorboard.

I keep waiting for Eirwyn to notice my peculiar behavior. Instead, she spends half the morning staring fervently out the window, hoping for a change in the weather.

"We should be searching for the fox," she mutters.

"Not even the best tracker is finding a fox in this storm," I tell her, picking up the log I've just carelessly dropped before adding it to the fire.

The wood basket is now empty, which means someone will have to brave the storm and venture outside to gather an armful or two from the rack. I'd send Brend if I wasn't worried about him wandering off and becoming a bear.

"The fox is our only lead," Eirwyn says. "If she is cursed like Brend is, then you might be able to turn her human. Then perhaps we can understand why Brend is meant to kill her."

"Yes, that all makes perfectly good sense," I acknowledge, smacking wood dust from my hands. "But, as I said, there's the matter of the storm."

"She must be taking shelter. Perhaps that will make her easier to find."

I breathe deeply, suppressing the urge to remind my sister how little she knows of tracking a fox or searching the western wood, considering she staunchly avoided the trees for four years. I'm glad to see that the grief spell keeping Eirwyn captive seems to have broken, but that doesn't mean I'm willing to spend useless hours being pelted by ice. Even if the weather was fair enough, searching the wood is unnecessary now that I know the identity of the red fox. If I want to find Colette, all I need to do is cross to the eastern part of Sugar Maple Village. And I will when the storm ends.

Or maybe a day or two later, when Colette's had enough time to heal.

Maybe a week from now when the tension between us has had time to fade. When she's ready to see me again. When I'm ready. Probably less than a week, though, considering the curses still need to be broken.

Soon. I'll settle for soon.

Rather than explain these rambling thoughts, I promise my sister that Shea and I will search the wood as soon as she returns from her fishing trip. Eirwyn nods, but not before declaring that she wants to search too. I insist this is fine, even though I'm lying.

As Eirwyn turns back to the window, I wipe my dirty hands on my leggings and decide, since I'm already feeling like the elder sister, I should make a trip to the wood rack. I don't want to face the cold, but I want to endure Eirwyn's pining even less.

I pull on my cloak, gloves, and boots and wrap my scarf around my head so that only my eyes are exposed to the elements. Outside, the wind is fierce, fighting me as I stumble toward the side of the cottage where we store our firewood. I keep my head down to protect my eyes from the hailstorm, shuffling through snow until my boots bump against the edge of the rack. Before I have the chance to start hefting logs, a low, moaning sound manages to reach my ears amid the blustery winds.

Shielding my eyes with a gloved hand, I turn toward the noise and spot a figure stretched out on the ground beside our well. In this weather, they are too far away to recognize, but my guess is they are one of those senseless villagers who tries to navigate a storm rather than hunker down in their cottage.

I hear another moan and run forward. Senseless or not, I can't abandon them to winter.

Once I'm close enough, I realize the figure is a man. A man close to Ma's age, of warm ivory skin tone and dressed in a brown wool coat with gleaming gold buttons and fine leather boots. He's no one I recognize from the village, though that doesn't say much given my history. His cap lies beside him, exposing wind-tousled brown hair that curls around his ears, reddened from the cold. I pick up the cap from the snow before the wind carries it away. There's a feather sewed to one side, light brown with darker brown stripes.

"Are you all right?" I shout against the wind.

All the man does is groan in response. His eyes are tightly closed. Snowflakes catch in his well-trimmed beard.

Tucking his cap into the pocket of my cloak, I hold out a hand to him. "Here, I'll help you up."

"No, no," he says, waving away my offer. I notice his gloves are fine leather too. "I can manage."

I very much doubt that, especially after he groans again. Without asking, I grab his hand and pull him to his feet. He's slight, so it's not hard. He wobbles and grips the edge of the well to steady himself. I notice there's a patch of ice where he laid. He must've slipped on it.

There's a break in the wind, so I'm able to hear his gruff "thank you," even though he murmurs it. "But as I said, I could have managed if you had given me a moment."

Some men think they need to do everything on their own. I've never been impressed by men like that.

I offer him the cap. "What are you doing by my well?"

"Your well?" He secures the cap so that the feather is only visible from one side, then points beyond me. "You live in that cottage?"

I nod, and the man holds out his hand. "My name is Silvain. I was attempting to reach your door when I fell."

I stare at his hand. "Why?"

Silvain frowns, appearing somewhat confused, but lets his hand fall to his side. "I am looking for someone."

I raise my eyebrows until they're covered by my scarf. "In this weather?"

He chuckles; it's an unpleasant, haughty sound. "Well, it is certainly not ideal. But I am only in the village for a few days, and I need to find my son. He is missing, you see."

Unease nips at me like frost. "What's his name?"

"Why?" Silvain leans forward. "Do you think you have seen him?"

The intensity of his gaze makes me think he's after treasure, not a reunion with his child. "Maybe." I shrug to appear unconcerned. "Sugar Maple hosts a traveler or two even in winter. I'd need to know his name to say for sure."

"Brend," says the man. "He is a boy about your age."

I feel myself stiffen, and I hope my reaction is obscured by my layers of winter clothes. Could this man truly be Brend's father? I can't ask Brend himself, seeing as he has no memories. But how else would Silvain know his name?

Then again, Brend knew my name even though we'd never met.

"I must find him," says Silvain when I haven't responded. "He left after—"

"Left?" I interrupt. Leaving implies a deliberate choice.

Maybe this is Brend's father, but maybe there's also a good reason Brend left him. "You said he was missing."

Silvain grimaces. "He *is* missing, where I am concerned. Now, have you seen him or—"

"How do you know he came here?" I ask, crossing my arms. The wind is picking up again. I itch to return inside where it's warm, but not before I learn more about this stranger.

"I am from the next village over," explains Silvain. "I thought Sugar Maple was the best place to begin my search."

I've never been to Violet Ridge, the village next to ours, but I've learned enough about it from Shea. Most of its people are as poor as we are. I highly doubt this man, with his gold buttons and leather gloves, makes his home there.

"Well, I haven't heard your son's name yet. I'll look out for him, though."

"Please do," says Silvain. "He must return home soon if he hopes to claim his inheritance."

Inheritance implies wealth. I remember the night I met Brend, surveying his smooth skin, hearing his stilted speech. One of my first suspicions was that he came from wealth. I want to ask how much he is set to inherit, but I don't have the nerve.

Instead, I ask, "If I happen to learn anything, will I find you at the Sugar Maple Inn?"

I haven't made up my mind about Silvain, but knowing where he's staying will be useful once I have.

Silvain's gaze narrows, but he answers, "Yes, the inn. And what is the name of the young lady who would be calling on me?"

I have no interest in giving a stranger my name, but I know

he won't be satisfied unless he gets one. "Meara."

A single, thick brow lifts. "Meara, you say? I shall try to remember that."

There's a thread of something dark in his tone, and I'm glad I gave him my aunt's name. "All right, well, the storm's starting up again. Do you need help getting back?"

I offer to sound polite; I'm hoping—and expecting—that he'll refuse my offer like he tried to refuse my hand. Someone truly polite would bring him inside to warm up, but I'm not inviting Silvain into my cottage. One strange houseguest is enough for me.

Silvain smiles, but it's not a kind one. "I will manage, thank you."

I watch him trudge slowly through the snow in the direction of the village. I wait until he's completely out of sight before returning to the wood rack to gather the logs. Inside, I find Brend sitting on the cushioned bench, practicing stitches with the scrap of cloth Eirwyn gave him after he expressed interest in learning how to sew. I nod to him in greeting, then drop the logs into the basket beside the fireplace. It won't be enough to last the night, but I'm not ready for another trip outside yet. Part of me worries Silvain might come back.

"Where's Eirwyn?" I ask.

"In the bedroom, folding clothes."

I'm amused but unsurprised that Eirwyn is too modest to fold undergarments in Brend's presence. I sit beside him on the bench. "Something happened you should know about."

"Go on," he invites, though he sounds wary.

I tell him about meeting Silvain. When I'm finished, Brend

sets his cloth and needle aside. "What should I do?"

I blink at him. "Why are you asking me?"

"You know him better than I do."

He makes a decent point. "Well, I don't trust him."

"You don't trust anyone," says Eirwyn.

Our heads snap toward the bedroom, where Eirwyn stands in the doorway, holding a pair of socks. "Sorry," she says, shrugging. "I couldn't help overhearing."

I roll my eyes. I never planned to keep Silvain a secret from my sister. I merely wanted to give Brend the space to consider things before Eirwyn could share her opinions. I know from experience how often she likes making decisions for others.

"So, you think I should meet with him?" asks Brend.

Eirwyn joins us on the bench, still clutching the pair of socks. "Right now, our only lead concerning your curse is a red fox. I think any opportunity to learn about your past is worth pursuing."

Brend nods, seeming pleased with Eirwyn's sensible advice. I can't stop thinking about that look in Silvain's eyes, like Brend was a prize to be won. He didn't come across like a father concerned with his son's wellbeing.

"What if Silvain is behind the curse?" I ask.

I don't know how that would explain Colette's predicament, but I can't rule it out. The encounter was too strange for me to trust.

"Anything is possible, I suppose," says Eirwyn. "But we won't learn anything by avoiding him."

"Eirwyn is right," decides Brend, looking at me. "I also think you are right not to trust him. I will meet with him, but I will not go alone. I want you both with me."

"All right," I concede. "Silvain said he's only here for a few days, so we should go as soon as the storm breaks."

As luck would have it, the storm breaks the following afternoon. Just as we're about to leave for the inn, there's a knock at our door. I pull Brend to the pantry, fearing it might be Silvain. When Eirwyn comes to fetch us, she explains Deidra was at the door, asking Eirwyn to watch Orla while she handles an errand. Normally, Deidra would bring the baby with her, but she's worried about the weather taking another turn.

"I couldn't refuse," says Eirwyn, shoulders slumping. "You'll have to visit the inn without me."

I grimace, disliking the idea of meeting Silvain again without my well-spoken sister. "Maybe this is a sign we shouldn't go."

"Nonsense," says Eirwyn, steering us toward the door. "You'll be fine. Don't do anything I wouldn't."

CHAPTER 15

I disregard Eirwyn's advice the moment Brend and I reach Maple Square.

To be fair, I wasn't expecting to see Colette enter the bakery, which stands two doors down from the inn. I know we're here to meet Silvain, but I can't ignore this opportunity. The storm gave me an excuse to avoid her, to avoid facing the fear that I'd lost her trust completely. Now the storm is over, and all I want is to repair what's fractured between us.

"Wait here," I tell Brend.

Inside, the warmth of the ovens immediately chases the winter chill from my skin. I breathe in, detecting a hint of sweetness beneath the smell of fresh bread. It must be pastry day.

The pastry counter is where I find Colette, slender fingers tapping the scuffed wooden surface as she waits for service. The hood of her blue cloak is down, revealing hair woven into tight braids, the ends decorated in beads that brush her shoulders.

I tug off my scarf as I approach her. "Colette."

She turns to me, blinking quickly before showing a hesitant smile. "Ro. I didn't expect to see you here."

I bite my lip, debating what to say in response. I shouldn't reveal the matter of Silvain until Brend's had a chance to speak with him, but I can't think of another reason I'd be here.

I settle for ignoring the comment. "How . . . how are you?"

I brace myself for her to dismiss me, to close herself off like she did the other day.

Instead, she answers, "I'm . . . all right. I've been resting."

"No" —I lower my voice— "changes?"

She shakes her head. "Not since that night."

Brend hasn't changed since then either. We still don't know what triggers the magic, only that I seem to be able to reverse it. Because I'm a faerie. I fight the urge to shudder at the reminder.

Colette adds, "I've missed you."

I grin, thoughts of roses and vines wafting away with the scents of baked goods. It's the last thing I expected her to say, but also the most perfect. I intend to mirror the softness of her tone, but my "I've missed you too" comes out in a rather embarrassing, giddy rush.

Colette laughs, reminding me of the day we met. I want more, want her laughter against my lips, and our hands entwined, but fear of rejection keeps me still. Colette seems to be in better spirits, but that doesn't mean she's forgotten our last meeting, the hurt and tension erected between us because of Brend.

"I'm glad I found you here," I admit. "I wasn't sure if you'd want to—"

"Ready, miss?" asks a baker's assistant.

I clear my throat and look down at the counter, embarrassed by the interruption.

"Two scones, please," says Colette.

"What kind?" he asks. "We have walnut and cranberry."

"Ro, is cranberry all right?"

"Yes," I breathe, looking up to meet her honey-bright gaze. I can't believe this is happening. It feels like a dream.

"Then two cranberry scones, please. And two cups of whatever tea you've got."

Before Colette can pay, I slide two coins across the counter, which the baker's assistant scoops up without hesitation. Colette blinks at me, clearly startled by the gesture, and I shrug. Eirwyn gave me the coin for *important matters only*, but this seems important enough to me.

We take our scones and tea to a vacant table near the front. I keep my cloak fastened because each time the door opens, a rush of cold air hits my back, but I'm not about to complain and risk losing this time with Colette.

"Thank you," she says, before taking a bite of her scone. Her eyes close as she relishes the taste, long lashes pressing against warm brown skin. I try not to openly stare, but I didn't know watching someone eat a pastry could be so . . . satisfying. I adjust my collar to hide the blush on my neck, then take a bite myself. It's the perfect blend of tart and sweet.

CALL FORTH A FOX

"I can't remember the last time I had one of these," I say once I've finished chewing.

Must've been sometime before I stopped selling vegetables with Eirwyn. Even before we lost Pa, our family didn't have much to spare on pastries. But sometimes Ma would bribe me to behave by promising me a scone.

"Maybe you should come to Maple Square more often," suggests Colette.

I frown, thinking of all that might come with a visit to the square. "I'm willing to go without fresh pastries if it means avoiding, well, certain villagers."

"I suppose I can't blame you for that." Colette sets down her scone. "Some people still can't help remarking how different I look from Mama, asking who my real parents are."

I scoff, indignant on her behalf. "They should all know better by now. You've lived here your entire life."

Shrugging, she says, "Doesn't seem to matter. That's one reason I prefer to forage in the western wood." She smiles. "The company's much better there."

I feel the flush on my neck spreading. "Truly?"

She nods, sliding her hand across the table. Carefully, I touch my fingers to hers. When she doesn't pull away, I grow bolder, taking her hand in mine.

"You were right to be angry with me about Brend." I swallow, remembering the blood on her sheets. "I'm so sorry, Colette. I was inconsiderate and defensive and a host of other terrible things when you needed my support. I made a mess of everything."

"You did," she agrees, and as much as that stings, I'm

grateful for her honesty. "But I know you didn't intend to hurt me. You're caught in the middle of something difficult and strange, same as me. I just . . . needed time to realize that."

"I'm glad you did. I want us to be united in this," I tell her. "The curses. Everything."

She squeezes my hand. "I want that too."

I have so much to tell her. About the faeries beyond the veil. About myself. The bakery isn't the place for it, but I could bring her to the western wood. We could find a quiet place to talk, and when we're done talking—

"How long were you prepared to leave me out there?" asks a voice from behind.

I pull my hand from Colette's as I turn to face Brend. The look in his eyes is that of a wounded bird. I forgot he was wait-ing outside. I should have been paying better attention to the door. I didn't hear it open. I didn't even feel the cold air.

"I got a little distracted," I admit, cutting a glance toward Colette, who watches Brend with a stare that makes me shiver.

"I'd better go," I tell her, rising from my chair. I notice her hands trembling against her teacup. Has seeing Brend triggered a change? "Will you be all right?"

"I'm fine," she says, but she doesn't meet my gaze. "It was good to see you, Ro."

"You too." I lightly touch her shoulder. The watchful eyes of Brend and other bakery patrons keep me from doing more. "Maybe I can come by tomorrow?"

She nods, but she doesn't smile. I don't know how to make real plans with Brend standing there, so I tug him by his coat sleeve toward the door, abandoning Colette and our half-eaten scones.

"That was odd," Brend says once we've stepped outside.

I don't know how to respond to his comment without jeopardizing Colette's secret, so I stay quiet. I rewrap my scarf and pull up my hood even though the inn is two doors away. I feel exposed. I want nothing more than to hide away. But I wouldn't hear the end of it from Eirwyn if I turned back to the cottage now.

I lead Brend to the inn. The interior is drafty compared to the bakery and smells nothing like fresh pastries. More like wet wood. I wrinkle my nose.

I recognize the innkeeper's daughter, Elsie, behind the counter. She's come for dinner a time or two, as she and Eirwyn are close in age. I thought she was pretty until she confessed she doesn't care for mushrooms.

Elsie is wiping down the counter with an old rag. She looks up with a smile as we approach, tucking a lock of red hair behind her porcelain ear. "Why, Roisin, what a surprise."

"It is Ro, actually," Brend corrects, and I nearly turn and bolt from the embarrassment.

"Right." Elsie's freckle-dusted nose twitches as her gaze lands on Brend. "And who might you be, handsome stranger?"

Brend's cheeks redden. I nudge him and he opens his mouth, but nothing comes out.

"My cousin," I mutter, begrudgingly playing along with the story Eirwyn gave me in case anyone asks. "Brend."

Elsie leans forward over the counter and extends her hand. She's short, so I bet she has to stand on her toes to reach him. "I'm Elsie. Nice to meet you, Brend."

"You as well," he says, frowning at her outstretched fingers.

I consider nudging him again, but Elsie drops her hand first, eyebrows lifted. "Well, then, how can I help you today?"

"We're here to meet with one of your guests," I say. "His name is Silvain."

Elsie taps a finger to her lips. "Hmm, I don't recognize that name. Let me check our records." She turns away to consult her book, red curls bouncing. I trade an uneasy glance with Brend. If Silvain's not here, I'm not sure what that means.

Elsie turns back to face us. "Sorry, Ro, but there's no one here by that name."

"Are you sure?" Brend asks. "Maybe he was left off your list."

She shakes her head. "That might happen in the summertime, but we don't host enough guests during winter to make mistakes like that."

Well, turns out I was right not to trust Silvain. Either he's already left, or he lied to me about staying at the inn. That means he could also be lying about being Brend's father. Whoever he is, and however he knows Brend, I doubt his intentions are good.

"Thanks for checking," I tell Elsie.

She brightens at my praise. "Sure thing." Then her smile turns sly. "You know, a little sparrow told me you've been spending time with Nanette O'Connell's daughter. Is that right?"

I scowl. I wonder where Elsie got her information. Maybe from Eirwyn, or Colette's mother. There's no use denying it.

Elsie would call me coy. "That's right."

"I'm not surprised you picked her," says Elsie. "But you sure kept everyone waiting, didn't you?"

She says the words lightly, as if in jest, but I know their true meaning. After years of confusion, I've finally chosen a girl, which means all the questions about me have been answered. To Elsie, I'm no different than Deidra and Shea. Of course, that couldn't be further from the truth.

If villagers suddenly saw me holding hands with Brend, I know the comments I would get—that I can't make up my mind, that I'm playing games, that I'm indecent. Then again, holding hands with Brend wouldn't look right for another reason, namely the fact that I'm telling people he's my cousin. But my point stands.

I want to correct Elsie's assumptions about me. I want to remind her that who I spend my time with is none of her business. I can't get the words out. Seems that my voice is only powerful if I use it in the western wood.

We exchange polite—if a bit awkward—goodbyes, and then Brend and I leave the inn. Outside, I expect him to ask what we should do about Silvain, but he surprises me with, "What did Elsie mean by her comment?"

"We don't have to talk about that," I say, drawing up my hood.

"She upset you."

"Lots of people upset me," I mutter, beginning a brisk walk away from the inn. "That's why I rarely come here."

Brend hurries to match my pace. "Eirwyn says that when you live in a village, everyone knows each other's business."

"Eirwyn's right," I say.

"So maybe you should be happy about leaving."

I stop abruptly, whipping around to face him. "Why would I ever be happy about that?"

Brend's eyes have that wounded look about them again. It's maddening but effective. I lower my shoulders and unclench my fists. Clearing my throat, I ask, in a much milder tone, "Why should I be happy about leaving the village?"

"In a town as large as Poppy, people are less likely to know you," he says. "That means they are less likely to know your business."

My lips twitch, threatening a smile that I'm not sure I can prevent. "For a boy with no memories, you have good reasoning skills."

He laughs, a deep rumbling sound that's far too pleasing to the ear. "I have no past to dwell on. I think that keeps me observant."

I nod, finally giving in. "You might be right."

We resume our walk home, and I think about how, before she left, Ma listed all the reasons Poppy will be good for our family. Eirwyn's echoed many of those reasons herself these past weeks. But Brend, a boy I only met this winter, was the first to suggest that leaving the village might also be good for me. Just me.

"Thank you," I tell Brend, nudging him with my elbow.

He nudges back. "You are welcome."

Though Brend and distance from Maple Square have put me at ease regarding Elsie's comments, I'm still troubled by my regrettably short reunion with Colette. I don't know where I stand with her, though the village seems to think we're well on our way to marriage. As evening settles over the village and we near the cottage, I become increasingly ready to hide away in my room, preferably burrowed beneath warm blankets. Since our plan to meet Silvain at the inn has failed, I know it's time to determine our next step, but I hope Eirwyn and Brend will spare me a moment or two to recover after my fraught afternoon.

That hope is dashed when Eirwyn meets us at the door.

"We have a visitor," she says, smiling tightly.

I look past her. Sitting at our dining table is none other than Silvain.

CHAPTER 16

"Why did you let him in?" I murmur.

Eirwyn throws up her hands. "What was I supposed to do? He caught me as I was coming home from Deidra's."

She could have told Silvain to go away or sent him to the inn, where Brend and I were already waiting. My sister has the unfortunate habit of being too polite.

To Brend, I say, "You don't have to meet with him."

Silvain is a proven liar. I would understand if Brend's feelings about speaking with him have changed. He can't hide in the pantry this time, but we have a cellar.

"And leave him alone with you?" he asks, eyebrows lifting. "No, I will not hide."

I roll my eyes, but before I can inform him that Eirwyn and

CALL FORTH A FOX

I are perfectly capable of handling this man ourselves, Brend steps past my sister into the cottage. Left without another choice, we follow him to the dining table. Brend and Eirwyn each take a seat across from Silvain, which leaves one seat for me beside the mysterious liar. I choose to stand.

Silvain leans back in his chair, one hand resting casually on the table while the other clutches a cup of tea. He smiles, appearing rather pleased with our arrival. "Ah, here he is." He gestures to Brend. "Reunited at long last. Does it not feel like ages since we last saw each other?"

Silvain's tone is light, but the hard set of his jaw tells me this meeting is a mistake. I wish we were at the inn, beneath the overtly watchful eye of the innkeeper's daughter.

"Oh, forgive me," says Silvain when Brend doesn't answer, though he looks the opposite of regretful. "For a moment, I forgot about your little . . . memory affliction."

Brend stiffens. Eirwyn places a gentle hand on his shoulder. Silvain knows that Brend can't remember who he is. That means that even though he lied, he and Brend are indeed connected somehow. A troubling realization for us all.

"Who are you?" asks Eirwyn.

"I already gave you my name." Silvain's fingers flit through the steam rising from his cup. "And my reason for being here."

"You haven't explained nearly enough," my sister insists.

"And you lied about staying at the inn," I add.

Silvain sighs like this conversation bores him. "Yes, yes, and that makes me quite an awful man. If only I had your honesty, *Meara.*"

I don't miss the emphasis he places on my false name.

What game is he playing? Thankfully, neither Eirwyn nor Brend rush to hand Silvain the truth.

"Please," says Brend, and his voice is quiet but pained. "Tell me who I am."

"I will not." Silvain straightens in his seat. "What I will do, is remind you that I issued you a task, which has gone unmet."

I scoff. It's no wonder the task has gone unmet. Brend can't remember what it is.

Silvain looks up at me. "Did you have something to add, Roisin?"

I frown at him as a chill dances up my back. Did he ever buy my ruse, or has he known me from the beginning? His fall beside the well seemed like an accident, but perhaps I didn't look closely enough. Perhaps it was a performance.

"What are you expecting Brend to do?" asks Eirwyn, and I silently thank her for deflecting Silvain's attention from me. "He's unable to remember whatever task you gave him."

Silvain nods. "Fortunately, he does not need to remember what the task is to meet it. All he must do is leave."

"Leave?" asks Brend.

"Yes," confirms Silvain, leaning over his tea. "Return to the wood. Instinct and fate will handle the rest."

I remember Colette telling me about her urges. I remember Brend's words from the night he nearly killed her: *To break my curse, I must kill the fox.*

Silvain knows about Brend's lost memories. He must know about the changes too. He must believe, same as Brend and the faeries I've met in the wood, that the curse will break if the bear kills the fox. But why?

I can't ask because I'm too scared I'll accidentally reveal Colette's identity. Silvain hasn't mentioned her, and there's a chance he may not even know who she is. I can't risk her safety to satisfy my hunger for information.

"You made a promise to see this through, whatever the outcome," continues Silvain. "A promise that goes unmet for too long will be met with consequences."

Eirwyn's hand tightens on Brend's shoulder. She recognizes those words as a threat, same as me. Brend places his palms flat against the table as if to steady himself. "What sort of consequences?"

Silvain chuckles. "Believe me, boy, you do not want to know. I came here to meet civilly out of respect for the girls' father, but I will not tolerate—"

"Our father?" Silvain's mention of Pa has my skin humming. "What's any of this got to do with him?"

"Ro," warns Eirwyn as Silvain scowls.

But I must know, especially after what I learned last night. "Tell me," I urge.

Silvain rises swiftly yet elegantly from his chair. "You have until midday tomorrow," he says to Brend. "Return to the wood, or I will return to this cottage, and I will not be civil."

"Wait," I say, following Silvain to the door even as Eirwyn and Brend call me back. I clutch fistfuls of the man's wool coat. My fingers press cold, gleaming buttons. "Please. You must tell me what you know."

Silvain isn't swayed by my desperation. His eyes flash with rage and he grabs me by the shoulders. Terror claws at my throat, smothering the voice that might have saved me.

Fighting his grasp, I push against his chest. I jerk and twist. But his hold is too strong.

I blink, and the cottage around us vanishes, replaced by a snowy clearing draped in shadows and edged in blue light. I'm beyond the veil, where the cottage must not exist. We both are.

Silvain has transformed with the crossing. Gone is the polished man with the well-trimmed beard. Now the creature holding me is covered in brown feathers. Tufts peak out from his head. A curved beak sits where a nose and mouth would. His yellow eyes are large and round. The hands that grip my shoulders are tan and wrinkled, displaying sharp talons that dig into my skin.

The sight of him pulls me into the past, back to Colette's story about a circle of flames and the great horned owl, watching from a tree. "You're a faerie."

"Not just a faerie." Silvain's beak clacks in a dark chuckle. It's eerie, witnessing him speak without his glamour. I don't understand how something so avian can talk as if he has a human mouth. "King of faeries. King of this wood. That rule extends to you."

King. Of course I'm dealing with a king. Of course Silvain can't be an ordinary faerie, as much as faeries can be ordinary. Finally, I gather the strength to wrench away from him. Or he simply lets me go. It's not like I have anywhere to run, here beyond the veil. "Am I a changeling?"

I hold my breath, dreading his answer, whatever it might be.

"I will share everything I know about you—about your father, even." His large yellow eyes narrow to slits. "If you send the boy to the wood."

But sending Brend to the wood might put Colette in danger.

As much as I want to know about my faerie blood and Silvain's connection to Pa, I must consider her safety. I can't betray her again. I swallow the lump of fear in my throat. "If I don't?"

"I will bring you here again," he says. "Your sister too. I will not let either of you go."

Before I can react to the thought of being trapped here, Silvain draws a single talon down my face. Lazily and without pressure, like he knows he can do whatever he wants to me and get away with it, but he's choosing not to harm me now. A tremor runs the length of my body, and I breathe in shakily, the scent of roses my only comfort.

"You are a prize indeed, Roisin." Silvain sighs, the force of it rustling the blooms in my hair. "But you have no role in this fight. Step aside. Command him to the wood if you must."

He takes me roughly by the chin, talons scraping and biting as he pulls me close enough that I'm forced to meet his round, owlish gaze. "Midday tomorrow," he repeats.

He releases me, and I stumble backward until I'm met with something solid. Warm, familiar arms wrap around me, and the rose scent that envelops me isn't one of my own making. "Ro," says Eirwyn, "are you okay?"

Certainly not. I lean against my sister, relieved to be back in the cottage with her. Relieved to be away from him. At least for now.

"What happened?" asks Brend. "What did he do to you?"

I gather my breath, then admit, "He threatened me. He said if I don't send you to the wood, he'll keep me beyond the veil. Eirwyn too."

Brend's swift nod is confirmation enough, but the words

are no less devastating. "I will leave in the morning, then."

"No," whispers Eirwyn, but it's weak, bereft of conviction. She knows we have no other choice this time. Brend must return to the western wood. Once he does, I'll find Colette and warn her away from the forest. Silvain didn't issue any kingly orders about that.

Brend stares at the spot in front of the door where Silvain vanished. "Perhaps we can share one last meal together?"

"Of course," I say when I realize my sister can't speak. She holds me tight, her soft cheek pressed to mine. There's a dampness on my skin that tells me she's crying. "Whatever you want."

Brend's smile is faint. "I'll see to the potatoes."

Dinner preparations are a quiet affair. I gather vegetables from the pantry. I show Brend how to rub dirt off the potatoes and parsnips with a wet cloth and how to properly peel the outer layers of an onion. Then I give him a knife, and his hand doesn't tremble as he chops. Eirwyn, meanwhile, visits the outdoor cellar for fish, and I make a trip to the well for water. I remain vigilant for signs of faeries, but we return to the cottage unscathed.

After moving logs with the iron poker until the flames are the right height for cooking, I put the kettle on for the water to boil. Eirwyn puts me in charge of seasoning, so I sift through our collection of dried herbs. Though I foraged them all during summertime, I don't have much experience using them. But I don't want to ask for my sister's help, so it's not until the vegetables are boiling and the fish is frying on the skillet that I'm confident I've chosen right. Well, fairly confident.

While I turn the fish over, Brend cleans up, brushing leftover vegetable bits into a compost basket meant for Deidra and Shea's garden, considering it will be of no use here now that we're moving away. Sizzling and crackling fill the space where voices might go, keeping us all silent. We can't make tea while food is cooking, so Eirwyn makes a second trip to the cellar for the jug of cider she purchased from Maple Square.

The world beyond the windows is fully dark by the time we're setting the table. While Eirwyn pours the cider, I place the plates and Brend places the spoons and cloth napkins. His shoulders are surprisingly relaxed, his fingers still as he pulls out a chair and claims his seat at the table. His face is calm, but there's fear in his eyes. Fear of what morning will bring.

A steaming plate of fish and vegetables sits before us. I can tell the fish turned out all right; I may have over-seasoned, but the smell is pleasing and Eirwyn made sure I didn't let it burn. The vegetables are once again overcooked, more like mush than recognizable potatoes and parsnips. It's all right, though. Food doesn't have to be perfect to fill you up. If village life teaches you anything, it's that.

We avoid the subject for as long as we can, muttering halfhearted comments about the food and the weather, but Eirwyn breaks first. "What will you do in the wood?"

Brend holds his spoon with a tight grip, knuckles strained. "I suspect I will change after I enter the trees."

"What happens if you don't?" I ask, knowing I plan to warn

Colette away from those same trees. If the red fox isn't in the wood to tempt him, will Brend still become a bear?

"I will not come back here," he says.

"No," I agree, before Eirwyn can protest. "But you could leave Sugar Maple. There aren't many villages on this side of the river, but Violet Ridge is the nearest within walking distance. You could wait there until the spring thaw."

Brend straightens, his eyes suddenly bright. "Then I could cross the river to Poppy, where you will be."

I expect Eirwyn to share Brend's excitement, but my sister remains oddly silent, staring at her vegetable mush she's hardly touched.

"Sure," I tell Brend, though I don't know how someone cursed to become a bear could fare well in a place like that. I might've been tempted to point this out when we were still newly acquainted, but the idea of dashing his hope now, however naive it might be, makes me feel wretched.

"We'll pack some provisions to get you started," I say, thinking of the food, clothes, and other supplies he might require. "We can spare a bit of Aunt Meara's coin too."

Eirwyn looks up at the mention of our aunt. "You gave Meara's name to Silvain, but he still knew yours."

I nod. "The man searching for his lost son was just an act. He knew Brend was staying with us."

"He knew us too," she says. "And Pa. Why?"

I shrug. "I don't know, because he's a king? He must know everything about the wood, and those touched by it."

My sweaty palm threatens the hold on my spoon. I wish Eirwyn wouldn't ask these questions, questions that might bring her too close to the truth. Because I suspect the reason Silvain knew Pa is me. The fact that I'm a changeling. Silvain wouldn't confirm it, but he didn't deny it either.

"What about your voice?" asks Eirwyn. "That must have something to do with faeries, don't you think?"

I gape at her, struggling to come up with an excuse or a way to deflect.

Brend clears his throat. "Perhaps I should begin packing."

Relieved, I sink back into my chair. "Yes, it's getting late."

Brend and I rise from the table in tandem, leaving Eirwyn to contemplate her questions alone. I lead Brend to Ma's bedroom for more of Pa's clothes.

"Thank you," I say once we're alone in the cold room.

Brend dips his head. "I know you are not ready yet, but you should think about telling her once I have gone." His fingers brush my shoulder, bruised from Silvain's hold. "You should not be alone in this."

"I know." I hug myself, seeking warmth. "For what it's worth, I'm sorry I couldn't follow through with our deal."

When Brend leaves in the morning, removing himself from our lives like I asked, he'll still be cursed. I was supposed to free him, but my voice has only managed to delay the inevitable. Silvain was never going to let him shelter here forever. He was never going to let Brend remain human.

"You will get another chance," says Brend, "once we reunite in Poppy."

Again, I hold back an honest response in favor of a brisk nod as I turn to Pa's dresser. "Right, let's see what's left that will fit you."

CHAPTER 17

In bed, I toss and turn, each fleeting dream a mere flash of memory.

The bear charging through the snow. Colette pressed against the tree trunk, her eyes yellow like a fox's. Nanette speaking of faerie gifts while scooping up a spoonful of soup. The bowl of water tinged pink with my blood. Pa telling me to use my voice. Waiting with him at the center of three trees. Silvain's sharp beak.

Halfway through the night, I decide to give up on sleeping. I stare at the ceiling as time passes slowly toward the hour when Brend will leave us, when it will just be Eirwyn and me again. Two sisters, one a faerie in disguise. I didn't lie to Brend. I do mean to tell her, but I fear what she'll say, what she'll think of me, the imposter who's invaded her home for nearly sixteen years.

I'm roused from my thoughts by tapping against my bedroom window.

My blankets are twisted around my legs like tree roots, tightening as I move. I untangle myself carefully, gathering my sheets in a bundle and kicking them to the foot of my bed. I brush loose tendrils of hair from my face, then pad to the window in sock feet, passing Eirwyn's sleeping form.

Moonlight paints the room with a pale glow, although it's not the only source of light. A yellow orb bobs before the window. A lantern held by a girl with raven hair.

I gape at Colette, standing on the other side with a smile edged in shadow. She beckons me with a gloved hand, then points at the window latch. Gooseflesh dances across my skin. Does Colette mean for me to come outside? At this hour?

Part of me wants to say yes immediately. The part of me that's pleased by Colette's smile, wants to be the reason for every one of her smiles. Another part remembers Silvain, his talons gripping my chin. *Command him to the wood, if you must.* I'm supposed to be warning Colette away from this place. Besides, there's Ma's one rule to think about. I've already broken it once to help Brend.

I'm ready to shake my head no, ready to return to bed. Then I meet Colette's eyes again, and an ache to be near her surges in my belly. We shared scones and tea. She let me take her hand across the table, even after I failed to walk her home that night Brend bloodied her with his bear teeth. Midday tomorrow is the deadline. We still have time. Before any other doubts creep in, I signal for her to meet me at the front door.

Colette nods vigorously, and the yellow orb of lantern light disappears.

I dress quickly by moonlight, throwing a thick sweater over my nightshirt and pulling long socks over leggings. The bedroom door creaks slightly as I slip through, but I'm confident the sound won't disturb Eirwyn. My sister didn't wake to Colette's tapping, so it's not likely she'll wake to a creaking door. She's always been a heavy sleeper.

I'm more worried about Brend. I'm almost certain he watches me tend to the fire, then sneak to the door. My shoulders are tense as I wait for the sound of his voice, asking where I'm going so late at night. But I don't hear a word.

Holding my breath, I remove my cloak from the rack and slip on my boots. I open the front door carefully, and intensely frigid air greets me. I wish I'd remembered my scarf. It's too late to go back for it now.

Colette is beside me as I close the door, wearing a smile so wide it squeezes my heart. I open my mouth to speak, but she presses a gloved finger against my lips. I feel a drop in my stomach. Instinctively, I lean in, but she withdraws almost as quickly, motioning for me to follow before she breaks into a run. I glance at my cottage door once more, then take off after her.

The night is still. Even our boots make little sound as they traverse the snow, as if we're trapped in one of my dreams. Colette's hood falls and her braids stream behind her like ribbons caught in a windstorm. I wish to twine my fingers in that hair, pull her close again, feel her finger on my lips—without the glove this time.

Breathless, we arrive at the tree line. I edge closer to Colette, wary of the dark. Wary of the wood. I haven't stepped foot past the tree line since I discovered my faerie blood. Whatever strangeness we may encounter tonight, I'm not sure I'm ready for it.

"Why are we here?" I ask, more than tempted to turn back.

I don't want to disappoint Colette or admit that I'm afraid. Yet returning to my dreams, however tangled and tormented they may be, suddenly sounds more appealing than following a fox-girl into the darkness.

She gestures toward the forest with her lantern. "We're foraging."

"I—I didn't bring my satchel."

She tugs at the quilted strap on her shoulder, embroidered with colorful beads. I recognize Nanette's artistry. "We can share."

"It's the middle of the night."

Colette laughs. "Do acorns hide when the sun goes down?"

"Well, no, but—"

She takes my hand, her grip firm and warm. "You didn't follow me to turn back, did you?"

The thrill of Colette's hand in mine chases away my fears. I shake my head.

"Then come on."

I let the fox-girl escort me past the tree line. A tiny cone of light shines from the lantern, leading us through the night. I can't see anything beyond it, not the trees nor the bushes nor the animals at play. But Colette is confident, turning at the right moment to avoid each collision.

During daylight hours, my feet recognize the many paths I've tread; my hands touch moss and know what direction the nearest stream lies; my eyes see the rotten logs that are likely to contain the best mushrooms. This forest, this night forest, is foreign to me.

Having spent most of my life heeding Ma's rule, I've never explored the forest at full night. With Brend, I had a destination in mind, I knew where my steps would lead me. Now I follow Colette, someone I hardly know, someone who hasn't spent years exploring the western wood.

I shiver. Not from the cold, but from a strange feeling. The same feeling that overcame me when the evergreen faerie's needles struck my face, when Brend stood over me as a bear, his heavy paw raised.

Weakness.

Frantic puffs of breath push past my lips. I shouldn't be here. I should turn back. My chest constricts, eyes darting from side to side. How will I find my way home in the dark? Will Colette lead me if I ask? Or will she laugh at my fear?

"Colette." My voice is so small, so thin.

She squeezes my hand. "I bet I can find bigger mushrooms than you."

Though my breathing doesn't slow, a smile pulls at my lips. "Bet you can't."

She releases me. "Let's see then, shall we?"

She takes off again, her lantern swinging with her steps and casting beams of light across the wood. I draw a deep breath through my nose, allowing the darkness to fall around me, forcing myself to embrace the night. This is my western wood.

If Colette isn't afraid, then I shouldn't be either. I'll get to know this forest like I've gotten to know my daylight forest. We can learn it together.

And we do. We find the few winter oysters that survived the storm and red oak acorns covered by snow. We pick hawthorn berries from trees that shelter woodland creatures, their eyes reflecting the glow of our lantern before they dart out of sight. We take turns hiding behind oaks and maples, waiting in the dark to be found. Then we share relieved laughs each time the game ends, having feared for a moment that we'd truly lost each other.

When tiredness pulls at our eyes, we drink from a nearly frozen stream, the water so cold it jolts us awake and turns our lips numb. We know of only one way to warm them.

In Colette's kiss, I find more than warmth. Her lips are like the forest, speaking a language of wildness and joy. In her embrace, I have no reason to fear the dark, to fear anything but the thought of forgetting this moment between us or waking to realize the night has been another one of my dreams.

But I feel Colette's hands gripping my waist, pulling me closer. The weight of my heavy cloak, a barrier I wish would disappear. My hand against the back of her neck, the soft hairs too short to make braids. The light press of her teeth against my bottom lip, making me gasp from the unexpected pleasure of it. I feel everything, and I know this moment between us is real.

When we finally part and our heavy breaths mingle with the dark, I decide I like the forest best when it's night.

By the time Colette's satchel is full, the black sky has lightened to blue-gray and birdsong fills the early morning air. I've long forgotten the cold; my hand is warm in hers. A light snowfall begins. The green and brown beads at the ends of Colette's braids clink together as she pulls up her hood.

"I forgot to say how much I like your braids," I tell her.

"I did them while waiting out that storm." Colette touches the beads with her fingertips, smiling softly. "Felt good to forget about the curse for a little while, remind myself that I'm still a girl."

I squeeze her hand. She squeezes back.

"I chose the beads for you," she says. "Forest colors."

My neck blooms with heat. I truly should have remembered my scarf.

Colette tugs on my hand, bringing me closer. "I wish we didn't have to worry about my curse. That we could be two normal girls exploring the forest together."

I smile. "And sometimes kissing?"

She laughs. "Not only sometimes."

Our lips meet again, the embrace cold and sweet and tingling. I hear the soft thud of Colette's unlit lantern hitting the snow as we pause beneath the muted light of dawn, hearts beating a rhythm the forest knows. My limbs are weary and my lips raw, but I've never felt more settled in my skin. Not even the western wood has had this sort of effect on me.

Breaking the kiss, Colette murmurs, "I hate that you spend every night with him instead of me."

I turn away, jaw tightening. "It's not like that between us."

Colette and I haven't discussed romantic attraction, but maybe she's heard about me from other villagers. She might think that because I can like a boy, that means I can't be loyal to a girl. Which is untrue, of course. But maybe she's never met anyone like me before.

"I'm sorry." Colette gently turns my chin back to her. "I'm just . . . frustrated."

I could tell her that Brend will leave come morning. I could tell her that I might never see him again. But that's beside the point. Colette needs to know that I'm capable of befriending and helping someone, without it being a threat.

"He's not staying with me because I want to kiss him," I say. "He doesn't have anywhere safe to go."

I wanted to be rid of Brend when I was hurt and scared. At the time, those were valid feelings. Looking back now, I'm grateful to Eirwyn for insisting he stay. Because no one cursed like that deserves the cold. If Colette didn't have her mother, I'd shelter her, too. If Silvain hadn't given us the deadline, I'd have kept sheltering Brend as long as it took to see him safe.

"You're right," she acknowledges. "It was wrong of me to say what I did."

I give her hands a light squeeze. "Can you accept that I want to help you both?"

"Yes." She presses her forehead to mine, then adds, "I'll try."

We kiss, and it's sweet, but I don't lose myself in it like I did before. I don't resent Colette for being honest with me about her feelings, but her words have disrupted the forest magic between us. I'm reminded of the hour and Brend's looming departure.

"I should get home," I tell her, pulling away. "I don't want Eirwyn waking up to find me gone."

"A little longer," she pleads, tugging me back to her. "This is the best night I've had since I was cursed." Then she smiles, suddenly appearing shy. "Maybe ever."

My cheeks burn from the praise. My chest aches, but in a good way, and I want to give back to her what she's given me. "This is the most fun I've had in the forest since I lost Pa."

The confession hangs between us for a moment, then Colette says, "He was a good father, wasn't he?"

I nod. My throat feels tight, but I choke out, "He was."

Her smile is soft. "Tell me about him."

"I will," I promise, "but not now. I need to get home."

I turn away, expecting her to follow.

But she asks, "What are we going to do about the curse?"

I hesitate, looking back at Colette. Do I tell her about Brend's recovered memory? Silvain? The ritual I performed? After a night of too little sleep, the thought of delving into any explanation is exhausting. But she deserves to know the truth, at least when it comes to her curse.

"I've learned a few things since you were last a fox." I gesture ahead, in the direction of the cottage. "I'll share them on our way back."

Colette shakes her head. "Tell me now." She's smiling, but gone is the relaxed set to her shoulders. Her body is rigid, her hands fisted at her sides. "This seems too important to wait."

Something's wrong. Sudden worry makes my heart thud harder in my chest. "Why don't you want me to go home?"

She blinks, her smile widening. It's forced; I can tell. "I already told you. I don't want the night to end."

"No, there's something else going on." I bite my lip, trying to find the words, trying to figure out what's changed. All that feels right is, "You're different."

Her lips part like she's prepared to answer, but she doesn't say anything. The sound of rustling comes from behind, like someone moving through tight trees. Before I can look over my shoulder, Colette says, "I knew he would come after you."

I stare at her, so thoroughly confused that I don't know where to begin. Who is she talking about? What is she talking about?

She sighs. "You say it's not like that between you, but I don't think he knows that."

The rustling from behind is louder. Then a familiar voice says, "Ro?"

It's Brend, emerging from the trees dressed in Pa's coat and boots. His hair is ruffled from sleep, but his eyes are clear.

"How did you find me?" I ask, still as confused as before, but now surprised as well.

"I followed your tracks." He gestures to the ground, where snowfall slowly covers my footprints. "I heard you leave earlier. I grew worried when you did not return."

"I'm all right," I assure him. "We were on our way back."

"No," says Colette. "I'm not leaving this forest. Neither is he."

She moves to stand between me and Brend. She's holding something. Her foraging knife, stained with mushroom shavings.

All the cold I wasn't feeling rushes back, spreading across my skin until it's the only sensation I know.

"Colette," I say, and then words fail me because I can't believe what I'm seeing. Is she prepared to use that knife as a weapon? Against Brend? Against me?

We spent the night foraging together. Moments ago, we were kissing. She told me this was the best night she's ever had. She asked about Pa.

My heart cracks like fissures in ice as a new realization dawns on me. She asked about Pa so I wouldn't leave. She needed to keep me here so Brend could find us. To set in motion whatever she plans to do with that knife.

Brend is completely still, his eyes wide and focused on me as if he's waiting for me to make a choice, to tell him what to do. I have no idea.

"Please don't hate me for this, Ro," says the girl who led me into the night. "But he must be stopped."

Her hand lifts, but I don't trust myself to go after the knife without one of us getting hurt. Instead, I dart forward to shield Brend's body with my own. I nearly tell him to run. But Colette doesn't strike us. She slices the knife into the palm of her hand, wincing as blood wells from the cut.

Then her entire body begins to tremble.

"No, stop," I say, but my voice is too late.

Colette drops her satchel and throws off her lovely blue cloak. The change overtakes her, and she falls on her hands and knees to the snow. I watch fox fur sprout from her skin. I witness her eyes change from honey-brown to yellow.

There's no time to think of what to do next. My back is still pressed to Brend's chest, and I feel him shudder. Panic grips me fiercely. It's happening to him too.

"Brend, stay with me," I say, turning to him and gripping his shoulders.

He shakes his head, eyes shut and lips twisted in pain. I'm too late again.

I back away from them both as their bodies crack and contort. As the magic of their curses courses through them, replacing every human thought and desire with something animal and dangerous. Until they are no longer the girl I kissed and the boy who said he liked my cooking.

When it's done, the red fox runs, and the bear chases.

CHAPTER 18

I chase after them.

I can barely hear the bear's thundering steps above the roaring in my ears, but I can follow his trail. I slog through snow, my palms scraping cold bark as I push off trees to gain momentum. My vision blurs, my ankles tremble. After a long night in the wood, my body screams for me to slow down, but I refuse to listen.

Sharp breaths sting my lungs, and the forest is dressed in shadows, but like Colette knows how to navigate the night, I travel confidently beneath the light of dawn.

Knowing the fox's quickness, I expect a lengthy pursuit, but a roar echoes through the trees, painful and near. I find the bear in a small clearing, writhing on his side in the snow. His left foreleg and right hind leg are caught in traps. Shea's traps, I realize. Two of many she set because Deidra saw signs of a bear in the wood.

Clever. A fox cannot overtake a bear with physical strength, but she can lead him to weapons that will wound for her.

The bear moans. I take tentative steps toward him, and saliva floods my mouth at the gruesome sight of the metal jaws embedded deep into his flesh. The snow beneath him is streaked with red. These are traps meant to bleed, not simply to hold.

The bear's amber eyes are cloudy and wild. I reach out to touch his fur but pull back as he flinches. Then growls. A warning to stay away.

I spin in a slow circle, searching for Colette. There's no sign of her.

The bear thrashes, frantic for release. He manages to stand for a moment, but his uninjured legs can't support him. He crashes to the ground, making clicking sounds with his tongue. I shut my eyes. The itch in my hands is almost painful, the desire to aid him overwhelming. But I worry what might happen if I get too close, if he lashes out.

I could try changing him back into a boy. That would lower the risk for me but increase it for him. His naked skin would be exposed to the elements. He might freeze before he bleeds to death, especially if I have trouble releasing him from the traps.

As I agonize over what to do, the thrashes and moans grow less frequent, but the bleeding doesn't slow. All around him, the snow is turning red. The tangy iron smell makes me feel faint, and my legs ache from standing, but the clearing holds no tree stumps. It wouldn't be wise of me to sit in the snow.

I approach the bear again, this time from behind. I bend and press a careful hand against his back. His coarse fur is drenched from rolling on the ground. The bear lifts his head and huffs weakly, then lowers it in defeat. His side rises and falls with increasingly shallow breaths.

"I'm here," I murmur, though I doubt my presence is comforting. At this point, Brend is so far gone he likely doesn't recognize me at all. He might be wondering why this girl isn't helping him. He might believe I'm responsible for his pain.

Maybe I am responsible. After all, I'm the one who followed Colette into the wood. I'm the one who couldn't stop the changes.

"It will not be long now," says a voice I recognize.

Behind me stands Tamsin. It's the first time I've encountered her on this side of the veil, and the sight of her in my western wood is unnerving. Unlike Silvain, she wears no mortal guise. White flurries pepper her thin fox coat, but the faerie gives no indication that she's affected by the cold.

My fingers twitch at my sides. "Where is—there was a red fox, and she . . ."

I stare at Tamsin as the pieces click into place like gears behind a clock.

She and Colette share the same slender face. The same dark hair. The same lean body, strong and graceful like a dancer's. Tamsin is a fox faerie; Colette can become a fox.

Tamsin nods as if sensing that I've put it all together. "Thanks to my lessons, my niece knows how to initiate a change, but not yet how to reverse one."

"Niece," I murmur, realizing what a fool I've been.

Tamsin told me that Brend isn't a faerie. I believed the same truth extended to Colette, and I was further convinced once I met her mother and learned about the rituals. Clearly, that confidence was unwise. I should have recognized the similarities between Tamsin and Colette from the beginning. Maybe I didn't want to, afraid of what it might mean.

"By the time Colette returns to herself," the fox faerie continues, "this will be over."

"What will be over?" I ask, as the bear huffs weakly behind me.

Tamsin sighs. She sounds so much like Colette that tears prick my eyes. "You care about them both, but only one can survive this."

I shake my head. "I refuse to believe that."

"Because you are young," says Tamsin, something like tenderness bleeding through her tone. "Young and foolish."

In a blink, her gaze turns hard, determined. "But death is the way to end their curses."

I spread out my arms, shielding the bear like I shielded the boy. "Don't touch him."

"I do not need to. Look," she says, pointing a single claw Brend's way. "He is already dying. Colette has completed her task. She has won."

Not if I can release Brend with enough time to get him back to Eirwyn. My sister healed his arrow wound. She can heal this too. She must. But if I start helping him with Tamsin here, she might try to stop me. That means I have to stop her first.

I stride forward. I grip her furred shoulders with my hands and stare into her yellow eyes. "Change," I command.

If my voice works on Colette, it must work on Tamsin too. I never intended to use my power this way—to force magic on someone who doesn't want it. But changing Tamsin is the only way to save Brend, and I must save him.

Colette's aunt tries to wriggle out of my grip, but she can't. She's older, but she's not stronger. The village and the western wood have shaped me. I'm grateful to Pa for teaching me to climb trees. I'm grateful to Ma for making me haul firewood from the square and water from the well.

"I won't be responsible for a boy's death," I tell her, echoing my sister's words from that first night with Brend. "Change, now."

She doesn't tremble. She can't get away, but she's resisting me. She has more control over herself than Colette. I must try harder.

I draw a deep breath. "Change, Tamsin."

Invoking her name proves to be enough. Tamsin crumples to the ground. She curses as her body is overtaken with shudders. She writhes in the snow, still offering enough resistance to make me question the power of my voice. I repeat the command once more in case it needs reinforcing.

Finally, she succumbs, the magic overtaking her. As soon as she's wholly fox, she swishes her tail and sprints away, disappearing into the trees.

The sight of her retreating form doesn't bring much relief. My eyes are dry and strained from being awake most of the night, but I assume that once I blink, I'll find myself beyond the veil again, where I always seem to end up after using my voice. Crossing will waste time, time I don't have, especially if I cross paths with a faerie while I'm there. Brend is still losing blood; he needs me now. Tamsin responded to my power, but she has control over her fox body that Colette doesn't. She could manage to return at any moment.

I remember what Tamsin said about commanding myself across the veil. Might that same power keep me here? Can I avoid the faerie realm entirely by issuing another command?

It's worth a try. I clear my throat. "I will stay here." Unlike the time Tamsin challenged me to use my voice, I don't let a hint of weakness into my tone. I speak with conviction. "I will help Brend now."

I blink hard. When I open my eyes, I see no blue light. I remain in the western wood, the forest I know. My idea worked. I grin, pleased with myself for finding a solution, for accomplishing what I couldn't before.

That grin falters when I turn to help Brend, only to realize he's no longer a bear.

He's human again and curled up on his side, his pale body slick with blood, snow, and sweat. My command must've made him change along with Tamsin. Maybe using my magic was the wrong choice. But I can't call it back now.

I kneel beside Brend. His eyes are closed, his breathing so faint I have to squint to see the rise and fall of his chest. I'm worried about removing the traps now that he's a boy. He's smaller and weaker. He has no protection from the cold. Freeing him is sure to incite further blood loss.

My knees quiver in the snow. If I can't bind his wounds well enough . . .

But if I go to Eirwyn for help, we may return too late. The jaws of one trap, clamped onto Brend's left hand, have forced his blood-drenched fingers to bend at sickening angles. If they aren't freed soon, he may lose them. The other trap, clamped on his right foot, shows skin turning sallow from blood loss.

He draws a sudden, shuddering breath, and I make my decision. Removing the traps is a risk, but he'll die if I do nothing.

"Hold on," I say as my vision swims. "Hold on, Brend."

The same day Ma taught me how to escape a bear, she also taught me how to escape a bear trap. I start with the one clamped on Brend's left hand. On either side of the trap's jaws is a spring, and I place a hand on each one, pressing down as hard as I can. I grunt with the effort, straining the muscles in my arms. My shoulders burn, but slowly, the jaws begin to loosen. Brend cries out as the tines leave his flesh.

"Pull your hand out," I instruct through gritted teeth.

He does as he's told, then lets his mangled hand drop onto the snow. I remove my hands from the springs and the jaws snap shut, making us both flinch.

One trap dealt with, and one more to go. Silently praising Ma for her thorough teachings, I gather my breath and move on to the second and final trap. My arms shake violently as I repeat the process, and Brend is slower pulling his foot free, but he manages to do so before my strength gives out and the jaws shut.

"Come on." I grip his bare shoulder, shake him so he doesn't close his eyes. "You need to get up."

I help Brend to his feet. He shouts when he puts pressure

on his right foot, but my quick scan of the clearing doesn't show any sticks to use as walking aids. He'll have to manage by leaning on me and favoring his left leg. His wounds drip blood onto the snow. I remember there are shreds of clothes where he and Colette changed. I can bind his wounds with those. In the meantime, I secure my cloak around his shoulders.

His head lolls backward, so I slap his cheek—first lightly, then with more force. Anything to keep him conscious. "Stay with me, Brend. Stay awake."

He nods, but listlessly, and I'm worried a few slaps won't be enough to get us home. I can't think of another solution, so I wrap my arm around his back and lead us, limping and staggering, hoping I'm strong enough to support him, and he's strong enough to stay awake.

When we reach the torn clothes, I wipe snow from a nearby boulder and lower Brend onto it for a brief rest. I use strips of fabric to bind his feet and his hands, to stop the bleeding of his wounds and protect his extremities from the cold. He growls at me like a bear, but I shove down my pity because I know bringing him back to the cottage without these bindings would mean his death. I tell Brend we need to move again.

I'm not sure how we make it back. So much of the return home is a blur of one foot in front of the other, of sweat and tears and grinding teeth. Of bloody footprints and trembling limbs. We don't encounter Colette, as a fox or as a girl. We don't encounter Tamsin. We don't encounter anything, as if the entire forest has cleared for our procession.

The sun is near rising when we stumble into the cottage, and I leave Brend to bleed on the bench cushions as I run for Eirwyn. I rouse my sister from bed, and she's dazed and wide-eyed as I pull her to the sitting room. She sees Brend and clamps a hand over her mouth but nods resolutely when I ask if she can save him.

I bring Ma's whiskey and the sewing kit, then clasp my hands so tightly the bones ache as Eirwyn sets to work. My sister removes my cloak and the bindings, tossing the soiled clothing into a pile. Brend remains listless, no longer protesting with growls or cries of pain. I shake my head in defiance of the anxious thoughts that run through my mind. I didn't make it all this way to watch him die.

Eirwyn's hands are eerily steady as she douses each wound in whiskey, but she bites her bottom lip so hard that there's red on her mouth. She stitches Brend's wounds with the same needle I used to prick my finger during the ritual. He slips into unconsciousness while she tends to him, his skin as pale as the snow.

When she's bound the wounds with proper bandages and says she's done everything she can, I run for the door. I barely make it outside before I'm sick, heaving and clutching my stomach, sour with grief and guilt. At this moment, I'd take a hundred years without the western wood before another night like this one.

"We're lucky. Shea's traps were old," Eirwyn says, laying a hand on my back. "Any sharper and he would've lost fingers. But I think I've managed to set the breaks. We'll have to watch for infection. There's a tea I can make that might help."

"Lucky." I spit the word onto the snow. "Nothing about this is lucky."

"He's going to live because you helped save him."

"You don't know what happened, Eirwyn." My voice is breaking. "You've no idea."

My sister rubs circles across my back. "Come inside and tell me."

CHAPTER 19

After tossing more logs on the fire, I peer at Brend, at his weak breathing and his bandages.

He's lost so much blood. Much of it covers my clothes. It's hard to imagine him well again. Hard to imagine those liquid amber eyes meeting mine, his rumbling laugh. Bile threatens to rise in my throat, and I swallow to keep it down.

We don't want to leave him alone, so Eirwyn and I sit on the floor before the fireplace, and I confess the secrets I've kept about Colette and the curses.

It's strange, revealing so much my sister doesn't know. Until recently, I've never kept anything from her. The moment I discovered girls make me blush the way boys do, I told her. Anytime Ma let slip what she was making Eirwyn for her birthday, I'd ruin the surprise. When I was young, and animals followed me home from the wood, I'd show Eirwyn after our parents fell asleep, even though she always made me return the creatures to the trees the following morning.

Hiding the truth from my sister used to be too difficult. When did that change?

There's no denying the judgment in my sister's gaze, the disappointment tightening her lips. "You should have come to me about Colette."

She expects an apology, and I'll give her one because it's owed. But I can't fail to remind her that she's not without blame. Mere weeks ago, Eirwyn ignored my bruises to tend to a strange boy with a curse. So yes, I kept secrets, because I feared my sister wouldn't choose Colette's side—my side—over Brend's. It's clear we've both strayed from the sisters we once were. We've made mistakes and put others before our bond.

I tell her this, and Eirwyn's shoulders move with her breath. "You're right, and that terrifies me. I don't want us to be like our parents."

I squint at her, unclear when or how they entered the conversation. "What do you mean?"

"Ma is . . . well, you know how single-minded she can get," Eirwyn says. "When she sets herself to something—like the move to Poppy, for instance—it's as if she sees nothing else. I suppose that's how I've been with Brend. I've been so—" She pauses to collect herself, to blush a deep shade of crimson. "So caught up in the mystery of him, of his curse, that I've neglected you as a result."

When she puts it that way, it makes perfect sense. With Brend,

Eirwyn has embodied Ma's focus, her dedication. Sometimes dedication can be taken too far, can leave others behind.

"You—you've been like Pa," says my sister. "He kept so many secrets. Helping Nanette all those years? I didn't know about that, and I'm certain Ma didn't either. Do you remember how he'd take you to the wood without telling us? We'd come back from Maple Square to find you both gone, without even a note or message left with Deidra to comfort us. Ma would be frantic, thinking of the faeries."

I bow my head, ashamed. I knew Pa never left word of where we'd gone, but that didn't stop me from following him to the wood. He insisted the secret adventures were all right if we returned safely. Each time that Ma forgave him for taking me, and Eirwyn forgave me for exploring without her, I saw it as proof that Pa was right.

But the secrets weren't all right because they hurt our family. Perhaps no secret is harmless—no matter how small, no matter how well intentioned. I might've started keeping secrets to protect someone I care about, but tonight those secrets nearly cost Brend his life.

I meet my sister's eyes. "I don't want to be like Pa."

Telling her about Colette was a start, but it's not enough. If we mean to be the sisters we once were, I must tell her *my* truth too. I must tell Eirwyn that I'm a faerie.

Eirwyn reaches for my hand. "Let's promise to be honest with each other again. Let's promise to trust each other again."

I squeeze her fingers once, then release them. "I want to make that promise, but first I must share something else." I bite my lip. "One last secret."

Eirwyn's eyes narrow. "Ro?"

I rise from the floor. "Actually, it's better if I show you."

I gather the clay bowl and the apophyllite from where I hid them under my bed, setting them before the fire as Eirwyn watches with a confused expression tightening her eyes and turning down the corners of her lips. I fill the bowl with water from the kettle and ask Eirwyn to clean the sewing needle she used on Brend.

"What for?" she asks, her tone thick with apprehension.

"Please, do as I ask." I point to the bowl. "You'll understand soon."

Eirwyn doesn't lose her frown, but she doesn't argue. She cleans the sewing needle with more of Ma's whiskey but lingers beside Brend rather than bring it to me.

"His breathing is stronger," observes my sister, resting a palm lightly atop his chest.

I want to believe her, but I continue to see red every time I blink. "You're sure his stitches will hold?"

I think of wounds opening while he sleeps, of blood-spattered sheets. *Colette.* A spell of grief engulfs me at the reminder of her. When she becomes a girl again, will she find her cloak and satchel in the snow?

"The stitches held well enough the last time." Eirwyn bends over Brend's sleeping form. Carefully, she lifts the edge of the bandage on his hand to peer at the wound. "See, look at—*oh.*"

"What?" I ask, grief doused like water to flame. "What's wrong?"

"The stitches," Eirwyn breathes.

Quick steps take me to my sister's side. "What about them?"

She removes the bandage entirely. Brend's lashes flutter, but he doesn't wake.

I'm faced with the unthinkable. Smooth skin. Pale-pink, flush. No stitches. No breaks. No wounds. Rather than wait for Eirwyn, I remove the bandage on Brend's right foot myself, only to find the same result. Ma's whiskey can't be that strong.

My sister's fingers skim the clean skin of his hand. "His arrow wound healed unnaturally fast as well."

"Not as fast," I counter.

"Still unnaturally fast." She bites her wounded bottom lip, deepening the dark grooves already there. "If the goal is for one to kill the other, why would Brend have accelerated healing?"

He wouldn't. The curse is already stacked in Brend's favor, with him being a bear to Colette's fox. What need would he have for healing magic? No, there must be another explanation.

My eyes dart to Brend, then back to Eirwyn. I think of her steady hands, of wounds that might've been fatal had they been tended to by someone else. I remember the bowl of water behind me, the crystal. Maybe I'm not the only Birch girl who must complete a ritual tonight.

I square my shoulders. "Come sit with me."

"Now?"

"Yes, now."

I can't change what happened with Brend, can't erase the mistakes I've made in keeping secrets, or reverse Colette's trickery. But I can help my sister answer this one question. I take Eirwyn's hand and pull her toward the fire. I gesture for her to sit on the floor across from me, the bowl of water between us.

Eirwyn picks up the crystal, turning it in her hand. Firelight dances in its clear shards. "Ro, what is this?"

Rather than answer her question, I ask my own. "Do you still have the needle?"

My sister sets the crystal aside to withdraw a cloth bundle from her pocket. She unwraps the cloth to reveal the needle, clean and gleaming. I pick it up and prick my finger, blood welling quickly.

My sister's eyes are wide as a startled doe's. "Why would you—" But she can't seem to finish once she witnesses the drop of my blood fall into the bowl.

I hold out the needle to her. "Your turn."

Eirwyn refuses me with a shake of her head so severe I'm momentarily dizzy. Or perhaps that's my exhaustion for having not slept much tonight. I hold the needle closer, but my sister merely leans back.

"Please, Eirwyn," I say through a groan, trying and failing to hide my frustration. "Trust me."

My sister purses her lips but finally accepts the needle, wincing as she pricks her finger.

"Now hold it over the bowl," I instruct.

"Yes, I gathered that." Glaring at me, Eirwyn holds her finger over the bowl until her drop of blood joins mine in the water. "Now what?"

"We press our fingers to the crystal."

"And then?"

"We lean over the bowl."

"And then?"

I clear my throat. "I make a request."

"What sort of request?"

I groan again. "Eirwyn."

She holds up her hands in surrender. "All right, go ahead."

Pleased, I set the crystal between us. I'm the first to press my bloody finger to the gem, but it doesn't take Eirwyn long to do the same.

"Are you ready?" I ask.

"Certainly not." Eirwyn scoffs. "I've no idea what we're doing."

"No matter what we see," I tell her, "we're still sisters."

Eirwyn hugs herself despite the warmth of the fire. "Ro, you're frightening me."

But when I lean over the bowl, she leans, too, blonde and auburn hair brushing. "Show us what is hidden," I ask.

Our reflections blur.

We find pointed ears.

Piercing green eyes.

A latticework of vines on our skin.

Roses in our hair.

My roses are red. Eirwyn's are white.

We are faeries. Somehow, we are both faeries.

I release a shaky breath, overcome with an aching relief. "I thought I was the only one." But I'm not. Whatever faerie blood I have, Eirwyn has too. We're still sisters, and not only in spirit. "Is it possible we're both changelings?"

"No." Eirwyn leans back from the bowl. Her eyes are no longer green, but the warm brown I recognize. "You know how Ma fears the faeries of the wood. She wouldn't have kept quiet about a switch."

I suck on my finger. "Then how?"

Eirwyn's hands tremble now. She covers them with the folds of her skirt. "Pa."

Of course. If we're faeries but not changelings, one of our parents has faerie blood. Who other than Pa, the man who believed so fervently?

I push away the bowl of water. I think of his stories. His advice to use my voice. His mysterious connection to Silvain. Pa was a faerie. Somehow, he ended up in this cottage with Ma. With us. Then he died before revealing the truth. Now Eirwyn and I are discovering ourselves without him.

Eirwyn stands, brushing soot from her skirt. "We should make tea."

I frown at my sister's calmness, her easy acceptance of what we are, what we've always been. I wait for her footsteps to carry her to the kitchen before I reach for the bowl again and look into the water, but the ritual must have ended, because I see the face I'm used to, a face with origins I never should have doubted. My lips—those are Ma's lips. And my hands holding the bowl. They are Ma's too. My strong nose is Pa's, as is the color of my hair. I'm no changeling, no intruder. I'm Ro Birch, and I was always meant to be Ro Birch.

"I remember something."

Startled, I rear back, and a strong wave of heat warns me that I'm too close to the fire. Brend watches from the cushioned bench through half-lidded eyes as I compose myself, scooting further from the flames. I never expected him to wake so soon. I suppose I can blame Eirwyn for that.

"The oak faerie told me about a girl with red roses in her

hair," he says. "He told me to find you. That you would help me."

The hint of a smile plays at the corners of his dry lips. "I wonder if I recognized you, even with your glamour in place. I wonder if that is why I knew your name that first night."

I hold his gaze, but I have no response to his musings. I can't say why the oak faerie would tell Brend to find me when I knew nothing of him—not until the night he turned from bear to boy in the snow outside my cottage. If anyone was waiting for someone like Brend to come along, it was my sister. Waiting for someone kind and interesting and magical, like the princes in her stories. But none of us are royalty.

Thankfully, I'm spared from answering as Brend drifts back to sleep, the ghost of a smile lingering on his lips.

I carry the bowl of water and the crystal to the kitchen, where Eirwyn prepares the tea. "Why didn't Pa tell us?"

My sister adds spoonfuls of the ginger spice tea blend to each cup. "Maybe he wanted to give us a normal childhood."

"No, he took me to meet the faeries before he died." I pick up a cloth to rub the blood from Deidra's crystal. "It didn't work, but he still tried. He wanted me to know, but he didn't want to tell me himself."

"It doesn't matter now." My sister returns the tea tin to its shelf, leaving the cupboard door ajar. "Pa is gone. All we can do is move forward."

"How?" I ask, an unexpected frustration rising in me. I thought Eirwyn and I would be united in this, but she seems to want nothing to do with the past when all I want is to understand it. "Can faeries even live in a town like Poppy? What if our glamour fails?"

"It hasn't failed yet," reminds Eirwyn. "Why should it now?"

"We didn't seem to have magic before," I point out. "But we do now. What if our glamour is the next thing to change?"

Eirwyn shrugs then carries the cups to the sitting room. I follow begrudgingly, because I know she expects me to lift the kettle from the flames. I yawn as I sluggishly pour the hot water, spilling some on the floor as my eyes briefly close. I thought performing the ritual with my sister would jolt me awake, but it's only drained me further.

It's not until we're seated with our steaming cups that Eirwyn gives me a genuine answer. "We'll learn how to control it. The magic."

I nod. Sounds reasonable enough. "How?"

She sighs into her tea. "Can that be tomorrow's problem?"

I gesture to the window and the light beyond. "It is tomorrow."

Eirwyn gapes at the realization of the night's passing. "I could've sworn it was still dark outside."

"I don't think it's been dark for a while." I set aside my tea, the act of sipping suddenly too burdensome. "We should sleep."

My sister pulls at the collar of her bloody shirt. "We should clean ourselves up."

Eirwyn drains the rest of her tea, then we scrub the blood off our skin with a damp cloth and change out of our bloody clothes. I consider dressing in Pa's old shirt but leave the garment in my drawer and go to Ma's room for one of her tunics instead. Eirwyn smiles at the fit—Ma is tall like my sister, while I'm quite short. Instead of settling past my hips, the hem ends well past my knees, almost like a dress. I don't mind.

Clean and warm, we return to the sitting room to snuff the oil lamps and draw the curtains. Eirwyn studies Brend's breathing a final time, and I draw the blanket higher up his chest. Then, exchanging a glance, we nod. We've done all we can. It's time to rest.

Yet we've taken a mere two steps toward our bedroom when a soft knock brings us to complete stillness.

"Deidra wouldn't come by this early," whispers Eirwyn. "Could it be Colette?"

"After how we parted in the wood?" I shake my head. "I don't think so."

Motioning for me to stay put, Eirwyn takes cautious, quiet steps to the window beside the door. I hold my breath as she draws back a sliver of curtain. Her muffled gasp has me at her side in moments.

Eirwyn moves so I can see through the window. "Is that him? The faerie you and Brend spoke of?"

"Yes," I confirm, recognizing the twisting branches and vivid green eyes.

The oak faerie is at our doorstep.

CHAPTER 20

I suggest leaving the faerie to the cold, but Eirwyn's politeness gets the better of her once again.

"Forgive me for intruding," says the oak faerie once she opens the door. "I only want to know how the boy fares."

"Why?" I ask before Eirwyn can make the foolish choice to tell him. "And why come by now of all times?"

He clasps his twig hands in front of him, branches creaking. "I know what happened in the wood with the fox. I know you freed him from the traps and brought him here. What I do not know, is whether he will survive."

Eirwyn opens her mouth, likely prepared to confess everything, but I put myself in front of her before any word of her healing or Brend's steady breaths can leave her lips.

"We'll tell you. We'll even invite you in. But we want something in exchange."

He holds up his hands as if to settle me. My lips twitch in irritation. "I cannot answer any questions about the curses," he says.

"Good. I wasn't going to ask about them anyway."

I don't require confirmation that King Silvain is the faerie responsible for Brend and Colette's predicament. He wants one to kill the other, and I don't understand why, but I know enough to be opposed. That's what matters.

I cross my arms. "I want to know about our father."

The oak faerie lifts his chin. "Ah, yes. I was wondering when you would start following that thread in earnest."

"Yes, well, we know we're faeries, and we're fairly certain he was a faerie." I pull at the sleeves of Ma's tunic. "But we don't know how he came to live here, on this side of the veil."

"Will you tell us?" asks Eirwyn, her voice honey to my bitter herbs. "Please?"

"Allow me to see the boy, and the story is yours."

This time I'm too late. "Come inside," invites my sister, nudging me out of the oak faerie's path.

I grunt my frustration. I would've made him tell us something useful before inviting him in, but I suppose I can threaten his oak branches with fire if he tries to betray us.

The oak faerie crosses the threshold, eyes searching the room until they land on Brend, still sleeping soundly on the cushioned bench. Without further invitation, the oak faerie crosses to him, bending to inspect him from head to toe. "He bears no wounds."

I roll my eyes. "Very observant of you."

"I healed him," Eirwyn admits.

The oak faerie's vivid green eyes latch onto my sister, causing me to shiver. "I suspected that."

Eirwyn tugs on her braid. "You know about my magic?"

He nods, rising to his full height. "Roisin's as well."

"Ro," I correct.

"Graeme," he replies with a smile.

"Eirwyn," adds my sister quietly.

"Now that we're all acquainted . . ." I gesture to the dining table. Graeme has seen that Brend is unharmed. Time to fulfill his end of things.

Graeme glances once more at Brend before joining Eirwyn and me at the table. Eirwyn pulls out a chair for him. "I'd offer you tea, but—"

"The kettle's empty," I say.

"You are kind, but this must be a brief conversation." Graeme sits, branches scraping wood. I wonder how he feels about sitting in something made of him, or at least made of something like him. The thought grants me an ill feeling. "I must return to my realm before the king suspects where I have gone."

"King Silvain knew our father," Eirwyn mentions.

Graeme nods. "He did. Early in his reign, his majesty collected faeries with talents he admired to be part of his inner circle. Your father possessed the gift of healing. A similar gift to yours, Eirwyn, though his affected plants and animals, while yours affects humans and faeries. He used his gift to enrich the western wood. Like all Silvain's confidantes, he could travel between realms."

The sound of shifting wood draws my gaze to the fire. A few logs have fallen too close to the edge of the fireplace. I leave the table and pick up the iron poker to push back the wood. "That's how he met Ma?"

"Yes," says Graeme. "As you must know, your mother grew up in this very home. Fearing faeries, she never strayed near the wood, until the day the family hound chased after a squirrel, and your father helped return him to the cottage."

The iron poker slips from my hand and clangs against the floor. "Ma knew he was a faerie."

"Yes," repeats the oak faerie.

Eirwyn draws an audible breath. Brend stirs but doesn't wake. I return to the table, my legs suddenly too shaky to hold me up. If Ma knew Pa was a faerie, she knows we're faeries. She lied to us like he did.

"They met each day afterward," continues Graeme, "in secret." His branches creak with his sigh. "Then your mother discovered she was with child."

I shut my eyes. Of course. Ma was seventeen when she had Eirwyn, much to her parents and Aunt Meara's disapproval. She and Pa were married before she gave birth.

"Upon learning this, your father requested that the king release him and allow him to live with your mother's family. Silvain did not like the idea of losing your father to humans, but he also knew how well-liked your father was among our kind. He did not want to risk angering his subjects, who are a fickle lot with thin loyalties. So, he proposed a bargain."

Now it's Eirwyn's turn to leave the table. She goes to pick up the iron poker I dropped, returning the tool to its hook.

"What was the bargain?"

"In exchange for his freedom, your father would promise his child to the king's service, to join his inner circle once she reached the age of sixteen."

Eirwyn covers her mouth with a trembling hand. "You mean, me?"

"Originally, yes," says Graeme. "My magic allowed me to know you would be a healer before you were born. It seemed to Silvain like a fair trade—one kind of healer for another. Your father agreed, and the king allowed him to leave."

"Originally," I murmur. "What changed?"

My sister clears her throat. "You were born, Ro."

Eirwyn's harsh tone unsettles me. I grip the arms of the chair, my body stiff with sudden defensiveness. "Is that true?" I ask Graeme.

"Yes," confirms the oak faerie. "When the king found out your mother was with child a second time, he was curious. That is when I learned that you, Ro, would have the gift of commandment."

Graeme must have shared that with Pa. That's why he always told me to use my voice. He knew what I would become.

"I mentioned that faeries of the western wood are a fickle lot." Graeme crosses his arms, sharp elbows balanced on the arms of his chair. "Silvain considers your gift more useful than healing. With the aid of your voice, he can make sure no faerie ever stands against him."

I take a quick sip of tea, hoping to chase away the sudden nausea. The last thing I want is to use my power to control others. The reason I fear my magic is the precise reason why King Silvain covets it.

Eirwyn scoffs. "He was allowed to change his mind even though the bargain was already made?"

"He is the king," says Graeme simply. "Your father was too wise to argue and risk his wrath."

"Cowardly is more like it," mutters Eirwyn.

"Eirwyn, don't," I chastise.

"What?" She throws up her hands. "You know it's true. He was too cowardly to protest the king and too cowardly to tell us the truth before he died."

But he wanted us to know. That must be why he took me to the wood to meet the faeries. For some reason, he couldn't say the words himself. Maybe he swore to King Silvain that he wouldn't. Maybe he didn't think I'd believe him on his word alone like I never believed his stories.

"And Ma knew," continues my sister, her cheeks turning red as she trembles with anger. "She knew everything and didn't say a word. What's the point of taking you to Poppy if you're meant to join the king in a matter of months?"

"Maybe she didn't know about that part." I'm angry, too, that our parents lied to us about our heritage, that Pa bargained one of his children away, and that said child is me. But I can't believe Ma would accept such a bargain. I can't believe that she would agree to lose me. "Maybe Pa never told her why he was allowed to leave."

"Well, you can ask her when you see her, right before you say goodbye." Eirwyn blinks hard, then swipes a finger beneath each eye. "Isn't it funny? You've been looking for excuses all winter not to leave, and now you have one."

I rise from the table so fast that I knock over my chair.

It hits the floor with a clatter. "I'm not serving any king," I insist.

I'd spend the rest of my life in Poppy before I agreed to something like that.

"You have no choice, I am afraid." Despite my outburst, Graeme remains calm as a lake in the summertime. "Silvain will hold you to your father's bargain. Though I cannot go into detail, the conflict between the bear and the fox is not unfolding as planned. Silvain's reign is weakening. He needs your power, Ro. He will not bend."

"Neither will I," I tell him. "You've answered our questions. You can leave now."

"Very well," says Graeme, the unexpected gentleness in his voice nearly my undoing. I shut my eyes tight so no angry tears can fall.

"Ro?"

I grimace at the sound of Brend's voice. All that shouting and furniture toppling must have woken him. I've no idea what to say, so I keep quiet.

"Glad to see you well," says the oak faerie, and even without looking, I know the words are for Brend. I suspect they knew each other quite well before he was cursed. Thanks to the events of last night, I'm beginning to suspect a lot where Brend is concerned.

Eirwyn offers to see Graeme out. Not even revelations about faerie bargains can topple her good manners. I wait for the sound of the door closing before I finally open my eyes.

My sister leans against the front door, arms crossed over her chest, her cheeks blotchy and glistening with streaks of tears.

"You know, before he died, Pa told me I'm not meant for the western wood."

I gape at her. "He did what?"

"Oh, Ro, don't act so surprised. You were always his forest daughter, while I was meant to find a decent trade and marry a decent man, have decent children." She says the word *decent* with so much venom that I flinch each time.

I want to say I didn't know, but that would be a lie. I never heard Pa say Eirwyn didn't belong in the western wood, but I certainly witnessed him favor my company over my sister's. So many times, he asked me to explore the forest without extending the offer to her. In truth, I can't remember Pa ever putting her first.

"You were always his favorite." Eirwyn says the words with a shrug, as if they're a simple fact we should all be aware of. But nothing about this is simple.

"Pa bargained because Ma was carrying you in her belly," I remind her. "He bargained so he could see you born."

Eirwyn sighs. "He made that bargain expecting he would lose me one day."

"But Silvain wants *me,* and aren't I the easier loss?" I pause, containing the quiver in my voice with a measured breath. "The girl who hates people and loves the trees? The girl who's never belonged to the village like her charming elder sister?"

"No one's kept you from belonging," says Eirwyn. "You've exiled yourself from any villager who's spoken to you wrong."

How can she blame me? The villagers make me feel strange. They make me doubt myself. They poke and prod, and when they don't like what they find, they poke and prod some more.

Until I'm raw. Until I have no choice but to withdraw into the wood.

But I can't withdraw to the wood now, because it's infested with faeries. Faeries who would see me serve a king, the very king who wants the boy I've befriended to kill the girl I've kissed.

I withdraw to my room instead. I sink to the floor, leaning against the end of my bed. Memories of Pa shift behind closed eyes. Him taking me to the wood, telling faerie stories at my bedside, bringing me to the three trees. He was preparing me for a life beyond the veil. A life he didn't want but was all right bestowing upon me. Because Eirwyn's right, isn't she? I'm the forest daughter. I was nurtured toward this very future.

"I'm such a fool," I murmur, bitterness souring my tongue.

"You are not," says Brend as he comes to sit beside me, hands gripping the blanket to keep it from slipping off his waist. I nearly laugh. A few weeks ago, I was embarrassed to see him unclothed. Now I've seen too much of him to ever be embarrassed again.

He places a hand on my knee. I'm torn between shoving it off and gripping it so tight that I reverse Eirwyn's healing.

"What do you know?" I wipe at my dripping nose with my sleeve. "You don't even know who you are."

I regret the words immediately, but there's no stealing them back. Shame coils low in my belly. I expect him to take offense or at least remove his hand from my knee. It's what I'd do.

Instead, he says, "Neither do you. We are quite similar, Ro."

I lift my eyebrows. "Well . . . at least I know how to wear clothes."

He first looks at me with a blank expression then surprises me completely as he erupts into deep, rumbling laughter. The sound is more soothing than I'd ever admit. I suck in my cheeks, but ultimately fail to hold back my smile.

Then the laughter ends, and the ensuing silence is heavy with what we need to say about the night, about the bear traps and the blood and Colette, about Pa's bargain with the king. "Did you hear any of what Graeme said?"

"All of it, in fact," he admits. "I was pretending to sleep from the moment he knocked at the door."

I grimace. "I suppose we weren't very quiet."

Brend murmurs his agreement, leaning his head against my shoulder. "So, let me see if I have it right. You and Eirwyn are faeries because your father was a faerie. You are promised to the king, who wants me to kill the red fox, who is Colette."

"Who is also a faerie. I swear, I didn't know about that part until last night," I murmur, breathing in the scent of him—earth and sweat and smoke. "Oh, and Tamsin, the faerie I thought was the fox, is her aunt."

"What am I, then?" he asks. "What is my part in this?"

I blow out a long, heavy breath. I've long wondered the same, but thanks to the many reveals tonight, I think I might've finally figured some of it out.

"Colette's adoptive mother told me her son, Callum, was born still," I explain. "I'm beginning to think that isn't true."

Colette and Brend must be the true changelings. That's how they're connected. The faeries didn't give Nanette a baby girl to remedy her loss. They made a switch. Colette, the faerie child, for Brend, the human one. What I don't know, is why one must kill the other. Pa's stories never mentioned anything like that.

"Callum?" The way Brend says it makes me think he must be frowning.

"I don't think it suits you either."

"Not at all," he agrees. "I prefer Brend."

I nod. "Brend is a good name." Then, surprising myself, I reach for his hand. His skin is warm and soft against my callouses. "I'm sorry for not telling you about Colette."

"You were trying to protect her."

"Yes, but I should have trusted you," I say. "You always trust me."

"You are easy to trust." The words are said with such tenderness that I'm left almost breathless. "But I have not been easy. I hurt you the night we met. I tried to kill the fox when I was a bear. Then I suggested killing her as a boy."

"Now she's hurt you," I say. "Now she wants you dead too."

"Whatever has cursed us to fight each other, we must end it before either of us is killed."

I'm relieved to hear him say that. Colette's actions tonight may mean that we never share another kiss, but I don't want her dead. I mean to free her still.

I want to figure out how, but I must have fallen asleep trying. I wake to the gentle caress of Brend's fingers across my cheek. "Someone new is at the door," he says.

CHAPTER 21

I tell Brend to stay hidden in the bedroom. Eirwyn is sleeping on the bench as I pass her to reach the door. She must be exhausted. From healing Brend to discovering she has faerie blood to the revelation of Pa's bargain, I wouldn't be surprised if she slept the rest of the day.

As I turn the knob, I'm jittery with fear, thinking a faerie might be on the other side of the door. But it's Nanette, her eyes wide with alarm, her long hair tied up into a hasty knot.

"Ro," she says by way of greeting, "is Colette here?"

I shake my head. I almost say I haven't seen her since last night, then decide against it.

"Oh." Her shoulders sag. "She told me she ran into you yesterday. When I found her room empty this morning, I wondered if she'd snuck out to see you."

"No," I say, though it pains me to lie to her when I can see how distraught she is. "I haven't seen her since the bakery."

Colette doesn't want Nanette to know about her. She betrayed me last night, but that doesn't mean I'm ready to do the same. I think of Brend, waiting in the bedroom, and part of me wants to ease Nanette's pain by informing her that her son most likely lives. But it's not my place. Brend should be the one to have that conversation with her if that's what he wants.

"She's probably foraging," I say. "I can look for her while I'm in the wood if you'd like."

Nanette smiles. There's relief in her voice when she says, "Yes, you're probably right. Thank you, Ro."

I bid Nanette goodbye then close the door. I press my forehead to the wood and release a long, strained breath. If Colette didn't go home last night, does that mean she's still a fox? Or is she somewhere in the wood with Tamsin?

A hand touches my shoulder, startling me. "Sorry," says Brend. "Was that Colette's mother?"

"Yes. I don't think Colette made it home last night. Nanette's looking for her."

He glances at the window. "You should try to find her."

I lean back against the door, weariness tugging at my limbs. It's late morning, which means I must've slept an hour or two. Nowhere near what I need. "I don't know . . . she might be with Tamsin. She's the one who told Colette to lead you to those traps."

"Maybe there is a way to convince them both that killing is not the answer."

I roll my eyes. "Sometimes you're too optimistic."

He rolls his eyes right back. "Sometimes you are too cynical."

I groan. "Fine. I'll look for her. Let Eirwyn know where I've gone once she wakes up."

I promised not to be like Pa. Despite the turmoil between us that knowledge of his bargain has wrought, I won't disappear on my sister again.

I pull on a pair of leggings and throw a sweater over Ma's tunic. My cloak is covered in blood, and Pa's coat is no more than shreds, so I slip into Eirwyn's and stuff my feet into boots.

Outside, I pause at the white and red rose trees. Bare for winter, it's hard to tell them apart now. Come spring they will show their colors, their contrast.

They are the remnants of our garden—what hasn't succumbed to wilt and decay since Pa's passing. I think of all the blooms we've clipped from their branches, of standing at the counter sanding thorns from stems and binding bouquets. Distilling petals into perfume. Along with Ma's soap, these two trees kept us from falling deeper into ruin. I should be grateful to them. I should smile as I look at them.

Instead, my lips are a tight line, and my shoulders fall as a new question strikes me. Did Pa plant these trees in honor of my sister and me, because he knew what we looked like beneath our glamour? Eirwyn's white roses, and my red ones. Another question not likely to be answered, more memories twisted and tainted by secrets.

A gust of wind shakes the trees, and a peculiar rattling sound sets me on a brief detour before I commit to my search for Colette. Despite the strong breeze, the temperature has risen some since last night. Melting snow squelches beneath my boots and drips from the roof of the cottage. New mushrooms will grow in the wood, taking advantage of the brief thaw. I bet villagers are moving about without their scarves and gloves, behaving as if rain and flowers and heat are not far away. They should know as well as I do that winter is far from over. Sugar Maple Village never meets an early spring.

On the other side of the cottage, I find the source of the noise. The latch on the cellar door isn't secure. I'm grateful to the wind for alerting me. The last thing I need right now is a horde of mice invading our cellar. I try to remember who visited last, myself or Eirwyn. I'm guessing the latter. She never remembers to shut a cupboard or close a drawer. Forgetting to replace the cellar latch isn't too different.

A new noise makes me fear that mice have already taken advantage of the unlatched door. When I take the stairs, I'm confronted with a foreign shape huddled in one of the back corners. A head lifts, and the daylight behind me illuminates Colette's tear-streaked face. Her eyes widen as she takes in the sight of me. She's got the burlap sack we use to hold potatoes wrapped around herself, and she's shivering. I can tell she's not wearing anything underneath. She must not have been near her cloak or a stash of clothes when she changed back into a girl.

"You must be freezing," I say, unable to think of anything else.

I light the cellar's sole oil lamp then pull the door shut. The air outside is warmer, but I don't want Eirwyn or Brend coming upon us before I have the chance to speak with Colette alone. I remove Eirwyn's cloak and hand it to her. Covering my eyes, I wait for her to fasten the buttons.

"Thank you," she murmurs.

I look at her, dressed in Eirwyn's cloak with the burlap sack covering her bare feet. Everything about her, from the beads at the ends of her braids to her freckle-dusted cheeks to her graceful hands, is familiar and yet unknowable. I wish I knew what she was thinking. I wish I knew *what* to think about all this. If she says she's sorry about last night, do I forgive her? Am I supposed to apologize too?

"Nanette came looking for you," I say. "She's worried."

Colette releases a shaky breath. "What did you tell her?"

I move to sit in front of her. The dirt ground is cold, but it felt strange to stand. "Nothing. I said you were probably foraging."

"Why would you lie for me?"

I shrug, wrapping my arms around myself because I'm feeling a chill without Eirwyn's cloak. "I didn't want to betray your trust a second time."

"Even though I betrayed yours?"

I nod. She lowers her head. I hear her sniffle.

"Was any of it real?" I ask.

She looks up at me. Her eyes shine. "What?"

"Your feelings for me." I swallow past an awful ache in my throat. "Were they real, or were you trying to get to Brend?"

Before I say anything else, before I make another choice, I must know.

"They're real," she insists. "I promise. Every kiss, every—"

"How am I supposed to believe you?" My voice wobbles and I shut my eyes, trying to collect myself. I want to be strong. I want to show her that she hasn't deeply wounded me, even though she has.

"I won't blame you if you don't." I hear her shifting, and when I open my eyes, she's kneeling, and closer to me than before. "But it wasn't my idea to use you to get Brend. I didn't want to go through with it, but Tamsin—"

"What?" I ask. "What did she tell you?"

If Colette is surprised that I know who she's talking about, she doesn't let on. "She said that Brend and I are part of some sacred faerie tradition. We're supposed to fight each other for a place beyond the veil now that we've come of age."

I nod, sorting the new pieces of the mystery within my mind. Colette's explanation fits squarely with my theory about she and Brend being changelings.

Fresh tears spill onto Colette's cheeks. "I met Tamsin the same night the bear had me in his jaws. She said I would die the next time he caught me unless I killed him first. So, I led you to the wood believing Brend would follow. Then I forced myself to change so he would, too, and I brought him to the traps I discovered while foraging."

"I freed him, you know," I say. "Right after I chased away your aunt."

She bites her lip. "So, you know about me then."

"That you're a faerie? Yes."

Colette moans softly. "That must frighten you."

I flinch, thinking of my own power. "That would be a bit disingenuous."

Her brows draw together in confusion. "What do you mean?"

I can't answer, silenced by sudden nerves. I don't know if what I have planned will work. I've called to the cursed and crossed the veil between realms, but I've never removed my

a
glamour. I close my eyes and picture my faerie self: the red roses twined in my hair as if the seeds were planted long ago; the points of my ears; the verdant green of my eyes; the spirals of vines around my arms.

I imagine every detail, then draw from a will deep within myself. A desire to show the part of me that's been hidden for fifteen years. The part that ties me to Colette, ties me to the western wood.

I hold that desire and mold it into the words I seek, "Let her see me."

Losing my glamour is like removing a shawl, a difference in weight that's not considerable but still noticeable. I hold my hands out in front of me, admiring the vines covering me like a second skin.

"Ro."

Colette meets my gaze unflinchingly, staring at me with so much awe that tears spring to my eyes. I feel . . . seen. Understood in a way not even the trees could offer.

She trails her fingers through my hair, the fresh scent of roses heavy between us. "You are lovely," she murmurs, lips now close enough to kiss.

I ask, "May I see you?"

Colette nods, her smile shy. I gather a new desire, a desire to see Colette as she truly is. For us to be open to each other, despite the barriers we've both enacted because of the curse. I hold the desire so fiercely my body aches.

"Let me see her."

Her glamour washes away like river waves upon sand. She keeps her brown skin and raven braids, but her eyes are now a muted yellow, her ears tall and copper furred. Her nails are black and curved, and short whiskers have sprouted from the freckles on her cheeks. She covers her mouth with her hand, gasping.

"What is it?" I ask.

Her lips part to show pointed canines. "Do I frighten you?"

"No," I say truthfully.

Seeing Colette, canines and all, makes me feel relief more than anything. Laid bare to each other, this may be the first honest interaction we've ever shared. That release—of secrets, of camouflage—brings upon a swell of boldness. I touch one of Colette's ears, and it's as soft as I imagined that first day in the wood. She closes her eyes, her body tensing.

I bring my hand back. "I'm sorry. Did that hurt?"

"No," she says, the word hardly more than a breath. "No, it didn't hurt."

I'm aware of the tension still lingering between us, of the many words left unsaid. Right now, I want to forget that tension, forget those words. I want my lips on hers, our hands on each other.

I lean in to kiss her, and she kisses back. I tell her I want more, and she says she wants that too. We lay together on the cold ground, one of her hands gripping my waist, the other tangled in my rose-dappled hair. We explore each other with fumbling, eager fingers and hot, desperate mouths. Her touch ignites and soothes with equal measure, and my lips graze all the places that sharpen her breaths. Her ears, her jawline, her collarbone.

Everything keeping us apart falls away as we discover each

other in ways no one else has, as we answer every need that's
blossomed between us since the day we first met.

Once we're spent from kissing, we lay turned toward each other,
our hands tucked under our cheeks and our legs intertwined.
Colette's fox tail brushes my hip, and I shiver.

"Does that—" She pauses, lips pressed tight, then seems to
reclaim her courage. "Is the tail too strange?"

"No," I say, laughing. "It tickles, though. What about the
thorns in my hair?"

"Sharp, but not completely unpleasant."

We both grin, but Colette's smile falters first. She closes her
eyes, and when she opens them, they are wet like before.

"Are you all right?" I ask, chest filling with dread. "Are
you . . . do you wish we hadn't . . ."

From my talks with Ma, I know Colette and I could have
gone much further than we did. Still, our time together was
the most intimate I've been with anyone. Despite how much
I enjoyed myself, and how much she *seemed* to have enjoyed
herself, perhaps it was too soon.

But Colette says, much to my relief, "No. I would never wish
that."

"Then what is it?"

"I made a mistake listening to Tamsin," she says. "A mistake
that almost lost me you."

"You haven't lost me." I cup her face with my palm, careful

not to crush the whiskers that brushed my cheeks when we kissed. "You haven't."

"She's my family, my blood. She's everything I've been looking for my whole life." Her body shakes from a rising sob. "But this morning, when I changed back and came across those bloody traps, I felt so awful. I don't want to be a killer, Ro."

"I know, I know." I try to make my words a caress, try to make her see that I understand. "I do almost everything Eirwyn asks of me, even things I question."

After he attacked me, I had good reason for turning Brend away, but I didn't. Because my sister wanted him to stay. Because Ma left her in charge of us for the winter. I know all too well the power family can have over you.

"I nearly killed him," Colette sobs.

"It's all right." Her lips taste of salt when I kiss her. Any qualms I had about forgiving her disappear. "Come inside with me. Talk to him."

"I don't know, Ro. After everything we've done to each other—"

"It won't be easy." Colette might've had the upper hand last night, but like Brend said, she's not the one who struck first. "He's still a bear; that makes him dangerous. But the way through this is to work together. I know he wants that too."

The question is, does Colette? Can she see a path toward forgiveness? The choice is hers, the same way it was mine after a bear battered me with his paws.

"All right," she says. "I'll come."

We tend to our messy hair and my disheveled clothes, then I

replace our glamour. Using my power this way doesn't bring me to the faerie realm. Though I can't fathom why, I'm grateful. Crossing beyond the veil would've been quite the interruption for me and Colette.

We hold hands as we emerge from the cellar. I feel strong and sturdy with Colette beside me, like an ancient and powerful oak. I don't know what we'll do next, how we'll break the curses, or how I'll avoid serving a dreadful king. But we're truly united in this fight now, just as I've wanted from the beginning. Colette and Brend will make amends, then we'll face this together.

We round the corner to the front of the cottage. I first notice the open door.

Then the pile of tattered clothes in the snow.

I drop the lantern and creep slowly inside, Colette's footsteps close behind me.

The dining chairs are overturned. Cups lie shattered on the floor amid puddles of tea. Peering closer, I believe there might be drops of blood among them. Whose blood it is, I can't say.

The tea kettle over the fire is bubbling over, water dripping onto the flames and making the logs hiss. I remove it from the hook, realizing too late that I've forgotten the cloth. I drop the kettle as my hand burns. Boiling water spills onto the floor. I wince and suck on my palm as smoke billows into the room.

The pantry door is closed. I rush to it, fling it open, hoping to find my sister.

The space is empty, save for the preserves and potatoes. Clean. Untouched. Unoccupied.

I slam the door shut. "Where are they?"

"I don't know." Colette shakes her head wildly, as shocked as

I am. "Maybe Tamsin came looking for—but she knows I have to be the one to kill the bear. She wouldn't risk coming after Brend herself."

I survey the cottage, searching for a sign. Something to tell me what happened. I shield my eyes from the light that shines through the cracked front window. Midday light.

Midday. Silvain's deadline, which I completely forgot amidst the turmoil of last night. The king must have arrived while Colette and I were in the cellar, the walls too insulated to allow sound from above. He saw that Brend hadn't left, and he enacted those consequences he warned us about. Only I wasn't here to face them.

If he's hurt either of them . . .

I clench my fists as a swirl of terror, rage, and regret surrounds me like a storm, forcing a scream from me. I call for my sister, for Brend. Of course, there's no answer.

I told Brend where I was going so Eirwyn wouldn't think I disappeared. But Eirwyn is the one who's gone this time. Eirwyn is *gone*.

CHAPTER 22

A t first, I think the snow-crunching sound of approaching footsteps must belong to Silvain, that he's returned for us. Alarmed, I reach for Colette, who links her arm with mine. Her closeness rouses strength within me. We'll face him together. We'll make him tell us what he did to Eirwyn and Brend.

But we don't get the chance, because the figure that appears in the doorway belongs to a mother. Not Ma, but as close as I'll get right now.

"What happened?" Deidra asks, face drawn with concern. I hear a gurgling noise and realize it's coming from Orla. The baby sits snugly in a pack on Deidra's back. "I heard you screaming."

I gape at her. I have no idea where to begin. But Deidra nods as if I've explained everything. Gaze determined and shoulders set, she says, "All right, come with me."

She ushers us outside and down the familiar pathway. In her cottage, there are no shattered cups or drops of blood. The furniture sits as it should, and the fire is warm.

Deidra places us on the bench and mumbles something about tea. Blankets are thrown around our shoulders. Orla coos from far away. I lean against Colette. She squeezes my hand so tightly it hurts, but I don't try to pull away. I can't lose her too.

Deidra hands me a cup I don't have the stomach to sip from, but at least the clay warms my hands. I stare into the fire. I ache for my sister.

"Tell me what happened," Deidra says, sitting on my other side. "Can you do that?"

We tell Deidra everything—everything we know about the curses, and more. We take turns recounting every moment since we first met eyes as fox and girl in the western wood.

Deidra listens. Even as Orla cries, she hears every word. She doesn't move away from us when we confess our faerie blood and doesn't show fear. If anything, she draws closer.

"The changeling explanation rings true to me too," she says. "Nanette always suspected the faeries were tied to you, Colette. Seems she was right."

"But we don't know why I became a changeling," says Colette. "Or why Brend and I are fighting for a place beyond the veil now."

I can tell Deidra's thinking by the way her lips press together. "And Tamsin didn't say anything more?"

"No." Colette sighs. "She didn't tell me much, really. Bits and pieces."

Just enough to make Colette do what she wanted. I shift

closer to her as a surge of protectiveness rises in me. Colette was vulnerable to Tamsin because she was alone. Brend had me and Eirwyn, but Colette was too scared to go to Nanette, and I wasn't there for her when she needed me to be. I won't let that happen again.

"All right," accepts Deidra. "The curses can't be our focus just now, anyway. We need to find Eirwyn and Brend. Now, I know you said Silvain might've taken your sister beyond the veil, but we won't know for sure what happened until we find Brend. The forest isn't safe for you girls until we do, anyway. So that's where we'll start." She nods as if to strengthen her resolve. "Shea's due back tonight. You know she can track anyone."

My eyes prick with tears. We've lied to Deidra for weeks, but all she cares about is helping us. "Thank you."

"No need," she says, rubbing my back. "You've each carried these burdens long enough. Time to share the load, and I'll gladly take some of it. Shea will too."

The last thing I want is to put Deidra and her family in danger, but I can't deny how safe and reassured I feel at this moment. I believe Deidra when she says Shea will find Brend. I believe her when she says she wants to help us, and I know she will.

"In the meantime, Colette, I have some clothes that might fit you," says Deidra. "Stay here and keep warm while I fetch everything."

Deidra withdraws to her bedroom, granting Colette and me a moment alone.

Colette pulls her hand from mine, angling her body in a way that ensures we're no longer touching. "I'm sorry, Ro. You were so busy dealing with me that you missed Silvain's deadline."

I shake my head. Colette made mistakes, but seeking shelter in my cellar wasn't one of them. "That's not something you need to apologize for. I'm glad you came to me rather than Tamsin." Lightly, I bump my knee against hers. "We were likely to miss the deadline anyway. Eirwyn and I were so consumed by Pa's bargain."

She bows her head. "I've made it impossible for you to trust me."

"Colette, I think we've learned by now that nothing's impossible." I lift her chin to kiss her softly. "If you can still trust me, I can trust you."

We've both made our share of errors regarding the curses and each other. What matters is that we're committed to righting them. Together.

She murmurs against my lips, "I don't think I'll mind it much."

Regretfully, I draw back to ask, "Mind what?"

She trails her fingers through my tangled hair as if imagining the red blooms hidden behind my glamour. "Being a faerie. Especially now that I know you are one too." She shrugs. "Who knows? Maybe we'd enjoy a life beyond the veil."

I stiffen, remembering something Silvain said to me yesterday. *You are a prize indeed, Roisin.* I don't want to be anyone's prize.

I shake my head. "You'd have to kill Brend."

Colette's hand falls from my hair to her lap. "What if there's another way to end the curses? A way that puts everything to rights?"

I don't begrudge Colette's desire to explore her heritage and where she hails from. Until I knew about Pa's faerie blood, I felt unmoored from my life. I wouldn't say the truth has set me on solid ground, but it's helped.

Yet there's Silvain to consider. Tamsin, too. "You'd truly want to live there?"

"I don't know," admits Colette. "All I know is that I wouldn't be satisfied returning to my life as it was before. Not after all that I've learned."

I reach for her hand. That, at least, I can understand. "I think we're long past that."

Whatever's to come next for each of us will be something new. I only hope that wherever that path leads me, Eirwyn will be there too.

I manage a few precious hours of sleep before night falls and Shea walks through the door, smelling of sweat and snow and fish. I hear her bags drop to the floor, then her footsteps as she crosses the room.

She kneels before us. "I saw the cottage. What happened?"

"We don't have time to get into the details," says Deidra, before providing her wife with an impressively brief explanation so that Shea is informed enough for our next step.

"I should've known," Shea says to me. "Questioned you more about the fox."

"I should've asked questions after I heard rumors about a

visiting cousin," Deidra adds, with a pointed look my way. "But how could we have expected all of this? Their story is strange even for our village."

"Don't blame yourselves," I say. "I should've asked for help sooner."

I claimed the curses as my burdens to bear, believing it would keep others safe. But what if I'd gone to my neighbors—two strong, wise women—straight from the beginning? Might they have helped Brend and Colette form an allyship? Might they have known a way to deal with Silvain and Tamsin? Might they have helped my sister and I discover our faerie heritage sooner?

"Maybe if I had come to you," I say to them—*maybe if I hadn't acted so much like my father*, I say to myself—"Eirwyn and Brend would still be here."

"Don't speak as if they're gone," Shea says. "We're finding them both. Tonight."

Shea, Colette, and I set off for the wood soon after, leaving Deidra to care for Orla and watch for Eirwyn and Brend in case they manage to return on their own. As I predicted, the warmer weather from this morning has vanished, and the winds are strong. I'm glad to be bundled in layers, though the cold is still biting.

We enter the forest with our lanterns, and Shea points to the ground. "Most tracks will be covered due to the wind."

"What do we do?" I ask.

"Find tracks that aren't."

We fall silent after that, accepting the circumstances as grim as they are. Shea steps carefully and searches thoroughly, tasting the night wind with her tongue. I focus on her movements and try not to imagine my sister beyond the veil, clutched in Silvain's taloned grasp, or Brend tearing her apart, the king smiling from afar.

The sky overhead is sprinkled with stars and the moon is bright, but the trees barely break the harsh gales slamming into our bodies. We push forward against the icy gusts, lips and noses turning cold, tears streaming from our eyes. We hold hands, fighting the night together. Our boots crunch snow that's hard underfoot, as if we're walking on stones.

I'm not sure how much time has passed when Shea finally spots a trail. My toes are stiff in my boots and my lips are ice. Shea kneels to inspect the tracks while I wait with Colette, my body quivering.

Shea looks up at us. Her cheeks are red even amid yellow lantern light. "Bear prints. Partials. Come. They lead this way."

The wind whirs and howls as we follow the trail. Shea loses the tracks to snow a few times, and although I groan, she remains patient and attentive. She always manages to stay on course until the tracks reappear. Yet with each step, the fluttering in my stomach grows and grows, almost to the point of aching. Eirwyn is out here somewhere, in this world or the next. My sister, who buys me ginger spice tea. Who braids my hair anytime I ask. Who shot a bear with an arrow to save me. Who used her faerie magic to heal a boy with a curse.

I make a vow to whoever might be listening: I'll do anything to see her safe. Abandon the wood. Let Brend stay in our lives forever. Answer any question villagers ask of me—

"Did you see that?" Shea's voice stops me from making more silent promises.

"See what?" asks Colette.

"A tall blur up ahead," Shea says, pointing. "It disappeared around that pine."

I take off, the lantern swinging wildly as I bolt toward the tree. Of course, Shea and Colette shout after me, and naturally, I don't stop or look back. I run against the wind and the night, toward the blur that might be Brend.

It *is* him, trudging naked through the snow, hugging himself to fight the cold. "Brend!"

He turns, eyes widening and shoulders sinking in relief. I rush forward and throw a coat around his shoulders, and then he gathers me in a fierce embrace.

"You found me," he says against my ear, his voice quiet beneath the roar of the wind.

"We did," I correct, pulling back and gesturing to Shea and Colette, who are catching up.

"You couldn't have waited?" asks Shea.

But Colette gets right to the point: "Where's Eirwyn?"

If Brend's surprised to see them with me, he doesn't show it. He pulls his coat tighter around himself and says, "Silvain forced me to start changing. He and Eirwyn disappeared before the transformation was complete."

Disappeared? There's only one place they could go.

"I was right," I say. "Silvain took her beyond the veil."

"Well, let's go after them," says Shea. "You can take us, right?"

Colette shakes her head. "You can't go, Shea. Humans aren't safe beyond the veil. Tamsin said the magic of that place is much too strong."

"She's right," I say. "I've felt the pull myself, and I have faerie blood."

Shea crosses her arms against her chest, her lantern banging against her hip. "What about Brend? He's human."

"As a changeling, he grew up with faeries," Colette explains. "He possesses faerie magic."

"Brend isn't going either," I decide, watching him shiver. "He needs to get out of this weather before he catches frostbite." With Eirwyn not around to heal him, I can't risk his safety.

Brend takes my arm. "I am the only one other than you who has spent time in the faerie realm."

"You're no help without your memories," I remind him. "Shea will take you home."

Shea's eyes are determined as they meet mine. "I don't want you doing this alone."

"I won't be alone," I tell her, claiming Colette's hand. "We'll find Eirwyn together."

Shea responds with a curt nod. I'm relieved she trusts me, even after all I kept from her. Addressing Colette, she says, "Look out for each other, then."

"We will," Colette answers.

Shea takes me by the shoulders. "Come back. You, Colette, and Eirwyn. All right?"

I press my forehead to hers, breathing in her scent, the scent of home. "All right."

"Brend can't last much longer in the cold," murmurs Colette.

I pull back. "Right."

Shea dips her head and heads in the direction we came, gesturing for Brend to follow. Instead, he lingers, bare feet buried in snow.

"I'll bring her home," I tell him.

"Be careful," he says.

I nod, and Brend finally turns to follow Shea. As they're swallowed up by the trees, I say to Colette, "Every time I've gone to the faerie realm, it's because I've called upon you or Brend to change. If I turn you into a fox, you might run away."

"Don't make me change," Colette says. "Think back to what happened in the cellar."

I blush as I remember our time together. "What do you mean?"

"You took away our glamour, but you didn't cross beyond the veil either time. Maybe that means you're learning to control your magic. If that's true, a command could be enough."

She's right. A command was enough to keep me here after I changed Tamsin, when Brend was caught in the traps. Maybe it'll be enough for this too.

I press a cold kiss to her lips. "All right, I'll try."

I close my eyes and see the faerie realm in my mind, sapphire-rimmed leaves and creatures with skin made of bark. I think of Eirwyn, of my desperation to see her well and whole again.

I say the words: "Take us beyond the veil."

CHAPTER 23

This time, crossing beyond the veil is like wiping a palm across a foggy window.

Despite the late hour, the world before me brightens with the aid of the blue light, and what was once dulled by darkness is now sharp. Each tree is defined. Each evergreen needle is distinct from the others in its cluster, and the stars overhead are so clear that they seem closer than the rest of the sky. Azure dust falls around us like snow. The cold has a taste, almost sweet like a pastry.

Night wind moves branches hemmed in sapphire light, every creak crisp in my ears. The trees sway to a thrumming beat I can feel more than hear, and the rhythm makes me want to run, run until I'm out of breath and my limbs ache, run until I'm consumed. As I said to Shea, even with faerie blood, the temptation to stray is nearly irresistible.

I notice a familiar scent in the air, the scent of roses. I look down at my arms and find the latticework of green vines. This time, crossing beyond the veil removed my glamour entirely.

Colette's glamour has also washed away. Grinning, she leans and bends like the trees, fox tail twitching. "I've imagined this place so many times since Tamsin told me who I was. I never imagined this."

Something sharp twinges in my chest. Colette's already enamored with the realm of her birth. But I don't want her to belong here, because despite how alluring this place is, I know I don't belong here. I don't want her to love a place that I'm not part of.

I squeeze her hand. "Let's start searching."

We leave our lanterns behind because we no longer need them to see. I try to track Eirwyn like Shea would, but there are no footprints to follow. Snow that once crunched underfoot remains perfectly intact like thick panes of glass. Our boots tap against the surface but can't break through.

I release a frustrated breath. "I don't know how to find her."

Colette's nose wrinkles. "Maybe I can catch the scent of her trail. I'm a fox, after all."

She pauses to sniff bark and branches, though nothing seems to spark her interest as we continue. Rather than hooting owls and rabbits rustling in bushes, long sighs, whispers, and bouts of laughter accompany our search, the sounds eerie enough to prickle my skin. I tug Colette closer to my side, certain we're being watched. No faeries stray onto our path, though they must be nearby.

I wonder what they see when they look at me: a girl dressed as a faerie or a faerie who pretended to be a human girl?

The longer we walk, the more exhaustion takes over. I rested while waiting for Shea, but clearly not enough. My vision turns hazy with the desire for sleep. I yearn to curl up atop the glassy snow and cover my ears against the sound of giggling, nap for a while beneath the cobalt stars. Perhaps when I wake, Eirwyn will be kneeling beside me, brushing back my hair, whispering that it's time to go home . . . .

A tug from Colette's hand jostles me out of my stupor. "You were veering off."

I stop dragging my feet and shake myself awake. "Catch anything yet?"

Colette shakes her head. I tell her to keep trying.

We travel through the blue-hemmed night, eerie chatter encroaching from either side. I'm lightheaded thinking of it swallowing us whole before we find Eirwyn, keeping us prisoner in the faerie wood until we're long forgotten by the village. We've already been here much longer than my past trips beyond the veil, and we're still a long way from finding my sister. Will I be strong enough to bring both Colette and Eirwyn back with me? I couldn't bear to leave either of them behind.

Colette's head snaps up. "Ro, I think I smell—"

"You should not be here," interrupts Tamsin, stepping out of the shadows. "This place is not safe for you."

I move to stand in front of Colette. "You are what's not safe for her."

Tamsin glares at me, yellow eyes narrowed. "You are lucky that I have made a vow not to harm you."

"Tamsin, please," says Colette. "Ro is not my enemy."

"But she is mine," argues Colette's aunt. "She ruined every-thing by saving that boy."

I clench my fists. "That boy's name is Brend, and I won't let you harm him again."

"Neither will I," says Colette, stepping out from my protec-tive shadow to stand beside me. "There will be no killing."

Tamsin plucks an azure-lined leaf from its bush and twirls the stem between her fingers. "Then you are as foolish as your friend."

Colette doesn't waver before her aunt. "There must be another way to end the curses."

"There is not, which is why you should not be here." Tamsin flicks the leaf away. It spins as it flutters to the ground. "Until you defeat the bear and claim your place, you are vulnerable to the faeries who would like to see you fail."

I shiver, thinking of the evergreen faerie and how she lamented the fact that I hadn't let Brend finish what he started. "Can't those faeries reach her on the other side too? You can."

"I am strong enough to cross between realms." She lifts her brow at me. "Most of us never come close to attempting such a feat, let alone mastering it. It is why we could do little as your village chipped away at our forests."

I roll my eyes. "We're not here to debate the strife between humans and faeries."

"Then why are you here?" asks Tamsin.

"To find Ro's sister," explains Colette. "She was taken by King Silvain."

Tamsin nods. "Yes, he holds her captive in his court."

I step forward, prepared to beg if I must. "Please, take us to her."

I don't like Tamsin, and I don't trust her, but I need to reach Eirwyn as soon as possible. Silvain may simply be holding her captive, but he could be doing a lot worse.

Tamsin chuckles. "You are a brave one indeed, Roisin. But you will never save her on your own."

"All right, then help us."

The faerie scoffs, crossing her arms against her fox-furred chest. "Why would I? Your sister would not be here if you had not interfered last night. If you had let the bear die, all of this would be—"

"Stop," I shout, because every minute I waste listening to Tamsin's condescension is another minute without Eirwyn. Because even while my skin is tight with exhaustion and my chest aches with desperation to save my sister, my limbs still beg for me to lose myself. To abandon all pursuits except the thrill of magic. The contrast is maddening, and I'm not sure how much longer I can stand it. "I didn't ask for any of this."

Tamsin's scowl deepens. I've offended her with my outburst. Colette knows it too. She touches my shoulder lightly, a gentle warning to keep my emotions under control. But how can I, with Eirwyn trapped in the court of a faerie king? With Colette and Brend's lives at constant risk?

"Tamsin," addresses Colette, "you're the first blood relative I've ever known. I trusted you, and for that, you nearly turned me into a killer." Colette pauses, and this time I lay a hand on her shoulder, a gesture to ask if she's all right. Gathering my meaning, she nods before facing her aunt once more. "But if you help us save Ro's sister, I might be willing to forgive you."

Tamsin's scowl falters. Her hands fall to her sides. A small hope blooms within me. Colette's words are affecting her.

"If you care for me at all—if this isn't about winning for you—then you'll help us."

Tamsin groans, fox face turned up to the dark blue sky. "Child, it is because I care for you that I so desperately want you to win. You are not safe until this conflict is over."

Unease turns the hope blooming inside me to rot. Appealing to Tamsin's emotions isn't enough. She's too sensible. She needs a worthwhile reason to help us rescue Eirwyn.

"What if I use my voice to end the curses in Colette's favor?" If Silvain thinks I'm powerful enough to secure his reign, I must be powerful enough to end his magic. I add, "Without any death."

Tamsin shakes her head. "You are gifted, girl, but you would need more time to reach the level of power required to end a curse, let alone two curses."

"Then we'll get time," I say. "Once Eirwyn is safe with us, we'll leave the wood. We'll hide until I'm strong enough."

We'll go to Violet Ridge like Brend planned to before he missed Silvain's deadline. If I haven't lifted the curses by spring, we'll cross the river to Poppy and I'll keep trying. Whatever it takes to see Brend and Colette free and alive.

"If there's a chance this can end without bloodshed, let us take it," Colette implores, striding to meet Tamsin. She grasps her aunt's unwilling hands. "When I'm free, I can return to you, and we can be a proper family. You promised you would tell me about my mother."

"Better that you run and not return," says Tamsin, fox nose twitching as she pulls from her niece's grip. "If Roisin manages to lift your curse, you will be safe from every faerie except the one who matters. Silvain will not like that you have tampered with tradition."

In that case, I want to promise that we'll stay away forever. As painful as it will be to leave the western wood behind, it's something I'll have to do anyway if I hope to avoid serving a king. Trouble is, I'm not certain Colette would agree to leave forever. She seems intent on knowing this realm, knowing everything that's been kept from her. She has every right to, but to me, her safety matters more. Her safety and Brend's. My own.

"Silvain doesn't have to know," says Colette. "You told me that when the curse ends, I'll come fully into my magic. If Ro can grant me that with her voice, couldn't my magic act as proof that Brend is dead, even if he isn't?"

"Perhaps." Tamsin crosses her arms, black claws tapping her shoulder. "He would need to stay away, and you would need to be very convincing."

Colette lifts her chin. "I've kept my curse a secret from Nanette. I managed to keep our acquaintance a secret from Ro until last night."

I cringe at the reminder that I was so well fooled. Colette notices and grants me an apologetic smile.

"All right." Tamsin's hands drop to her sides. "I would prefer you proceed according to tradition, but I am not like the king. You are my blood, the blood of my sister, and I will not force your hand. If ending the curses without bloodshed is your wish, I will allow you to try."

Colette beams at her aunt, fox tail swishing. "Thank you, Tamsin, truly."

"And my sister?" I ask.

Tamsin's lips press together for a concerningly long moment. She glances briefly over her shoulder. "Very well. I will help you retrieve her."

Before I can thank her myself, she adds, "On one condition."

"Fine," I grant, wary but willing.

Tamsin blinks slowly, then waves a hand in Colette's direction. In the same instant I register what's occurring, she disappears from the land of blue light.

I gape at the remaining fox faerie. "What did you do?"

Tamsin grins, exposing pointed canines. "Why, I sent her back across the veil. As I said, this place is too dangerous for her. I will not allow her to go anywhere near Silvain's court until she's come fully into her magic."

Burning with indignation, I stare at the place I last saw Colette, debating whether I can use my voice to bring her back.

"Come now or lose my help." Tamsin's tone is frustratingly nonchalant. "It matters not to me what you decide."

She ventures off the path, vanishing into the blue-edged night. Years' worth of stories remind me that nothing good ever comes from following a stranger into the dark. But Tamsin knows where to find my sister. She promised to help me rescue her. It's not like I have another choice.

I run to catch up with her, then match her brisk pace. Tamsin leads me through clumps of swaying trees, her fox claws clacking against the glassy snow. Faerie chatter starts up again, a blend of more voices than before. We follow the sound, follow it to a clearing, and finally, I can match that chatter to mouths.

Hidden from view behind a cluster of bushes, I observe a group of faeries large enough to inhabit a small village. Faeries dressed in ash bark and willow tree vines. With rabbit ears and squirrel tails, raven-black eyes and thorns poking out of skin. Lounging on toadstools the size of beds. Sharing laughter and sipping from flower petal cups. Tossing sticks into a blue-flamed fire.

My eyes stray to a willow vine faerie whose arms reach briefly to the sky; the next moment, a cone of rain showers her companion. The violets in his long hair are drenched, and the willow faerie laughs. The violet faerie smirks and the willow faerie turns to stone. I shudder.

Seems like most faeries have gifts in addition to their flora or fauna natures, like my voice and Eirwyn's healing. Perhaps Colette will have one, too, once her curse is lifted.

Beyond the gathering, Silvain sits upon a massive stone chair draped in blue-laced lichen. A blend of rage and terror burns through me at the sight of him. I don't see my sister anywhere. Beside the king, a small stone throne remains vacant.

Following my gaze, Tamsin murmurs, "That throne is meant for the victor."

Thrones are meant for royalty. I swallow. "Does that mean—"

"Yes," says Tamsin. "Colette is the king's daughter, and Brend is his changeling child. Silvain's magic runs through them both, by blood and by gift."

The missing pieces of the curses finally fit into place. Colette and Brend compete for more than a place beyond the veil. Unbeknownst to them, the bear and the fox are challenging each other for a faerie throne.

"Why did Silvain make his daughter a changeling?"

Experience tells me faeries don't think much of humans. Silvain could have raised Colette here, under his influence, yet he chose to give her to Nanette. I'm glad Colette was raised by a kind woman rather than a cruel king, but I don't understand why Silvain would want that too.

Tamsin's gaze softens to something like sadness. "Each heir must be tested. My sister did not know of this when she fell in love with the king and bore his child. It had been so long since Silvain's own trial, and faerie memories are delicate. But Silvain will not accept Colette until she has proven herself. If she fails, and Brend overcomes her, then he is most worthy to inherit the throne."

"That doesn't seem fair," I argue. "Brend grew up here. Colette thought she was a normal village girl her entire life."

Tamsin nods. "That is why the king revoked the boy's memories. The test is not one of magic. It is cunning versus strength."

Cunning versus strength. The fox versus the bear.

Yet Brend regrets his acts of violence, and Colette regrets tricking Brend into those traps. Neither is suited to the natures dictated to them by this trial.

"Does Colette know?"

Tamsin's eyes snap to me. "She does not know, and you will not tell her. That would violate the rules of the trial. She is already at a disadvantage thanks to your meddling."

As prickly as her insult makes me, I also can't help but understand Tamsin better now. She's giving Colette the chance to prove her wrong, but Tamsin clearly believes the only way to save her niece is through Brend's death, and because I don't want anyone to die, I'm considered a threat. If not for her vow not to harm me, I expect Tamsin would've gotten rid of me by now. Silvain leads with violence, so his subjects must see violence as the solution to every conflict.

I can use my magic for violence, but I can also use it to make peace—to call a lost soul back to themselves, to lower barriers and dissolve secrets. Maybe, if I manage to end the curses with my voice rather than anyone's death, Tamsin will learn there is always another path, another choice.

"Enough talk," says Tamsin. "Silvain sits upon his throne now, but he could decide at any moment to pay a visit to your sister. We need to act while she is the least guarded."

She's right. "What's your plan?"

"Your sister is in the small clearing behind the king's throne," explains Tamsin. "There is enough foliage between them that no one should see you, but you will have to take care of the guard."

My eyes widen. She can't mean—but then again, she wanted Brend to die in those traps. "Take care of, how?"

Tamsin sighs. "With your voice, Roisin. What else?"

"Right," I say, cheeks warming as embarrassed relief moves through me. "What will you do?"

Tamsin sets her gaze on the king. "I will distract Silvain."

CHAPTER 24

Wary of being discovered, I try to move slowly and quietly through the forest that borders the faerie gathering, seeking the smaller clearing Tamsin spoke of.

Once I reach it, I'm supposed to wait for her signal before I rescue Eirwyn. Tamsin will loudly approach the king about something, and that's when I'm meant to use my voice on the guard. Their conversation should obscure any noise our confrontation makes. Then, once the guard is no longer a threat, I'll bring Eirwyn home.

The plan seems manageable until I see the clearing. As I crouch behind a clump of juniper bushes, I get my first glimpse of who guards my sister.

It's the evergreen faerie; the one who spit needles at my face. I had to pull them from my skin like pins from a sewing cushion as blood slipped down my cheeks. A bolt of fear strikes me at the thought of facing her again.

Eirwyn sits upon a snow-covered log. Her glamour was also removed by coming here, and the white blooms in her hair shine brightly amid the blue-hued night. From this distance, I can't see any cuts or bruises. She doesn't look like she's in pain—only frightened.

The evergreen faerie's gaze is severe, determined. Based on her rigid posture, she's alert for any sign of trouble. Trouble, meaning me. The evergreen faerie already knows I can cross beyond the veil, and Silvain knows about my voice. He's probably told all his subjects about me.

I haven't made enough noise to garner the evergreen faerie's attention, but I need to remain as still as possible while I wait. These juniper bushes seem thick enough to shield the red blooms in my hair; still, the distance between us is a bit vast for my liking. Once I hear the signal, I'll need to move quickly before she spits needles at me again.

"How much longer?" Eirwyn asks.

The sound of my sister's voice tempts me to forget the plan and charge into the clearing. Maybe I could take her hand and bring us back to our realm before the evergreen faerie has the chance to strike. Yet I know the thought is foolish before it's over. My magic has never worked that quickly or seamlessly before. I've grown stronger since I first changed Colette from fox to girl, but each act of magic still comes with struggle.

"I would not be so eager to hear his majesty's judgment of

you," says the evergreen faerie in reply. "King Silvain is not known for his mercy."

Clearly shaken, Eirwyn falls silent, and the urge to intervene grows. I shift uncomfortably in my crouched position, the muscles in my legs already aching. When will Tamsin act? Before we parted, she was concerned about not having enough time. Now she seems to be wasting the little time we do have.

Unless this was all a trick, and Tamsin never intended to help me rescue Eirwyn.

Perhaps she's quietly alerting Silvain of my presence as I wait. I'm the fool he'll capture, too, and no one on our side will be able to reach us—not Colette, not Brend, not Shea or Deidra. The changeling conflict will continue without interference, and either the bear or the fox will die.

With dark thoughts like these, acting before Tamsin's signal seems more appealing with each passing moment. I press my palms to the glass-like snow, ready to propel myself forward.

Then a muffled shouting starts up, and I can tell it comes from the large clearing where the faeries are gathered. I recognize Tamsin's sharp tone as she confronts the king, though I can't comprehend what she's saying; I'm too far away. Besides, the content of their conversation isn't what I'm meant to focus on. Eirwyn is the priority.

As the evergreen faerie turns her head toward the sound, I launch myself forward. Juniper branches catch on my clothes and the rose vines in my hair, but I don't let them stop my momentum. I burst into the clearing and tell Eirwyn to cover her ears. After what happened to Brend in the traps, I don't want to risk her changing along with the evergreen faerie.

Eirwyn looks startled to see me but doesn't question the order. She covers her ears as I open my mouth to issue the command, "Change."

The evergreen faerie's head snaps in my direction. Her eyes blaze with rage. "How dare you—"

"Change," I say again, relieved as the faerie begins to tremble. Too late, I realize it's not because of my magic.

Needles spray from her body. I shout for Eirwyn to get down, but I slip on glassy snow as I attempt to evade their path. My back hits the ground with a sickening thwack. Dizzy with pain, I watch the needles soar over me. I don't hear Eirwyn scream, meaning she must have moved in time. That's one thing to be grateful for.

But it's over; I've failed. I can't make another stand against the evergreen faerie. The pain in my back is too intense to fight through. Besides, someone from the other clearing must have heard me shouting. They'll be here soon to assist with my capture. Tamsin was right; I might be gifted, but I'm not strong enough to rival the faeries of the western wood.

A hand covers my shoulder, tender but urging. "Get up, Ro," says Eirwyn.

Heat blooms where she touches me, but when it's over, all the pain in my back has subsided. "How—"

"Her name is Lydie," says Eirwyn. "If that helps."

My sister pulls me to my feet. It's not only the pain from the fall that's gone. My exhaustion has left me too. The evergreen faerie is hunched over, heaving loud breaths. It must have taken a lot of strength to send that spray of needles at me, and she doesn't have a sister to heal her.

Reinvigorated by Eirwyn's magic, I issue a new command. "Change, Lydie," I say, putting all my new strength behind those two words.

Her body starts trembling in a familiar way. I'm relieved as the change rapidly overtakes her. I've never tried to compel faeries with flora natures. I've only ever changed faeries to their animal selves. So, I suppose I have the right to be a little shocked when Lydie the evergreen faerie becomes an evergreen tree.

"She'll be able to change back, right?" asks Eirwyn.

"I think so," I say. "I hope so."

The evergreen faerie terrifies me, but I don't want her to remain a tree forever. Just long enough for my sister and I to escape.

"Worry not. She will return to herself in time," says a new voice. "In fact, you will be here to witness it."

Eirwyn mutters a curse. My heartbeat spikes to a faster rhythm. I was right; someone heard our confrontation. The very someone I was hoping to avoid. With my newfound strength, I'm confident I can dispatch another faerie like Lydie.

King Silvain is a different matter entirely.

Together, we turn to face our adversary. He hasn't come alone. Graeme stands beside him. The oak faerie betrays no noticeable concern for our predicament, twig hands clasped loosely at his middle. The king, however, simmers.

"Roisin, I am impressed," says the king, sounding anything but. "How did you convince Tamsin to aid you? She has such intolerance for most folk."

"Perhaps the Red Rose promised her something," suggests Graeme, his tone cold and distant. Nothing like the gentle faerie who sat at our table and spoke of our father.

"Ah, yes." Silvain snaps his talons, the crack loud enough to make Eirwyn startle beside me. "Perhaps you promised to help my daughter defeat the changeling boy? Much as I admire my girl's cleverness, I must remind you that interference is against the rules."

"Daughter?" murmurs Eirwyn, and I squeeze her arm, a silent vow to explain everything so long as we make it through this.

"I want nothing to do with your cruel traditions." I make the declaration clear and loud. Though I fully intend to end the curses, it's safer if Silvain and his subjects believe I'm done meddling. "I only want to take my sister home."

Silvain's feathers ruffle. "I would rather you both stay. Your sixteenth birthday cannot be too far off, can it?"

I let every ounce of my revulsion seep into my first command. "Change, King Silvain."

Perfectly still, the owl faerie chuckles. "You will have to do far better than that."

Eirwyn's hand settles upon my shoulder. Warmth pulses through me. I try again: "Change, King Silvain."

This time, a visible tremor ripples across the king's feathers. His round yellow eyes blink once. "That is quite enough, Red Rose."

He lifts his taloned hands and a wall of fire ignites between us, stretching so high that the king is almost entirely obscured from my view. The blaze is startling, but I don't let the loss of visibility deter me. "Change, Silvain."

The fire's smoke makes me cough, but dropping his title

seems to improve the effect of my magic. Through the haze of flame, Silvain struggles to contain himself. "Change, Silvain," I say again, my voice a rasp. Eirwyn lays another hand on my shoulder, and my next command is clearer. "Change, now."

The king grunts and a flame leaps from the wall of fire, headed toward us. Eirwyn screams, ducking to avoid being burned. I stagger at the loss of her magic, my throat hoarse again, the nearness of the flames searing my face with incredible heat. I don't know if I have another command in me.

But maybe I've done enough. "Graeme," says the king, the name unsteady as it leaves his beak. "Do something."

"Of course, your majesty," replies the oak faerie, before shoving the king toward the fire.

I stare, open mouthed and gasping against a flood of smoke, as the king's own flames singe his feathers and he cries out in agony. The smell of him burning is nauseating. I cover my mouth and nose with both hands as I try not to gag.

Behind the screaming king, Graeme shouts, "Go. Go, now!"

"Ro," says Eirwyn, shaking me. "Come on."

I blink rapidly then voice the words, "Take us home."

The smoke and screams disappear, replaced with a dim, cold wood. Eirwyn and I cough into the quiet, bent over with our hands braced against our knees. Even in the predawn dark, I can see that our glamour has returned. No vines trace the back of my hands. The bite of smoke is the only smell in the air.

"We need to run," gasps my sister, "before he follows us."

"I don't think he can," I say.

"Do you need more healing?"

I almost tell her yes. But then I'd have to clarify that I don't require healing in a physical sense. The smoke in my lungs is already clearing, but perhaps not the damage done by witnessing a king ravaged by flame.

I meant for Silvain to change. I meant to burden him with his animal form while I saved my sister. Yet my magic began a chain reaction of so much more. So much more violence than I intended. I judged Tamsin for only seeing one path forward, and I ended up on that same path.

Numbly, I follow my sister through the shadowy wood as dawn approaches. I'm in no mood for conversation, but I make sure to inform her where Colette's allegiances lie. Unlike my initial reaction to Brend, Eirwyn is ready to give Colette another chance, proving again who is the kinder sister.

Then Eirwyn provides the details about her ordeal with the faerie king. She and Brend were having tea when Silvain appeared inside the cottage. He yanked her from her chair and drew a dagger down her arm, making her bleed until Brend became so distraught his limbs started trembling and he was forced to leave the cottage. Then the king brought Eirwyn beyond the veil.

"He wanted to know where you were," shares my sister, "but I didn't know, and Brend wouldn't tell him."

"I was in the cellar with Colette," I tell her. "We didn't hear a thing. I'm so sorry."

"You don't need to apologize." Eirwyn presses closer to me as she avoids a tree branch heavy with snow. "We all forgot about the deadline, and everything happened so fast. I'm just glad you found me."

"We found Brend first." I shiver, remembering his bare

feet in the snow, even though Eirwyn's the one wearing only a sweater and skirt. "He told us that you and Silvain disappeared. We knew that meant he'd taken you beyond the veil."

As we near the edge of the wood, Eirwyn explains that Silvain put her in the clearing to await judgment for her misdeeds. "I was prepared to ask for a cloth to bind my wound, but the cut had already healed."

"Then you healed me with one touch after I fell," I add. "You know, Lydie changed faster than anyone else I've commanded."

I still needed to say her name, but that's nothing compared to how much I struggled with Tamsin.

"The faerie realm must strengthen our magic," concludes my sister, grinning. "I wonder if it's permanent, or if repeated trips beyond the veil are necessary."

Thanks to our encounter with Silvain, I'm not thrilled by the idea of more visits to the faerie realm, or the idea of strengthening my magic, even though that's what I've promised Tamsin I'll do in order to end the curses. But I don't mention my reservations to my sister, who's endured enough tonight. If the thought of fortifying her magic is lifting her spirits, I won't ruin that.

We leave the forest, intending to go straight to Deidra and Shea's cottage, but light in our cottage windows draws us to our own door instead. Inside, we find Colette scrubbing blood and tea off the floor. The broken cups have been swept up and the chairs returned to their upright positions. The fire burns bright.

Colette turns when the front door closes. A few of her braids cling to her sweaty cheeks. She also wears her glamour, fox ears and tail hidden by magic, the dust of freckles on her cheeks free of whiskers. She's a faerie, yes, but right now she looks like the girl from the village who makes me blush. After all I've seen tonight, and all I've heard, the sight of her is a balm.

Colette drops her rag onto the floor. "I didn't know what else to do while I waited."

I run to her, throwing myself into her embrace. I press a cold cheek to her warm one, drawing comfort. Compared to me, she's slight. But she's steady like the trees, and we fit together in a way I didn't know was possible. I never want to let go.

"You smell like smoke," she says, holding me tight. "What happened?"

The words leave me in a rush: "Silvain is your father."

CHAPTER 25

I'm not surprised when Colette immediately pulls back from me, her honey eyes wide with shock. Though I never intended to keep Tamsin's secret, I hadn't planned on shattering Colette's world the moment we reunited.

"Sorry." I wince. "I could've said that more delicately."

I just hated the idea of keeping any more secrets from her.

"No, I'm glad you told me." Colette puts a hand to her temple as if she's already developed an ache. "I suppose that makes a great deal of sense."

"There's more," I say. "But I think Brend needs to hear it too."

"Let's go to Deidra and Shea's," suggests Eirwyn. "We should all be on equal footing about this."

Colette helps me put out the fire, then the three of us trudge through the snow to reach Deidra and Shea's cottage. Inside, hugs and relieved greetings are exchanged, except between Brend and Colette, who regard each other warily. When everyone else moves further into the sitting room, Colette lingers by the door. I return to her and take her hand. Her skin is clammy.

"It's all right," I murmur gently. "He won't hurt you."

Brend approaches cautiously, hands behind his back, lips tight. "I do not feel a change coming on. Do you?"

Colette shakes her head, but her discomfort is clear. I'm not exactly pleased with the situation either. Neither of them trembles now, but with a fox and bear in the same room, anything is possible.

"I want to take this opportunity to apologize," Brend says then, "for all the times I have chased you, and hurt you, as a bear."

"Thank you." Colette draws a noticeable breath. "I'm sorry for leading you to those traps. I won't try to put you in danger again."

I squeeze Colette's hand and grin at Brend, proud of them for taking this first step toward reconciliation. They've each been influenced by faeries and faerie magic, but they're choosing not to let those influences win. While I may not see friendship in their future, the potential for allyship is promising.

We all take a seat at the dining table, Orla swaddled in Deidra's arms. As best I can, I relay what I learned from Tamsin regarding the changeling conflict, and then Eirwyn shares what happened with Silvain.

"Do you think he's dead?" asks Shea, arms crossed as she leans back in her chair.

"No," I admit. I never saw him change, so I have to imagine that once we crossed back to our side, Silvain found the will to put out his flames. I *have* to imagine that, because to believe otherwise . . .

A shiver runs through me. It feels impossible to even think of another outcome.

"At least we know he is not infallible," says Brend.

"Doesn't mean we can risk staying here," murmurs Colette. "We should keep our promise to Tamsin. Find a place to hide so you can strengthen your magic, Ro."

"We might've already found a way to do that." Eirwyn nudges my shoulder with hers. "The faerie realm invigorated our gifts. Maybe, if we get far enough away from the western wood, we can cross safely to gain more strength."

"Does the faerie realm exist anywhere else?" Deidra wonders aloud.

"We'll find out," declares my sister. "So long as we're all agreed, the four of us will leave for Violet Ridge once we've rested."

Shea's eyebrows slant. "The four of you?"

Eirwyn stammers, "You don't mean to come with us?"

Shea scoffs. "I'm not about to let you travel on your own. I happen to know someone in Violet Ridge. A fellow fisherwoman who might let you stay in her cottage while she's away. I'll take you to her, and I'll only leave once I know you're safe."

Deidra places her hand over Shea's in silent agreement. "You also need time to gather supplies. The folk of Violet Ridge struggle just as we do. Even if Shea's friend can offer shelter, you aren't likely to find any handouts in the way of food or clothes."

"All right," says Eirwyn, "then we'll leave after we've gathered and packed enough for the journey. Agreed?"

Though I'm still sorting through my feelings regarding my magic, I know leaving Sugar Maple is the safest course for Brend and Colette, so I murmur my assent along with everyone else. Everyone else except Brend.

"What is it?" I ask him, curious to know his reservations, to see if they match my own.

His voice is hushed as he says, "Perhaps we should not run."

"Are you not keen on having your curse lifted?" asks Colette. "Or are you disappointed that our plan means you won't inherit the faerie throne?"

"I have no desire for a throne," Brend assures her. "I simply wonder if now is not the best time to strike at Silvain again, while he is weak. If we kill him, we do not have to run. Our curses might even be lifted with his death, since he is the one who enacted them."

Seems our reservations are hardly similar at all. I'm worried my magic is growing beyond my intentions, while Brend speaks calmly about ending a life. He promised not to harm Colette. Maybe I was wrong to assume there'd be no more talk of violence. Perhaps there's more bear in him than I realized.

"You can't know that for sure," says Eirwyn.

Brend shrugs. "But would his death not be helpful regardless? It would give us time to figure out the curses without us being under threat, and we would not need to run."

Across the table, I meet Colette's wounded gaze. She only just learned the identity of her father. He might be cruel and unyielding, but he's her blood. My own father lied to me about so many things. Bargained me away to a faerie king. And still, I'd use the power in my voice to call him back from the dead if I could. It helps to have good memories to balance the bad, but I know how much Colette wants to understand her past. Silvain's death would mean so many of her questions left unanswered.

"No," I decide. "Going after Silvain is too risky. I saw how many faeries he has under his command. Running is the better choice."

Brend doesn't voice any protest, but tension hangs in the air, dissipated only by Deidra's heavy sigh. "There's another matter we should discuss. The matter of protection until you leave here." Deidra glances at her wife, lifting her eyebrows in a silent question. Shea bites her lip, then nods. I watch their wordless conversation, remembering how Ma and Pa used to do this too. I'd try to decipher the meaning behind each glance, but never could.

Addressing the rest of us, Deidra says, "Since we brought Orla into our lives, I've spent more time studying wards—gems and even household goods that can keep a faerie from entering the home. If we put up these wards and they hold, they can protect against any faerie intrusion while we prepare the supplies you'll need for Violet Ridge."

After successfully using the apophyllite for the glamour ritual, I trust whatever crystals Deidra has to offer. "All right, let's do that."

"Do we have enough wards for both cottages?" asks Eirwyn. "That way Brend and Colette won't have to share a space."

"I'll have to sort through what I have, but I think it will be enough," says Deidra.

"All right, then Colette will stay here with us," says Shea. "Brend can keep staying with you, Eirwyn."

"What about me?" I ask. "I can't be in two places at once. What if someone changes?"

"I think you're better off staying with Brend and your sister," says Deidra. "If Colette changes, Shea and I can handle a fox better than Eirwyn could handle a bear."

I swallow my disappointment. Deidra's logic is, unfortunately, sound. I hate the idea of being parted from Colette, but if I insist we all stay in the same cottage, I'll put everyone in danger.

"It's nearly morning," says Deidra. "Let's place the wards here, then get some rest. We'll work on the other cottage after we've all slept."

While Shea excuses herself to change Orla, Eirwyn and Brend follow Deidra to where she keeps her crystals, leaving Colette and me lingering beside the dining table.

We step into an embrace without speaking, arms wrapped tightly around each other. "I hate this," murmurs Colette.

"Me too." I brush my lips across her cheek. "But we'll be together once we leave."

Colette stiffens against me. "For how long?"

The fact that she's even voicing the question tells me that, despite what she's learned of her father, she plans to return here as soon as her curse is lifted. She's already made peace with inheriting a faerie throne if it means knowing her heritage, her past. She suspects I feel differently because following her would mean serving the king. Her suspicion is correct.

But I used all my boldness rescuing Eirwyn and facing Silvain. I'm not ready for another confrontation.

Stepping out of Colette's embrace, I say, "Let's see if Deidra needs help with the wards."

I make sure to leave her before her eyes can name me a coward.

Under Deidra's instruction, we sprinkle salt along the front doorway and every window ledge to prevent faeries from crossing inside.

Then we place quartz at the North-, East-, South-, and West-most points of the cottage, along with selenite outside the door. The crystals will protect against outside magic, meaning Silvain, or any faerie like him, won't be able to cross from the faerie realm directly into the cottage like he did when he stole Eirwyn.

The wards don't affect faeries already within the home, so those of us with faerie magic won't be forced out. But for one of us to leave, we have to disturb the salt line, which will temporarily lift the ward and require someone else to repair the break.

The sun is rising by the time the wards are set, but we can't sleep until we know they work. I become the ward tester. Deidra disturbs the salt line, and then I wait in the early morning cold while she repairs it. She calls for me to attempt crossing the threshold, and I warily approach the open doorway, hands splayed out in front of me as if feeling for the knob of an oil lamp in the dark.

"Don't be shy about it," Deidra says. "We need to test the

strength of these wards, and the best way for you to do that is to act as if you don't know they're there."

I draw a deep breath and let my hands fall to my sides. Then I stride forward with purpose, only to be knocked backward by an unseen force as I try to enter the cottage.

I fall to my bottom, sending a spray of snow into the air. Deidra gasps but a startled grin stretches Colette's lips, having witnessed me taken down by a line of salt. She must notice my scowl because she risks a trip outside to offer me her hand. She's not wearing her boots, so she bounces from foot to foot while waiting for me to grasp her fingers.

"Come on," she urges.

Maybe it's the fact that we're about to be parted again, or I'm simply delirious from the last few adventurous nights, but I have another idea in mind. Without warning, I grab Colette's hand and yank her down to the snow with me. She yelps as I erupt in laughter.

In retaliation, she tosses a handful of snow at my face. Ice-kissed lips sputtering, I smack the ground with my hand so a wave of fresh snow descends upon her, prompting Colette to shriek. I'm grinning so wide my cheeks hurt, and she seems equally gleeful. It's so rare that we're able to have fun together like this.

"All right, enough playing," Deidra says, stepping over the threshold. "We have more wards to test."

I look at Colette, and Colette looks back at me.

Deidra realizes our unspoken agreement too late, lips parting in protest only to catch a mouthful of snow.

After truces are promised and faces wiped clean, we decide to test the crystals. I step outside again, then close my eyes and utter the words that take me beyond the veil.

The cottage is gone when I open my eyes to the faerie realm, replaced by a clearing of glassy snow so bright that spots dance across my vision until my eyes adjust. It's my first visit here during the morning, and the rising sun is blue like the moon, but a paler shade that brings more light to the realm. I lift my chin, basking in the strange rays of warmth.

I check for signs of faeries, scanning the line of trees leading to the western wood. When my search brings up nothing, I move to stand where the cottage would be if it were in the faerie realm with me. I command myself to return to my realm, but nothing changes. I try a few more times to be safe, but I can't cross back.

If I can't cross, that means other faeries can't either, so our plan will work. Thanks to Deidra's wards, we'll be safe in our cottages until we leave for Violet Ridge. That also means Deidra, Shea, and Orla will remain safe after we've gone.

Brimming with hopeful energy, I return to where I first crossed the veil, but before I utter my next command, I see a spot of color in the distance. As that color moves closer, I discern the copper fur and raven hair of a familiar fox faerie. *Tamsin.*

"Clever," she says by way of greeting, one sharp black claw pointing to the space behind me, where she must know Deidra and Shea's cottage resides in my realm. "Most villagers do not believe in wards nor understand how to use them."

"Is it enough to protect us until we leave?"

Tamsin's lips purse as she considers. "The wards should hold against the king's subjects, so long as you keep them in place."

A bit of relief joins my hopeful feeling. A bit of pride, too, for Deidra's wards. Then I realize what Tamsin hasn't said.

"What about Silvain?" I ask.

"He requires a day or two to recover, but after that . . ." Tamsin sighs. "There is no ward strong enough to defy him."

All my hope and relief drain away until my stomach feels sour with dread. "Then we'll gather what we need quickly."

"See that you do." Tamsin turns, presenting a fox tail that's lost half its length, the new tip coated in dried blood. I suck in a breath through my teeth, horrified.

"He will take the rest if I disobey him a second time." Tamsin faces me again, and I'm grateful not to have to look at the severed tail any longer. "He could do worse to Colette. Until she inherits her full power, she is vulnerable. You all are."

"I understand." I bite my lip, hesitant to make the offer, but knowing Eirwyn would chastise me if she learned I didn't. "Why don't you come with us?"

I can't say I enjoy Tamsin's company, but I don't want Colette's aunt to be tortured again.

She shakes her head. "I belong in my realm. Besides, I am working as discreetly as I can to find supporters for Colette. She'll need them if you succeed but Silvain finds out the trial was ended without bloodshed."

"I hope he doesn't."

"Hope is a fickle thing," says Tamsin. "I would trust your magic over that."

I speak my command then, having heard enough, but Tamsin's dark warnings and bloodied tail seem to follow me back to my realm.

Though I inform Colette of my unexpected meeting with Tamsin, I don't mention her aunt's torture at Silvain's hand. The last thing Colette needs after a night of no sleep is to lie awake feeling guilty that Tamsin helped us. A better time to explain will come.

Besides, Tamsin's warning is troubling enough. If Silvain needs only a few days to recover, that means either we didn't hurt him as badly as we thought, or he's stronger than we realized. Whatever the case, we can't risk facing him again. We must leave here before he attempts another confrontation.

With the wards successfully tested, it's time for much-needed rest. The cottage has one bedroom, so Shea brings armfuls of blankets to the sitting room. Eirwyn sleeps on the cushioned bench, Brend on the floor before the fire. Colette and I lay blankets near the dining table.

Colette falls asleep with her forehead pressed to my shoulder, but it seems like I can't keep my eyes closed for more than a few minutes at a time, continually jerked awake by the terror that someone will change while I'm sleeping, or that a faerie will somehow find a way past the wards.

It doesn't help that the world beyond the cottage is so bright. The curtains are drawn, but tiny beams of light slip through, reminding me that I'm trying to sleep during the day. It also doesn't help that I'm on the floor rather than my bed, and that there's a pretty girl beside me, dark lashes fluttering against her soft brown skin as she dreams.

Restless, I rise to tend the fire, trying not to think of Silvain as I do—his wall of flame, the acrid scent of burning feathers. I'm quiet as I shift the coals to make room for new wood, but not quiet enough for Brend. He sits up as I'm reaching for the log.

"Ro?" he whispers.

"Yes?"

"I have not asked if you are all right."

I place the log on the fire and wait for the satisfying crackle as it catches before answering, "And?"

"Are you all right?"

"Yes," I say, then, "No. I don't know."

I pad across the room, past a sleeping Colette to the kitchen. I grab a knife and cut into a loaf of bread before slathering a piece with cherry jam. I stuff the slice into my mouth, tartness flooding my tongue as I chew.

Brend joins me then, glancing briefly at the mess I've made on the counter before remarking, "I wonder if you sometimes eat to avoid conversation."

Pointing to my full cheeks, I shrug. I can't answer either way.

Brend picks up the knife and cuts a much neater slice, then manages to make the act of spreading jam appear elegant. I glare at him, still chewing, as he takes his first bite.

I swallow and wipe my mouth free of crumbs. "Would you truly kill Silvain?"

Brend clears his throat. "If I felt there was no other choice, yes."

"He raised you."

His brows draw together. "I have no memory of that."

I hold back a groan, mindful that the rest of the household still sleeps. "But you will, once your curse is lifted."

Brend nudges crumbs into a tiny pile on the counter. "Silvain hardly seems like the fatherly type. I doubt any of those memories will be pleasant."

"What if some of them are?"

"That is something I would have to live with."

I shake my head, then grab the knife to cut another slice. But I stop halfway through the loaf when Brend says, "This will never come to pass, though, because you will not allow it."

I point the knife at him. "Because Colette doesn't want to see her father killed."

He sighs as if he was expecting that. "Even if Colette agreed with me, you would not consent." Gently, he takes the knife and cuts the rest of the slice himself. He spreads an even layer of jam, then offers the slice to me.

Once I've taken it, he says, "You want Silvain to be spared because if your father were here, you would spare him. But their misdeeds are not the same. It is not wrong to judge them differently."

I nearly choke on a bit of cherry. Of course Silvain and Pa are not the same. Has Brend lost more than his memories? "I have no idea what you're talking about."

Brend glances over his shoulder. "I am going to try to sleep again. You should too."

He leaves me standing in the kitchen to stew over his wrongness. My hands are sticky. I have the strongest urge to wash them in the snow, but I also can't bear the thought of stepping outside into cold brightness to face the daylight.

Instead, I drop my half-eaten slice of bread onto the counter and return to my blanket. Colette wraps an arm around my middle and tugs me close, pressing her face into my hair and breathing deeply, as if I don't smell truly awful. As if I'm everything she needs.

My eyes sting with unshed tears. I bring Colette's fingers to my lips and kiss them, determined to keep hold of them until I finally fall asleep.

CHAPTER 26

I startle awake as Deidra and Shea emerge from their bedroom. Colette's weight against my back tells me she hasn't become a fox. I breathe in relief, then nudge her gently.

Though it's late afternoon, Deidra lays out a breakfast spread, and we gather around to eat before it's time to ward the other cottage. Deidra must have noticed the crumbs and dirty knife I left behind, but she doesn't remark on the mess. I avoid meeting Brend's gaze across the table, certain that if I do, everyone will be able to read the conversation we shared earlier.

You want Silvain to be spared because if your father were here, you would spare him. What a ridiculous thing to say.

After everyone's finished eating, I decide it's time to speak with Colette. While Deidra gathers more salt and crystals,

Shea feeds Orla, and Brend helps my sister clean up the kitchen, we sit before the fire, and I quietly tell her what the king did to her aunt.

"She didn't deserve that." Colette shudders, and I take her hand into my lap. "Her methods haven't been perfect, but all she wants is to see me safe."

"I know." I brush my thumb soothingly across the back of her hand.

Suddenly, Colette's troubled expression transforms into one of panic. Her hand tightens in mine. "What if Brend is right? What if the only way to keep everyone safe is to kill Silvain?"

Alarm tugs at my gut. "Colette—"

"I mean to return once you lift my curse," she says. "He'll be there too. Even if he accepts me as his heir, he'll be the same cruel faerie who tortured my aunt, who was fine with losing me."

"Yes," I agree, because it's the truth. Silvain isn't likely to change. "But you don't need to take on the burden of who your father is. No one expects you to."

"What if you're wrong? What if his subjects hope for change?"

"Then they can make it themselves," I say, bristling at the thought of faeries forcing Colette to challenge the king. Forcing her to do anything. "You don't owe them a death. They all stood by while Silvain left you in the village."

"Maybe they didn't have a choice," she argues. "Tamsin didn't. But she left Nanette gifts, and she wasn't the only one. There are faeries who would see me as their princess, their future queen."

I swallow, disliking where this conversation is leading us, and knowing I need to stop it before we're carried too far. "It's too early to be considering all of this. Our priority is your safety and lifting the curses."

The slant of Colette's mouth tells me she doesn't agree, but she doesn't pursue the issue either. "I need to let Nanette know we're leaving. She's likely still worried sick over my absence."

I nod. "We can go tomorrow morning if you'd like. That's when Shea is planning to gather supplies for Violet Ridge."

With Silvain still indisposed and our departure looming, it will be our best and only chance to visit Nanette. Deidra and Shea may not like it, but I hope they understand that this is something Colette must do. Nanette may not be her birth mother, but she's still her family.

"Thank you," says Colette, leaning in. "I would like that very much."

I hesitate before our lips meet. "I'll try to be brave for you, whatever happens."

Colette smiles softly. "I know you will be."

We share a tender kiss, and as fearful as I am of the future, I know I've spoken true. Colette makes me want to be more than I've been. More than the shy, messy child hiding in the forest. More than the girl the village likes to gossip about.

More than the girl bargained to a king.

While the others stay behind, Deidra accompanies Eirwyn, Brend, and me down the path to our cottage to help us place the wards, a relatively simple process now that we all know what we're doing.

Afterward, Deidra and Brend volunteer to build a fire and make tea, while Eirwyn and I go to the cellar. Shea sent us home with a supply of smoked fish that will feed us for a week in Violet Ridge so long as we keep it cold with fresh snow. We'll use Ma's old vegetable cart to transport it along with our other perishables, but for now, we pour the fish into a barrel, then start hauling in buckets of snow to cover it.

"I gave Shea a bit of Aunt Meara's coin for supplies," says Eirwyn, climbing down the cellar stairs with a filled bucket. "Enough so she can purchase salted meats for our journey."

I shovel snow from my bucket into the barrel, grateful to be wearing gloves. "Good thinking. Meat will keep longer than fish."

"Right." Eirwyn sets down her bucket at the bottom of the stairs, then brushes back a strand of loose hair that's fallen into her eyes. "I believe we'll manage fine in Violet Ridge, so long as you lift the curses before spring."

I wipe my gloves on my cloak to dry them. "I plan to," I tell her.

Eirwyn worries at her bottom lip. "Have you thought about what happens after?"

"After?"

"After you lift the curses. After Silvain's no longer a threat."

I frown. "He'll still be a threat to me. He wants my magic."

Grunting, Eirwyn lifts her bucket. "So, what are you planning to do?"

"Cross the river to Poppy," I say, "to get further from the king."

"Ma said she'd be on one of the first ferries after the spring thaw." My sister joins me at the barrel. "What if you miss her?"

I shrug. "Deidra and Shea can let her know where we've gone and why."

"Or I could tell her."

I scoff. "How would you manage that?"

"Because I'd come back."

"To tell her?"

"To stay."

I nearly drop the bucket onto the fish. "You've been in favor of Poppy since the beginning."

Eirwyn sighs. "That was before."

"Before what?"

"Before I returned to the western wood." She sets her bucket down again, this time on the ground beside the barrel. "That day Brend and I went searching for you felt like waking up from a four-year sleep. I started remembering everything I loved about our forests: the sharp scent of pine, the snap of my bow when I hunted, how it felt to come home dirty and spent and smiling after a full day of exploring with you."

Her grin falters. "And to think I kept myself from those feelings for years because of Pa. To honor someone who told me I didn't belong with the trees." Eirwyn shakes her head as if disappointed in herself. "I supported Ma's decision because I believed what Pa said. Not anymore."

My eyes are wet. I wipe them with my glove but get snow crystals in them, which I hastily blink away. "So, you'll stay in the cottage alone? What will you do?"

We're supposed to leave for Poppy because we can't afford to stay. Our garden is failing, and without my foraging, Eirwyn will have only herself to rely on for food. She can't be thinking of hunting in the eastern forest. One clean shot to a bear aside, she's too out of practice to compete with other hunters.

Eirwyn draws herself up, back straight and shoulders set. "Well, you know the village healer is growing old. I'd like to become her apprentice and use my faerie magic for good."

I set my bucket on the ground and take up hers. I need something to do with my hands, so I start shoveling snow again. "Won't someone ask questions after you heal their broken arm with one touch?"

"I've thought of that," she says, nodding. "I'm going to practice controlling my magic. A lot of it seems to do with intent, so as a healer, I'll start small. I won't pour everything into one touch."

She's put more consideration into this than I expected, but of course she has, because she's Eirwyn. She always thinks things through.

"What about Brend?" I ask. "He's going to choose me."

The words are a jab at my sister, and maybe I'm rotten for saying them. But if they convince her to come with us to Poppy, I don't care. If she joins us because of Brend, I won't be jealous this time. Only grateful. She's my sister. I've never lived without her.

But Eirwyn's smile is soft, sad. "Brend chose you a while ago, Ro. He's not my prince. I've accepted that."

I scowl at the snow-covered fish. He's not my prince either.

Eirwyn reaches for my hands, and reluctantly, I let her take them. "I'd hate to be parted from you, but I understand why you need to leave. I hope you'll show me the same understanding."

At winter's start, I never imagined Eirwyn and I would trade places. I never imagined that I'd be the one willing to leave the western wood, while my sister insists she stay. So much has changed since Ma left, all the changes put in motion by a conflict between a bear and a fox.

I've always hated change, but it'd be wretched of me to resent Eirwyn's reclaimed love of the forest, or her plan to use magic to help the villagers of Sugar Maple. It'd be a lie to say I regret growing close to Colette, even to Brend.

Change can be good. I guess if there's anything I've learned this winter, it's that.

I pull my sister in for a hug, and I tell her, "I'll try."

After a blessedly uneventful night behind the wards, I return to Deidra and Shea's for Colette the following morning. The moment she learns what we've planned, Shea is staunch in her refusal to allow Colette and I to visit Nanette ourselves, claiming it isn't safe nor smart with a forest of faeries after us. I refuse to let on that she might be right, but that doesn't stop her from deciding we'll make a joint venture to see Colette's mother and purchase supplies from Maple Square.

Colette's hand in mine, I follow Shea deeper into the village, any fear I held about encountering faeries lessening with each step. I doubt even the faerie king would be so bold as to attack us here. If he were powerful enough to take on an entire village, he would've driven us out years ago. Unfortunately, my fear of faeries is replaced with a fear of crowds. The moment Maple Square comes into view, I drop Colette's hand.

"Ro," she murmurs.

"I'm sorry," I tell her, mouth dry, "I can't."

"It's all right." She brushes her sleeve against mine. "I'm with you even when we're not touching."

Overcome with gratitude, I squeeze Colette's fingers a final time before tucking my hand into the pocket of my cloak.

As we visit vendors and shops for the supplies we'll need for Violet Ridge, Colette and I are met with a few irritating comments about our recent closeness, but nothing Shea can't deflect on our behalf. Perhaps it's a lucky day, or I've simply endured one too many hellish nights with faeries, but spending time in Maple Square isn't entirely unpleasant. I don't go so far as to reclaim Colette's hand, but I don't mind when our shoulders brush in the company of villagers, or when her laugh makes me blush with its loveliness.

Mostly, villagers ask if I'm well and if I'm missing Ma, and my throat feels achy when I tell them I do miss her, very much. A few also ask about Brend, our mysterious cousin, and Shea rolls her eyes every time.

Once we've settled our business in the square, we move on to visiting Nanette. Upon sight of her daughter on her doorstep, Nanette hugs Colette so fiercely I'm worried she might faint. Shea and I wait in the sitting room while mother and daughter have a tense conversation in the kitchen. I'm not sure how much Colette reveals about our situation, but it's enough that when they join us, Nanette's cheeks are ruddy and her eyes are wet, but she nods to me and Shea like she understands.

Colette asks me to help her pack a few things for Violet Ridge. I follow her to her room, and it's not until I hear the soft sound of her door closing that I ask, "How much did you tell her?"

"I couldn't tell her everything." Colette picks up a quilted satchel from the floor and crosses to the dresser. She opens a drawer and begins stuffing the satchel with what appears to be a random assortment of clothes. "I explained that I have an opportunity to understand where I come from, but that I have to go to Violet Ridge to do it, and it's better if she doesn't come with me."

That sounds incredibly vague. "She's all right with that?"

Colette nods. "I promised I'd only be away for a short time."

Worry seeps into my skin like a nasty chill. "But long enough to lift your curse, right?"

Colette doesn't answer. She moves on to another drawer, but I doubt she has room left in her satchel for a single sock.

"Colette?" I draw forward, placing a hand on her shoulder. "If I can't free you and Brend by winter's end, we may need to get further away from Sugar Maple. Silvain's bound to find us in Violet Ridge at some point. Poppy might be safer."

Colette turns to face me, lips taut and gaze hard. "I'm not going to Poppy."

"You might have to," I insist, because unless she has another way to break the curses without killing anyone, my magic is our only chance.

"No," she says simply. "If I follow you that far, I'm afraid I won't be able to return."

I let my hand drop to my side. "Would that be such a bad thing?"

"For me, yes." Colette brushes past me, her stuffed satchel knocking against my hip, but she stops short of opening the door. She whirls around. "I meant what I said to Tamsin. I want to know her as my family. I want to know about my mother— my *faerie* mother. After years of waiting and wondering, I want answers. I want to belong somewhere."

You could belong with me. I'm too cowardly to say the words, because I fear I'm not enough. I can't possibly make up for the family she seeks.

"What about Silvain?" I ask.

"Maybe he'll learn to accept me as his heir. Maybe there's some other trial I can undertake that doesn't involve killing someone."

"He won't agree to that."

Colette hasn't witnessed Silvain's cruelty firsthand, but I have. I could never forget the grip of his taloned hands on my shoulders, the coldness with which he spoke of his daughter and Brend, his wall of flame. Silvain doesn't strike me as someone who could learn to accept anything that he doesn't already want to.

"Well," she says, hefting her satchel over her shoulder, "it's a risk I'm willing to take."

Desperate, I capture Colette's hands and hold them to my chest. "You once said you wished we could be two normal girls. We can be those girls in Poppy."

Away from the wood, Colette and I would have the chance to make whatever we want of ourselves.

"That was a dream." Her voice has turned hollow. She wrenches free of my grip. "We were never going to be those girls."

"All right, our faerie blood means we'll never be quite normal," I concede. "But we don't have to let it dictate our lives."

"Don't you realize that running is just as bad as agreeing to serve the king?" Colette throws up her hands. "He'll still control your life. Every choice you make will be to avoid serving him."

I stagger back as if I've been pushed. "Better to hand myself over, then? Is that what you're suggesting?"

It's clearly what Pa wanted. And now Eirwyn wants to stay in Sugar Maple too. Brend has agreed to follow me, but that wasn't his first impulse. Maybe no one thinks I should run. Maybe everyone believes I should accept my lot and serve the foul king. Serve him or kill him. Are those the only fitting options?

But Colette says, "No, of course not." She pulls at her braids in frustration. "I'm only saying that neither choice is perfect."

"I don't need perfect. I need to belong to myself." I know my voice will break on my next words even before I say them. "And I need you."

Her shoulders fall. She draws close, gentle fingers lifting my chin. Her kiss is soft and sweet and aching. She whispers against my lips, "You can have me if you stay."

Then she steps back, and all her tenderness has turned to stone like the willow faerie in the blue-hemmed clearing. "Or you could command me to go with you."

Her words steal the breath from me. They are a dark challenge, one I never imagined I'd have to meet. "Colette, I would never do that to you."

Much as I want to see her safe, I would never force her to follow me anywhere. I would never force her to choose a life with me. That would make me no better than my father.

But she reminds me, "You've commanded me before." Her voice is trembling, like she's afraid of me. "You've used your voice to make others do what you want."

"To help you," I argue. "To help Brend and my sister."

I thought she understood that. Every call, every command, every plea has been made in the name of aiding them, protecting them. But Colette isn't sure of that. And if she isn't sure, maybe Eirwyn and Brend have similar concerns. Brend once claimed he was certain of me, and I assumed that wouldn't change, but I remember what he said about killing Silvain: *Even if Colette agreed with me, you would not consent.* As if my approval is all that matters.

"I know that's what you believe, Ro." Colette sighs, appearing almost apologetic. "But what happens when you decide the only way to help us is to keep us in Poppy?"

I gape at her. "I won't, I'd never—"

"I'm only trying to say that your magic isn't good or bad. It's both. Just like any choice you make can never be completely good or completely bad. Like my decision to come back here. The choice comes with risks, but it's also what I need to do."

Colette straightens her shoulders. There's an elegance to the way she holds herself. Almost like royalty. I suppose that's what she is. "You can have me if you stay," she vows again. "But if you cross that river, you'll cross without me."

CHAPTER 27

On our way home, Shea surprises me by asking if I'm all right. It's surprising because Deidra is usually the one who asks after my feelings.

Colette walks ahead of us, straight-backed and unyielding. We haven't spoken since we left her bedroom. I could hardly find the words to bid goodbye to Nanette. I hardly have any for Shea now.

You can have me if you stay.

"Ro, talk to me." Shea clears her throat like she's uncomfortable, which she probably is. I am too. Our relationship has always been more practical than emotional. "Did something happen between you and Colette?"

I draw a breath of courage. "Have you and Deidra ever

disagreed about something so strongly that you didn't know if you'd survive it?"

Shea blinks. Clearly, the question was unexpected. "I . . . yes, in fact."

"What did you do?"

"Well." Shea hoists her bag of supplies higher on her shoulder. "I suppose after a lot of nasty squabbling, we became so exhausted that we sat down together and found a compromise."

She makes it sound so easy, even the days of squabbling. "How do you find a balance between two different desires?"

"It's not always even," answers Shea, a twinge of ruefulness to her tone. "Sometimes one person compromises more than the other. Sometimes the other person only gives a little, but enough that it's better than whatever options you had before."

I can't imagine any instance where either Colette or I would compromise about Poppy or Silvain in a way that makes either of us satisfied. "What if there is no compromise to be had?"

What if there's no trust either?

"Then you need to make a tough decision." Shea sighs, her gaze trained on Colette. "If there is no possibility for agreement, you either choose her and abandon your desire, or you choose yourself."

And abandon her.

Silence falls between us as I weigh the choices Shea placed before me. It's not until we're about to part ways between our cottages that she adds, in an uncharacteristically soft voice, "I won't tell you what to do, Ro. I only ask that you make your choice out of love, not fear."

I set my hands on my hips. "So you're asking me to choose her."

All that talk of compromise and tough decisions, and she wants me to side with Colette anyway.

Shea shakes her head. "A love choice doesn't have to be about someone else. It can be made for yourself."

"I don't understand."

Shea ruffles my hair. "Think about it some, and maybe you will. Now get inside before it's too dark. I'll see you in the morning."

I wait until she and Colette are safely inside the cottage before heading to my own. I may not understand everything Shea said, but I'm lucky that she even said it. I'm lucky that even though I lost one parent to illness, and another is away, I still have guardians who love and look out for me.

I don't show my appreciation for them half as much as I should, but I hope they know that Eirwyn and I wouldn't have made it this far without them.

That evening, safe behind the wards, Eirwyn and I pack our belongings while Brend clears the table and tends to the dishes. I notice that my sister leaves half her clothes in her drawer, while I empty mine completely.

With a faerie bargain looming over my head, I can't see the forest ever feeling like home again, but the reminder that I'm leaving without expecting to return still brings an ache to my limbs, still thickens my throat with fear to know I might never see this cottage again. That I might forget the paths my feet have known for years. I won't press my palms to trees I watched grow with me. I'll no longer belong to them.

When it's time to climb into our beds, Eirwyn appears to drift off easily, while I struggle to find sleep.

I need my rest for the morning's journey, but I can't seem to quiet my mind. Bits and pieces of the day's conversations tumble over each other, wrestling for my attention. *Their misdeeds are not the same . . . I supported Ma's decision because I spent years believing what Pa said . . . You've commanded me before.*

Is refusing the bargain no more freeing than accepting it? If my magic makes Colette fear me, can it ever be good? Do some misdeeds deserve death?

My breaths quicken, my skin turning hot and clammy. I don't have the answers to these questions, but I can't stop asking them. I throw back the covers, hoping to cool my legs. I'm warm even lying still. My feet itch. My eyes are watery. A sort of scream builds in my throat.

Out. I must get out. Out of this bed, out of this room.

I slip from my bed, steps light as I exit the bedroom, but I trip as I cross in front of the fireplace. I grasp the mantel to avoid falling, then look down to find that the crack in the floorboard I made all those years ago with the kettle has grown wider, far enough to catch the tip of my sock foot.

I grimace, certain this must be the result of dropping the kettle after I discovered Eirwyn and Brend missing. Peering closer, I see a glint of silver that catches my breath.

There's something beneath the floorboard.

I half-expect Brend to wake and call me mad as I grab the iron poker and use it as a lever to pry away the cracked wood. But he doesn't stir even as I toss the floorboard aside. In the space below rests a small garden trowel. The tool was Pa's. I remember Ma looking for it the spring following his passing. She resorted to borrowing Deidra's to tend the garden, half-heartedly blaming the faeries for its disappearance. Pa must've placed it here before the fever took him. Why?

He was foggy in the days leading up to his death, but now I know the visit to the three trees wasn't some fit of delirium like I once believed. He had good reason to contact the faeries. So what was his reason for this?

Then I hear it, an echo from the past. *Mind the garden, Ro.* His last words to me.

The trowel belongs to the garden. Pa told me to mind the garden.

Tool in hand, I hurry to the door. I stuff my feet into boots, throw on my cloak, and light a lantern. I agonize for what feels like the longest and shortest minute of my life, staring at the line of salt, knowing that if I break it, there will be no one to repair it while I'm outside. Waking Eirwyn or Brend would mean explaining what I'm about to do, and that'll take too long. I need to be in that garden now. I need to know why Pa left a trowel beneath the floorboard. I need to know if it has something to do with faeries, with me.

I promise myself I'll be quick. Silvain is still recovering from his wounds, and I didn't have any trouble running errands with Shea and Colette. There's nothing unique about the night, except that I've uncovered a message from my father, a message I must follow. Besides, the other wards are still in place. I'm not leaving Eirwyn and Brend completely unprotected. The door is the only entry point, and I'll be able to see that from the garden.

I make a small break in the salt line with the toe of my boot then pull the door behind me as I leave the cottage. I fall to my knees atop the barren garden, brushing away snow and pushing the trowel into nearly frozen dirt. As lamp oil burns, I dig up old roots and rocks, decayed seeds that never sprouted, and curled up worms waiting for the spring thaw. I dig and dig and dig, until the shovel clangs against a metal tin. A metal tin I open to reveal yellowed parchment with cluttered, half-faded handwriting. Pa's writing. His letter is addressed to me.

What if I had left without finding this? I could have gone my entire life never reading his last words. The idea of it leaves me dizzy.

Ma is the one who insisted I learn to read. Her lessons were endlessly boring, and I've never been interested in stories like my sister, but I'm grateful for the skill now, because the thought of someone else reading my father's letter to me, even Eirwyn, is unbearable.

The letter reads:

Dearest Ro,
Your first steps took you into the forest.
That day, I was knee-deep in soil and seeds while Eirwyn slapped mud between her hands, pretending to make cakes for the faeries. You crawled away while my back was turned, and Eirwyn pointed a muddy finger your way. I turned around, but I did not stop you. I could see where your crawling was taking you, and I thought maybe—just maybe.

Grass stained your palms and knees. Wind blew back wisps of your dark hair. Lyricists so often describe the laughter of children as music or bells or birdsong. You did not laugh—you cackled as you crawled, unabashedly and marvelously. I rose from the garden and followed but did not chase. I wanted this choice to be yours alone.

Then you reached the tree line. You stopped as if a cord of rope had tugged you still. Your laughter died with the wind. You stared, still and silent, at the evergreens and the oaks.

Somewhere within the forest, a bird trilled its song, and you put dirty palms on a fallen log and used it to help you stand. Then you tottered forward, palms gripping bark to use as your guide as you ventured into the western wood for the first time.

That was the moment I realized you belong to the trees in a way I never could. In a way your sister never would.

It would take pages to tell you everything I wish to say, but I have so few moments of clarity these days, and this is the last of our parchment. I trust that any answers you seek, you will find. Knowing how determined you are, I would not be surprised if you have already found them by the time you are reading this.

What I will say is this: I have never once regretted my choice to leave the realm of my birth to start a family with your ma. Even though it made me fallible to human sickness. Even though it meant bargaining with a king. But I no longer regret making that bargain, because as the fever takes me, I am comforted by the knowledge of your future. My selfishness will not be a curse to you as I once feared, but a gift. A gift I knew you were meant to receive the moment you stepped into the western wood on your own.

My only sadness is that I will not be there to witness what you become.

All my love, Pa

I read the letter a second time. Then a third. Yet it remains almost too difficult to comprehend. To accept.

A gift. Pa referred to the bargain he made without my knowledge, in which I'm meant to serve a faerie king for the rest of my life, as a *gift*.

I crumple the letter in my hand. I wish I had Silvain's fire so I could burn it to ash. Our fireplace will have to do.

I stride toward the cottage. Brend meets me at the door.

"What are you doing?" he asks.

I ignore him, stepping over the salt line and leaving him to repair the break. My only focus is the fireplace, the flames that will devour my father's last words.

I pull back my arm, prepared to hurl the letter into the fire, but a hand clamps over my fist. Brend's hand. I struggle against him, but he's strong for a gangly boy. He refuses to let go.

"Stop," I groan.

"Tell me what is on that parchment."

"It's none of your business," I hiss.

"Ro, please." He grunts against my struggle.

I won't give in. I'll see that parchment burn if it takes every ounce of my strength. If I have to turn Brend into a bear for him to release me.

He must sense this, because he calls, "Eirwyn," and the summons sounds desperate. "Eirwyn, please come."

The bedroom door bangs open. My sister stands at the

threshold, braids half-undone, eyes heavy with sleep. "What is going on?"

"She is trying to burn something," answers Brend. "I think it is important."

In a fury, I shout, "Let me go!" and there's magic behind the words. Brend releases me, staggering backward.

Before I can toss the parchment into the flames, Eirwyn places herself before the fire. She glances at the hole I left in the floor, then my tight fist. "Ro, tell me what this is."

I can think of so many words to describe Pa's letter. A betrayal. A violation. A farce. Certainly not a gift.

"He doesn't regret it," I murmur, staring past my sister into the glow of the flames. "He's not sorry."

Brend believes Eirwyn will stop me, but she's angry with Pa too. He claimed she can't belong to the forest. She will understand why I must do this.

But all she says is, "Ro?" and her gentle voice is my undoing.

Heaving a sob, I drop the crumpled letter to the floor, then I stumble into my sister's waiting embrace.

Later, after Eirwyn's comforts have quieted my tears, after she's read and subsequently hidden the letter and returned to bed, I sit on the cushioned bench with Brend. Whereas before his loud, heavy breaths were an annoyance, they now belong to the cottage as much as the crackling wood and the creaking furniture. I would miss them, were they not here.

"I'm sorry," I tell him. "I shouldn't have commanded you like that."

For a brief yet significant moment, I'd decided burning Pa's letter—satisfying my angry desire—was more important than Brend's free will. A wretched betrayal. A violation. I recall what Colette said, about what could happen if I decide Poppy is the only safe place. I thought she was overreacting, but now I know she was right to question me, my magic. The power is stronger than I realized, and I'm much weaker.

Brend hasn't answered. He must not be certain of me any-more. I swallow past an ache in my throat. "I understand that you can't ever trust me again."

Since the night we met as bear and girl in the wood, he's endeavored to earn my loyalty. Tonight, I ruined any chance of keeping his.

Yet he places his hand over mine, the touch of his fingers light but warm. "I trust you, Ro. One mistake cannot change that."

I pull away. Not because I want to, but because I feel I don't deserve the comfort. "What if I can't trust myself?"

He leaves his hand in place, like he's hoping I'll come back to it. "I felt that way after I hurt you and Colette."

I study his profile. Firelight flickers off his fair skin. Short, fine hairs line his jaw. He'll want to shave again soon. Eirwyn taught him how to hold Pa's old blade, but he always manages to nick something. "Do you still feel that way?"

"No." His lips curve into a wry smile. "Because you are beginning to trust me now, and I do not want to lose that trust. I make each choice with that in mind, and so far, it has not led me astray."

I only ask that you make your choice out of love, not fear.

Brend already follows Shea's advice. It's time I started following it too.

I cover Brend's hand with my own, but only for a moment. "I need to leave for a little while. Can you come repair the salt line?"

Without question, he follows me to the door, then waits with the salt can while I slip into my boots.

"If she wakes before I get back, please tell Eirwyn not to worry."

Brend nods. "I trust you, Ro." Then he hesitates before adding, "But my trust is not all you need, is it?"

I shake my head. I'm relieved he understands. Trusting him to repair the break, I step over the salt line and into the cold.

I'm ready to make my choice.

CHAPTER 28

I take the path to Deidra and Shea's. The sight of the western wood, flanking my progress, makes me wonder what pulled me to the trees the first time I walked. The scent of pine and the song of birds, or my faerie blood?

Whatever the reason, it was enough for Pa to write the story of my life before I could even speak. Well, it's time I write that story myself, with a little help.

I knock on my neighbors' door softly, not wanting to wake everyone in the household. Colette must be sleeping on the bench, and I hope she still has some of her fox hearing when she's a girl. After a few minutes of anxious waiting, the door opens. Colette's braids are pulled up and covered by a fabric wrap, and she's dressed in one of Shea's long-sleeved tunics and a pair of Deidra's woolen leggings. Both hang on her slim form. She must be saving her own clothes for Violet Ridge.

"Ro," she says, yawning. "It's the middle of the night."

"I know," I tell her. "May I come inside?"

In answer, she disturbs the line of salt barring my entry and I step quickly over the threshold, leaving her to repair the break.

I choose the dining table for our conversation; the bench is too close to the bedroom. Colette takes the seat across from me, and perhaps she's still waking up because she reaches for my hand despite our earlier conflict.

"You're trembling," she notices, squeezing my fingers. "What's wrong?"

I slip from her grasp, then tell her about the letter.

Colette shuts her eyes, lashes pressing firmly into soft brown skin. "Ro, I'm sorry. You must feel awful."

"I do, and not only about the letter," I admit. "You were right, Colette. No choice I make is free of consequence, especially not any choice made with my voice."

Her slender eyebrows lift. "So, what does that mean?"

"It means I'm not asking you to leave with me, and I'm certainly not going to command that you do. All I'm here to ask is, what do you want to do next?"

She leans back in her seat, face scrunched in confusion. On anyone else, the expression would be off-putting, but Colette always manages to retain her loveliness. "About my curse? Or about Silvain?"

"Either." I shrug. "Or both."

I've been so intent on fighting this curse my way. Protecting Colette my way. Yet if my actions tonight prove anything, it's that the decision shouldn't always be left up to me. Good intentions or not. And if I want her to trust me again, I need to let her take the lead for once.

"I want the chance to speak with my father." Her tone is reticent, but upon my silent urging, her voice grows bolder as she continues, "You've all had that opportunity. You've all been able to determine his character firsthand, and what I know of him has been filtered through you. So I want to meet with him myself, and I want to make my next choice based off that conversation."

It's a reasonable request, but one I might've bristled at yesterday or even an hour ago. It stands in direct opposition to my plan—which is to get as far away from Silvain as possible. But my plan is just one option. It's not the only path. We can try Colette's first.

"Then let's go talk to him."

Her lips part in shock. "Now?"

"Yes." I push back from the table, rising from my seat. "He's still recovering. I'm not saying this will happen, but if the conversation takes a bad turn, it'll be easier to get away."

"That's smart," says Colette.

Movement beyond the kitchen window catches my attention before I can fully appreciate her praise. I draw closer until I discern a shadowy figure standing just beyond the glow of the outdoor lamp. At first, I think Brend has followed me. Perhaps I've taken too long, and he's grown worried.

Then the figure steps forward.

Wrinkled hands. Sharp talons. Curved beak.

"Silvain," I murmur.

Patches where feathers were singed by fire expose tan, leathery skin, but he otherwise appears recovered from our last confrontation. Perhaps there's another faerie who can heal in the western wood. Or Silvain is just that resilient.

The sound of soft footsteps prompts me to glance over my shoulder.

"The king?" Colette asks, joining me in the kitchen. "Here?"

"Yes," I say, alarm coursing through me. "Get down before he sees you."

She crouches low, one knee pressing against my leg. I watch Silvain's beak open like he's speaking, but I can't hear him through the window. Two more shadowy figures approach the light. I hold my breath, hoping the shadows don't belong to Eirwyn and Brend.

But the evergreen faerie, Lydie, is illuminated first. My eyes close in relief until I remember there's one more figure, a figure that could be someone I love. Cautiously, I open my eyes.

Nanette stands beside Lydie. The faerie's needled hand grasps her arm in what looks like an uncomfortably tight grip.

The sight of Colette's mother is unsteadying. I grip the kitchen counter to keep upright. Nanette is the last person I expected to see. Before we left, Shea told her to ward her cottage. Did she not listen? Or was Tamsin right when she said even wards cannot stop Silvain?

Whatever the case, she's the perfect captive. Perfect because I won't see Colette's mother—Brend's mother—harmed.

I'm going outside, and that's exactly what Silvain wants. He brought Nanette here to draw us out.

I turn away from the window. Colette grabs my ankle,

preventing me from taking another step toward the door. "Where are you going?"

"Outside," I tell her. "Nanette's with him."

"Mama?" Her eyes widen. "I'm coming with you. You said I could speak with him."

"This isn't the time." It pains me to deny her when I'm desperate for her trust, but circumstances have changed. "Whatever he has in mind is nothing good."

"He's my father," she argues. "And she's my mother."

"I know, and that's why you should let me speak with Silvain first. Let me figure out what's going on."

I need to know exactly what he wants before I involve Colette.

"But—"

"Colette, please." I shut my eyes, searching for a way to convince her. "Your mother wouldn't want you to put yourself in danger, even for her. Wait here."

I half-expect her to refuse, and I wouldn't blame her for it. If that were Ma out there, I would charge through the door. But she releases her grip on my ankle. "Don't let him hurt her."

I tell her I won't, even though it's a promise I can't truly make. "Repair the salt line, then wake Deidra and Shea."

She nods and follows me out of the kitchen. When I open the door, a rush of cold wind stirs the salt sprinkled across the threshold. Colette picks up the salt can below the coat rack, waiting for me to leave so she can sprinkle a fresh line. I give myself a moment to turn back. If it were only Silvain and Lydie outside, I would. But Nanette is out there too. I can't hide from that.

I make a break in the line then cross the threshold. I don't look back to make sure Colette is repairing the ward, fearful my resolve will crumble at the sight of her misty eyes. I veer off the path that would take me to my cottage to meet the faeries and Nanette. The outdoor lamp illuminates all of us, casting our shadows across the snow.

Now that I'm closer, I can confirm that Nanette hasn't been harmed. Her eyes are glassy with terror, though, and her cheeks are red and wet with tears. She wears a wool robe over her nightdress, and her chestnut hair is gathered in a messy bun atop her head. Did Silvain pull Nanette from her bed? I can't imagine how terrifying that must have been.

"Ah, Roisin." Silvain's owlish head cocks to the evergreen faerie. "Lydie believed the fox or the bear would be first because of our captive, but I am not surprised to see you, knowing how much you enjoy interfering."

I won't rise to meet his taunt. If there's any hope of diffusing the brewing storm, I can't be combative. "Colette wishes to speak with you."

"Wonderful. She may join us at any time. You have all hidden behind wards long enough." Silvain's feathered brows turn downward. "She and the boy must finish what they started, or else Lydie spills the blood of their lovely mother onto the snow."

I press my hands tight against my sides, willing myself to remain steady. The threat can't be real. Silvain must know that Nanette's death would make Brend and Colette turn on *him* rather than each other. This is all a ruse so he may finally witness the bloody end he's been waiting for.

"Release Nanette, then you and Colette can have a conversation."

"You forget than I am your king, Roisin. You cannot give me orders."

A single nod from Silvain has the evergreen faerie pressing the tip of one needled finger to Nanette's throat. Nanette winces, and a drop of blood drips down her neck. I stiffen, worried I might be wrong about the king's intentions.

"Retrieve them," Silvain says, "or Lydie cuts deeper."

"No," gasps Nanette, breaking her silence. "Don't listen to him."

"Quiet." He points a talon at Nanette, but the woman is undeterred.

"Neither one of them can die. Promise me, Ro. Promise me you—" she breaks off with a wail as Lydie draws three fingers down her arm, carving ribbons of red.

"Stop," I shout, the word consumed by panic rather than magic. It will do nothing to deter the king.

"Gather the changelings," he orders.

"Bind her wound first." Blood falls from Nanette's finger-tips. One sleeve of her robe is soaked with it. I swallow to clear a foul taste from my mouth. My knees quiver, the snow below me suddenly a tempting place to rest. "Please."

"Your sister can heal her once everything is settled," snaps the king, his beak clacking disconcertingly with every word. "How many wounds will need tending is up to you."

His head turns sharply toward Lydie and Nanette.

"No," I cry, foolishly reaching out as if I can stop what's about to happen.

Lydie slices into Nanette's cheek. She screams, rivulets of blood spilling from the new wound, further soaking her clothes. I bite into my fist against a rising sob, knees bending dangerously close to the ground.

This time, I push more than panic into the words, "Lydie, release her."

The evergreen faerie promptly steps back. Nanette falls to her knees, keening in pain. I never intended to use my voice tonight. I wanted to give Colette her chance, the chance she's owed to take charge of her fate. But I couldn't watch Lydie inflict pain upon her mother.

I swallow the satisfaction of my command's success. I'm not finished yet. "Lydie, do not touch her again."

The evergreen faerie holds her needled hands behind her back as Silvain watches with narrowed eyes. "Well done," he remarks. "Most faeries cannot access such magic so young. I was wise to choose you over your sister."

I shudder at the reminder of the bargain. "Leave us, or I'll use that magic on you."

He chuckles. "Will you, now?" He stretches his arms wide, long feathers draping them to give the appearance of wings. "It worked so well the last time."

Anxious doubt weighs on me like snow on a pine branch. "Leave us, Silvain," I command.

The king doesn't even flinch. Lydie, still held in place by my magic, grins.

"This is my final request," says the king. "Retrieve the changelings or the woman dies."

No. I can't offer up Colette and Brend knowing one of them

won't survive. I can't watch them take on their animal forms and chase each other through the wood. Not again.

But I'm not giving up on Nanette either. I wring my hands, willing myself to be stronger. "Leave us, Silvain. Leave us, now."

"Roisin."

The sound of my name in Silvain's beak makes me feel wretched, because I know it means my command has failed again. Nanette draws shuddering breaths through her teeth. Tears mingle with the blood on her face. She nods to me, her gaze steady as if to say, *You stay right there, Ro Birch.*

I once questioned Nanette's love for Colette when I heard about the rituals, the threats to send her back to the wood. I never should have doubted her. When it truly matters, Nanette is more than prepared to sacrifice herself for her child, for her two children.

I force myself to stand straighter, to hold my hands at my sides. I want to be strong for her, as strong as I can be despite my failures. "No, Silvain. I will not bring them to you."

For a moment, the king doesn't falter, perhaps believing I might change my mind. When I don't take back the words, he strides to Lydie, grabbing her by the shoulders before shoving her toward Nanette. This seems to snap the evergreen faerie out of the trance my magic bestowed upon her. She pulls a struggling Nanette to her feet, her needles at the woman's throat once more, eager for the king's final command.

"Wait."

The word is a terrible thunderclap on an otherwise clear day. Defeated, I watch Brend leave the cottage path to stand at my side, hands lifted in surrender. How long has he been watching this scene unfold? Certainly long enough to know I was prepared to sacrifice the woman who birthed him.

Shame heats my face. What must he think of me? What must Colette think of me?

"Let them go. I will finish it," Brend announces. "I promise you."

"Brend, you can't," I begin.

Silvain holds up a wrinkled hand. "Not another word from you."

I fall silent, pressing a hand to my chest, where an ache blooms like a rose. I vowed to protect both the bear and the fox, but in the span of minutes I've lost all control. At least Colette is still safe behind the wards. She's safe with Deidra and Shea. They won't let her join us out here. They won't let Brend hurt her.

"Become the bear, kill the fox," says Silvain, "and I will spare the woman."

"Brend, no." Desperation leaks into my voice. "You can't."

"I told you to be quiet," says Silvain.

His taloned hand points directly at me, and the snow in front of me ignites into flame, spreading until it forms a ring around me. I hug myself tightly, trying to make myself smaller to avoid the fire's touch. The flames are half my height, and if Silvain closes the fiery snare, I will burn.

"Do not hurt her," calls Brend. "Please."

"Then cease your foolishness," says the king. "Retrieve my daughter so the trial may continue."

"No," Nanette gasps through her pain. "I don't want either of my children to die for me."

Brend visibly stiffens, and hope sparks within me. Might her plea change his mind?

"That's right, I know," continues Nanette. "They told me everything."

"Silence," Silvain warns.

"I'm so glad you're alive, Callum." Her voice breaks when she says his name. "My boy."

Brend shudders. "I am sorry, I—"

"Enough." The king's feathers ruffle with his impatience. "One of you must die. Tradition demands it."

The heat of the flames makes sweat break out across my forehead. I'm already coughing from the smoke, so I tear off my gloves and rub them in the melting snow around my feet. Once they're drenched, I hold the wet fabric against my nose and mouth, taking small breaths. The fire isn't closing in yet, but if I make a move that the king doesn't like, he'll let the flames consume me.

Through the flickering orange haze, movement beyond Silvain attracts my attention. Colette emerges from the shadows, the glint of a kitchen knife in her hand. She must have snuck out the sitting room window to make her approach. She's moving toward Silvain now. She means to strike him.

I need to keep him distracted. I lower the wet gloves and say, "What if I agree to serve you now in exchange for their protection?"

I would never make such an agreement, but he doesn't need to know that now.

But he answers, "I require no bargain to make you serve me," and the fire jumps closer, so close that I could touch the flames if I lifted my hand. "I maintained such courtesy for your father's sake, but you are erasing every bit of goodwill he had with me."

The heat of the fire is searing. Smoke engulfs me, and the effectiveness of the wet gloves seems to be waning. But Colette is lifting the knife. I can't stop Silvain, but she will. I hold my breath, wishing I could cheer for her.

But Silvain isn't who she's aiming for. Colette brings her arm down, and the blade sinks into Lydie's shoulder. The evergreen faerie cries out, staggering away from Nanette. Colette shouts for her mother to run.

She does, nearly making it to the cottage's front door before Silvain puts a ring of fire around her too. Then another around Colette, and one more around Brend.

We're all trapped.

"Children," he says, dipping his head to Brend and Colette. "I do not wish to restrain you. But I cannot have you acting against me. Assure me that you will continue the trial, and I will free you. Refuse, and I will let the fire take the mother. Then, if necessary, the Red Rose too."

Brend's gaze meets mine, panicked and pained. "Don't do it," I say. I know everything seems hopeless, but I won't condone his or Colette's death.

"There must be another way," pleads Colette. "Another trial."

"I am sorry, daughter," says Silvain, in a rare moment of gentleness. "There is only this. I have never wished to see my blood perish, but perish you must, if you are not strong enough."

"I am strong enough," declares Brend.

Silvain's feathers ruffle, as if he hoped those words had come from Colette instead. But he says, "Very well."

My eyes snap to Brend as the ring of fire at his feet disappears. He moves to pick up the bloody knife from where it landed in the snow. Stunned, I watch him walk past Lydie to stand before Colette, whose ring of fire has also vanished.

I call for Brend to stop. He doesn't. I call for Colette to run. She shakes her head. Her expression is fierce as she faces Brend. As much as I want her to, she's not going to be the fox this time, sprinting through the forest to escape the bear.

"It's okay," she says, and the words flood my eyes with tears because I know they're meant for me. "This way, you'll be safe."

But Colette won't be. She told me once that she's not very brave, but I think this is braver than anything I could ever do.

"Go on." Her words are directed at Brend this time. "Save them."

"Finish it, boy," encourages the king.

"Ro," says the bear-boy, lifting the knife, "I am sorry."

I say nothing. I don't care what his reasons are—I will never accept his apology. He promised he wouldn't hurt her again. He promised he wouldn't hurt *me* again, and this will do more than that. This will break me. I will never forgive him, never trust him.

As I make this vow to myself, the blade turns, and Brend drives the knife into his own heart.

CHAPTER 29

Brend falls to his knees before Colette.

His mouth moves, muttering something I can't hear above Nanette's screaming. Colette must understand, because she nods and steps forward. Wide-eyed, she pulls out the knife, dropping it to the ground as Brend splays a hand over his chest. Blood streams between his fingers and splatters the snow. Too much blood. The bear drove the knife, but the fox delivered the fatal blow.

Colette closes her eyes and crouches low. She wraps her arms around herself as if hoping to disappear.

Instead, the flames disappear. The flames around me, around Nanette. With no regard for Silvain, I run to Brend, coughing against cold air and lingering smoke. Nanette must be sobbing for her son, but all I hear is my pounding heart and his wet gasps of breath. I put my hands to his wound. If I press hard enough, maybe I can stop the bleeding.

But I'm no Eirwyn. My hands cannot heal, so his blood leaks past my fingers, makes red lines down the backs of my hands, and soaks the cuffs of my cloak. The thick tang of iron stings my nose and tempts me to retch.

"Do not die," I say, choking on the words. "Please. Stay with me."

My voice is as powerless as my hands, too weak against the changeling magic wrought by the king. Brend's amber eyes meet mine as he falls onto his side. I follow him to the ground, and snow seeps past the layers of my clothes. Icy cold spreads up my back, but it's not nearly as powerful as the grief gripping my body in a hold so tight, I can scarcely breathe.

His skin is turning sallow. I should take his hand now; I know he's dying. But my own hands are drenched in his blood, and I can't stop looking at them, can't hold them steady.

He's gone before I can tell him I'm sorry. He didn't hear my vow to never forgive him, but I still made it. Even if I unmake it, he'll still be dead.

Why didn't I know this would happen? The signs were there, and yet I stubbornly clung to the false belief that Brend would always be that terrifying bear I first encountered in the wood, rather than the kind boy I grew to know, fighting the violence of his curse.

I bow my head. Brend's chest, drenched in blood, remains unmoving. His eyes are glassy and vacant, unblinking. His hand, the hand I should have grasped, lies heavily on the snow, unfeeling. My bloody hands become a blur. I promised I would free him.

"The trial has ended," announces Silvain, with a heavy sigh that expresses his disappointment. Despite the king's many threats, he didn't get the bloody battle he desired.

Lydie rises to her feet, wincing through the pain of her wounded shoulder. "The heir has been decided. Colette, you may take your place beside the king."

Startled, my eyes find Colette. She no longer wears her glamour, and her fox tail slashes behind her like a sword. A layer of copper fur covers her brown skin. She looks even more like Tamsin now. A proper faerie. "Will you accept me?"

She won the trial, but only because Brend forced her hand. I'd ask the same question of the king.

"I have no choice," murmurs Silvain. "Your methods leave much to be desired, but the boy's actions prove he was never meant to rule. I will think of other ways you may impress me."

He holds out his taloned hand. "Come."

Colette hesitates.

"Now." Silvain spares a weighty glance my way, implying a threat he doesn't need to voice. "I will not ask again."

Colette crosses the snow to join the king—her father. Helpless, I watch as she places her furred hand in his wrinkled one. Then they and Lydie vanish, the blood left behind the only proof they were ever here.

I scrub my blood-soaked hands with snow, but they remain stained. They might be stained forever. Maybe they should be. I've failed everyone. Brend is dead, and Colette's beyond the veil with Silvain. He wasn't pleased with how the trial ended. Heir or not, she might still be at risk.

Footsteps crunch the snow behind me, but I don't turn. Whoever it is, I can't face them or their tears.

Eirwyn comes to kneel at Brend's other side. "Oh, Brend." Tenderly, she brushes back his mop of brown hair.

"Where were you?" I demand, suddenly furious. Eirwyn should have been here to heal him. To keep him alive when I couldn't. She's the elder sister. She supposed to take care of things.

She startles at my words. "He made me promise not to intervene. I wasn't going to listen, but when I saw the flames around you, I couldn't—you're my sister, Ro. What was I supposed to do?"

Her face crumples, and I feel horrid, berating her for choosing me over Brend, choosing me like I've always wanted her to. We cling to each other over Brend's still form. I bury my face into my sister's neck, but her rose oil scent isn't enough to comfort me this time.

"It's too much," I say, the grief so overwhelming. "I promised him, Eirwyn. I promised them both that I wouldn't let either of them die."

Eirwyn jerks away from me suddenly. I expect her to call me the failure I know myself to be. Instead, she says, "Ro, open your eyes."

Her voice is insistent, so I do as she says. My sister is dressed in rose vines and white blooms. Azure-framed stars wink at us from above. We're beyond the veil. All three of us. I must have brought us here. I don't think I issued a command, but—

Wait.

I promised him. I promised them both that I wouldn't let them die.

Maybe I can still keep that promise. Maybe the power in my voice knew it first.

The idea pierces me with such clarity that a wild, hopeful smile tugs at my lips. I move Brend onto his back, giving me a clear view of his bloody chest. It's terribly gruesome. Bile threatens to rise in me, but I shove it down. Because this will work. It must.

"What are you doing?" asks Eirwyn, the words barely more than a croak.

I meet my sister's vivid green gaze. "We're bringing him back."

Her brows rise. "Ro, are you mad?"

"No, I'm a faerie beyond the veil. So are you. Our gifts are stronger here, remember?"

Eirwyn looks down at Brend, whose empty eyes stare up at the sapphire-hued sky. "Not strong enough."

"You're wrong." I trust my voice. It's not always right, and it might have failed against Silvain, but it brought us here for a reason. "Put your hands on his wound. I'll give the command."

"Ro—"

"You've healed him so many times, as many times as I've compelled him with my voice." I grip her shoulders to make her look at me. To make her see that there's no doubt in my faerie eyes. Only faith. Faith in us. In our magic, and our sisterhood. "We're bound to him, Eirwyn. We've been bound to him since that very first night. Together, we can save him."

She shakes her head, white blooms rustling, her expression pained.

"Please, Eirwyn. Try. We owe him that, don't we?"

She draws a breath. "All right."

I grin, hope flaring as she presses her hands to the wound and closes her eyes. I cover her vine-laced hands with my own. I clear my throat of the last lingering traces of smoke from Silvain's fire. I draw a rose-scented breath.

"Come back, Brend," I call. "Come back to us."

I watch him, but his chest remains still, his skin remains sallow. My ears grow hot, and my sister bows her head in dismay, but I refuse to give up. I refuse to let Eirwyn move her hands.

I attempt a different plea: "Heal him, Eirwyn. Make Brend whole."

The words feel right this time, flawlessly complete in a way a command has never felt before. My sister's breaths grow increasingly labored. Her arms begin to shake. Tears leak from her eyes. The press of her teeth pales her bottom lip. My call echoes around us, though I spoke it only once.

Something is different. Something is working. I can feel it.

Brend draws a ragged breath, and I scramble backward, hands painfully scraping snow. My chest shudders like leaves battered by the wind. Brend is breathing. Brend is *breathing*.

"It worked." Eirwyn lifts her hands from his chest. She draws them through the snow to clean away the blood before wiping her eyes and the sweat from her brow. "We did it."

"Eirwyn." Brend's voice is barely above a whisper, but his chest wound has closed. "Ro."

"We're here." My sister squeezes his shoulder. "You're here."

I'm too numbed by bewilderment to say anything. He's *breathing*. He said our names. A dead boy, speaking. A dead boy with life in his eyes. I wanted it to work. I wanted our gifts to bring him back. But it's one thing to want, and another to *see*.

I rise to shaky legs and help Eirwyn lift Brend to his feet. I'm only realizing it now, but the command has drained me. I don't think I've ever felt so weak, the exhaustion pulling at my limbs, begging me to slow. But I manage to bring us back to our realm, and we half-drag Brend across the snow to Deidra and Shea's cottage door.

Flashes of that first night follow me with every step. The roar of the bear. The arrow in his shoulder. The naked boy lying in the snow. Eirwyn asking, *What have I done?*

I see what she's done now, what we both have. Brend was dead. His blood still stains my hands, and I watched the life slip from his eyes. He wasn't unconscious. He was truly gone, or else the trial wouldn't have ended.

Yet we brought him back. We opened his eyes and filled his chest with breath.

I kick open the door to the cottage, and we stagger in. We're lowering Brend to the cushioned bench when I finally register the loud banging sound coming from the direction of Deidra and Shea's bedroom. Familiar voices call for someone to open the door. There's wailing, too, which must be Orla.

I turn away from Brend and my sister, catching the glint of a key on the fireplace mantel. Colette must have locked them in before she crawled through the window to strike Lydie. My sister murmurs words of comfort to Brend as I insert the key into the lock. I open the door, and Shea barrels out, looking angrier than I've ever seen her. Deidra follows, a screeching, red-faced Orla in her arms.

Shea glares at me. "Want to explain why we were locked in our bedroom?"

I helped my sister bring a boy back from the dead, but I still feel like a tiny, misbehaved child in Shea's commanding presence. I point to the door. "Nanette's outside. She's hurt."

Shea's eyes widen. She leaves without asking further questions.

"Where's Colette?" asks Deidra, rocking her baby daughter as she slowly calms.

My lips part to answer her, but I don't know where to begin. Brend's sacrifice. Colette's transformation. What my sister and I did in the faerie realm—

"Ro?"

Brend calls me to his side. His skin is slightly pale, his eyes half-lidded. His hand lies over his chest, over the place he gave himself what was meant to be a fatal wound.

"I'm here," I tell him, covering his hand with my own.

"Curse-breaker," he murmurs. "You did it."

I frown at him, concerned. "You ended the curse, Brend, not me." I hope momentarily dying hasn't made his memory worse. "And you should know I'm terribly upset with you for that."

I'm relieved he didn't use the knife against Colette, but using it on himself wasn't any better. What if mine and Eirwyn's magic hadn't been strong enough to revive him? What if we hadn't known to try?

"The bear was one part of my curse. My lack of memories was the other." He squeezes my hand. "A dead boy has no memories, but I am alive thanks to the Birch sisters, and I remember everything."

I blink at him, stunned. All I hoped for was his life. He lost the trial. I didn't expect his memories to return. But I recall what I said after I told Eirwyn to heal him. *Make Brend whole.* He didn't feel complete without his memories. He was held captive by what he lost. Now he's free. I *am* the curse-breaker. I really did keep my promise after all.

"I'm not sending you away," I tell him, tears mingling with my smile. "Even though that was part of the deal."

"Good, because I never meant to listen." He briefly returns my smile, then his lashes flutter as he drifts off.

Shea appears in the doorway, her arms supporting Nanette as the pair crosses the threshold. I hurry to move a chair near the bench so Nanette may sit beside her son. Once she does, I guide her trembling hand over Brend's healed chest. He's sleeping now, but there's no doubt he's alive.

"Oh," says Nanette, as fresh tears spill onto her cheeks, as her hand rises and falls with her son's steady breaths.

Shea begins tending to Nanette's injuries, though I'm sure Eirwyn will end up healing them herself. For now, my sister leans against the fireplace mantel, her normally pale complexion flushed with heat. I bring a chair for her, too, which she gratefully falls onto. I debate claiming my own seat, taking a moment to rest.

Then Shea says, "I demand an explanation," and I'm reminded of everything left unfinished.

"You'll have to get one from Eirwyn," I tell her. "I'm going after Colette. I need to make sure she's all right."

Silvain claims to have no choice but to accept her, but that doesn't mean acceptance will come easy. He also vowed to think of ways for her to impress him. I can't imagine anything that impresses King Silvain can be achieved honorably.

Colette may not want my help. She may want to deal with her father on her own. If that's the case, I'll stand aside, as much as it will grieve me. But if there's any chance she needs me, I will be there for her.

"At least let me heal you first," Eirwyn says, reaching for me.

I let her take my hands, and I feel the strength she pushes into me, miraculous and invigorating. I reclaim all the power I used to save Brend. Maybe it's too optimistic of me, but I feel as though I might have gained a bit more.

"Whatever one of you has, remember to share it with the other," murmurs Eirwyn, reciting one of Ma's rules, handed to us as squabbling children. She sinks back into her chair, spent but smiling. "Now I'll be with you, whatever happens."

"I know you will be," I say, filled with so much love for my sister that I might burst from it. But that will need to wait.

There's a fox faerie princess I need to see.

CHAPTER 30

As the sun rises beyond the veil, I run through a stretch of blue-hemmed forest, ignoring strange rustles and peals of laughter, until I nearly collide with a familiar faerie.

"Good, you are here," says Tamsin, beckoning me forward. "We do not have much time."

"Why, what's happening?"

"Silvain means to put Colette before the court, but not as their princess," she explains as I follow her deeper into the wood. "After more than a decade, his favorite consort is finally with child. We just learned the news. Silvain has no reason to name Colette his heir now, especially with the trial being such a disappointment."

All that talk of Colette impressing him, gone with the news of a faerie babe.

"What does that mean for Colette?"

"Silvain will convince his subjects that she has not proven herself. He will deem her heir-in-waiting until his new child comes of age. Then another trial will begin to determine the true heir." Tamsin laughs, which sounds eerily like the laughter echoing in the forest around us. "All the while his reign will endure, especially with the aid of your voice. He is as clever as he is cruel."

I hasten my pace, galvanized by the reminder of the bargain. "We can't let that happen."

"I was hoping you would say that." Tamsin pauses behind a thick oak tree. "The court is gathered where you saw them last, in the clearing up ahead. Thanks to my efforts, half are prepared to defend Colette's legitimacy, but they will not act until Silvain is dealt with."

"Dealt with?" I worry at my bottom lip. I don't want to use my voice against Silvain. Not only did it not work last time, but I'm not sure it's what Colette wants. "Have you spoken to Colette about this?"

"No, foolish girl," snaps Tamsin. "He has not let her out of his sight, and I remain ill-favored." Behind her, the half of her fox tail that remains slashes through the air in irritation. "But I can aid you from the periphery."

"How?"

"Think back to the day you discovered Colette was a fox. Do you remember the storm?"

I nod, though I don't know why that's relevant now. The storm was indeed strange. The weather was clear outside the wood, but winter raged within the trees.

Tamsin grins, fox whiskers twitching.

I gape at her. "That was you?"

She crosses her arms, looking pleased. "My gift allows me to affect the weather. Dispatching Silvain's fire will not be a problem."

I'm relieved to know that I won't have to contend with the king's flames again, but there's still the matter of dealing with him.

"Colette hoped to have a conversation with Silvain, so they could settle matters without bloodshed," I confess. "I said I'd support her."

Tamsin sighs. "If there was a chance of that succeeding, the opportunity has passed." The fox faerie takes me by the shoulders, turning me until I face the clearing ahead, where Silvain prepares to put Colette before the court. "My niece has the spirit of a queen in her. And a good one, at that. But she cannot claim her rightful place while Silvain's rule endures. You must use your voice, Roisin. You must remove the king from his throne."

Alone, I confront a court of faeries.

Faeries dripping in moss. Faeries with fangs. Birch bark skin. Swishing raccoon tails. Maple leaf hands. They differ in expression as much as appearance. Some look intrigued, others bored. Some grin, others glare with such hostility that I shudder.

I spot the evergreen faerie among them. Lydie's needles

are raised like daggers, ready to strike at any moment. A faerie with antlers dips his head to me, and I wonder if he's one of Colette's supporters. I don't see Graeme. I wonder if the king punished him for helping us like he did Tamsin. Perhaps he even killed him. I wish he was here. We need all the allies we can get.

A hush falls over the murmuring crowd as a single voice rises: "Ah, Roisin. Just in time for my decree."

Silvain's deep voice is unmistakable. I stretch my gaze beyond the court to find him lounging upon his throne, talon hands resting on either arm. The throne beside him is meant for the victor of the trial, but Colette doesn't claim it. Instead, she stands before the court, shoulders back but whiskers twitching with uncertainty. As we meet eyes, I'm gripped by the urge to charge forward and steal her away from the king. But I won't act before I know what she wants.

"Will you not join us?" asks Silvain. "This matter concerns you too."

The crowd splits to form a path directly to the throne. I catch whispers of Pa's name as I make my way slowly toward the king. I remember Graeme saying Pa was well-liked. I hope that appreciation extends to his daughter. I'll learn soon enough.

I stand before the king, but I don't bow like I'm one of his subjects. I'll never bow to him. By the way he sits rigidly upon his throne, talons scraping stone, I think he must know that.

I gesture to Colette, mere feet away from me now. "Your heir has completed her task. She's proven herself. That should be your only decree."

I can't help but wince as Silvain's beak clacks with dark,

awful laughter. "Proven herself, how? By pulling a knife from the chest of a dying boy?"

Before I can manage a suitable retort, Colette surprises me by saying, "I don't need to kill to win. I proved that today. If given the chance, I can also prove that leadership doesn't need to be defined by violence. There are other ways to rule."

A round of cheers lifts from the crowd, and rightly so. She responded to her father's taunts better than I ever could. I stand straighter, bolstered by her words and the crowd's support. Tamsin wasn't lying when she spoke of allies.

Silvain leans forward in his seat. "You dare speak against me, girl? I could rid this realm of you if I saw fit. You are not my heir, yet you have the chance to become my heir because of my mercy, and mine alone. Do not forget."

"There's no mercy in forcing her into another trial," I argue. "Making her wait years until her sibling is old enough to kill or be killed."

"That's right," Colette agrees. "What sort of king pits his children against each other? And for what reason?" She faces the crowd as she continues, "I'm sixteen, the proper age to be named my father's heir. I completed the trial, even if it wasn't to his liking. I deserve this."

Colette is a marvel to behold, her voice clear and her reasons sound. Her determination palpable. The crowd must like her, too, because they abandon all notions of respectful silence. Faeries cheer and shout. Some call for the king, but many more voice their support for Colette.

Yet Silvain manages to regain his composure. "A powerful statement, indeed. But words will not be enough to turn this crowd. I have been their king for years. I have led them well. They trust my leadership."

At this, more court faeries take up a chant for the king. Too many. Enough to make me doubt.

"You will return to your human village to await your next trial," orders the king. "Before you go, I will recall every memory you have of this place and your heritage. When your sibling is old enough, I will do the same to them. Then you will compete as tradition demands."

Colette's panicked gaze finds mine. It's bad enough making her wait for another trial, but to steal her memories too? Her only solace through this endeavor has been trusting she would eventually claim the realm of her birth and learn her heritage. Connect with the family Silvain tore her from. Now he wants to take those possibilities away with her throne.

The urge to grab her and flee returns, now twofold. But I continue to resist that instinct, because to Colette, running would be no different than losing her memories. She would still be separated from what she desires. Allowing King Silvain to dictate her path.

What Colette needs is more time to convince the faeries of this realm that she can make a better regent than her father. That can't happen if she runs away or loses her memories.

Time . . . it seems I'm always fighting for more of it. When Pa was ill with fever, I fought to keep him with us as long as I could. I fed him soup, kept him warm, and brought him gifts from the western wood to remind him of the forest. Each time I ran from villagers or dodged their questions, I fought for more time to understand myself so I could face them with certainty.

Whenever I argued with Ma about moving across the river, I fought for more time in the western wood I love.

I lost those battles with time. Pa died. The village made up its mind about me without my say. Ma left for Poppy.

Yet there is a fight for more time that I've won. With the magic in my voice, I kept the changeling conflict going for weeks when it could have ended in nights. Each time my voice interfered—turning bear to boy, fox to girl—I won time for Brend and Colette to make choices about their futures. Choices Silvain wanted to take from them. I won time for Eirwyn and me to strengthen our magic so we could bring Brend back to life. To forgive a boy who once hurt me, to care for a girl who calls me brave.

I can win Colette the time she needs. But I can't do it alone.

"Colette," I murmur. "Do you trust me?"

I won't act without her blessing. This has to be her choice too. Colette glances at her father, then back at me. Her hand lifts as if to reach for me, but we're too far apart. Still, I lift my hand too. We can't touch, but we're connected. Woven like the threads of a quilt, like the branches of an oak. She smiles softly, then nods.

I draw a deep, rose-scented breath, summoning a power that is mine and directing it toward one adversary. "Change," I say to the king.

Silvain rises from his throne. "Do not challenge me."

I cringe at the avian sharpness of his tone. I touch one of the roses in my hair, the soft petals steadying me. "Change," I say again.

A ring of flame ignites around me, searing and close. But a

dash of rain puts it out in moments, leaving the king stunned while I silently thank a certain fox faerie.

"Change, Silvain."

He grabs a fistful of my hair and yanks me to him. Terror makes me choke. Rose petals tumble to the ground like bloody snowflakes.

"Quiet," he seethes, wrapping a taloned hand around my throat.

My skin burns where he touches me, and I scream, abandoning the command.

But Colette shouts, "Keep going, Ro."

And I want to, even as Silvain's burning talons press into my skin, as his beak presses against my ear and he says, "You will die like the changeling boy."

I smile. If only he knew.

"Change, Silvain," I say, shouting above the burning pain, above the crowd of faeries, above the king's magic, "and do not change back."

His hand drops from my throat. The owl king releases an unintelligible screech. Amid the turmoil, Tamsin has joined us. She shouts for the crowd to keep back. I reach for the princess, finally take her hand and pull her close so I can tell her that Brend is alive and they will both be free.

Colette presses her lips to my cheek. "Thank you," she says.

We watch the change. The snapping and stretching. The screeching and contorting.

When it's over, an owl stands before the throne.

As the bird takes flight, the court erupts into chaos.

Faeries clash—teeth and claws, branches and vines, whirl-winds and spears of ice. Lightning strikes and boulders hurled through the air. The king's supporters against the ones Tamsin won for Colette. Perhaps Colette and I managed to win a few of them too.

Escaping the fray, Tamsin guides Colette and I behind the stone thrones, and I'm shocked to find Graeme waiting for us. "We must all get away from the fighting," he says.

Tamsin nods. "I will take the queen to safety."

I've barely registered that she's called Colette *the queen* when Tamsin pulls her away from me and they both disappear, presumably to the human realm. My lips part, preparing a command that will let me follow.

But Graeme catches my wrist, stopping me. "Let them go. You have done your part."

"I can't abandon her," I say. "This is all happening because I used my voice against Silvain."

"And his supporters might soon call for your death, the vil-lage girl who overthrew their king." Graeme's oak fingers press hard against my skin. "You freed Colette from her father, but once the fighting subsides, she must return to unify the court and claim her throne. You cannot be part of that. For now, you must distance yourself from this realm."

And from her. I blink back tears. All this strife, just to be parted.

Graeme's expression softens. "I have the gift of foresight, you know. Years ago, when I touched your mother's hand, I saw more than what your gift would be. I saw you shelter the changeling boy I helped raise. I saw you confront a bear to save a red fox. I saw you install a new queen with your voice."

The gift of foresight . . . that must be why he told Brend to find a girl with red roses in her hair. Graeme knew I would be Brend's ally. He's known what I would do for years, and he let it happen. He wanted it to happen.

"I shared everything I saw with your father," he says.

The revelation is dizzying. Pa knew what I would do today. He knew that I would love the forest, but he also knew that I would resist his bargain. Pieces of his final letter return to me in a rush: *I no longer regret making that bargain, because as the fever takes me, I am comforted by the knowledge of your future. . . . My only sadness is that I will not be there to witness what you become.*

Graeme still holds my wrist. "What do you see now?" I ask him, because if I must leave without Colette, I need to know that it's not forever.

"You will reunite," he says. "I swear it. Right now, I must take you home."

The confirmation grants me hope, settling my urge to follow the fox faerie queen. After one last look at the fighting court, one last breath of rose-scented air, I tell Graeme, "All right, I'm ready."

CHAPTER 31

The first breeze of spring is at my back, gently nudging me toward the forest, toward the clump of trees I can disappear into if I just move my feet.

I make my body rigid and dig my boots into the mud and melting snow. Though one step will take me beyond the tree line, I promised Graeme I wouldn't enter the forest, nor use my voice to cross beyond the veil.

The western wood slowly wakes from the long sleep of winter. This morning's warm rain carved tiny streams through what remains of the snow, rivulets of water with a latticework of ice drifting lazily along the surface, waiting to melt. More water drips from branches dotted with green buds. Birds swoop and dip, gathering twigs for their nests. I watch a squirrel paw through the slush to reach what remains of its winter storage. Trees groan and stretch, basking beneath the golden light of the afternoon sun.

I should be waking up with my forest, a satchel slung around my shoulder, eyes bright with the excitement of discovery. Yet I sleep. I've slept since I left the faerie realm, since the moment I had to leave her.

The sound of boots squelching in mud pulls me from the memory. Eirwyn rests an arm around my shoulders, drawing me close.

"Shea says the river will finish thawing today. Ma might be on tomorrow's ferry." She sighs. "You don't have to go back with her, you know."

It's not the first time she's said so.

"I know," I tell her. "But you understand why I will, right?"

For years, I believed my life would be meaningless without the western wood. Then I found meaning apart from the trees: growing close to Colette, helping Brend, and learning the secrets of my blood and the power of my voice. Now I must see what I can become when I'm truly separate from the forest. I don't know if it's what Pa would've wanted for me, but he knew of Graeme's visions. He knew I wouldn't accept his bargain, and he didn't try to stop that from happening. He died accepting the choices I would make.

Now free, I can take the ferry to Poppy with the certainty that I will not be running. I'll be exploring, discovering. My feelings about Pa might always be messy, but maybe with time the scars of the wood will fade, leaving forgiveness in their wake.

Admittedly, I don't know if Poppy will be any better than the village square I've avoided for years. But if I can face a faerie king, I think I can overcome ignorant questions and assumptions too. It may not be easy, but I like to remind myself of what Brend said once before—in a town as large as Poppy, people are less likely to know your business. Perhaps less likely to care about it too. I believe it'll be worth it for me to find out, one way or the other.

"Of course, but you can't blame me for wanting you to stay." Eirwyn squeezes me tighter. "We've never lived apart."

I breathe in my sister's rose oil scent. "I'll come back."

She kisses the top of my head. "You better."

I've no doubt I will. While my relationship to the western wood has irrevocably changed, I can't imagine saying goodbye to my sister forever. Or to Colette, who's the reason I'm at the tree line now. I've long accepted that she won't be coming with me, but I want us to say our farewells properly, preferably with kissing.

"I saw Brend in Maple Square while I was running an errand for my apprenticeship," mentions Eirwyn. "He told me that Graeme visited last night to say goodbye, and Nanette let him stay for tea."

"Must've been strange," I say. "Nanette and Graeme in a room together."

The woman who birthed the boy, and the faerie who helped raise the bear.

Though Brend has spent the last weeks of winter in Nanette's cottage so they could get to know each other, he's coming with me to Poppy. With his memories returned, he seeks a life apart from the wood too. Graeme did his best to offer comfort and guidance, but Brend's childhood was anything but pleasant under Silvain's rule. The threat of the trial was always looming, as well as the promise of either a throne or death—neither of which he wanted.

Nanette wishes him well, but she won't leave the village where she buried her husband and raised her daughter.

Eirwyn was vehemently against Brend leaving, but not out of any notion that he might become her prince. Bringing him back from death instilled a new sort of protectiveness in her. The idea of him being so far out of reach was breath-stealing. But she relented the day I tried teaching Brend to chop wood only for him to foolishly cut his hand on the axe, and she realized she can no longer heal him. A consequence for saving him, we think.

Now she yearns to be parted from him, because my sister can't bear the thought of seeing him hurt and not being able to do anything about it. I've since discovered that I can no longer command Brend, either, but I don't mind. I prefer that our friendship be on equal terms.

In fact, my plan is to never command anyone again. Colette helped me realize the true weight of my power. I understand now that continuing to exert my will on others, even with their consent, would ultimately take too much of a toll, would twist me into an authority I've never desired to become regardless of my intentions. Instead, I'm seeking ways to use my voice for good without influencing others. I began by calling to the seeds of Pa's barren garden. They've sprouted now, and I'm confident the magic will remain strong for my sister long after I cross the river.

Eirwyn tugs on my sleeve, bringing me back to the moment. "You know how Nanette sometimes uses the name 'Callum?' Well, Brend says that every time she did, Graeme looked around the room as if there was a guest he couldn't see." She laughs.

I laugh, too, then I clear my throat. "Do you know if Graeme said—"

"No. Nothing about what's happened beyond the veil."

I try not to sound too disappointed. "Oh, all right."

A stronger breeze lifts my hair. I tuck a few loose strands behind my ear, then wrap my arms around myself, regretting my choice to leave my cloak on the rack. The thin sleeves of my tunic seemed like the right idea when I looked through the window this morning to see snow melting beneath the bright sun, but spring brings its own bite.

My sister rubs her arms, affected by the wind as well. "Deidra invited us for the midday meal. Walk back with me?"

"Not yet," I tell her, still searching the forest.

"All right," says Eirwyn. "If you insist on keeping vigil, let me at least bring your cloak."

I nod, and my eyes burn as I watch her follow the muddy footprints back to the cottage. I hug myself tighter, missing my sister's warmth. Leaving her will be much harder than leaving the western wood. The forest taught me adventure, but Eirwyn taught me goodness. The value of sisterhood.

I turn back to the trees. Standing between two evergreens, as if I've summoned her with my very thoughts, is the girl I seek. Her hair is unbraided, the tight curls framing her face. Dressed in her human glamour, she even wears her lovely blue cloak.

"You're here," I say, knees weak with the shock of seeing her again after so much time not knowing if she was all right.

Colette points to the muddy ground. "The spring thaw's happening beyond the veil too. I wanted to see you before you left."

So she knows I'm leaving for Poppy. I wonder if someone told her, like Graeme, or if she merely guessed.

"Thank you—I mean, I'm glad," I say, cheeks growing warm. I press my cold palms to my face, having nearly forgotten how easily flustered I am around Colette.

"I'm sorry I couldn't come sooner." She looks over her shoulder to the wood. "Establishing order took longer than expected."

"But everything's all right now?"

She shrugs, stepping out from beneath the trees. "The arrangements are ongoing, but most faeries have accepted me. I've made it clear that those who don't are free to leave the wood. There will be no more bloodshed while I'm queen."

I believe her. While I'm committed to leaving, part of me wishes I could witness her reign over the western wood, witness her claim her birthright in full.

"Do you know what happened to Silvain?" I ask.

"A few of his supporters caught him and tried to change him back, but they failed. Your magic remains strong."

I'm glad to hear it. I didn't want to cross the river, leaving my loved ones behind, without knowing for sure that the king was no longer a threat. And yet . . .

"I'll change him back, if that's what you want."

The offer is difficult to make. With Colette's blessing, I put an end to Silvain's cruelty to protect her and those I love, and I'd prefer they remain protected. And Brend was right to point out that Silvain's misdeeds should be judged differently than Pa's. But it's not for me to say whether Colette's father deserves a lifetime of punishment. That's why I never considered using my voice to take his life.

"Thank you, I appreciate that." Colette glances up at the trees as if she expects to find a great horned owl perched on one of the branches. Concerned, I follow her gaze, only to be soothed by the sight of a sparrow. "I think he should remain as he is for now. I might change my mind one day."

"That's fair," I grant. "Any calls for my death?"

Graeme warned me to keep my distance. I'm curious to know if that was warranted.

She frowns. "No, but plenty of calls for you to join us beyond the veil."

"I see." I look down at my boots as they slowly sink into slush.

"Ro." Colette's voice is gentle. "So long as Silvain remains trapped in his animal form, he cannot enforce the bargain he made with your father. You are under no obligation to serve me in his stead."

I clutch the collar of my tunic as a heavy breath of relief whistles between my teeth. I didn't believe Colette would ever make me serve her, but I'm glad to hear the words aloud.

She cocks her head in the direction of the wood. "Walk with me?"

We don't wander far past the tree line. Colette stops at a fallen log covered in wet moss, and we sit together, close but not yet touching. I don't think either of us is ready for that. We've been apart for more time than we were together, and we're certainly not the same as we were when we shared our first kiss. She was a cursed girl, and I was clinging desperately to the western wood. Now she's a queen, and I'm ready to leave these trees behind.

With all that's changed within us, what might've changed between us? I'm afraid to find out. She might be too.

"Tamsin told me about my mother, my faerie mother," says Colette. "After I was born, and she learned about the trial, she appealed to Silvain to change his mind. He had one of his subjects take away her memories, and then he exiled her to the human realm."

Just like Brend, only Colette's mother wasn't part of any changeling conflict. Silvain simply wanted to be rid of the woman who challenged him. Well, now the western wood is rid of him as king, and that woman's child is queen. I take immense pleasure in that.

"Once I came into my magic, I started having these . . ." Colette trails off, running a hand through her curls, perhaps searching for a way to explain. "Well, visions. Visions of her."

This must be her faerie gift, like my voice and Eirwyn's healing. "Graeme told me he has the gift of foresight," I mention.

Colette shakes her head. "No, I spoke to Graeme, and it's not that. He says I'm not seeing the future. I'm seeing the present."

The notion is just as compelling. "Have the visions told you where she is?"

"Not completely," says Colette. "I know she's not in a village like ours. Every time I see her, she's surrounded by people on a busy path, with stone buildings on either side instead of wood."

Maybe it's because I was already thinking of it, but realization sparks within me like the strike of two stones. "That sounds like—"

"Poppy, I know," she says, grinning. "I could be wrong, but it seems like a good place to start. So . . . do you think there's room on the ferry for one more? I want to find my mother, and I want you by my side when I do."

Forget distance, and who cares what's changed—I take Colette's hand, and my breath is nearly stolen by the thrill of touching her again. "What about your throne?"

"The throne will wait," she says, and now I want to kiss her too. "I mean to embrace the role, but breaking my curse was never about becoming queen. All I've ever wanted was to know my family, who I came from. So I've elected stewards to rule in my place. They'll take care of things while I'm gone."

"In that case, yes," I breathe, because it sounds like a dream. Maybe not a forever kind of dream, but a dream worthwhile. "I'm certain there's room for you on the ferry."

"Good," she says, drawing closer. "I can't imagine doing this with anyone else."

We kiss then, cold lips warming quickly despite the steady spring wind buffeting our bodies. Where they were once dim, the sounds of melting snow and twittering birds become crisp and clear. Like my forest, I'm finally waking up.

While I don't want to ruin the perfect moment between us, I know from past experience that honesty is our best course. "Brend is still coming to Poppy. He'll stay in my aunt's tavern until he gets his footing. Will you be all right with that?"

"So long as he is," says Colette, smoothing out her cloak. "I can't promise we'll be friends, but he cares for you. That means something to me."

I grin. "You're a lot more mature than I am."

She laughs, loveliness in its purest form. "Comes with being queen, I think."

While I agree that friendship may not be their future, I don't think we'll run into much trouble where the former changelings are concerned. I care for Brend more than I ever believed I could, but he knows my heart belongs to Colette. I've already teased that there must be at least one girl in Poppy who will draw his eye, and he surprised me by saying perhaps there might even be a boy. With his memories returned, each day Brend seems to rediscover himself in a new way.

As for me and Colette, we might part ways after she finds her faerie mother. Perhaps the two will return beyond the veil, and I'll stay in Poppy with Ma and Brend to find a trade. Who knows, I might even try my hand at cooking in Aunt Meara's tavern. Stranger magic has occurred.

Or maybe I'll have had my fill of Poppy by the time Colette and her mother are reunited, and I'll join them in the faerie realm. I'll bind myself to Colette not because of a bargain, but out of love, and I'll stand by her side as she rules the forest, a queen of her own making.

I have time; I don't have to decide now. But I know that when I do, it will be my choice and my choice alone. I think Pa would be proud of that.

Colette and I rise from the moss-covered log and turn away from the western wood. The breeze has changed course and is once again at our backs, stirring locks of dark auburn and raven hair.

Pushing us in a new direction.

THE END

ACKNOWLEDGMENTS

This novel's journey from graduate creative thesis to debut publication was possible thanks to the support of many lovely people in my life. As a reader, you're part of that journey, too, so first and foremost: thank you.

Lauren Knowles, thank you for embracing the book of my heart. I'm endlessly grateful for your insightful feedback, which was always in tune with my vision for this story. I couldn't have asked for a better editor and partner. Shoutout to Kumari Pacheco, who polished my words and made the copy-editing process a breeze. Thanks also to the entire team at Page Street YA for lifting up queer stories, especially Laura Benton, Rosie G. Stewart, Lauren Cepero, Jane Horovitz, and Shannon Dolley for their part in bringing this book to the world.

Thank you to my agent, Tricia Lawrence, for recognizing the value of my writing and my potential as an author. I love having you as my champion. Thank you to everyone at Erin Murphy Literary Agency who supports me and my work.

Gaby Verdooren, you illustrated a cover that gorgeously evokes my story's characters and world. Your art is magic.

Huge thanks to the Hamline University MFAC program, faculty, and community. In particular, this novel wouldn't exist without the incredible teachings and guidance of my advisors Anne Ursu, Emily Jenkins, Jacqueline Briggs Martin, and Eliot Schrefer. Thank you to my cohort, The Qaudropus, for your encouragement and friendship, especially my critique partners Kalena Miller, Elizabeth Selin, Lisa Frenkel Riddiough, Katie Dunlop, and Ari Tison.

Special thanks to Sherrie Weller, my creative nonfiction professor at Loyola University Chicago, for recommending that I pursue my graduate education at Hamline. In a sea of writing instructors obsessed with literary fiction, your respect for my storytelling was a lifeline. And to Patricia Lantier, for taking the writing I did as a teen seriously and continuing to cheer me on.

So much love to all my family and friends for believing in my abilities as a writer. Most of all, thank you to my parents for always encouraging my pursuit of this passion. To Jackie for being my best friend and lifting my spirits with Instagram reels. And to Matcha and Kava for being the best and worst writing companions a cat mom could ask for.

Finally, the utmost gratitude and love for my fiancé, Anton. Thank you for your unwavering support; for seeing me completely and loving every single part of me; and for building a life with me that makes this dream possible.

ABOUT THE AUTHOR

Markelle Grabo retells the fairy tales that frustrate her, which, based on that guideline, could include nearly all of them. She earned her master's degree in creative writing for children and young adults from Hamline University and lives in Illinois with her partner and their two cats, Matcha and Kava. *Call Forth a Fox* is Markelle's debut novel.